# The Silver Highways

Also by Malcolm Macdonald:

*On a Far Wild Shore*
*Tessa D'Arblay*
*For They Shall Inherit*
*Goldeneye*
*Abigail*
*Sons of Fortune*
*The Rich Are with You Always*
*The World from Rough Stones*

# The
# Silver
# Highways

## Malcolm Macdonald

Based on an idea by Peter Gilmore

St. Martin's Press
New York

WB

Library of Congress Cataloging-in-Publication Data

Macdonald, Malcolm, 1932–
    The silver highways.

    I. Title.
PR6063.A1594S5   1987      823'.914      87-4594
ISBN 0-312-00680-2

First published in Great Britain by Hodder and Stoughton Limited.

First U.S. Edition

10 9 8 7 6 5 4 3 2 1

*for*
# Kathryn Falk
*whose encouragement
has meant so much
to so many writers*

# CONTENTS

PART ONE

Childhood's End                                    9

PART TWO

Over the Water                                     63

PART THREE

A Rare Oul' Race                                   121

PART FOUR

On the Anvil                                       239

PART FIVE

Impossible Times                                   323

PART SIX

Remarkable Occurrences                             443

ENVOI                                              493

# PART ONE

## CHILDHOOD'S END

# CHAPTER ONE

WISH I WAS A LADY FAIR," she sang, "to lie twixt sheets of silk. For 'tis a cruel and winter air . . ."

It was, in fact, a grand morning in May. A warm south-west breeze blew steadily up from Kilfenora carrying flocks of thin, small clouds that did nothing to hinder the sun. She sat on Poulaphuca moor, upon the warm stone of the Oul' Kinnel, facing north, and sang her sad song, thinking all the while how good life was. She watched the pale cloudshadows ramble up the sides of the distant hills, the Moneen Mountains to her left, the even higher Turlough Hill to the right. Where else but in County Clare would the hills be raised higher than the mountains – and the gentry brought lower than the peasants!

She hugged her knees to her chin, luxuriating in the warmth of the sun as it soaked into her back. Actually, life wasn't all *that* good. This place was a bit of a prison; her father, who really was in gaol, was in a way much freer than her – free to read all he wished, to write prospectuses of his lovely, ridiculous notions. For all his confinement, he was still *The* Flinders of the Barony of Inchiquin in County Clare. He still led the life of a gentleman. Yet the world would call her the free one – free to tend the goats, cut the turf, till the soil, carry the produce to market . . . free to slave from sleep to sleep.

She sighed. How could a land as wide, as high, as open as this, be so imprisoning? Yet it was. If she stayed here, she'd become just like the rest of them, nothing for supper but dreams – and breakfast from the leftovers. She had to get away before this poverty had its tendrils around her soul. But where *was* "away," and how did anyone get there?

The beauty of the scene diverted her thoughts; on a day like this you could almost love it – the vast, blue-grey domes of barren rock that rose a thousand feet and more out of the sparse bogs and the meagre valleys that ringed their feet. In winter they seemed brooding and sullen, as if they'd like to give one good heave and shake off the rash of little cottages that dotted their lower slopes, flaunting their limewashed walls. Those pinpoints of white often seemed to her like little cries of astonishment that survival was even possible in this grim, beautiful land, which demanded so much and yielded so little in return.

When men first came to Ireland they must have wandered as far as the country that surrounds this waste of naked rock, the good, soft country where Kinvara and Gort, Corofin and Ennistimon now stand. Who would then have ventured farther? Only an eejit. If ten thousand times ten thousand giants had fought in battle, and if their dead had been turned to stone, then this was their battleground and resting place. And that was the best of the land, in the foothills. On the mountains themselves, on those great, bald, limestone skulls, nothing could grow, except where the frost and rain had scoured deep cracks in the surface; there, where blown soil and the dung of goats and rabbits could lodge, there and there alone did a sparse, outlandish, outcast vegetation take root. Who would leave those gentle lowland acres and settle here instead? Only eejits like the Flinderses.

"Poor I may be yet I'm honest . . ." She began a new song, a virtuous song, to complement her wishfulness.

Down below, at the foot of the slope beneath Poulaphuca, she saw the figure of a man. A wandering monk. He was walking toward her, not on the new road but on the road built in olden times, which vanished in the moor where a saint had once hurled a bit of a rock in a fight with another saint. Not that she believed those papist superstitions.

"Mary! Mary!" From away to the west she heard her mother call her home. She gauged the length of her own shadow among the heather and saw that it was time to bring in the goats for milking. "Coming!" she shouted.

Where in God's name were the creatures, anyway?

Ten idle minutes later the question was answered as they came leaping up onto the moor, driven ahead of the man she had seen. Now she saw he was no wandering monk; what she had taken for his cowl was, in fact, a small wheelbarrow, strapped to his back. He was a common labourer. When he was almost nigh she made out other details – a pick and shovel tied across the barrow, a billycan dangling by its handle, a bundle of clothing to cushion the hard edges.

"Come home! Come home!" she called to the animals, not taking her eyes off the man. They pranced and trotted past her, putting her between them and the stranger before they turned to watch with wise and goatish curiosity.

"That's a grand day," he said in Irish, halting about a dozen paces off. He was old, more than thirty, with a rugged, kindly face.

"God be praised," she replied mechanically, also in Irish. "Where are you from?"

"From Gort."

"There's more work there than here."

"Would you be knowing a Mary Flinders?" he asked.

"I might," she said. "And then again, I mightn't. If I did, who is it wants her?"

"Steam Punch, ma'am. So they call me." He strolled over until he was at her side, where he turned his back to the Kinnel and rested his burden upon it. He gave out a great sigh. "God be praised!"

"That's a fierce burden," she told him.

"It puts beef in the belly and wool on the back."

"And by God it'd want to! The weight that's in it."

He sized her up. "I have word for Mary Flinders from England."

"England is it? Who would she know there?"

"A bold young lad by the name of Ignatius Murphy."

She frowned, then gave out a great laugh.

"You have two grand sets of teeth," he told her.

"Ig-naaa-tius is it! Could that be Con Murphy in his Sunday best? Ignatius, would you ever stop!"

From the inner reaches of his coat he drew forth a letter. As he was on the point of handing it to her he said, "I'm to ask you to describe some mark or feature of the man."

13

"Of Con Murphy?" she asked truculently. "The biggest thing about that one is his own opinion of himself."

Steam Punch laughed in agreement, but shook his head, asking for more.

"His face was opened by a knife," she said. "Hasn't he a scar here" – drawing a finger down her brow – "and a white blaze in his eyebrow where it crosses, and just the tip of it on his cheek."

He handed her the letter. It was in English, of course; Con was a Leinster man. She read a line or two – *Dear Miss Flinders, How are you? Well, here I am in London. The man who carries this letter will tell you* . . . – and folded it inside her bodice. "Let's bring these goats home before they ramble again. You'll sup with us?"

"Gratefully. That's a longer walk from Gort than I thought now."

"It's that land for you – it promises a mile and it gives you two. If it did the same with the corn, we'd all be rich."

"Isn't it the truth." He shouldered his burden again and went to stand between the goats and the road. She circled them on the other side, gathering them into a tighter bunch, squeezing them homeward.

"Even the English don't want it," she went on. "Sure you could walk all day and never rest your eyes on a landlord house."

"Praise God for a little mercy."

"The English or the O'Lauchlins, there's a poor enough choice for you."

He spat crosswind, away from her, agreeing without words. The goats darted and stood, darted and stood, never certain whether they were being driven or were going voluntarily. "How many acres have you?" he asked.

"Oh God, a fair few," she replied.

"Is it just yourself and the oul' woman?"

"Did Con Murphy tell you about my father?"

"He said he's in gaol for debt."

"For dreaming! I have three brothers. One's in Ennis, one's in Liscannor, and one is ploughing a salt furrow somewhere between here and here-again."

"A fisherman?"

She shook her head. A certain reluctance seemed to overcome her. "Ship's officer," she said at last.

"Well," he said in surprise, looking her over carefully, as if he

thought he might have missed something about her. "And the other two, then?"

"Michael, the one in Ennis, he's a court clerk. And Jimmy's a bailiff and bookkeeper." They had reached the lip of the hill. She paused and stared down into the valley, over the backs of the goats as they tumbled down the paths ahead of her. She raised her arm and pointed at a grim-looking stonewalled farmhouse nestling among some wind-bent sycamores and ash trees. "Didn't you know?" she asked ironically. "Didn't Ig-naaaa-tius tell you? My father is *The* Flinders of the Barony of Inchiquin in County Clare. We're *gentry*!"

"That's where you got the reading and the writing," he said evenly.

She laughed. "You're a practical man, Mr. Punch. They're like hen's teeth in these parts."

"The father in Ennis Gaol and the son a clerk of the court . . ." he said.

She led the way down the kindest of the paths. "He wants for nothing," she said. "For some men liberty's more ruinous than gin."

"So," he said, "when you go to England . . ."

She turned to him in astonishment. "Why in God's name would I do that?"

His momentum, what with the slope and the weight on his back, carried him into her. For a moment they teetered, like a pair of lunatic dancers, and then just managed to regain their balance. She laughed. "To England?"

"Sure isn't it all set forth in that letter? And haven't I a draft for five guineas for you, payable in Ennis? I thought you read it all."

She clutched his arm in disbelief. "To London? Con Murphy wants me . . . he's given you five guineas . . ." Hastily she pulled out the letter and read it.

Indeed, Con wanted her to come to London, had loved her from the moment he saw her – blether blether . . . a whole page of lovewords she'd read later in private. No one had ever sent her a love letter before. He had worked his way into a position of trust with Lord Tottenham, heir to the Marquis of Enfield, had saved, could afford to keep her in a manner beyond even her father's dreams, all that unfortunate misunderstanding with the army now forgotten and done with . . . no more running . . . would send this and five guineas for the journey by the hand of Steam Punch, a navigating man, trust him with your life. Sent from Mother Redcaps, Camden Town, this 14th day of February, 1789.

"Is he a gentleman now?" she asked.

He looked at her askance. "Something less honest than a rogue, I'd say."

She folded the pages with care. "And who is Mother Redcap? Was it herself penned this letter, for I'm sure Con hasn't the writing?"

"'Tis an alehouse in a village outside London."

"God, I hardly know the man," she burst out.

But she already knew she was going to London. Chances like this didn't come ashore on every tide. As to marrying Con Murphy, well, that was another matter entirely. You could plan your life too much; that was her father's downfall – he never stopped his scheming and dreaming.

Steam Punch asked, "How did you chance to meet that man?"

She looked at him warily. They resumed their walk down the hill. "Did he not tell you?"

"Not in three words. I fancy he killed a redcoat?"

"It was a perfectly ordinary streetfight," she assured him. "That's where he got that scar."

"He's a fierce man to cross."

"The captain told my brother Michael he was glad to shed the man, the soldier. He was nothing but disorder on two legs. One of the king's bad bargains, he said. They didn't search out Con Murphy above six hours."

"Did you shelter him?"

She nodded. "For a week or two, while the cut healed. It was the other man's fault."

As they came to the farm gate she asked, "Who's Lord Tottenham?"

"A man to be feared, they say."

"And what does Con do for him?"

"He's a prizefighter, the best." Reluctantly Steam Punch added, "Among other things."

## CHAPTER TWO

SHE MILKED THE GOATS before she brought Punch indoors. She thought, as she worked.

London! What would that place be like? Grand people being carried around in their chairs . . . lords and ladies as thick as you'd want them, drinking tea and chocolate, giving out Secret Signs with their fans, subscribing their names to all the new books, killing with a glance, languishing at balls . . . oh, doing every sort of grand thing altogether.

Did the prospect not frighten her, just a little? Begod, it did not. To tell the truth, she couldn't wait.

"London," she said, casually. "Would that be far?"

She had seen it in the atlas, of course, but since she'd never travelled more than twenty miles from Poulaphuca, the span of a hand across the engraved page meant nothing.

"With your five guineas," Punch said, "you could get passage out of Galway to Cork for a crown, and from Cork to Wales for seven shillings or to Bristol for eight. Your fares the whole way would be a pound, and it would take you a week. Ten days at the most."

"Is that the way you'll be travelling?"

He was silent. She looked up at him, wondering if he'd heard. There was a remoteness in his eyes, a strange flatness in his voice as he answered: "It was. But I had . . . business in Gort that consumed the fare."

"I'll pay for you so," she said gaily, not wanting to attempt the journey alone.

"You will not! I'll leg it and catch what work I may along the road. There's the new canal to Carlow, now."

17

"Then I'll leg it too, by God!" She laughed. "And with what's saved I'll buy some pretty fashions in Dublin. Will we pass through Dublin?"

"We will, of course." He nodded. "What'll the oul' woman say?"

"Good riddance, I should think. She can set the farm and go over to Liscannor. They've need of a dame school there."

The last dribbles fell into the pail. She rose and looked around the lean-to. "They're better housed than ourselves," she said. "Come away in and you'll see." She paused and added, "My mother only has the English, or so she pretends."

They drove the goats out through the gate, letting them wander back onto the moor. Punch hoisted two full pails, leaving her the third, half filled, to carry.

"You never drink it all," he said. Now he spoke English, too.

"We sell the cheese in Ennis and so purchase my father's vittles for the week. And I'll tell you now – there's not a happier man in the whole County Clare, so there isn't."

As they went indoors her mother, who was scalding the pans at the range, said, without turning round, "Did you get wet? I'll take the skin off you."

"It isn't even raining. This now is Mr. Steam Punch, so it please you. He's come out from Gort, bound for London – and he has news of – guess who – Ig-naaa-tius Murphy!"

Punch, already fairly sure he was among heathens, searched nonetheless for a bowl of holy water; finding none, he began a wary search of the room for other marks of faith. But there were no saints, no holy pictures, no crucifix. Instead, he found Mrs. Flinders's eye fixed sharply upon him.

"Ye have some grand oul' shticks of furniture, ma'am," he said to explain his scrutiny.

She smiled, not deceived. "And divil a horn nor tail among us. Come in, come in." She took the pails from him and carried them to the range. "You'll have the thirst on you after such a walk?"

"I was wondering was there any danger of a drink," he agreed jovially.

The woman nodded at her daughter, who went out across the yard and returned a short while later with a stoneware cruse of poteen.

Punch grinned at the pair of them and gulped the fiery liquor as if his life depended on it. He chased it down with mild ale, the brewing of which was one of Mary's tasks. The women sipped their portions, savouring every drop. They ate bread and their own make of cheese, and potatoes mashed in goatsmilk.

"*Steam* Punch?" Mrs. Flinders said. "Now that wouldn't be your baptismal name?"

"Indeed it is not, ma'am. 'Tis a navigator's name I got in a fight I ended in glory. That was in me fightin' days."

"And when were they?"

He winked encouragingly. "You may rest aisy, Mrs. Flinders. I'm not your man for a brawl. And this year's fight is fought and won."

"That was a bold man who took on *you*."

"*Was!*" he chuckled at the emphasis.

"And your real name?"

The humour left him. "Moore, I was baptized. Declan Moore."

The women exchanged sudden, knowing glances. "From Gort, you say?" Mrs. Flinders went on. "Are you *that* Moore?"

He nodded. His troubled eyes flickered between them and the cruse.

"Fill your cup so, Mr. Moore," the mother said earnestly. "We're sorry for all your trouble. That was a terrible, terrible thing."

"It was, ma'am. I'm obliged."

"To return home to such a woeful occasion!" Mary said. "Did they get word of it to you on your journey?"

"Divil a breath of it until I arrived."

"The mother *and* six children!"

He nodded and drained his glass.

Mrs. Flinders went on: "I always said those cottages were ripe for such a tragedy. The straw thatch does be so quick to fire. And when you think of all the good reed thatch there'd be in Castle Lough . . ." She shook her head and refilled his cup. "That's from Doolin, now. Ireland's best."

Mary took her chance. "He's brought us word from Con Murphy, who wants to marry me," she said. "He's sent five guineas for me to come and join him in London. Punch will bring me there he says."

"Marry you!" Mrs. Flinders exploded. "That *soup*-Protestant!

In case you need reminding, my girl, *we* have been Protestants since . . ."

"He's as good a Protestant now as ever he was a papist," Mary interrupted. To Punch she added, "Saving your presence."

He agreed: "There'd be little rejoicing in either fold at the return of that stray sheep."

She turned back to her mother and said in a more conciliatory tone, "I wouldn't be obliged to marry the man if I didn't want to. If we leg it to London, I'll have the most part of his money intact to hand back to him. And what we spend on the sea crossing I could soon make good."

"Out of what, pray? Dreams and nightmares! You're a Flinders right enough."

"I can read and write. And cast up an account. I have a little Latin. I can sew. I can speak and act as dainty as any Miss Pale out of Dublin. I can recite after Dryden and Pope and Shakespeare. I can sing and play the harp. And if I carry letters from Reverend Pearce and from the justiciary in Ennis, wouldn't the daughter of *The* Flinders of the Barony of Inchiquin in County Clare soon be in the way of paying back a few shillings to the like of Ignatius Murphy!"

"Would you ever listen to her!" Mrs. Flinders beseeched the ceiling. "She's that clever, she'd herd mice at a crossroads." She scooped up the breadcrumbs and rolled them into a ball, which she popped between her lips. "Dreams!" she added scornfully.

Punch watched them in fascination. He saw that, for all her apparent scorn, the mother was proud of her daughter's waywardness; yet the daughter could not see it.

Mary did her best to contain her anger. "You're the dreamer, mother," she said quietly. "You complain about father's wild, impractical notions and the way they always strand us in debt, you seek to fill every waking hour with meaningless tasks, but . . ."

"Dreams, is it!" her mother cried. "What woman after four children the likes of you – not to mention twenty-eight years with such a man as that – what woman I say would have the pick of a dream about her still?" She turned to Punch and said, as conversationally as if she were saying, *I've run out of sewing thread*, "I haven't a dream left me, 'clare to God."

Mary spoke sharply. "Nothing's ever right for you. You must

have this changed, that changed. We need new thatch. The hinge of the gate has dropped. Oh God, there's a new rathole. The turf was better firing last year. Why are the hens laying smaller eggs – is it to spite us or what? This petticoat is ruined after only five trips to the tub. Lord, I'll swear the sun isn't so warming this year as last! You never stop."

"But it's all true," the older woman protested.

"It's all dreams. You dream of everlasting linen, and hinges that never wear, and a world without the rats . . . and all the rest of it. Your days are ruined with dreams of what isn't and what never can be, so you've no time left to love what is."

"Love!" Mrs. Flinders gave out a sour smile; her eyes flickered briefly toward Punch. "She'd argue the cross off an ass's back."

"Would you be interested, ma'am, to hear of Con Murphy's doings over the water?" he asked.

"Scantly." She jerked her head in Mary's direction. "He's *that* one's ruin, not mine."

Mary told her anyway: "He's working for Lord Tottenham, as a prizefighter, and making good money, and his lordship is heir to the Marquis of Enfield. So!"

"So, indeed! So my daughter's to become a prizefighter's moll! Mary you were christened and Moll you'll die. Don't look for my blessing."

Mary clenched her jaw and stared at the ceiling.

"Will you give up the farm?" Punch asked.

"I will not!"

"She thought you might move to Liscannor."

"Hop from the bakepot into the skillet? Oh no!"

Still not looking at her, Mary asked, "And how will you manage here, alone?"

"Will I be alone? Wouldn't Peggy Walsh lepp at the chance to put five more miles between Christy Miller and that daughter of hers?"

"Pamela?"

"The same."

Mary burst into laughter. "I yield, mother, I yield. For twenty years I've had Saint Pamela Walsh held before me as the living image of all that's good and great in the holy estate of daughterhood. And now, before the rain can fill my leaving footprints, she's to be gaolled in my stead. Lord, I'm well content!"

Punch, seeing the glint of ancient battle in both women's eyes, now rose and said, "There'll be much that wants doing, ma'am, I make no doubt of it – ground to till, thatch to mend, and though 'tis early for the turf, sure we might shake a fist at it if this weather but holds."

He stayed four days. Mary had heard legends of the navigators, the men who built canals, of their prodigious feats of strength and endurance. She might have guessed at their truth from the size of Punch's travelling burden, or from the massive, rippling muscles that seemed to make up his entire body; but not until she saw him at work over those days did she truly grasp their meaning. Work that would have taken other men hereabouts a week, he managed in a morning. Where they would walk, he ran; where they ran, he flew. He cut a ton of turf (which is five tons of water beside). He set out a half acre of potatoes. And in the evenings, for a desperate want of idleness, he dug new shores, rebuilt walls, tore out old thatch and put in new, cut heather for bedding, rehung the gate . . . jobs that had wanted such a hand as his for years. He ate his way through an entire goat, not to mention six quartern loaves and all that week's cheese; he drank half the goats' yield plus a gallon of kitchen ale each day. And Mary had to take the ass over to Doolin for more poteen. But Lord, wasn't he worth every gulp and gasp of it!

On her way back from Doolin she cried in at her brother Jimmy's in Liscannor. He pretended to be appalled that she was even thinking of going off to London. And as for marrying that ne'er-do-well Con Murphy . . . But she could see, underneath it all, he envied her the freedom she was taking. When he saw he couldn't shake her he promised with good enough grace to get word to Michael in Ennis, so he'd have the letters from the minister and the justice ready when she passed through. There were tears at their parting.

# CHAPTER THREE

ON HER LAST NIGHT in the old home, restless at the thought of leaving it, fearful of the world yet excited at its prospects, she rose and went outdoors. The night air was balmy with a gentle southerly breeze; high in the skies above, a full moon was falling among ribs and streets of fine, thin cloud. The farm was profoundly at peace; she wanted to remember it thus.

Tiptoeing past the outhouse where Punch was no doubt sleeping the sleep of the justly exhausted, she let herself out by the newly greased gate and followed the little goatpath up to the moor, to the Oul' Kinnel.

One of the nannygoats came up, sniffed at her, tried to bite, and got a sharp slap for her love. "Don't imagine I'll be sorry to leave you," she told them brusquely.

She would, of course. Or rather – she would and she wouldn't.

Just like being gentry – she was and she wasn't.

Or loving her mother – she did and she didn't.

Or marrying Con Murphy – no, there was no chance of that. Dear God! What did she want at all?

There was a long silence in her mind, and then the thought occurred to her: She wanted *everything* to go on being possible for as long as ever it could.

Fame and fortune – that is what folk would say. "Mary Flinders? Sure, didn't she go over the water to seek her fame and fortune."

"And did she find it?"

"She was presented to his majesty last week."

"She has dukes and God knows what else attending on her

23

with offers of castles and marriage, and she won't say yes and she won't say no."

"That's our Mary right enough!"

*Obscure* fame was what she really wanted.

And *humble* wealth.

The thought crossed her mind as she went back to her bed that London might be a million miles from either of those strange commodities.

Next day, at the hour of parting, Mrs. Flinders was plainly determined to permit no vulgar show of emotion before the itinerant Steam Punch. "You may take the ass," she said when she saw the size of Mary's load.

"Sure I can buy one in Ennis when I have the draft cashed. I'll manage fine until that."

But her mother insisted. As she helped settle the load on the creature's back she went on, "Would you feel the weight of those books? Is it a famine of paper in London then?"

"They're to read along the way," Mary answered grumpily.

"And isn't the Bible enough?"

"Ah, the print's too small when you're walking. It's just a few pomes and Dean Swift and things. Some of them are for my father, anyway. He'll be glad of a change."

"And the harp?"

"I may have to sing for my supper."

Her mother frowned. "Rather sing to repay the Murphy creature. Never forget that you are one of the quality, my child – of the Barony of Inchiquin. None should buy *you* for five guineas."

Mary was gripped by a confusion of feelings – part anger that her mother would not dignify this parting with an open show of loving grief, part tenderness for one so crippled by bitter disappointments.

Her mother stumbled on toward an oblique confession: "You now have all the opportunities I threw away when . . ." Her voice broke; she forced herself to smile and shooed her daughter away. "Oh, along with you, now! Along with you!"

"I'll bring your love to my father."

The humour faded. "Yes. Of course."

"And I'll send word what way I can – a letter if I can afford it."

At last the moment of their parting was too sharp for any

artifice of words to blunt. The smiles died completely, leaving an emptiness between them you could touch. It trembled there, in that dwindling space, upheld by the magic of its own surprise: a real emotion between them at last – and when each of them least expected it.

The surprise of the one fed the surprise of the other until at length the tension became so unbearable that only tears could dissolve it. They hung upon each other in awkward astonishment, racked by a grief that frightened them, giving it scope, letting it dissipate.

Mary broke free and laughed, said this would never do, kissed her mother, made all her promises yet again, and then set herself resolutely forth upon the road.

Mrs. Flinders called, "Wait – I'll go the length of Poulaphuca moor with you."

They talked of the weather, the fine day it was, the good omens, the last-minute did-you-bring-this-and-that. It petered out to silence as they passed the Oul' Kinnel; there Mrs. Flinders stopped. Mary's last view as the trail twisted out of sight was of her mother, sitting on the capstone. They were too far apart for such details to be seen, but Mary knew the tears were in her eyes again.

"Never look back," Punch said.

Could people just do that? she wondered.

"Would your brothers not pay off the oul' fellow's debts?" he went on as they began to step it out.

"They can, of course. And they have, these many times. Sure he'll get a legacy this month or next, or next year, then he'll be out again, full of wild new designs to cast his fortune away on."

Punch, who had heard some of these "wild designs" over the past few days – the noble vineyards, the carriage works, the perfume manufactory said, "There's a grandeur in it. You have to give him that."

"Oh yes – strangers love him at sight."

"There's a hard streak in you, woman."

"Wouldn't there have to be!"

He grinned and nodded a small concession. After a long, easeful silence, he said, "The oul' woman does be needing him though. You should bring him out and find some way to govern him. For the oul' woman's sake."

Mary foundered between answers that ranged from too knowing to excessively naïve. He gave her arm an avuncular squeeze. "One day you'll understand."

It annoyed her. How could she show him she was no longer a child?

## CHAPTER FOUR

THE DEBTORS' GAOL IN ENNIS was housed in a corner of the regular county gaol, but a few privileged prisoners, gentlemen mostly, whose families could pay for it even if they could not discharge the entire debt, were lodged on their own parole in the house of the head gaoller. Naturally *The* Flinders of the Barony of Inchiquin in County Clare was among them. Their rooms were the former servants' quarters in the attic, the servants being boarded out.

Mary put the ass in the stables and eased the load from its back. Punch left off his burden. And together, carrying the books and such victuals as they had bought after cashing the draft, they ascended the steep and narrow staircase to the garret where The Flinders was lodged.

"I'm coming, you're going, I'm coming, you're going . . ." Punch intoned in time with his footsteps; to the same rhythm he mimed a strange gesture, raising his clenched hand to shoulder height and bringing it sharply down, halting it suddenly a few inches from the banisters.

"Is that a secret society?" Mary asked.

He laughed. "That's Con Murphy – and it's certainly no secret, I may swear to you. Just say those words anywhere in London – 'I'm coming, you're going . . .' – and you may watch the faces turn pale!"

"But what does it mean?"

"It's Con Murphy's way with the debtors – not his own debtors, of course, but his lordship's."

"Lord Tottenham's?"

"The same. Gambling debts, mostly. Debts of honour they call them. And when they don't pay – in goes Con Murphy with his cry of 'I'm coming, you're going.' That's his lordship's way with the debtors." He looked about them at the substantial and well-kept house. "Your oul' man's the lucky one."

"But why d'you keep swinging your arm that way?"

The man gave a confidential wink. "Doesn't he be carrying a lump hammer, a seven-pounder such as a stonemason might use. And with it he'll be knocking out the banister pieces as he mounts the stair."

Mary paused at the stairhead. "Con Murphy?" she asked.

He nodded.

"But what if Lord Tottenham finds out?"

His laugh told her she had asked a childish question. Annoyed, she tried to distract him. "But it must terrify the debtors."

"Sure isn't that his aim? The first visit, 'tis only goods and chattels is destroyed on the fella. The second visit, which is a rarity, 'tis arms and legs for the breaking. The third visit, which has never happened yet praise God, your man would be taken forth in a box."

"I can't believe it," she said.

But alas, she could. The time he'd killed the English soldier it had been eight of them onto him. Eight to one, and he'd licked them all into fits – and left one accidentally dead. At least, he'd said it was an accident. He was the most powerful man she'd ever met, more powerful even than Punch. And on top of that – and quite unlike Punch, who was soft-hearted underneath all his muscle – Con Murphy just radiated menace. You only had to draw near him and you were thinking of ways to bolt.

"Sure you believe it," Punch said.

She gave a knock to her father's door. "Come in!" he chirped brightly. She smiled, glad he was in a good mood – seeing the day that was in it.

He was still struggling into his wig as she entered. The air was stale. She crossed the room briskly and flung wide the casement before she bent to kiss him. "You'll never be told," she said.

"You know full well you'll catch a consumption if you live day and night in your own bad breath."

"That's your mother speaking," he said jovially. "And who have we here?"

"This is Steam Punch, father. Mr. Declan Moore from Gort, who has brought me word from Con Murphy that we sheltered at Poulaphuca this twelvemonth, and I'm bound for London where he has secured me introductions to Lord Tottenham and others of the nobility."

It cost the old man some effort to absorb this stream of intelligence; it cost him even more to evoke a sentimental mist into his eyes and then, raising his hands in patriarchal weariness, cry, "Ah, my poor, sweet child!"

She laughed and gave him a further kiss for trying. "Poor I am, sweet I may be, child I'm not." She glanced firmly at Punch as she spoke the words. Then she turned back to her father. "And you know as well as I do now, you're as pleased as a dog with two tails to have me off your hands."

"I have been somewhat agitated, I must allow, at the thought you might never have dowry enough to marry. Your face must be your fortune." He touched her cheek tenderly and added, ". . . which is just as well." Then he dismissed the matter with a flash of a smile and, turning solemnly to Punch, said, "If you're the Moore I believe you to be, sir, then I owe you my family's deepest condolences."

They shook hands and froze in a moment's silence.

Then, recovering all his earlier briskness, he said, "And so it's over the water, eh? You both look fit for the journey, I must say. And what would your trade be, Mr. Moore?"

"I'm a navigation labourer, your honour, sir. I do be digging the canals."

"Canals!" The Flinders's eyes lit up. "But how extraordinary, my dear fellow! You are not to know this but at any moment I expect to receive a substantial dividend that will free me from these purely temporary but pestilential constraints" – he waved at the comfortable arrangements all about them – "and I shall then be in a position to implement a grand new scheme that is entirely of my own devising – a scheme to insulate the Burren by means of a canal! There now, what d'you say to that? Is it not magnificent in its daring?"

"Have you used up your chest elixir?" Mary asked, running her eye along the shelves. "Or have you just hidden it again?"

"Oh, do be quiet girl!" He shook his head forgivingly at Punch. "They can't help it," he explained. "The female brain is only three-quarters the size and weight of the male's. They simply cannot support a grand idea – and so they can't abide one, either. What d'you say, Mr. Moore, you who are so well versed in the whole business of the canals?"

Punch cleared his throat awkwardly. "Well now, your honour . . . your honour called it 'daring.' And daring it certainly is!"

The Flinders threw up his hands in delight. "A kindred spirit!" he chortled. "And a man who *knows*!"

"But" – Punch screwed up his face to suggest he was scraping the bottom of the barrel to find even a tiny objection – "you might have some little trouble husbanding the water now – seeing the miles and miles of bare rock that does be covering the place."

The old man smiled triumphantly, like a schoolboy who knows every word of his lessons. He searched among the litter on his desk and drew forth a parchment which he unfolded and spread before his visitor. Upon it was a sketch, unmistakably of one of the Burren hills, a thousand-foot skull of bare rock. And crowning its stony pate was a veritable rash, an orchard, of windmills.

The Flinders chuckled. "The one thing those hills are not short of, sir, is wind!"

"Especially Poulaphuca Hill," Mary said solemnly.

"Just so, just so," her father said, pleased that she took any interest at all.

Punch had to bite his lip to stop himself from smiling.

"I shall get my water free, d'ye see!"

"But who *wants* a canal across the Burren?" she asked.

"All the sailors who'll be spared the journey around Black Head."

"But that's only another four or five miles, father! And the wind that fills your canals for nothing does the same service to their sails." She closed her eyes and turned aside, adding more to herself than anyone, "I should know better! I should not be talking like this."

"Quite right," he answered sternly. "You've no respect. And, indeed, no memory. There's another reason for my canals. Aren't you forgetting the gold and silver?"

"True," Mary agreed with sarcastic enthusiasm. "And the lead."

Punch frowned in puzzlement.

Mary explained. "The hills of the Burren are only filled with minerals just waiting for the ring of a pick and shovel. We're all living on a metallic paradise out there."

"She doesn't believe it, Mr. Moore," her father explained. "She's only mocking me. But one day she'll wake up to a great surprise. Besides, the Burren Canal is only the acorn from which a mighty oak will one day grow. I have plans here for the insulation of the whole of Ireland – Dublin to Galway, Belfast to Cork. And with the proceeds I intend to buy Gort House, you'll be interested to learn, Mr. Moore. Not that I'm at all taken with the demesne, but they own a hundred thousand acres up in the Slieve Auchties, where I believe African hardwoods might be induced to grow very prettily." He smiled forgivingly and added, "Oh, the money I have thrown away in my time! And the fortune I could make if I had but a tenth of it back again!"

Mention of money prompted a further line of thought. He turned to Mary. "This Lord Tottenham, er, has he great wealth?"

Mary looked at Punch, who shrugged and said, "He's on that road."

"Capital!" The Flinders scrabbled further among the papers on his desk, found a pile of solicitations beginning *Dear (blank)*, wrote "Lord Tottenham" in the space, sealed it, and passed it to her with a seraphic smile, saying, "Will you be so good, my dear?"

"The usual news from Nonsuch," she sighed as she tucked it up her sleeve.

He affected not to hear.

"Will you look at the books I brought and pick what you will?"

He was delighted with the entire choice. He promised to get some more elixir and to send out his washing and to have his wig fumigated before summer and to let the boys know if his living conditions took a turn for the worse – and above all not to fret her mother more than he could help. She felt even sadder to be leaving him behind than she had felt about her mother. But now there were no tears; it was a sadness that lay beyond their help.

At the threshold she turned and impetuously pressed a golden guinea into his hand. And then, before he could say a word, she fled down the stairs.

When Punch joined her in the stables he remained silent, but she knew he had seen the transfer of the coin. "If we're legging it, I have money to spare," she said.

He shrugged. "I hope so. You could as well have sent it from London, when you'd be sure 'twas spare. Your man above has scant enough need of it."

"I'll be more miserly with what's left," she promised. "You'll see."

"I don't know which of ye is the worst. Would you look what he gave me?" He held forth a piece of paper – a six-month bill of exchange for a thousand guineas. " 'You might need a little loose change along your journey,' says he! Begod but he's a real gintleman."

She could not tell whether he added this as a balancing compliment or in irony. She took the worthless scrap and, with an impatient shrug, said, "Some fool might lend us twopence-halfpenny upon it."

Next she went to take leave of her brother Michael, who was usually far too busy on court business to grant her more than a moment of his precious time. But today, forewarned by Jimmy, he closed his office at once and took her home. There he gave her the letters of recommendation from the justice and the minister. He also handed on an old coachman's overcoat he'd lately acquired; its dense cloth would keep her warm, for there could yet be a late frost or two at night. He also gave her a strip of oilcloth as a groundsheet. She tried to give him two shillings to buy their mother a replacement ass, but he said he'd take care of it. Jenny, his wife, gave her a cake and a pot of honey and, for the ass, a bag of roots.

Jenny said their best way was surely to go down to Cork and take a packet boat to any port in the west of England. Michael said why wouldn't they go down to Limerick, then up the Shannon to Athlone, thence into Dublin by the main west road, which ran clear of the bog almost all the way. Punch said nothing. He thanked them and withdrew. Michael and his wife were still arguing the matter when Mary, feeling as well set up as any queen, set off in Punch's wake, catching him up at the edge of town – which was only a few hundred yards from its centre.

"Which of them's right?" she asked.

"Both," he replied. "And neither. In Ireland aren't there always three ways to anywhere, whether it's Dublin or heaven you have in mind."

"And what's the third way to heaven?" she asked.

He laughed. "Sure isn't that the one we're *all* seeking – the short cut!"

She joined his laughter. "And have we a short cut to Dublin?"

"You may say so. Short and grand. The Grand Canal is out to Monasterevin now. Being the trade I'm in, I may ride free, and you with me, on any boat into Dublin."

"And the ass?"

"Sell it at Monasterevin, of course."

They took the back way down toward Killaloe, at the foot of Lough Derg. To soften the road they talked of her father. Punch said what a great shame it was that such a fine gentleman with such a great understanding should be so wanting in plain sense.

"You jest of short cuts to heaven," she told him, "but that's his ruin. He's forever seeking the short cut to fame and fortune. Yet wasn't he born with both! He inherited a fair-sized estate, did you know? We once owned all the land between us and Leamaneh. As far as Inchiquin, and I'd tell no lie. But it was all dissipated on . . . well, you heard yourself now. The insulaaaaaaation of Ireland! Most of it went before I was born, so I never had taste nor sniff of the landlord life."

"But you have the blood, sure."

"That's true." Then, in case he might think she was giving herself airs, she added, "Or d'you believe all that?"

"Ah, well now. I do and I don't. There's believing and then again there's believing. It may happen, when you get to London, you'll learn quick enough if the blood is there or isn't it."

She asked what he might mean but he would not be drawn further. He changed the subject by saying her family hadn't lost much, for it was poor land between Poulaphuca and Inchiquin. She looked all about them, at the land through which they were now travelling, which was fine for both tillage and pasture. With the spring so well advanced, the green of it was almost hurtful.

"This has it bet into a Kerry kettle," she said. "Is all Ireland as green as that?"

"The easter you go, the greener it is. There's places in Wicklow you'd never stray without a good steel hook and a stone to keep it honed. Turn your back on the grass and it'd spring up and *eat* ya!"

When they had exhausted that day's budget of conversation, they made their nestle for the night in a little coppice a half-mile short of Tulla, which wanted five leagues or more to Killaloe. In all they had walked sixteen Irish miles that day. She hobbled the ass and turned him free to graze the long acre; the roots would keep in the case God's fodder ran out. She'd be sorry to sell the creature at Monasterevin; she'd hand-reared it from a few weeks and it was one of the family, a tractable creature, and very affectionate to her.

She was glad of Michael's two gifts, the oilcloth and the overcoat; between them she'd be kept both dry and warm. There was neither rain nor the smell of rain upon the wind, which still held south and fair. They ate some bread and goatsmeat, followed by cake and honey. They drank clear water from a running stream and warmed the tail of it with a nip of poteen. The stars were out by the time they settled. Punch vanished into the ditches for fifteen minutes or so – to answer the call of nature, she thought. But in the small hours she heard the rabbits scream as they ran foul of his snares, and he bounded up to still the noise before some prowling gamekeeper might think it more than a fox that held them.

Would he teach her the secrets of poaching, she wondered? Or was there a rule that only men could do it? Would he think her a child for asking?

Fatigue cast its mantle over such questions and soon had her drowned in sleep.

# CHAPTER FIVE

THE TWO RABBITS made a grand breakfast, which, eked out by an occasional bite of cake, kept hunger at bay all that day. Mary's shoes pinched her swollen feet. She wanted to kick them off and go barefoot, as she did often enough at home; but Punch told her to rub a little (and he stressed "little") poteen into the sore spots and to soldier on, or she and her feet would never be friends. She tried it and was delighted at the ease it brought.

His resourcefulness amazed her. When they stopped for a bite of cake around noon, a mile and a bit short of Killaloe, they could find no water that was not clouded by mud and alive with leeches and larvae of every description. "Don't be fretting," he said. And he plucked several handfuls of last year's grass – wild hay, as he called it – which he combed with his fingers so as to align all the stems. This he made her grasp, one clenched hand above the other, in a tight column over his billycan. Into the top of the column he slowly poured the muddy water; what emerged at the bottom was clear and sparkling – and quite innocent of livestock. He knew a thousand such travelling dodges.

At Killaloe bridge they hailed down an empty grain barge that was returning to Portumna at the head of Lough Derg, twenty-odd miles away to the north. The master, Fergus O'Donnell by name, agreed to take them for fourpence a head – a shilling including the ass. But as soon as they were under way, and the crack began to flow, he found he was a third cousin to Mary's mother and so halved the fare.

"Begod," Punch said. "Talk on, talk on – if there's a first cousin in it somewhere, we'll go for free."

From the inexhaustible depths of his travelling baggage he brought out a fishing line, which he baited with shreds of sinew off the rabbit skins. And for no more effort than the trailing of it over the side, he brought inboard their supper – a fine fat bream and a pike that must have weighed all of ten pounds. He had a way of fishing such that even the keenest-eyed bailiff with the strongest telescope would have to be quick to see the fish move from water to deck.

The bream gave good sport but the pike came out like a branch of wood and lay between his boots, yielding up its life with hardly a twitch. "'Tis the same with people," Punch pointed out. "There's some as will tear your eyes out for the last sod of turf, and there's others will lay down and beg you to wipe your boots."

Throughout the voyage the ass stood at the very prow of the boat, sniffing the breezes, a living figurehead. From time to time it looked back with such deep intelligence in its mild, dark eyes, Mary knew she could not possibly sell it at Monasterevin.

It is arguable whether Lough Derg is a true lake or just a widening of the Shannon. Both banks are well in view for all of its length, and a man even halfway handy with the oars could cross its widest reach in under half an hour. Mary thought she had never seen so many different sorts of green – the trees, the grassy hills on either side, the reflections in the water, and even the water itself – there was every shade and tint and hue in the whole of Nature's palette. And as for the wildfowl, even the autumn madness on the slobs at Lahench, during the height of the migrations, was as nothing to the everyday birdlife among the thick reedbeds that fringed both banks. The endless chatter of tufted duck and crested grebe – and pochard and goldeneye and scaup . . . the whole fowler's vade-mecum of names – filled every silence of the day; at times the sky seemed black with wings, and when the creatures settled, not singly but by the thousand, they silvered the water with their commotion.

"Wouldn't that be a grand sort of a country if we owned it now as once we did?" O'Donnell said.

"Who does own it?" Mary asked.

His finger pointed out the demesnes, wagging like a priest's blessing: "Palmer, Cooper, the M'Donaghs, Lord Avonmore . . . and, to be sure, the Marquis of Clanricarde. He owns the whole of Portumna."

"And what sort of a man is he?" Punch asked.

"Sure we never saw the hide nor hair of him. But I'll tell you this – if he got a shilling at his baptism, he has it about him still." In the same laconic tone he said quietly, "You may pull up your line now, Mr. Moore, and you, Mary Flinders, take those fish under your skirts awhile."

A water-bailiff was rowing out directly into their path, plainly with intent to stop them. "George McGrath," O'Donnell informed them. "The Cromwell of Lough Derg."

He tightened the sail into the wind until it fell slack. Though the boat lost headway, the breeze still pushed it north at a fair pace.

Punch dropped the flap of his breeches and concealed the line down there. Mary gritted her teeth and stuffed the fish into the tops of her stockings at the backs of her thighs. O'Donnell laughed as loud as he dared. "By the saints, ye'll have well-seasoned fish and a well-baited hook when that man's gone!" He raised his voice and shouted: "That's a grand day for counting your flocks, Mr. McGrath!"

The bailiff threw them a line, which Punch caught and held fast. "Haul me closer," he commanded gruffly as the momentum of the boat carried them on past him. "Who are those people?"

"That woman's a cousin of mine. That man is her man."

"And their names?"

Mary stood tall at the gunwale. "I'm the daughter of The Flinders of the Barony of Inchiquin in County Clare," she said, in tones of remembered gentility. "And your name, good man?"

For a moment it threw him out of his stride – a tribute as much to the number of eccentric gentry in Ireland as to the conviction in her accent. But one look at their clothing, at the ass in the prow, at Punch's tools of the trade, and he was jack-in-office again. "Your business?" he asked.

Punch stepped in and said, in more humble tones, "An it please your honour, sir, haven't I work on the Carlow navigation from Robertstown."

McGrath frowned. "Then you're out of your way by miles. The road to Carlow is through Nenagh and Maryborough."

"Saving your honour's geography, we may join the navigation at Monasterevin, so we're bound off through Borrisokane and Kinnity."

"Show me your hands. Haul me alongside now."

Punch took good care to let the rope slip a few inches at each haul; his hands, by the time McGrath was close by, smelled of nothing but tar and lakewater. Mary, realizing his purpose, went forward and petted the ass, letting it lick her hands free of any taint of the fish.

The bailiff saw he was defeated and that further bullying inquiry would only pin the ass's ears on him. "I'll swear I saw the flash of silver back there," he muttered darkly.

"Isn't it the joy of the spring itself that's in them," Punch said.

Mary reached into her bosom and pulled out her purse. She came aft, toward McGrath, spilling its coins into her hand. His eyes popped at the sight of so much gold, the best part of a year's wages to him. "Would we poach your lake?" she asked, "when we could buy every fish that's in it!"

Deliberately she dropped a sixpence in the bilge. Punch was quick to seize the chance, he stooped to trap it before it vanished, "inadvertently" letting slip the line. O'Donnell ran to trap the rope as it paid out but, "alas," fumbled and missed the chance. Without a hand at the tiller the boat yawed side-on to the wind, which caught up the sail and began pushing her northward much faster than McGrath could row. O'Donnell ran back to the helm. "Will I come about, Mr. McGrath?" he called amiably. "Will you give me the indemnity with Mr. Williams?"

Mr. Williams was Lord Clanricarde's agent and was known to resent McGrath's frequent interference with the grain boats as they plied up and down the lough. The bailiff waved them on with an angry flourish.

"God be good to you, sir!" Punch called out cheerfully. "May you never have a son that's blind!" Under his breath he added: ". . . without a crippled daughter to lead him!"

The sun was down by the time they reached Portumna.

"I'm in the Barony of Longford in County Galway," she said, as they stepped ashore, "and that's the second county I've been in in my life."

Punch pointed to the old wooden bridge across the Shannon. "And over there will be your third – County Tipperary. The Barony of Lower Ormonde."

O'Donnell wouldn't take a penny of the fare, and even said they could sleep the night in the boat; he pulled a tarpaulin over the bows to shelter them, for there was the smell of rain on the air, he believed. They turned the ass free to graze and all three went into the town together, O'Donnell to his home, the two travellers to buy victuals. But as they passed a tavern, of which there were several in the one main street, Punch took a shilling from her and said he'd buy O'Donnell a jar or two for his pains and she could make a start on baking the fish.

"Just the one, mind," O'Donnell said with politely feigned reluctance. "I'm wanted at home."

This banishment to the scullery, as it were, angered Mary. "Well I'm no sugared plum of a bog Kathleen," she told him sharply. "Ye have but thirty minutes. If you come later than that your fish'll be burnt, for I'll not move one scale of it from the fire."

O'Donnell laughed but Punch looked furious. She herself was so angry as she set off again for the grain basin that she almost forgot her marketing.

But the balmy ease of the evening, the tranquillity of the lake, and the promise of fresh-baked fish soon mollified her and she set about the cooking with a will. First, using Punch's shovel, she scraped out a hollow for the fire. She gutted and beheaded the fish before she went down to the bank and, again using the shovel, gathered marl from just beneath the water. In the first few handfuls she took care to wrap the offal before hurling it as far as she could into the lake; with the rest she completely encased the fish, which she then lay flat in the fire hollow. Around them she built a pyre of dried twigs. There was a cottage close by, where they collected the tolls for the bridge. She carried some tinder up there and brought it back glowing in its box. The man kept her talking for most of the half hour she had allowed Punch; she was annoyed all over again. She wanted to burn his supper and teach him a lesson.

Twilight was well advanced and the fire had died to a glow when she heard his footfall upon the highway above. Stubbornly she refused to turn and greet him. She leaned forward, intending to take out the first of the fish, when she heard his voice cry "Ahaa!"

But it was not his voice.

The blood seemed to freeze in her veins.

She turned and found herself staring up into the malevolent eyes of George McGrath – the Cromwell of Lough Derg.

# CHAPTER SIX

HE MADE NO MOVE. He simply stood there, staring at her. Terrified though she was, this pause allowed her to gather sufficient of her wits to take up Punch's pan, place it over the flames, and break into it a little knob of butter. While it melted she raked out one of the par-baked potatoes from the fire, taking care to poke the ashes even more thickly over the clay that encased the fish. Then she sliced the soft, creamy flesh into the now sizzling fat. She was fairly sure the two fish, tightly cased as they were, and baking very slowly, would give out no smell; but even if they did, the frying potatoes would now mask it.

McGrath saw her purpose. "Take that off, girl," he commanded.

"I will not," she told him. "D'you own the long acre itself?"

He stood above the flames and sniffed the air suspiciously. She saw he was uncertain how far to assert himself with her; also there was an odd look in his eye, as if for two pins he'd try to befriend her. "Ye took up fish from the lough today," he said. "That's as sure as tomorrow's dawn."

He strolled a short distance away, to the water's edge, where he rooted around among the reeds, seeking, no doubt, the fish-heads and offal. Pretending to a complete unconcern for him, she began to sing, "The lark in the clear air . . ."

He turned to face her, head on one side, smiling. "That's as sweet as the lark itself," he said.

She picked up a short length of cut reed and with its help turned over the slices. He came back to the fire. "Isn't that a grand reek! Ah isn't the potato your only man for the hunger."

"Isn't hunger itself the grandest spice," she replied, not taking her eyes off him. For some reason, her gaze disconcerted him, forcing him to look away. He squatted on his haunches and stared out over the darkling waters. " 'Tis three months since the oul' woman went to her reward," he said.

"I'm sorry for your trouble, Mister McGrath. Have you children?"

"Two left to rear. They're with the grandmother." He shook his head as if seeking to dislodge ideas that were stuck too fast to utter. "I thought the trade of water-bailiff was lonely enough, but . . ." He sighed.

She wagged the pan vigorously, to stop the food from sticking. "We're never burdened but for some purpose," she told him.

He seemed not to hear. "The work drives off all companionship, d'you see? A bailiff's a bailiff every hour God sends – but what other occupation is there? Sure I *want* to be a reasonable man, without being too aisy, if you follow. But let me give e'er an inch, they'll take a mile, and we'll all end up in gaol. And where's the good in that, I ask you?"

"It must be hard." She yielded him the merest smile and gazed anxiously up toward the road, cursing Punch and every public house in town. The ass stared down at her, mild-eyed, contented.

McGrath seated himself, too close for her comfort. "Is your fella good to you?" he asked. "Or does he beat you or what? Is he a drinking man?"

"He's not my man," she said. "We're bound off for London, where I'm to marry into the household of Lord Tottenham."

As soon as the admission was out she knew it had been a mistake. McGrath's eyes lit up. "So he's not your man! Yet you lie by him each night, I'll wager?" He looked her up and down, seeing her in quite a different light, frankly undressing her with his eyes.

"I do no such thing!" she protested. But she could hear how querulous she sounded – and fear in every quaver. It merely encouraged him.

"You needn't be frightened, now," he said soothingly. "I'm not one of your drunken brutes." He winked and grinned. "I can be as gentle as any young lord out of England. The oul' woman,

Lord-a-mercy, she'd have told you – I have a grand stroking way with me . . . and divil a woman to practise it on. Is it too much to ask?" He put a hand to her boot. The merest contact with her brought him out in trembling. She saw he was at some threshold. An inch or two more and whatever was driving him would become uncontrollable.

What was best? Humour him? Try to put him off? Seize the initiative and return two guineas of threat for every shillingsworth he offered? She lacked any experience that might guide her.

"I know there's fish in it," he was saying. "You have them sealed in clay beneath the embers – sure, haven't we all done it? But I'll say nothing. D'you hear me now? I'll leave you go in peace. We only pass this way but once – why can't we do each other a little kindness? You'd be wanting to do me a little kindness in return . . . surely?"

His grip moved up to her ankle. He was trembling all over now. His voice strayed up and down the scale. His throat was dry. There was a mute pleading in his eye that almost softened her – not into yielding but into saying something kindly, or not too wounding to his pride.

"Listen, I'm sorry for you," she told him gently. "You're as dacent a man as any in these parts, I'm sure. And if you'd only show your good heart to some woman of your own kind – as you've shown it to me . . ."

He let go her ankle and stood up, proud of the bulge in his breeches. Should she take up the pan and give it a clout?

"I'll show you I mean no harm," he said, and with the toe of his boot he began gingerly to rake aside the embers.

She snatched the pan to one side, aware that their little drama was approaching some kind of climax but having no inkling of its shape or form, wondering frantically what to do.

His toe dislodged the pike, the larger of the two that were cooking there. Its casing was quite hard and it moved in one rigid bundle without cracking apart. "There!" His triumph was mild, generous. "You may eat it in peace. Be his lordship's guest – *if* I may be yours."

"Sit yourself down, Mr. McGrath." Her voice was all over the place. "You'll be hungry, no doubt. It will be cooked to perfection."

"Perfection," he repeated dreamily as he unbelted his breeches. "Ah – you'll have kept it warm for me these long years."

She swung the hard edge of the pan against his shin with all the force she could muster. He let out one great bellow of pain and then fell on her, pinning her helplessly to the grass. Up on the road she heard the ass bray.

He tore at her bodice. She held it closed tight with her hand. He reached down between her legs and threw up her skirts. When she struggled to push them down again he went back to her bodice. And thus, bit by bit, her two hands being four too few for such work, he began to gain his object. In between these struggles he poured out his hatred. "That blow will cost you dear . . . I'll take your gold, too, so I will . . . and when my pleasure is done, 'tis the lockup for you – I'll see you transported . . . I'll see you dancing gallows-high."

He took her purse and flung it away into the dark, where he could retrieve it at his ease. As she reached out in one last futile gesture to prevent him, he tore the few remaining stitches that held her bodice together. She knew then that the struggle was hopeless – that is, the awareness of it began to creep in at the edges of her mind. Now she had a twin battle – with his lust, with her own despair.

He caught up her skirts and petticoats, holding a bunch of her hems in his mighty fist, the same fist as pinned her down by the shoulder. Not all her struggling beneath that unshakable weight could pry the fabric from his grasp; worse still, the fire prevented her from rolling herself out the easy way, down the slope. In one superhuman effort she tried to heave him onto it instead, but he guessed her purpose and spread wide his feet, pinning her more firmly than ever.

She became aware that her squirming was only exciting him further. His spittle fell in strands upon her cheeks and neck. To push his head away she had to remove both hands from the struggle to pull down her skirts. But that only gave him the chance for which he had been waiting – to thrust his trousers down to his knees. Now they were flesh to flesh.

*Why do I not scream out?* she wondered. Shame, of course. Even in the sticky thick of this loathsome struggle some inner voice was telling her that the public shame of it would be laid at her door, not his.

There came a terrible moment when all the fight in her petered out in weariness and resignation. Unbidden by her, every muscle relaxed. *Very well, be gentle with me now . . .* the words were in her mind, mustering themselves upon her tongue. She felt herself, her true self, shrivelling inside, abandoning her body to him, seeking refuge in some withdrawn knot of her innermost being, some stubborn, inviolable cranny of her person.

And at that instant she, McGrath, the dying fire, the river's edge, the moonbanked clouds – all seemed to pass over into a land of nightmare. She opened her eyes and looked up – and there, squatting over them, his curved horns impaling the skies, was none other than the Earl of Hell. His infernal breath was hot on both their faces. McGrath felt it, too. She sensed the terror as it seized him. He wrenched his neck as he turned to look; she heard the gristle crack. For a moment he and the Devil stared each other in the face, their noses almost touching.

Then he gave out a little, high-pitched scream, so girlish it would, in other circumstances, have been comical. The Devil opened wide his jaws; she saw the filthy teeth as they closed, giving one great bite to the man's neck. Without a whimper, McGrath fell upon her, senseless.

And the Devil raised his head and brayed the moon.

When she saw it was only the ass she laughed and wept and laughed again, all in the one breath. She rolled out from under her attacker and, leaping to her feet, placed her boot firmly on the man's neck. But there wasn't a stir out of him. She relaxed a little. The ass came to her side and nudged her gently with its long, soft nose. She gave it a hug and stroked its ears and made every sort of a fuss of it altogether.

Then, seeing what danger she still was in, she stooped and sought among Punch's gear for a ball of twine she knew he kept there. In the dark she took an agony of minutes to find it but still McGrath did not stir.

She wondered if he were dead and realized she cared not a jot – a response she never thought to feel toward another human soul. When she found the twine, it was a matter of moments to bind his wrists behind his back. Then she took it up in a loop around his neck and so down to his ankles, the way that, if he tried to straighten himself, he'd choke – the way Con had shown her once for a cod.

Finally she opened his jaws, forced the stiff fragment of reed between his teeth, like a horse's bit. She tied the two projecting ends, looping the string behind his neck. He was breathing, she noted. Now, if he tried to cry out when he recovered she could stuff his mouth with clay and grass without his biting her or being able to spit it out.

The moon sailed forth from behind the cloud; by its light she saw his tiny, shrivelled manhood. If you tied a knot around it tight enough, she wondered, would it dry out and drop off the way the parts of the young rams do? Wouldn't it only be a boon to every female in the barony.

There was a footfall, some way off, along the highway. "Punch?" she called out.

He heard the edge to her voice and came running. Quickly she gathered together the torn edges to her bodice and wrapped a shawl over them, tying tight the knot as she went up the bank to meet him.

"What's that?" he asked, seeing the hunched body in the grass.

"McGrath," she replied. "And the seven curses of Quilty upon him!"

"Is he dead?"

"To the world. He's breathing yet."

"Did he find the fish?"

She sniffed. "He was after more than the fish."

He turned to her, wide-eyed. "Your gold?"

She remembered her purse suddenly and dashed to the spot where she fancied it had fallen. While she hunted she said, "More than that even." She raised the shawl to show her torn bodice; he looked away in embarrassment.

"By all the saints, what did you do to the fella?" He went down the bank and stooped to examine the way she'd tied the body. "You're a mistress of the gaoler's art, I'll give you that," he said.

She found her purse and, retying the broken thong, put it once more around her neck; it was cold between her breasts but the comfort was never greater. She was on the point of telling him what the ass had done when it struck her that it might be no bad thing if she had the reputation of being able to put a man out cold like that. And it'd show him she was no child.

"I hurt him where it wouldn't blind him," she said lightly. "Only he was so sudden at me he'd never have torn this. What's to do with him though? He could still bring trouble upon us."

Punch thought it over. Then he looked at her bundle, where the poteen cruse was hidden. " 'Tis a waste of good hard shtuff," he allowed. "But sure we've no choice."

He got a reed from the bank and, with one of his mason's chisels, pushed out the pith from the core of it, leaving a stout, hollow tube. He took out his knife and cut one end on the slant. "We'll fill him full of the sperrits and leave him on one of those islands to sleep it off," he explained.

Just at that moment, McGrath stirred and gave out a little moan. He tried to straighten himself. When the cord tightened around his neck it choked him wide awake. He looked up at them and the panic of bewilderment gave way to the terrors of remembrance.

"Sure, this is better still," Punch said as he cast aside the reed. He helped the man up into a sitting position and then, kneeling beside him put the knife to his throat. "One whisper outa you and I'll furnish you a new mouth to breathe by," he warned.

McGrath, squinting down at the point of the blade, nodded as vigorously as he dared.

Punch tipped his head toward Mary. "You may free his mouth."

"Are you sure?"

"I'm sure. And then you may bring a jar of the poteen. Wet it with enough water that he'll be able to drink it down."

While she complied he turned his attention back to their prisoner. "By rights I should kill you for what you sought to do to that one," he said. "But we'll be merciful. We'll leave you dead drunk on one of those islands. When you stir in the morn, you'll have to swim ashore. And you'll find your boots and breeches in County Tipperary, by the Ferry Inn, where the roads divide."

"Ah God, leave us the breeches," the man pleaded. "If the Kellys who gather the tolls see me bare-arsed, I'd as well . . ."

"You're lucky to be left with your life," Punch told him roughly. "Now houl' your whisht or I'll take new counsel."

Mary returned with the cup of slightly diluted spirits. Punch held it to the man's lips. "You'll drink the full of this," he warned. "Spit out one drop and I'll cut the ear outa ya."

McGrath managed half the cup before his gorge rebelled. Desperate not to spill it he backed off slowly, making urgent noises in his throat. Punch relented.

"At least pull my breeches up while the lass is here," McGrath panted.

"You were proud enough to show it off ten minutes ago," Mary told him.

"Ten minutes?" He closed his eyes, shook his head gently. "Jasus!" He opened them again, his memory rekindling. "What was it? God I'd swear it was the Divil himself with his great eyes like carriage clocks, and the horns on him like a heathen, and the stink outa him like all the cess in town."

"There was nothing," she said innocently. "Your own bad conscience, like as not. I had you bet, fair and square."

"Then you're a witch, so," he told her.

She drew back her hand and slapped him hard.

"Aisy! Aisy now." Punch intervened. "You – drink down some more o' this."

On the man's empty stomach the liquor soon took effect. His head began to roll; he wheezed; his eyes wandered.

"You may free him of his boots now," Punch said.

McGrath looked at her, too unsteady to assist even had he wished it. "Why did you?" he asked, and then stood the question upside down. "Why wouldn't you? 'Tis the sweetest music."

"A few more swallows," Punch said.

". . . and we'll make this man's summer!" Mary laughed.

Soon McGrath was out to the world again.

"It would be a shame were the fish to spoil," Mary reflected.

Punch laughed. "Begod but you're the cool one!"

She found a handful of potatoes still among the embers, overbaked but edible. The fish were done almost to perfection, just a little dry. They washed it down with the clear limestone waters of the Shannon – and soon felt like royalty.

"No two fish were harder got – nor better ate," he said.

"'Twas meself had the hard getting, and you had the better eating," she pointed out.

"Sure, I was obliged to wet your man's whistle – and he after bringing us all the way from Killaloe at no harm to our purses."

"Well, well . . ." she half-conceded.

"But I'll not leave you again," he promised.

"Ha! I know you – you'll promise Christmas in December."
He rose and, looking down at the snoozing, half-naked body,
he chuckled. "I wouldn't cod you now, girleen. Aren't you a
better companion than any man that ever I shared with the road?"


# CHAPTER SEVEN


As a matter of prudence they resumed their journey the
moment they had the drunken McGrath safely snoozing among
the bulrushes on a little island within wading distance of the
Tipperary shore. They walked a short piece along the Terryglass
road before dumping the man's breeches and boots, to make it
appear they had taken that way instead of the Parsonstown road,
toward which they now cut across the fields. They reached
Parsonstown itself at dawn.

For the first hour or so of that moonlight journey Mary fought
the compulsion to speak of her experience. Punch held his
counsel, too. Their talk was all, "Isn't that a fine, sturdy
ass . . ." and, "Would you look at those fields, such grand
country altogether . . ." and, "Those clouds have a fierce air
about them . . ." – they spoke of anything but McGrath and what
he had sought to do. But at last, Mary could hold herself back no
more. "Is all the world beyond like that?" she asked.

"Well, I want to tell you about that," Punch replied, "for it has
me perplexed entirely. I'd have sworn that a woman could walk
unmolested from Slyne Head to the Point of Howth, safe
through every inch."

"He wasn't even drunk." She laughed and added, ". . . when
he arrived, anyway!"

He joined her laughter. "We put right that small fault. Did he
say nothing?"

She was about to tell him of the death of McGrath's wife but then, remembering Punch's own bereavement, merely said, "Ah, it was a mixture of bully-talk and sweetness. He didn't say above twenty words before he had one hand round my ankle and the other at his buttons."

Punch chuckled. "You mean, two *hundred* words and you'd have considered the request. Two thousand and it was as good as granted?"

"Not twenty, anyway. And him such a stranger."

"Well now!"

They walked on in easy silence. After a while, Punch said, "Give the divil his due, that man was right about one thing."

"What was that?"

"It is 'the sweetest music.'" He let her digest that before he added, philosophically, as if they were discussing some overhead snippet of scholar's talk on the behaviour of a remote and primitive tribe, "The mystery is that the men can hear it everywhere. They hear it in the fields, along the ditches, up the street, in chapel, in the tavern, at cockcrow and sunset, midnight and noon . . . for the men it's music as common as the wind."

The silence forced her to ask, "And the women?"

"You know yourself," he said. "Aren't your ears stopped against it? Even when a woman has heard it once, or a score of times . . ."

"Aha – a musical score!" She laughed.

He was not deflected. ". . . the stopping is still there. They'll hear it – but deny it's there. A woman does need a particular musician, a particular concert, and a particular conjunction of the planets and her whims before she'll admit Old Pan is playing his pipes."

"Can you understand that?" she asked.

"Not I! There's three classes of men will never understand the women: young men, old men, and men of the middle years."

And that was all they said on the subject that night. She lightened the road with the old song:

> *Is it true that the women are worse than the men –*
> *That they were sent down to Hell and were threw out again?*

. . . all forty-eight verses of it.

As they walked into Parsonstown the rain began to fall in rivers.

They took breakfast at Dooly's, where they stabled the ass and, shortly afterwards, settled themselves down in the hay to sleep out the morning. After a bite of lunch they had the luck of a new farm cart that was being delivered to Frankford; but for that they would not have reached Charleville, on the outskirts of Tullamore, by evening.

Mary thought Parsonstown a gem of a place, quite unlike Portumna, which had seemed mean and drab. When she said as much to Michael Hoctor, the driver, he told them it was the difference between a town where the landlord was an absentee, like Portumna and the de Burgh-Cannings, the marquisses of Clanricarde, and a town where the landlord was resident, like Parsonstown and the Parsons family, the earls of Rosse. "And 'tis a game ye may play the length and breadth of Ireland," he said: "Who's with us and who's beyond."

The rain eased off soon after they reached Frankford, and by the time they were in sight of Charleville, a good drying wind had removed all evidence of it. They camped for the night on an island between the old wooden bridge and the new stone one by the Charleville back gates, where the river divides. Mary, for whom the few hours in the hay at Dooly's had not made up for last night's lack of sleep, nodded off as soon as their supper was done. Punch went out to set his snares in the Charleville woods, which Michael Hoctor swore had grown unhindered since Ireland left the Creator's hands. From the mighty softness of the woodland floor, he could well believe it.

Back at the encampment he lay on his bedding of fronds and leaves and watched the dying firelight as it played over Mary's sleeping face. She was but three or four years older than the eldest of his daughters, who had died in the fire. That filled him with paternal longings toward her, an urge to protect her, to see her well set forth upon her own path in life. But she was also only a dozen years younger than that darling woman, the most warm and wonderful wife a man could have wished for, who had perished in the same blaze. And that memory filled him with longings for Mary of quite a different order. As he lay and watched her, he could feel both urges inside him. He was aware that as they walked the roads of Ireland together, he was forever juggling the two feelings in his heart, teasing his baser nature with the one, reviving his nobler parts with the other, keeping all possibilities alive.

As he sank toward sleep he was in fatherly vein, wondering what would she make of her life. Would she get the measure of that Con Murphy, who, in his opinion, was a gobshite of the lowest rank? Should he warn her, or would that only set her more firmly in her ways? You never knew with women.

He decided to say nothing unless she asked. Her lack of curiosity – about Murphy, about London, about what life might hold for her – was only amazing. Still, the lass could look after herself in *one* way – begod, but she'd proved that!

# CHAPTER EIGHT

IT WAS A SOFT DAY. They cooked and ate their rabbits in a chill dawn. The first time they had breakfasted on poached game, back at Tulla on the road to Killaloe, it had seemed to her as harmless as eating berries out of the hedgerows. Now, since the brush with McGrath over the fish, it felt like the worst of crimes. She bolted down the meat and could not throw away the bones quickly enough nor far enough for her peace of mind. Some magistrates, if their own parklands had been marauded lately, would even transport you for it for life. She had never before realized how narrow is the divide between the criminal and the respectable. If anyone were to catch them now, then she, merely for taking up these few morsels of flesh, could be sent to Virginia for life! Or was it Botany Bay, nowadays? Anyway, the very thought was enough to make her feel reckless; what did lesser fears matter when one's fate hung by such a delicate thread? Of what use were minor constraints? Life was there to be enjoyed before the axe fell and the men with the darkness arrived.

They spent half an hour hunting for the ass. But then they made good time over the Bog of Allen, through the baronies of Geashill and East Offaly, arriving at Monasterevin late that afternoon. Having for the moment exhausted their conversation, as well as her repertoire of song, extensive though it was, she passed most of the journey in reading to Punch out of the books she had brought from home. He enjoyed *Robinson Crusoe* but after they rested for a bite at noon he asked her would she save the remainder of the story for those next days. So in the afternoon, between the showers, they polished off the whole of a much shorter novel called *Old Nick*.

He considered it the best tale ever, a perfect blend of morality and the other thing. He asked who had written it. She pointed to the title page and, thinking to teach him at least one word, said, slowly, "Anon."

He was amazed. "The world's gone mad altogether!" he said. "You'd never suppose one of them ladies could dream up such a tale as that."

At Monasterevin they got a night's lodging in the stables of the Drogheda Arms, in whose bars Mary earned their supper with her harp. She had a clear, young voice with a fine shake in it and a cutting edge that silenced hard-bitten men and made them think of their mothers and recall innocent, gentle, carefree days long gone. The curate who brought round the drinks, a wild young fellow off a farm in Carlow, taught her a new song, "While goin' the road to sweet Athy . . ." that had savagery in every verse. She thought she would like to learn more such songs . . . indeed, would like to keep the young man's company at least a day or two more, rough though he was.

"Where would be the harm in it?" she asked Punch.

He watched the budding of this miniature romance and was again torn between his own two selves. One half of him seethed with jealousy, such pangs as he had not felt these many years, but the other half wished to encourage it – not too much – just enough to show her how little she really felt for Con Murphy. In the heel of the hunt, Old Necessity made their choice for them. There was a boat bound for Dublin at four next morning. On it they could be at the City Bason by noon, which would leave them a day and a half in Dublin before the mail packet sailed from the Custom House Quay. "Little enough time for that big place," he told her. "And we still have the ass to sell."

They had an argument about that, of course, which he ended by saying he'd forgotten what cantankerous eejits women were. But she kept the ass.

Next day the locks were in their favour all the way and they made better time than predicted, arriving in the City Bason at just gone eleven.

"And now I've been in six counties!" she said delightedly. "Clare, Galway, Tipp – King's, Kildare, Dub! Six counties in five days – it's a wonder I'm not giddy with it all."

"And are you not?" he asked, casting a morose eye toward the ass.

The City Bason was at the extreme western edge of Dublin, among the market gardens around Mount Brown. Their first sight of the place was grim indeed: up Cutt Throat Lane, past the Bedlam, beside the Workhouse, and along by the Bridewell – all the official dumps for the city's human rubbish. Unofficial dumps there were, too, in plenty. Their walk along the lane beside the fields led them among clusters of decrepit cabins that seemed to float on a tidal sea of children in every last state of wretchedness. Their mothers leaned in the doorways, crying out for alms. Most had a child at the knee, another on the hip, and yet another to swell out their bellies; they seemed too exhausted to do anything but beg. She fingered her purse but one look from Punch was enough to quell the impulse. "God, they'd be onto us like travelling rats," he warned. "You'd best accustom yourself to those sights now for you'll run such a gauntlet in every town from that to London – and in London worst of all."

When they reached Kilmainham Lane she looked back and hoped that, in her eyes at least, such scenes would never grow stale, hoped she might one day have money to spare.

Along St. James's Street her sense of wonder rekindled. In all the breadth of Ireland, walking from town to town, the largest place they had come through was Parsonstown, which took under ten minutes to cross; the whole of it could have been lost in that one Dublin street. And the buildings! These were not the fine places she knew from the engravings in her father's books – the

Castle, the Parliament House, Trinity College, and the Duke of Leinster's new palace – these were ordinary private dwellings and commercial premises, chandlers and merchants with great warehouses out the back. The mixture of rich and poor amazed her. Up near the Watch House at St. James's Gate stood a row of elegant new houses; but right in the middle was a dirty, narrow passage, Cherry Tree Lane, that gave views into a sort of earthly purgatory, dark, filthy, and overshadowed – worse than the hovels by the canal for at least they had fresh air and fields about them.

"The stench!" she said.

"Lord that's not from there," Punch told her. "That's from Dunghill Lane where the city middens are."

She looked at him askance, not entirely believing it.

"Sure," he said, "if every man, woman, and child went out with a spade each day, the way it is in the country, they'd turn every bare sod from Kilmainham to Irishtown inside the one week!"

"So the whole city goes to the one place?"

"No! Do your fine books teach you nothing! They empty the soil into the carts each night and they tip the carts out there. How else might they go about it?"

The stench of the middens did not diminish until the two wanderers were past the Cornmarket, through the old city wall, and in sight of Christchurch. The cathedral was the first building she recognized from the books – what little she could see of it over the roofs of the houses and stables. When they drew level with it, they turned right and went down Nicholas Street; there, in Draper's Court, a mean little yard at the bottom of the hill, they got lodgings until the morrow. It was Punch's regular "skipper" in Dublin; there was also stabling for the ass. Just before they turned into the place she looked farther down the street and saw the familiar outlines of the city's other cathedral, St. Patrick's. "We should go and pay our respects to Dean Swift's house," she said.

But when they emerged once more, after a light refreshment, it was back up the hill that she directed her feet, toward Dames Street and the fashionable milliners' houses. There, at the corner of Crane Lane, was a workshop where cast-off ladies' dresses were renovated and sold cheap – or less expensively than when new. She had never seen so many fine articles. After an agony of "Shall I get this or what about that?" – which drove Punch to the alehouse and left her in peace and ecstasy – she bought a gorgeous bodice, ruched in glittering peach-coloured satin all across the front and edged in golden piping; it had lace at the cuffs with perfect little apples and flowers embroidered into the cruilles. And then there was a torn silk dress she was sure she could mend – the same general colour as the bodice but of a darker hue. She toyed with the notion of getting a wig, too, but, alarmed at what she had already spent, she decided she could always hire one until she had money enough to buy. Anyway, the wigs they had for sale looked more like nests for mice.

When she left, the woman who owned the place surprised herself, and astonished her downtrodden little assistant, by making a present of a small bangle. There was little enough value in the trinket but it was years since the woman had been moved to such an act. There was something so appealing about this happy, innocent young country girl. Her usual customers, the poor-but-ambitious respectable womenfolk of petty traders, would pick sourly over the cast-off clothing and look as if they were trying not to vomit. But this simple colleen's unaffected delight had been so infectious, the jaded old storekeeper had not been able to help herself.

Mary took directions and returned by a more roundabout way, past the Castle gates and down Warburgh Street. She had wanted to see the city north of the river but, or so her informant told her, a big faction fight had been going on all week between the butchers of Ormonde Quay and the tailors of the Liberties, and all the bridges were impassable on foot. Since the battle was neither religious nor political, the soldiery did nothing to hinder it. Still, she had to allow that the men, all in their scarlet tunics, and the officers, laden with gold braid and plumes, made a brave sight in the afternoon sun. The Castle sentries stared at her with frankly hungry eyes; and the officers, too, looked her up and down in a way that was becoming familiar, almost tiresome. If she were wearing the clothes that were now bundled under her arm, after a bit of mending, to be sure, then they'd see she was really a lady. *Then* they'd not dare not look her over with that superior carelessness. No – there'd be less certainty in it, more humility, more of a plea . . .

She luxuriated in the dream of it. If Con were some sort of favourite of Lord Tottenham, and if his lordship were well up among the likes of officers and such crowds . . . well, who could tell what might transpire?

Swift's house in St. Kevan's Street was a disappointment – a house like any other. You could pass it every day and never guess what marvels of sedition, spite, and exuberance had issued from it. The same was true of his birthplace up in Hooey's Court, to which she now returned (having walked straight past it in her daydreaming). But sure what else could you expect of bricks and plaster? The military comings and goings in the Main Guard at the head of the court were more interesting. She drifted back in that direction.

Hard by the guardhouse was a bookseller's stall. She would never have been tempted inside if she had not seen, newly gilded among a row of faded spines, the title, *METAMORPHOSES or The Golden Ass, a New Translation*.

If asses had stars, they were high in her firmament that week.

The bookseller, not knowing she could read but supposing rather that she was a servant sent out by her master for a selection of recent titles, thought it amusing to lay so dirty a tale in such innocent hands – where it could surely do no harm. When he learned the truth, he was mortified; but by then he had seen the bag of gold around her neck and could not choose but let her browse to her heart's ease.

Her next choice was a second-hand book called *The Fortunes and Misfortunes of the Famous Moll Flanders, &c. who was Born at Newgate, and during a Life of continued Variety for Threescore Years, besides her Childhood, was Twelve Year a Whore, five times a Wife (whereof once to her own Brother), Twelve Year a Thief, Eight Year a Transported Felon in Virginia, at last grew rich, liv'd Honest, and died a Penitent. Written from her own Memorandums, by Daniel Defoe.* It was obviously a moral tale that promised much instruction in matters that had never been talked about but which, she felt daily more convinced, ought to be known to her. Besides, the name was too close a coincidence for her to ignore.

She saw the scandalized look in the bookseller's eye and so added to her pile of purchases, *The New Whole Duty of Man, Containing the Faith as well as Practice of A Christian . . . Authorized by the King's Most Excellent Majesty* . . . She tried to give the impression that this was indeed the book she had come of a purpose to buy.

Then her eyes fell on an old collection of poems. The pages were torn and stained, but the title page alone induced her to buy: *THE ARBOR OF amorous Devices. Wherin, young Gentlemen may reade many plesant fancies, and fine devices: And thereon, meditate divers sweete Conceites, to court the love of faire Ladies and Gentlewomen By N. B. Gent . . . 1597.*

It would be well for her to know the tricks and "sweete conceites" of gentlemen, she thought; it would be even better to be able to tell if those gentlemen who might pay her court were truly of good blood or were mere rogues. She added it to her pile.

To explain the choice to the bookseller, she pointed to the author's name and said with an offhand smile, "My family is closely related to the Gents."

"There's many would wish to claim that," he said, suppressing a smile. The child's eclectic browsing fascinated him; and her utter lack of guile was quite charming.

Moments later she returned with a brand new book, fresh in that morning: *The Amazing Tablet of Memory, shewing every Memorable Event in History from the Earliest Period to the Year 1790, classed under distinct Heads.*

"Everything that ever happened!" she said in tones of awe as she placed it on top of her pile. "And all in one volume!" Then, in a more businesslike tone, she turned and asked, "How much is that now?"

When she heard the addition she turned pale. He saw it, saw how she looked again at the titles, wondering which to put back. To his dismay she picked not just one but three. "I'll tell you what," he said smoothly, clamping the pile together again and removing only the *Tablet of Memory*. "Buy the rest and I'll make you a gift of that one, a free and gratis gift to a *connoisseuse* of good books and a lady of exquisite discrimination! A feminine Mæcænas to literary genius!" While he mouthed these flatteries he calculated the gesture would would cost him eighteen pence. But then his profit on the remainder was four times that at least.

Moments later, white about the gills, shivering with an emotion that was neither fear nor awe but a little of each, she walked back along Bridget's Alley, clutching her books and clothes.

Of her five guineas – or a hundred and five shillings – there remained but twenty-seven shillings and threepence farthing.

# CHAPTER NINE

WHEN THE PACKET BOAT, with all her five sails bent, slipped the Custom House Quay, immediately below Christchurch, a brisk nor'wester pushed her smartly down the Anna Liffey and out into Dublin Bay. A following sea athwart her stern and running almost even gave her a queasy, lopsided yaw. Punch, no great sailor, clung to the rail and tried to keep his eyes on the horizon. Mary, too excited to worry about seasickness, watched the dwindling of the Wicklow Mountains and Howth Head. *Now it begins!* she told herself, wondering what *it* might be. Lucius, as she had decided to call the ass (after the Golden Ass of that scandalous book she had bought), was tied fast to the rail; he was content with life as long as she was beside him and a bag of roots was hung about his neck.

When the land had paled to a memory, Mary left off her reverie and turned to Punch. "Ask me the name of any lord mayor of London since 1758," she challenged.

He grunted.

"Ask me when any university was founded – any one you like."

He grunted twice.

"Ask me any battle in history, anywhere in the world. I've got them all set down here. Go on, ask me."

He groaned.

"Very well, I'll ask you. Did you know the date of Noah's Deluge? It began on the twenty-fifth day of November in 2348 B.C. and it continued three hundred and seventy-seven days. And Noah left the ark on the eighteenth day of December the following year. There now!"

"That man was a triple saint!" Punch said. "A year on a boat with all them animals!" He glanced sternly at Lucius.

The argument with the ship's officer over letting the ass on board still rankled – especially the audacious way Mary had gallivanted with the fellow, casting sheep's eyes at him until he was confounded entirely. The worst of it was she had no idea what she was at; she couldn't picture herself the way men would look at her; all she could see was that this kind of a smile, this tone of a voice, this fluttering of an eyelash, had a persuading effect on them. It bent them to her will – indeed, to her merest whim. So naturally she had favoured the officer with that kind of a smile, cooed at him in that tone of a voice, put just that ardent tremor into her eyelids . . . until the poor man was fluthered. Fortunately he seemed a dacent enough fellow, with a wife and family at journey's end in Holyhead. It sufficed that Mary flattered his self-esteem with such attentions.

But before many days were out she'd surely meet the other class of a rogue, who'd take her as a filly good for a canter over any hurdle and best of all on the back stretch.

Meanwhile, here she was at the ship's rail, prating on: "I expect not many people would know that in the Year of Our Lord 1571, Marcley Hill near Hereford was moved from its situation on a Saturday evening and it continued in its motion until the Monday morning, and it carried with it all the fields and hedges and cattle on its surface, and it overthrew a chapel in its path, and it formed a large hill, twelve fathom high, and left behind a forty-foot chasm where it had formerly stood. Wouldn't that have been a sight for pity and terror!" After a moment she added, "I wonder where is Hereford?"

"Oh turn all the pages," he replied. " 'Twill be recorded in there somewhere."

She ignored his sarcasm. "The title page doesn't even say who wrote the book," she complained. "He must have a long head on his shoulders the size of Howth itself."

"Then he's afraid so."

"Of what, pray?"

"That some man of good sense would take him out to sea and sink him and then build a lighthouse on him – where he'd be more use to mankind in general and me in particular than he ever is now!"

She laughed and, throwing her arms around him, gave him a tight hug, saying, "God love you, Punch, but you're a fierce oul' shtick-in-the-mud."

He shrugged himself reluctantly out of the embrace. "Ah, away with you! Put aside your *Tablet of Memory* and read us a tale outa the other book, the woman who was twelve year a whore."

"My, isn't this a new song! When I told you the title yesterday, you said there was little purpose now in reading the tale itself for wasn't it all there on the first page."

"It isn't for me you must read it, girl, but for your own sake – for the cautions that's in it."

"And do *I* need cautions then? I'm sure Mister McGrath wouldn't think it!"

"You do so. Listen while I tell you now, if that ship's officer wasn't the dacent man he is, you'd be on your back in the sail locker this minute, fighting him off and wishing to God you'd heeded me and your Miss Moll Flanders."

For a moment he dented her confidence, but soon the smile was back. "You'd be my St. George," she replied. "Didn't I see the murder in your eye by the lake in Portumna, when I told you what had passed between McGrath and me, and you had the man asleep at your feet? Anyway," she added, "a ship's officer is almost a gentleman."

He grew angry with her. "Sure there's nothing more danger-ous abroad than a woman with sharp eyes and a thinking box behind them that's as empty as a snake's slipper – and her with as much experience of the world as a gnat might pilfer."

She was chastened at last.

"The more so," he added in a gentler voice, "when the lass in question has a fortunate face and the figure of Venus and hasn't the first notion of . . . ah well, you'll learn soon enough. God send it's . . ."

"No – go on – I haven't the first notion of what? What'll I learn?"

"We've spoken of it before," he said awkwardly.

"When? I don't recall it."

"You do so. We spoke of the music men hear, above and below and beyond. Well, I want to tell you – the seeing of you, and the hearing of you, and the *being* of you, is like a whole flurry of fiddlers playing that same music to the most of mankind."

"But how? That's what I don't understand. What do I do that makes it so?"

"Nothing. You needn't do a thing. Just when you walk even, the way you move, just to watch you – dear God, it's like watching two rabbits fighting in a sack!"

"Away with you!" She laughed gaily and her face coloured up. "Enough of this. We'll make a start with Moll Flanders, an it please you."

By the time they slipped into Holyhead harbour she had quite a circle of listeners around her, sprawled on the deck, sitting on their bundles, hanging on the sheets. An impromptu collection, quite unasked for, brought in tenpence farthing, which got them both a decent night's lodgings at the inn near Four Mile Bridge, a bath, and a goodly breakfast the following day.

Before they set off she washed out one of her petticoats and hung it over the bundles on Lucius to dry as they went along – a condition it achieved only four miles later, at Llanynghenedl. At a stream just beyond the village she washed out a second petticoat. She had to run to catch up with Punch, who had been hard enough to persuade into the tub the previous night and who had absolutely no patience with such frivolities as the laundering of clothes that had been worn a mere week. "When you'd throw a shirt at the wall and it'd lodge there – that's time enough for a wash," he said.

Before they reached the ferry at Menai that evening, where they crossed over to the Welsh mainland, she had all last week's clothes fresh and bright once more. A few miles down the road they came into Bangor, where they decided to rest for the night. Once again, her skill with the harp and her fine voice earned them their lodging and a little over – quite a little over, in fact.

All that day they had trudged toward the mighty, misty-blue outlines of the North Wales mountains, with Snowdon towering over them all – still, as its name half-promised, capped with snow. The following morning the English road from Bangor led up, up, interminably up, into the very heart of those highlands.

When about mid-afternoon they reached the summit of the road, she gazed at the peaks that soared far above them still, some so high they were lost in the clouds; it seemed impossible that after climbing most of the day they had still reached only the feet of those enormous slopes. At last she understood why so many English writers, when they referred to the Wicklow mountains, or the Slieve Auchties near Poulaphuca, often put the word *mountains* between quotation marks; they were, indeed, pimples compared with these titans of rock and snow.

"I'd hate to come this way in winter," she said.

"Oh, you can't at all," he told her. "You have to go along the coast to Chester."

He seemed to know all of England. Since he never read a book or looked at a map, she wondered how the information was tucked away in his mind; she could not think of even that part of the journey they had already completed without seeing it as a line on the map.

The rest of that day was mercifully downhill, to Betsy-Coed, where they broke their march for the night. Again, her singing brought in a handy surplus over the cost of their lodging. The innkeeper offered Punch three pounds for her.

"I all but took it," he confessed. "In Ireland I would, but here in England I have a reputation for fair dealing to keep up."

Next day they still tramped through wild country, though not so bleak as at the summit of the road. They passed four people in all that time, until they drew near Llangollen, where the landscape grew suddenly more tame and there was even a sprinkling of gentlemen's houses.

"Tomorrow," Punch told her, "we'll be in Shrewsbury, and from there we may travel by navigation and canal all the way to London."

The surplus at the inn that night, added to earlier surpluses, had recouped her purse to the extent of twenty-two shillings, bringing her fortune back to almost half its original size. On learning that they still had the best part of one hundred and sixty Irish miles to tramp before they reached London she calculated that, at this rate of earning, she'd be able to hand Con back his five guineas and still have coins to jingle.

In fact, she found herself thinking before she fell asleep that night, why go to London at all? Why stay with Punch? She and

Lucius could travel independently about the country, and she singing for their supper. It needn't always be in taverns, either. The way it would happen would be she'd come to some place and a young duke travelling home and much troubled in his mind would hear her and be charmed and he'd take her to his palace and there she'd sing for him. And perhaps he'd fall in love with her. Or even if he didn't, one of his guests would hear her and give her an invitation to his castle . . . and so she'd go on, from one big country mansion to another until she knew every noble family and every gent in England . . .

The word *gent* made her pause. She suddenly realized. Of course, that was what it meant on the title page of *The Arbour of Amorous Devices*. N. B. Gent – "N.B." were the man's initials; "Gent" was simply his rank. Punch had been closer to it when he'd joked that the book was written by No Bloody Gent! She remembered how she'd boasted to the shopkeeper of being "closely related to the Gents." Now it made her want to scream. She threw the old coachman's coat up over her head and shouted *No n-no* . . . over and over in her mind to mask her embarrassment, until at last she fell into merciful sleep.

In her dreams she was indeed taken up by a young nobleman, who carried her away to the most splendid castle. It was surrounded by a rose garden in which roamed all the most ferocious animals in the world. They came rushing at her but when they heard her sing they were pacified at once. She told the young lord she wanted to bear his child but he said he wouldn't spoil her, she was so perfect. It made her angry, but he gave her a potion that he swore would get her with his child if only she sang the right tune while she swallowed it. But he wouldn't tell her the tune and she was afraid to swallow the potion in ignorance of it.

It was a stupid, shameful dream. She awoke very grumpy.

# PART TWO

# OVER THE WATER

# CHAPTER TEN

ARON M'GROTTY SAT on the opened barrel of blasting powder smoking his clay pipe. He knew it was dangerous, of course, to himself even more than to any of the workmen under him; but that only made it the more exciting. He felt brave, even dashing, devil-may-care. He gained a sense of power. He was challenging God, and God always shrank from the contest – so far. And it revealed his power over the men, too; no matter how much they feared the explosion of the powder, they feared him more. Not a man among them dared speak out, for Aaron M'Grotty was their charge hand; Aaron M'Grotty had power almost of life and death over them.

They had now been digging this tunnel, on a branch of the Rugely & Coalbrookdale Canal, for two weeks, and had reached more than half a dozen fathoms into the hillside: eight labourers, four mining carpenters, two mason's carpenters, and four stonemasons. Eighteen men, all of whom would be glad to see him dead, and not one among them with guts enough to speak out. Scum, the lot of them. The sweepings of the country's gaols and rookeries.

Aaron M'Grotty puffed his pipe contentedly, blowing sharply back down the stem so as to create a dangerous shower of sparks. He watched the men all freeze. "Come on, ye dogs!" he cursed at them. "The next man I see stretching his back is for the long walk and the cold kipper. Now let's *move* some of this clay!"

Scum, every man jack. He hated them – singly, together, side-by-side, near or far . . . he hated them. And none more so than Matt Sullivan, the professor. "Silent" Sullivan knew a better way to do everything under the sun. Anything you cared to set before him, he could improve it. He never talked much about it, he'd just stand and watch the fools making a mess of things, and then he'd step in and – straight off, no practice go at it, just as if he was born to it – do it better. It was his silence that was so infuriating; cool, contemptuous, superior. What the women saw in him was past all comprehension.

Aaron M'Grotty hated Matt Sullivan with a passion that exceeded all others in his sour, dark soul.

Matt, in turn, had little liking for Aaron M'Grotty. Not that he wasted much time thinking about the man. Or any man. Or any woman, come to that. Women were all right; they seemed to find him fascinating – for which he was grateful, and not a little puzzled. But at least it meant he didn't have to waste much time actually *thinking* about them.

Matt spent most of his time absorbed in the endlessly fascinating behaviour of the world of things. At the moment, for instance, while his body was mechanically shovelling out the clay and shale brought down in the last detonation of blasting powder, his mind was pondering a problem the stonemasons had set him – quite unintentionally – on his way into the tunnel that morning: How to construct its arch?

If the line of the intended canal had gone straight into the hillside, at right angles, there would be no difficulty. A conventional arch would do. But this particular tunnel ran into the hillside at an angle, so that one of the foundations for the arch was skewed forward of the other by about five feet. One of the masons said they should bring the other foundations forward, too, out into the open air; then build an ordinary right-angled arch and back-fill over the top with clay and topsoil – in short, what he proposed was to artificially square off the hillside at the tunnel mouth. The other wanted to do something more fancy, to build the arch of the tunnel as a series of stone rings, each one skewed a little to one side of its neighbour, so that the foundations, seen in plan, would have a zigzag outline. In the end they decided to wait until Mr. Croxley, the engineer, came . . . see how he wanted it done.

Matt had heard the argument but, as usual, said nothing. The first mason's idea – to artificially square off the hillside – was the idiot's way out. It was like saying to Nature, "My genius knows but one trick – and you must play it with me." Beneath contempt. The other dodge, to skew each arch, was a poor solution, too. Not only would it demand much thicker courses, but each block of stone would have to be dressed on two exposed faces. There must be a better way. His mind wrestled with the problem all morning.

When they paused for their snap Jacko Kinch muttered, "That bastard's going to get us all killed." He had to say it several times before Matt surfaced sufficiently to ask, "Which bastard?"

Jacko laughed. "How many d'you know on this working, then?"

"Oh . . . him."

"Someone should do something."

Matt nodded.

"No point talking to old Silent Sullivan!" Seth Corley chuckled and jerked a thumb toward Matt. "He'd likely scheme a better, quicker, and more effectual way for M'Grotty to kill us all off!"

Matt nodded again, as if he agreed. Actually, he was close to solving the problem with the tunnel arch. And, indeed, while they were strolling back to the working face the answer suddenly came to him. Don't skew the foundations – skew the courses!

Alas, a moment of further reflection revealed that matters were not so simple. There would then be a weakness at the oblique angle at the very mouth of the tunnel. But his instinct told him that his idea of diagonal courses was fundamentally right.

After some further mental wrestling it occurred to him that the weakness could be overcome if the courses were cut narrower toward the foundations. Why? He couldn't say. He just *knew* it was so – felt it in his bones.

Yes, but why? that was all he now needed puzzle out.

He was deep in silent argument with himself when M'Grotty leaped back upon the powder barrel, took out his tinder, rekindled his pipe, and looked pugnaciously around, challenging any one of them to speak out.

Jacko nudged Matt. "That bastard's at it again!"

M'Grotty saw Matt's gaze turn his way. All morning he'd been trying to catch that fellow's eye. Now he gave an extra hard puff, followed by an extra fierce snort, and the shower of sparks almost engulfed him and the barrel. The men winced and cowered in fear.

Matt walked straight over to the charge hand. M'Grotty waited for the humble request, the grudged politeness, the fawning, "If it please you, sir, Mr. M'Grotty, sir . . ." Never in his life would he have imagined that a common labourer would simply grab the pipe from his mouth and toss it into the mire of the tunnel floor.

The silence was sudden and absolute. Every man straightened. Every face turned toward the pair of them.

"Get back to your work!" M'Grotty yelled over Matt's head, his eyes flashing in the candlelit dark.

No one moved.

The charge hand felt a moment of panic. Authority that was not absolute, fear that was not total – these were worthless to him. He turned to Sullivan and asked in a low, menacing tone, "What d'you suppose you're doing?"

"You're a dangerous lunatic, M'Grotty," the man answered evenly.

"Mister M'Grotty to you."

The other said nothing.

M'Grotty laughed, though it came out more like a gasp of astonishment. Suddenly he lashed out with his fist. But Matt was expecting it; he moved his head aside and the great paw whizzed harmlessly by his ear.

M'Grotty had put every ounce of muscle into that punch – it certainly had enough momentum to jerk him from his perch and, after a moment or two on the very edge of his balance, it sent him sprawling at Matt's feet. A great cheer went up from every man in the tunnel.

Swiftly Matt put his boot upon the fellow's neck, fetching from him a great bullroar of pain. "Hark'ee," he said calmly. "I'm leaving. No more trouble, eh? Your word on it?"

M'Grotty struggled to rise. Matt gave a vicious jerk with his boot; the sinews in the other's neck cracked like pistol shots.

"Yes!" M'Grotty conceded in a great howl of pain and rage. "My word! My word!"

But as soon as the pressure of Matt's boot was removed he made a grasp at Matt's other leg and, sinking his teeth into the calf, brought him down. The moment his head hit the clay, M'Grotty's hand shot up and grabbed the family jewels.

Matt's scream rang down the tunnel. He almost passed out with the pain as he thrashed around, desperately seeking to get out of that vicious hold. If his boots had not accidentally found contact with M'Grotty's own tender parts, it would all have been over in seconds. As it was, they both lay there, writhing and gasping. Matt was bathed in a cold sweat; every muscle shivered from the shock of what had just happened.

"Watch out!" several voices warned.

Risking the pain, Matt lashed out again with his boot. But this time it was his knee that made contact, bursting M'Grotty's lip wide open and knocking out two of his teeth. The blood began to flow. The pain in Matt's groin was still so fierce he had to roll over onto his stomach before he could even think of rising to his feet again. It was a mistake.

M'Grotty lurched up and fell onto Matt's back before he could get even one knee under him. If those teeth had still been intact, Matt would have lost an ear. As it was, M'Grotty put an armlock on him while the fingers and thumbs of his free hand came round in search of Matt's eyes. The man's breath fouled the air about them. Blood streamed from his lip onto Matt's neck, into his hair.

He kicked out but found only emptiness. He reached feebly behind him but even when he caught part of the man's clothing there was no leverage in his joints. He squirmed and wriggled, caught in the pincer of M'Grotty's thighs; a champion jockey could not have clasped him tighter. He buried his face in the clay, tilting it so that his eyes were covered but his lips could just manage to breathe within the space created by the arch of his neck.

With a slowness and a silence that chilled the onlookers, M'Grotty began scooping up the clay and filling that space. It formed a cold, clammy pillow that grew and grew – and grew.

Eventually Matt had to lift his face simply in order to breathe – and that was the moment for which his assailant had been waiting. Those eager fingers and thumb went straight to Matt's eyes and began to gouge and press.

This new torment was beyond all bearing. It was to the earlier pain as that had been to a mere pinprick. As he began to pass into merciful unconsciousness, in a blaze of stars and auroras, he knew that when he regained his wits – if, indeed, he ever did – he would be blind. But in those final moments of his agony, before his senses deserted him, he heard, from infinitely far off, an angry voice shouting, "Stop this!" over and over.

He felt, or imagined, a sharp kick in the ribs. The pain of it was so much less than the pain of his eyes that it came as an absurd sort of relief. The weight of M'Grotty was removed, Matt rolled over and opened his eyes. It made no difference; open or shut, all they saw was a swirl of stars and fiery mists. Perhaps he was already blind. He stumbled to his feet. Somewhere in there, among the giddying fires, he could just make out the mouth of the tunnel. He knew it by the masons' formwork. Even in his blinded agony he remembered briefly the problem with the stones and the skewed courses of the arch . . .

"And what, pray, is the meaning of this, you curs?" The engineer's voice cut into his thoughts.

The fires were growing dim, their motion less violent. Dark was returning, bringing with it, paradoxically, the gift of sight. But he had a headache that would fell an ox.

"Nothing sir, Mr. Croxley, sir. It was nothing." That was M'Grotty's voice. Like all bullies he was an abject sycophant to anyone in authority over him.

Dimly Matt saw, or half-saw and half-guessed, that Croxley was looking at him, waiting for his plea. Though he could still discern almost nothing his eyes began to hunt the floor, seeking the pipe he had thrown there. Croxley followed his gaze and saw it almost at once. Its ghost-white clay was phosphorescent in that gloom. "What's this, then?" he asked as he stooped to pick it up. "And still hot!"

"'Tis his," the charge hand said quickly, nodding toward Matt. But a roar of disagreement from the others put an end to that line of retreat.

In any case, the engineer would not likely have been fooled, for his next words – pointing the broken stem at M'Grotty – were: "I've warned you of this before, you rogue. Were you smoking this anywhere near that blasting powder?"

The man made no reply. Croxley turned to Matt. "Is this what you were fighting about?"

Matt shrugged. "Personal, sir."

"You fucking great idiot!" his mates shouted, but it was too late. Pity briefly flushed the engineer's eyes. "You're a fool, Sullivan," he said. "I could just about tolerate you back in the gang if your quarrel was over this. But . . ."

Matt ignored the rest as he went back to the face to retrieve his pick and shovel. *Time to move on, anyway,* he thought to himself.

Croxley was saying, "It goes for you, too, M'Grotty. You're away now, this very minute."

The charge hand stared at him, gaping in disbelief.

"You've earned French wages, man," the engineer insisted. "There's no second warning on any contract of mine." His eyes roved over the gang in general. "Let every man understand that."

He turned back to M'Grotty who was sputtering, "But . . . but . . ." He gave him a rough push toward the mouth of the tunnel, toward the rapidly dwindling figure of Matt Sullivan. "You're turned off, man. Just get that notion into your thick skull. Shake a leg or I'll keep back whatever's due to you."

At the mouth of the tunnel Matt passed the two masons. He could not resist the temptation. With his shovel he turned up a sod of clay, which he quickly fashioned into a half-cylinder lying on its side – a solid representation of the empty air of the tunnel. With the tip of the shovel he cut the end of it obliquely at about twenty degrees – the same angle as that between the hillside and the tunnel.

The two masons gathered close and watched him. Their tolerant smiles were almost sneers.

He held out his hand and, with a lift of his eyebrows, begged one of their trowels. The taller of the two, the one who wanted to build the skewed arches, handed over his. Matt put the point of it upon the clay "tunnel," at the top dead centre of the arch at its daylight end; and then he scored a line at right angles to the slant of that end, a line that, naturally, curved back and down over the half-cylinder until it reached the ground – which would be the foundations of the real tunnel. On each side he drew a further line, parallel to the first and about an inch from it. Then a further two, also parallel, but somewhat less than an inch from the first pair. Then two more, still parallel but now a mere three-quarters of an inch from the previous pair. And so he went on down each side until the lines were no more than an eighth of an inch apart, at which distance they remained until the entire surface near the tunnel entrance was covered with spiralling lines.

He stood, grinned, nodded, returned the trowel – all without a word – and continued on his way.

The shorter mason, the one who wanted to re-landscape the hillside to match his elementary skill, snorted contemptuously. "Stone courses that slant up and down! It'd tumble in if anyone but sneezed beneath it!" He raised his voice and shouted after Matt, "Labourer, stick to thy trade!"

He was about to trample the clay back level when his colleague stopped him. "No no, the man's got something. We must think on this."

Matt stopped and tried to ease his aching head. M'Grotty caught up and passed him by. The two antagonists squared up but made no move to close the gap between them. The ex-charge hand's eyes were filled with a dark hatred. "Get yourself transported, Sullivan," he warned in a voice slurred by his battered lip and missing teeth. "There's no navigation in this land where they'll take you on."

Matt just stared at him; if he felt any emotion it was pity. He wondered if he should tell the man the trick to replant teeth and make them grow again.

M'Grotty continued in that same soft, menacing tone, "One day, Sullivan, one day I'll repay you this treachery. I'll see you ruined. I'll hound you to the very gates of hell." He spun his heel in the clay and squelched off.

Matt watched him out of sight before he set off for the coppice where he and the gang had been kipping of late. It belonged to the landowner whose income would be doubled, and redoubled again, by the new cut of the canal – so he was willing to tolerate a brief trespass, and even a little gentle poaching, by the lads who were digging it.

Before Matt reached the end of the cutting he turned for a last look. The engineer and the two stonemasons were all squatting on their haunches, examining his clay model and talking ten to the dozen. Their hands were sculpting great blocks of stone in the air.

Later that evening, his last in that camp, he went out for a twilight stroll. Habit, or a total disregard for his surroundings – for he had really come out to get away from the inane fireside chatter and profanity of the other navigationers – brought him back to the canal workings. At the mouth of the tunnel he saw the masons' benches already set up with the rough-hewn stones upon them. They had even started on one of the blocks. The face of it, he was amused to see, was being cut at twenty degrees to its sides. Beside it, neatly sliced from the ground and placed on a plank, was Matt's clay model. He chuckled.

"Aye – well may you laugh!"

The voice came from the dark of the tunnel but he recognized it at once as Croxley's.

Matt stood and waited.

The engineer came out into the light, or what little was left of it. He pointed to the model and said, "That is most ingenious, Sullivan. And like all truly ingenious discoveries, it is so simple, so obvious – once someone else has shown the way. I'm sure it'll work."

Matt nodded.

The engineer looked at him, somewhat surprised at his silence, and went on, "It's the reduction in the thickness of the courses from the apex that is so clever. I see how you do it. You take the cosine of the angle with the springing line and apply it to the unitary measurement of the keystone, so that at sixty degrees it is a mere half of the initial thickness. So simple! So simple!"

Matt nodded again.

Croxley, unnerved by this continuing silence, gabbled on. "Naturally, at that rate the courses would tend toward an infinitesimal thinness as they approach the springing line – so your practical compromise is to cease the reduction at seventy-five degrees, thirty minutes, when they reach one fourth the thickness of the initial course. That is brilliant, too – a brilliant discrimination between the theoretical and the practical." He paused and eyed the other shrewdly. "So tell me, *Master* Sullivan – why are you here, masquerading as a simple navigationer?"

Matt shook his head. "No masquerade, sir."

Croxley's eyes begged for more; when nothing came he gave a resigned sigh. "I had to turn you off, you know. The directors of the Rugely & Coalbrookdale are sticklers against brawling."

Matt nodded.

"Where will you go next? I may be able to . . ."

"South," Matt said.

"Oh? It's not your home country, down there – you sound more like a Northerner?"

"As much as anywhere."

"And how long ago was that?"

"Long enough."

"And you've been on the navigations always?"

Matt shook his head. "I was in Cornwall, working the engines."

"Oh? For Mr. Watt? D'you know him?"

Matt pulled a face. "We got on famously, Mr. Watt and I. For a while." Watt had complained he could not find a millwright to bore a cylinder with sufficient accuracy that a shilling coin would be prevented from slipping down between the piston and the wall. Matt had showed how it might be done, but then the pair of them had fallen out – a little misunderstanding concerning Mrs. Watt, who had lost her head. He had no urge to tell Croxley these things.

The engineer's bewilderment deepened. "You carry an odd conviction, Sullivan."

"Just habit." Matt laughed.

"What else have you done?"

"I worked with the Darbys for a while, in Coalbrookdale."

He had heard of their difficulties in casting their steel. In fact, all they had lacked was a good half-vacuum – also an effective chaperone for the daughter of the house, who had become a great nuisance to him.

"And how did you fare with Mr. Darby, then?"

"Well enough – for a while. Then I went to France."

"Did you, by Jove! You seem to be a dissenting sort of man, Sullivan. You even dissent with the Dissenters."

Matt made no reply.

"And whom did you tangle with in France? M. Cugnot and his steam carriages, no doubt!"

Matt smiled to himself at the choice of words. Cugnot's sister had, indeed, been a "tangle" – and certainly not of his making. "I did have a slight tiff with that man, yes. But it was the aeronautical balloons as took my fancy. And then I got interested in gases."

"And let me guess – you no longer see eye to eye with the Montgolfiers, either! Or was it Professor Charles?"

"We did fall out, that's true," Matt admitted. How to explain about Mme. Montgolfier's maid? Best not to try, perhaps. He was still more than a little puzzled by the whole sorry business.

Women did these things and he always seemed to get caught up. And then caught.

"D'you fall out with everyone in the end? Even scum like M'Grotty?"

Matt shook his head. "They fall out with me. I wish no man ill."

Croxley, finding no conversational toehold in such laconic bursts of fact, said, "Well, we shall see, eh? It's all in the hands of the gods."

"'Tis my opinion the gods have lost interest in mankind. Though I don't suppose they ever had much to start with." He looked at his own clay model and added, "Did you ever think our world might be just the one they *practise* upon?"

"And where's the real one?"

Matt waved his hand vaguely at the darkening sky.

The engineer shuddered. "You have a chill vision, Sullivan. If you're bound for any particular working down south, I may be able to help."

Matt was evasive. These questions touched on his own increasing desperation. "This dark is most kindly to my eyes. When I was working at Sapperton Tunnel last year, I left some papers with the landlord of the tavern. That's my first port of call. After that—well, we shall have to see what the future may bring."

And we must hope, he added to himself, that the landlord had by now forgotten the incident with the serving wench.

## CHAPTER ELEVEN

MARY CAME TRIPPING DOWN the outside stone staircase of the warehouse in which she and Punch had passed the night. It was going to be a bright day with clear blue skies, though her view of them was at present obscured by the overhead awning.

Indeed, her view of almost everything was obscured, for thick convolvulus had tangled itself around the uprights and now infested the open side of the staircase. All she could discern was the gravel of the waggon way immediately beside the steps. When she was about halfway down, the canopy of green became thin and she could begin to make out two horizontal patches of colour – the towpath and the nearer edge of the canal. Cutting across them were the stark verticals of a pair of legs, seen from behind – not precisely vertical, in fact, but spread somewhat apart. She recognized them as Punch's legs, or at least they were his breeches. Between them, rust-coloured against the grey-green face of the canal, fell a doughty, tinkling stream.

This entire scene she took in between one step and the next. The following step revealed the dark shape of his jacket. But only one arm was visible, the one that was directing . . . operations. The other arm did not come into view until she was almost at ground level; raised above his head, it held a tankard of ale, tilted into his mouth, which was stretched skywards like a cook's funnel.

This tableau, with the ale going in at one end and something very like it – in colour, anyway – pouring out at the other, struck her as so comical that she could only stand there, hands on hips, and roar with laughter. The sudden noise from behind caused a moment's hesitation in the outflow, but it resumed at full strength the moment he identified her voice.

"Come away out of that," she cried. "You'll poison all the fish."

He gave a great sigh of satisfaction. "Didn't I think you were above," he said, dressing again before he turned.

"What is that place? I forgot."

"Stroud." He pointed westward down the valley, toward the small town whose edges were just visible at the bend in the canal and river. Then he pointed in the other direction. "And London's that way. There's a tunnel somewhere down there, Sapperton Tunnel, the longest in England." As she drew near he lifted his jacket, revealing two fine trout hanging from his braces. "Breakfast," he said.

She went over a little clap bridge and down to the River Frome to wash herself; then she returned and saw to their breakfast. When the fish were nearly cooked he came up and said, "Well? Did you count it?"

"It's bad luck," she said evasively.

"Less than a pound, anyway."

"I have three shillings and fourpence left," she told him, a defiant edge in her tone.

He snorted. "Your father won't die while you yet live!"

She shook her head, as if agreeing with him about some remote, spendthrift acquaintance of them both. "Where in God's mercy has it gone? I had it all planned out that I could hand Con back his five guineas and still have coins to shake by the time we reached London." She passed him his fish, speared on a fork. The merest tip of a smell of it made her mouth water so fiercely she could hardly speak.

"Didn't I tell you," he said almost dreamily, for nine-tenths of his concentration, too, was reserved for the fish. "A ball gown! If you've the need of such an article at all, which is another question that begs its own answer – a ball gown'd be half the price in London. *And* you'd forgo the carrying of it. And nor did you need the new bag. The day we walked into Gloucester, well that must have been the patron day for those city merchants! Put ears on you now, colleen, for what I'm going to tell you . . ."

"Ah wheesht!" she said crossly. "I heard you last year. I'd have been all right but for that little Welsh hoor – didn't he rob me blind?"

"And wasn't I after warning you so at the time? You've paid a quare old penny for that, I said."

A faraway look stole into Mary's face. "Ah, but hadn't he the mildest gaze though!" she said dreamily. "And the eyes on him – like wet coals by a silver moon." She shivered and grew brisk again, returning to present business. "Sure it can't be far to London now."

"Only a hundred miles. That's not but a hump and a skimp and a jump to a grand spending lady like yourself."

"Why will the Welshmen pay so handsomely to hear a girl sing and the English nothing at all?"

"The English have but one use for a young girl such as yourself, and her voice isn't in it," he warned. "You'd do well to remember it. Aren't they the worst at that caper – and known to *be* the worst, the whole world over."

She hardly listened. Indeed, she did not want to listen, preferring instead to wallow in her own fecklessness, as if she could now stand apart from it. "I still can't understand it. Haven't

I given out against my father all my life for the way he's let the money slip between his fingers. And when we set out on this road together with the five guineas intact . . ."

"Four," he interrupted brutally. "You were after giving him the fifth within the hour."

"Well, never mind that. Didn't I plan it all out the way I'd guard it and earn on top of it, and . . ."

"You've seven guineas' worth of goods about you – and a half-guinea of food inside you – so I'll grant you that. You'll have the way of earning it without stooping to the tricks of Moll Flanders and the likes o' them jades. But, make it or spend it, you're the one who'll never put it by!"

She stared at him fiercely, trying to gather the shreds of her former confidence about her. "You'll eat those words one day, Steam Punch," she vowed.

"God send I do, mistress. There'd be none more eager for that diet, and I'll tell you no lie."

"Well," she said, businesslike yet again, "if we buy nothing but food between that place and London, we'll manage well enough, I'm thinking, on under the three shillings."

The glint in his eye said he'd believe it when he saw it.

As they were about to set off along the towpath a narrow boat came into view from the direction of Stroud, behind them. They waited.

The young fellow leading the horse was dark-haired and wild. From the moment he saw Mary until he was almost level his eyes never left her; but they did not, as with so many other young men, run up and down her body; they dwelled in her face with an intensity that made her acutely uncomfortable – but which she yet found exciting. She stared him out, relishing the tiny triumph. He pretended he was checking the towpath for obstructions, of course.

"We're bound for London," Punch told him.

Without pausing he nodded back over his shoulder and said, "You'll 'ave to ast the old 'un."

"You're a Londoner yourself," Punch added.

He nodded and passed on, still gazing back at them over his shoulder. Again his eyes dwelled in Mary's and now he grinned. She smiled back. He began to whistle, a melodious country tune full of trills and warbles, as good as any penny-whistle man back in County Clare. It would sound well, she thought, with the harp. Perhaps, if any sort of a friendship might develop between them, they could wander the land together, earning their keep by the music – until, of course, she caught the eye of some gentleman, who would rescue her from her chaste and simple poverty.

The narrow boat, named the *Roger*, drew level.

"We're bound for London, master," Punch repeated.

The man scowled, looking them up and down as if he might discover some cause to ignore them. But the sense of obligation all canal people feel toward the navigationers who create their waterways overcame his distrust and he said, morosely, "You may put your impediments aboard, of course. And help leg through the tunnels. We're stoppin' at the warehouse up ahead."

"And the girl?" Punch added. "May she not ride with you?"

The master sniffed and looked her up and down again. "What can she do? Can she launder?"

"God she never stops. And loves it!"

"Can she cook?"

"Fit for a French queen. There's nothing makes her happier."

"Can she darn a shirt?"

"You'd never know it was tore. And she can sing a song or tell a tale that'd charm the owls to silence."

"Here, I'm just the farmer's cow!" Mary protested.

The man said, in the most grudging tone – though she could see he was delighted, "She'd best come aboard then and make a start. The ass may join the horse."

She stood her ground. "I'll not slave from dawn to dusk unless I get my keep into the bargain."

"You can bloody leg it, then," the man told her.

"I will, so!" She gave Lucius a light tip, to make him step out.

After a moment the master relented. "Chokey-chokey. You can 'ave your keep."

"And cover at night," she added.

He laughed as he steered the *Roger* toward the warehouse basin. "You'll be trampled to death by volunteers, my darlin'!"

At the warehouse they offloaded two barrels of rum and a consignment of carpets, taking on in their place several dozen cheeses and a crate of porcelain. Mary, already sorting through the clothes to be laundered, watched the son at work. Aware of her admiration, he stripped to the waist and flexed his muscles far more than the job required. The master's dirty clothes smelled sour, worse than the cheeses; but the young fellow's had the tang of vigour and strength.

There was little enough to wash, though. Even before they left the basin every article was hanging between the masts, swiftly drying in the bright sunshine. By now Punch and the master had struck up a friendship, which they proposed to cement in the taproom of the nearby tavern.

"You watch the cargo," the old man told his son, who did not seem to mind being excluded from the spree.

"And what of me?" Mary called after Punch.

"You mind the lad!" he laughed.

She snatched up one of the master's shirts and busied herself at darning a rent in the tail of it. The young fellow came and sat cross-legged at her feet. "You needn't mind me," he told her.

"I'm sure I don't."

"What's the tag?" he asked.

Puzzled, she held her needle and thread toward him. "Cotton."

"No! Your handle . . . your sob . . . what they call you?"

"Oh – Mary."

"Moll . . ."

"*Mary*," she insisted. "And yourself?"

"Hal." It sounded more like *how*, the way he said it. "Where you from?"

"The County Clare in Ireland." She no longer recited her proud lineage for such common people. It only caused them mirth.

"What's that in Wales, is it?" he asked. "We don't never trade there."

"Next door to it you might say. You have a sweet whistle, Hal, when you want it. Like a bird, that tune you had. What's the name of it?"

"I have another whistle," he said with a wink. "It plays even sweeter – the oldest, sweetest tune in all the world."

Her spirit sagged. "Is that all you think of?"

"That other cove, is he your old man?"

"How many days is it to London? Because this could soon weary me, I want to tell you."

He sniffed heavily and, pretending he had to work it out, said, "Lemme see. I count in females, not miles. There's Jinny at Latton. There's Peg of Oxford. And Sweet Sue of Reading. Not forgetting Roxie of Maidenhead – and that's a laugh all on its own. And last but not least I raise my glass – and one or two other things beside – to Barbara in Isleworth. How many's that?"

She went on with her sewing. "It's not worth the counting."

He dabbed a finger toward her and chuckled. "My sentiments exactly, Moll. Help me round it up to five, eh?"

"It's five already."

He laughed. "See – you counted! Come on – what d'you say?"

"No."

His grin lost no confidence. "Every mott's the same – you all says no when what you means is yes." He narrowed his eyes, as if giving away secrets. "Tell you what, Moll. Before this day is run, you might hear that old sweet tune yourself. There now!"

She finished off the darn and bit through the thread. "Is that the truth!"

He nodded confidently. "In Sapperton Tunnel – the Tunnel of Venus, I calls it." When she said nothing he prompted, "Want to know why?"

"I can't wait to hear."

"Last trip – no, I tell a lie – last trip but one, we lifts another little mott along the way. And when we comes to Sapperton, me old man walks the nag over the hill whilst I legs the narrow boat through. Know what I mean?"

"You walked along the towpath, pulling it through?"

"Nah! There ain't no towpath in the tunnel. No, I legged it. You lies on your back, on the top of the cabin, and the roof of the tunnel, see, is only that much above you." He moved his hands some thirty inches apart. "And the bricks in it is all like sticking down. And then it's just like walking, only upside down." He lay back on the deck and showed her the movement.

"Like walking on air," she said.

He nodded and lowered his legs. "That's what we calls legging it. Anyways, I'm lying there up on the roof, right? And I'm thinking omigawd, how long's this bloody tunnel, when this little mott, I'll remember her name in a mo, ripe and plump she was, she climbs up beside me – and then on top!" He whistled. "After a certain amount of necessary dishabilitation, as you might say, there she is, mortised – and me, tenoned. And does she move? Not a muscle! And I've got to go on legging it, haven't I."

He repeated the movement, now with his eyes closed. "Right

leg . . . left leg . . . right leg. . . . Can you picture it, Moll? Can you *feel* it? Eeeeeeh! Her lying there, not a twitch out of her, but moaning like the wind and the sweat pouring off her like a brewer's nag. And me wishing they'd built the tunnel four mile long! Never mind your walking on air!"

She watched the muscles on him ripple as he repeated the movement. He sat up and grinned at her. "The offer's open, girl. Say no more about it."

Then, to her surprise, he changed the subject completely, ceased to ogle her, dropped no more heavy innuendoes. He talked of life on the canals, how they were opening up the countryside . . . the way people came down and walked with them a mile or so, gathering the news, passing on their own . . . the inland docks that were springing up everywhere and the prosperity it was bringing to remote little villages that had hardly changed since the days of Billy the Conk.

"Are there so many canals here?" she asked. From her knowledge of the situation in Ireland, she expected him to say there were half a dozen or so.

"Twenty or thirty at least," he told her. "They must have dug out over a thousand miles these last forty years, men like your old cove and his mates. But I don't reckon that's nothing, when set beside what's coming." He shook his head, unable to express the vastness of it all. "The money what's going to be made in the next foo years – it'd break your heart. If I had a hundred pounds now, I'd have a thousand by the new century, I tell you."

"Will I tell you something, Hal?" she said.

He looked up at her.

"I like you when you talk of such things. I didn't like you before."

He lay back again and laughed, unrepentant. "Talk is just the bill of lading," he said. "It's the cargo you must judge, the cargo and the performance."

He was teaching her some of the canal songs, *The Old Rose of Oxford* and *D'Arcy's Cut*, when a somewhat unsteady master and Punch returned from the tavern. But drink had mellowed the old man; he was delighted with the mend that Mary had done, simple enough though it was. They cast off shortly and began their stately, silent journey to London. Punch curled up on deck and went to sleep at once.

"Did I hear there was a tunnel ahead?" she asked the master.

He broke into a broad grin and chuckled. "Told you about that, did he?"

She blushed. "Punch mentioned it."

"Oh, ah."

"Is it far?"

"You'll have to curb yourself a while or so yet, my darlin'." He spat into the water and, raising his voice, nodded toward his son and added, "'Course, it's all in 'is mind, you know. It never really 'appened."

# CHAPTER TWELVE

WHEN MATT SULLIVAN emerged from the Sapperton Tunnel he looked around at the delightful sunlit valley of the Frome and decided he might as well stop the night here as anywhere else. He hopped off the obliging canal boat at Frampton Common, by Trillis Farm, where a pair of narrow footbridges spanned both canal and river. The evening promised fair so he put up his tarpaulin as a windbreak rather than a tent. He had noticed a rabbit warren at the edge of the wood beside Sapperton graveyard. Now, risking a thrashing from the local landowner's warrenders, he set off with his snares.

No man can walk a dozen yards in the English countryside without being observed – certainly by a fox and almost certainly by another human. Matt decided that a navigator walking along by the canal would rouse less suspicion than a rough-living fellow striding across the common; and that is how he came to be on the southern bank when the *Roger* went by. He had decided that the afternoon was still an hour too young for the setting out of snares, so he was, at that actual moment, stretched at full length in the grass, considering the prodigious energies of the sun and wondering how it might be more effectually harnessed for the benefit of mankind.

He had seen the *Roger* before, several times on various canals, during the course of his travels, but never with a woman aboard. She was not the sort of woman he'd forget, either. Young. Cheerful. Bright eyes. Good skin.

Lazy, sun-stupefied, he gave the passing *Roger* a cheerful nod, scratched himself – and wondered what it was about this particular young woman that awakened his interest.

"A grand world for some!" she shouted after him, giving the mat she was holding an extra hard crack on the gunwale.

They always had to draw attention to how busy they were, how the world would fall to bits without them.

"Why fret?" he shouted back. "There'll be fresh dirt on it tomorrow."

"Sure no one could say the same of *you!*"

They always had to have the last word, too.

Watching him, Mary wondered if he owned the land – lying there so lordly and indolent. She felt a momentary urge to jump off and join him. Why was everyone else's life so pleasant and assured?

At that moment, a man – a parish constable by his hat – came riding toward them along the towpath. "Ho!" he called out in some agitation. Punch came suddenly awake.

Hal, who was now leading both Lucius and the draught horse in ill-matched tandem, pulled them to a halt. His father and Punch leaped ashore and hauled at the braking line. Mary was surprised to see how far the boat dragged two such strong men before they brought it to a halt. By then the constable had drawn level. His mare was in a fine old lather.

"Thomas Cousins, masters," he said breathlessly. "Constable of Edgeworth, yonder." He pointed east, toward a hill that seemed to block off the end of the valley.

"At your service, constable," the master replied.

"Pray tell me, sirs, have two men passed this way? One mounted, the other on foot. Bearing a sack or two between them."

There was a general shaking of heads. "Not this last while."

With narrowed eyes the constable looked at them, one by one. Each shook his head again by way of reinforcement.

"What was in the sacks?" Mary asked.

"Is there a price on the men?" the master cut in.

Cousins sucked air vigorously. "Soon enough, I'll wager. My Lord Ferrers, the banker hisself, will swear out a warrant against them both."

"For what?"

"What are their names?" Mary and Punch spoke together.

"Why, Sir Jack Horley and his son young Jack Horley – both of Aston Hall." He pointed to the southwest, to the downs above the steep and wooded valleyside. "And as to what they've done, why they've been and gone and stolen their own family silver – that's what!"

His hearers looked at each other in bewilderment. "How may a man steal his own property?" the master inquired.

"Well now . . ." The constable, seeming to forget he was out upon an errand of some urgency, licked his lips and told the tale with relish. "The family plate, see, was forfeit to my Lord Ferrers in default on a debt. And now, come the morn, young Jack Horley is to wed with . . . ah . . ." He hit his forehead in vexation. "Oh, her face is as plain before me as your own . . ."

"Never mind the woman's name, man," the master cried angrily.

Master Cousins bit his thumb. "She's that wench from Tetbury – oh, her name'll choke me in a minute . . ."

"Yes, yes, yes!" the master shouted. "Young Jack Horley is to marry this Tetbury wench, and . . ."

"Well, Long Newnton, to tell the truth," the constable said, "which is as good as Tetbury, being only . . ."

". . . and they wanted back the family silver to grace the occasion, I suppose? And they seized it by main force, eh? Hence a man may steal his own property. Was that the why and the wherefore of it?"

"Oh . . . she's a cousin to my next-door neighbour but one . . . Corinna? No! It's an uncommon name."

"Are you sure they came this way?" Punch asked.

"What size reward would it be?" the master persisted.

"Ten guineas?" Hal put in hopefully.

"Cora?" Mary suggested, trying hard to keep a straight face. The others looked daggers at her.

"They'd have to come this way," the man replied, but with little confidence. "Or here or up on the downs there. Connie? Carnelia . . ."

"The reward, man!" the master screamed. "For the love of God!"

"Oh." Cousins scratched his head. "Why, 'twould be one twentieth part of the value, to be sure. It begins with a C – of that I'm as near certain as . . ."

"And the value is . . . ?" Hal pressed.

"Ah . . . four hundred pounds, or so I'm told. Cynthia? No . . ."

"What's a twentieth part of four hundred pounds?" Hal asked. The men's eyes glazed over or vanished into their skulls as they began muttering their calculations.

"Twenty pounds," Mary told them. "Would it be Christobel?"

"Crystal!" the constable shouted in delight. "Crystal Coker. That's the very wench! Crystal Coker of Bickerstaffe's Farm, Long Newnton. Well!" He heaved a sigh of vast relief.

The others were going noisily insane by now.

"Twenty pounds!"

"What do they look like?"

"Young or old?"

"Tall or short?"

Mary glanced across the canal to where the indolent, unwashed landowner, who had sauntered up to join them, was watching it all with weary amusement. She smiled.

With a lift of his eyebrows and the tip of a raised finger he indicated a copse halfway up the hill on their side of the canal. She followed his gesture, saw what occasioned it and, cutting across the commotion among the men, said, "There's another mighty argument going on up there. D'you think they could be trying to bury it under that sapling?"

They soon saw what she meant. One particular tree was thrashing about as if in a full gale; its neighbours merely stirred in the gentle breeze.

The master wasted no more time but leaped the ditch and began striding up the hillside. "You mind the boat, Punch," he called.

But Punch and the constable were only half a dozen paces behind him. Hal quickly unhitched the draught horse and tied part of the loose hauling line around a willow, effectively tethering Lucius, too.

"Look after the boat, Moll," he called as he sprang upon the creature's back and, holding tight to its collar, spurred it forward; soon he was gaining on them all.

Mary, aggrieved at being left alone, looked across the water at Matt and said, "Aren't I as entitled to that reward as any of them?"

He nodded.

"And I've a desperate need for the money."

"A common complaint."

"And sure it's not a private fight. Anyone can join in."

He offered no argument.

"Well, I can't stand here chatting away like this!" She laughed. "Would you ever guard the boat for me?"

He shrugged. She picked up a deck hammer and, gathering her skirts, untied the ass and leaped on its back. Lucius, being a gregarious beast and having taken a deep liking to the draught horse, needed no spurring to set off in pursuit of the others. "I'll halve my share with you," she called over her shoulder.

What life was worth *any* share of twenty pounds, he wondered?

Their return, ten minutes (or an hour?) later, took him by surprise. He was lost in contemplation of the ripples that advanced steadily eastwards along the canal. Why were they so evenly spaced and all of a uniform size? How did each little wavelet "know" where the one before and the one behind it were – so that it could place itself exactly halfway between them?

"Did you see me hit that big fellow?" the woman's voice cut excitedly through his musings. Moll, the other cove had called her.

Punch laughed. "There'll be no wedding tomorrow, I want to tell you that!"

Matt saw the party was one short. "Where's the constable?" he called across to them. If the constable was hurt, he wanted to be twenty miles away by nightfall.

"We'll send out the doctor," the captain shouted back. "They're best not moved."

"Send for the parson," Hal said brutally. He leaped aboard and, without pause, upended his sack over the tarpaulin that covered the storage hold.

A treasure-trove of gleaming silver spilled out upon the dark canvas. Soon it was doubled as Punch did the same with the sack he had been carrying.

They stood and gazed at their haul in awe.

"Four hundred pounds!" the master said.

"And all we'll share is twenty," his son added in disgust.

"Which," Mary pointed out, "is twenty more than any of us

owned at breakfast time this morning. I'll be content with my five."

"*Your* five!" the master exploded.

"*My* five!" Her fingers tightened upon the shaft of the hammer, which she still held fast.

"We could melt it down," Hal said. "Tony Church, out Hackney Marshes – he'd give us five-score for it."

"We can't just keep it," Mary protested.

"Who's to say out *we* got it?"

"The constable for one."

"Nah! He was out cold before we even spied where the sacks was."

"And when he comes to? And sees the villains lying there and the silver gone? He'll simply forget all about us?"

Hal gave a reluctant shrug. "You're right," he admitted and, leaping ashore again, faced his horse back toward the copse. "Hold fast here. Get that loot out of sight."

"What's your lay?" the master asked.

"What d'you think! I'm going back to finish off the bastard. I'll purpose to leave the cudgel in one of the villains' hands."

"Listen, I'll have no part of this," Mary warned. "The minute we reach that village ahead, I'll jump ashore and tell the magistrate the truth. Why can't you be satisfied with an honest fiver?"

"I'll take care of you when I come back," he told her contemptuously.

"Punch!" she called out.

Without a word he began transferring their belongings from the boat to the towpath. "What they do is their affair, mistress. We weren't on this vessel, we don't know these people, we were never by this canal . . ."

"Oh yes – very likely!" the master sneered. "And the first village you come to you'll peach on us to the traps and claim the reward!" He leaped upon Punch and, rolling in the dust of the towpath, began what would have been a most unequal contest but for the fact that he managed to seize up a rock, with which he repeatedly beat his opponent around the head.

Mary gave out a whoop and made for him with the hammer held aloft. But before she could get ashore Hal, having doubled back, leaped from his horse and sent her sprawling over the hold. The hammer went skittering away in the bilge.

The sight of her with her skirts thrown up and her bare thighs struggling for a new footing put all thoughts but one out of his mind. "All talk, was it?" he crowed. "Well, Moll, it's your lucky day!" He had the flap of his breeches down in a trice. She was still groping blindly for the hammer when she suddenly felt him collapse and lie still.

She did not see Matt put away his catapult.

Her first thought was that Hal had been struck by an ague. Then she saw the blood as it streamed from his ear. She screamed. In her panic to get out from under him she half rose, staggered backward, fell over the gunwale, and plunged into the canal.

There were so many skills she had never learned that yet would have eased her progress through the life on which she had lately embarked.

Among them was the ability to swim.

The evening sky turned green and dim. She noticed the change long moments before she felt the coolness of the water. The world, and her awareness of it, were strangely out of joint.

*You're drowning*, she told herself, but it had no meaning. The shock had somehow caused her to sever connections with her body; she remained she, it became it.

*It* did not struggle as it sank into the darkening world. *She* felt herself already turning from it, turning to that other world, where dark and light, cold and heat, resistance and submission, also had no meaning. She was already wondering, half-fearful, half-eager, what the next world would be like.


## CHAPTER THIRTEEN


IT WAS LIKE the smell of rashers frying.

Like the screech of an owl.

Like the reek of smoke and the sound of branch-wood crackling merrily in a fire.

Her lungs wheezed and gurgled. She had a monstrous sore throat – as she discovered when she tried to clear it.

Somehow she knew she was not alone.

She could feel that she was wrapped in a blanket. She opened her eyes and saw her own clothing scattered on the bushes around the fire. Wreaths of firelit steam curled upward and vanished into the dark of the night.

To one side of the blaze . . . a man, squatting – frying rashers, in fact. The direction and colour of the firelight gave him such a vulcanic cast that several moments went by before she recognized him as the indolent fellow who had been sunning himself on the bank . . . when? She had lost all contact with . . .

Suddenly it all came back to her – the constable, the silver, the fight in the wood, Hal and . . .

The man saw she was awake and gave a tentative little smile. It must have been he who took off her clothes to dry them. As she struggled to sit up, clutching the blanket to her, she was relieved to discover she still had her shimmy on.

He pointed to her clothes. She thought he was about to make some joke about undressing her but all he said was, "Threadbare. Trapped no air."

"Ah," she said. He was no landlord; even the briefest survey of his little encampment showed him to be a tramping labourer like Punch.

"I owe you my life," she said.

"You made no struggle," he commented.

"God, wasn't I half-kilt with the drowning."

"In five foot of water?"

"Oh." She pulled a face.

"As you'd have learned if you'd but struggled."

She remembered that time with McGrath, the moment of resignation when she had simply given up the fight. And now this. She had, indeed, yielded to the notion of drowning. Also, come to think of it – how seriously had she resisted Hal? A disquieting fatalism seemed to lurk within her, the worst enemy of all.

"Then I surely owe you my life," she told him.

"You owe that to your long hair." His hand relived its plunge into the water, its grasp on her locks. "The anchorage of hair in skin is an amazing phenomenon."

*Phenomenon!* Here was no ordinary tramping man.

He asked, "What do they call you?"

"Mary – Mary Flinders. I'm the daughter of The Flinders of the Barony of Inchiquin in County Clare."

"A lady."

"By birth, aye."

"Is there another way?" he asked. Perhaps he *was* a gentleman, after all – down on his luck like herself. "I'm Matt Sullivan." He flipped a rasher onto a battered pewter plate and added a hot potato, raked from the embers. She looked for a knife. He smiled. "Eat it 'fitty-like,' as they say down in Cornwall."

"Where are the others? And Lucius? And all my things? What happened to the *Roger?*"

"Vamoosed."

"And Punch – the old man who was with me?"

"Old?" He bridled at the word. "They hauled him aboard, alive or dead I couldn't rightly tell. There was a lot of blood about his face. Eat up."

The food tasted scrumptious and was soothing to her throat, but she was in no mood to relish it. "What of the men we left injured in the wood?"

"They'll live."

"You mean you went up and saw them?"

He nodded.

She took another bite. "It's all my fault."

He offered no comment. This woman was like no other he had met, yet he could not put his finger on the difference.

"Oh God!" She put a hand to her breast. "Was there e'er a purse slung about me here – a leather purse that hung by its drawstring?"

He shook his head. Some women were indifferent to him; some grew belligerent; some lost their heads. A few dwelled awhile in all three of those inscrutable territories. He was used to the arrangement. But this Mary Flinders – where did she fit?

"That was all the money I have in the world." She shut her eyes, sick with dread. "And everything else, I suppose, is still on the boat? All my books."

"Books?" he echoed in surprise.

"And my clothes."

"Books, eh?"

"Everything!" The full truth of her situation was just dawning upon her. "My letters of introduction – it's all gone. Nothing left but these damp clothes!"

"And your life."

"Yes. And that's in pawn to you."

He laughed. "Among the Ancient Vikings that would have made you my slave."

Pinning the blanket with her chin she offered him both her wrists, to receive imaginary shackles. Then she gave a shy laugh and plucked them back.

She was good company, grant her that.

"You're a man of learning then," she said. "Tell me though – did anyone send after the *Roger*? Another constable, or the watch?"

"More than likely. One good thing about seeking a barge: It can't grow wheels and vanish across the . . ."

He fell to silence.

She popped another morsel into her mouth and sat watching him curiously. He was staring into the fire, allowing his own rasher to burn. She leaned forward and pulled the pan out of the flames. "Is aught amiss?" she asked

He looked at her and grinned. "A canal boat with wheels – just fancy that!"

"The *Roger*? It would be my sort of luck if she had."

"No, no! But just suppose! Picture it – canal basin, cable winch, or steam, lift the boat – set of axles, team of horses, gee-up, and away she goes, wheeeest!" His childlike excitement was infectious; she began to realize how lucky she was to have fallen into his company.

Surprisingly, the moment he had made his idea public, he seemed to lose all interest in it. He looked about, searching for some other topic. She pointed to the pan she had rescued from burning. He made a vague noise, a sort of prototype thank you, before he lifted the rescued rasher above his lips and dropped it in one big mouthful. He ate noisily, swallowing a lot of air, which he then belched up, only half-discreetly.

"How we fine apples swim – said the horsedung!" she commented.

He had no idea what she was talking about.

"You could have done with a swim yourself," she went on.

"That shirt has more marks than a fiddler's notebook." It was covered in small brown spots of dried blood where the fleas had bitten him. "Have you soap? I'll wash everything you have first thing tomorrow."

"No call for that," he answered in alarm. "I'll be up in Manchester within the week. Time enough then."

She wondered why he did not disgust her more, dirty and ill-mannered as he was. And easily over thirty. As old as Steam Punch. But when he sat like that, staring into the fire, there was an odd nobility about him, a wisdom lurking behind his eyes. He reminded her of saints she had read about, mystics who lived wild and rough. Those old hermits must have reeked worse than all the goats in Christendom, but somehow they made it seem unimportant; indeed, you felt that if you met them, they'd be . . . well, very like this fellow. Their silences could make wisdom itself seem thin. Their sanctified dirt would turn your own cleanliness into some kind of fussy obsession.

"Are you a gentleman or a holy man?" she asked.

"Holy?" He smiled and continued to stare into the fire. "I wholly doubt God's existence."

"You're not a common labourer – though you have the manners, dress, and implements of one."

He shook his head. "How d'you know what I am or am not?"

"I will when you tell me."

He gave a morose shrug. "If you must know, I'm at the end of my . . ." He paused and scratched his ear. "I'm not begging for help, now."

She smiled encouragement. The firelight dancing in her eyes was enthralling – but not as it would have been with other women. What *was* the difference?

He began to tell her things he would have revealed to no one else on earth (except, to be sure, to the Duke of Bridgewater).

"I have a scheme for the improvement of canals."

Her heart sank. She almost asked if it included windmills.

"I can't seem to get anyone to listen to me," he added.

"Perhaps because you talk so little?"

He looked at her with an odd kind of gentleness that made her catch her breath. "I can talk with you, Miss Flinders, I don't know why. With most women there's only one topic, even if it's never mentioned in so many words. But with you . . ."

"What?" she asked eagerly.

"I feel I can really talk."

She flushed with pleasure. "That potato's helped my sore throat. Is there another?"

He reached behind him, pulled a fresh one from a bag, and poked it into the embers, raking them over it. "Canals," he said. "They're very young. How old are you, Miss Flinders?"

"Three weeks older than your shirt, I'd say."

He ignored the provocation. "D'you know how all this spate of canal-building began?"

She shook her head.

"Well, some years before you were born, the Duke of Bridgewater – Dux, as they call him – up in Manchester, took coals to the city – ten miles – by horse and waggon. Cost? Twenty shilling a ton! Then – a grand notion: Worsley, his mines . . . coal depot in city – same level! Build a canal. Lots of water – one thing that's never scarce in Manchester! Only trouble was the River Irwell. In the way. Need a cascade of locks down – cross over the river . . . another cascade up again on t'other side. No good. Then – stroke of luck. He met this genius, the Father of the Canals, they call him – James Brindley."

"Is the duke an old man?"

"Then? About your age. Brindley? Fifteen, mebbe twenty, years older than what I am."

"And how old are you?"

"You have an obsession, miss. I'll kiss thirty soon enough."

*He must be lying*, she thought.

He continued: "Well, Brindley was in his mid-forties. Said to Bridgewater, 'Live up to thy name – build a *bridge* to carry the canal over the *water!*' Old Dux liked that."

"Ah yes, I recall it now. I've seen an engraving of the scene."

"Anyroad – coals now sell in Manchester at twelve shilling the ton. Dux is the richest man in the North, they say."

"I hope he didn't forget Mister Brindley."

"Nobody did that! Gentlemen from every county – begging him: do us a canal! They'd have laughed in his face but for Dux."

Mary observed him closely. He had undergone some remarkable change in telling this story. His eyes shone. That holy remoteness had evaporated. To encourage him she asked, "Is that

why you're going to Manchester? Hoping this Duke of Bridgewater will hearken to your ideas?"

The firelight twinkled in his eyes. "Those were the days, lass!
People listened then. This'll show you. When they had to get the
Bridgewater Canal Bill through parliament, their lordships
objected that the water would all leak out of the canals and flood
the fields. Learned folk were that ignorant, see?"

"Well, I tell you no lie, I've been wondering the same thing
myself those last days. Why don't canals leak?"

"Old Brindley showed them. Took a bag of puddling clay.
House of Lords! Puddling clay! Built a canal in miniature on the
floor."

"A Lilliputian canal!"

"I don't know what he called it. Anyroad – filled it with water.
It leaked, of course. Everywhere. Laughter all round. 'Told you
so!' But then he puddled it. D'ye follow me?"

She shook her head.

"Well, with a real-life canal, we drive flocks of sheep or
yearling cattle up and down. Chuck buckets of water over the
clay. 'Puddling,' they call it. Puddled clay is impermeable to
water. So Brindley puddles his toy canal using his fingertips. Fills
it with water . . . and, *le tour est joué!*, nothing leaks! Aristocratic
eyes falling out all over the place! 'I'm hungry,' says Brindley,
drawing a little mark in the clay at the water line. 'Let's go and
have us dinner. And ye may lock that door.' And when they
come back, after how-so-many hours it takes for a flock of lords
to sup, the water level hasn't dropped by the thickness of a hair!"

"They got the bill through, I suppose."

He nodded, eyes aglow, as if the triumph had been his. Then,
appearing to recollect himself, he shot her a guilty glance. "You
must sing out if I grow tedious, Miss Flinders."

"On the contrary!" she assured him heartily. She felt a small
pang of jealousy; here was a man who knew exactly what he
wanted in life. And when he got it – as he surely would – she'd be
miles away, still wondering what it all amounted to.

"And what is your idea?" she asked. "The one no one will
listen to."

He took a kettle filled with water and an empty jug of about
equal capacity. "A lock," he said, pointing to the kettle. "You
know how a canal lock works, of course?"

She grinned. "I've pushed enough lock gates those days that went by!"

He poured half the kettle water into the jug and threw the rest away.

"A device to spare water!" she guessed excitedly.

He looked at her in a mixture of surprise and admiration.

Suddenly she saw it all. "And on the refill . . ." she said and, picking up the half-filled jug, poured half its contents back into the kettle. There she hesitated. He was watching her intently. At length, she put down the jug without pouring out any further water. "Of course, only half of it would be able to flow back. Still – you save a quarter of the lock's contents each time."

His face fell and he peered at her suspiciously. "Have you read that in a book? Is it already printed?"

"No!" She was surprised. "You just showed me."

"You've a swift mind then."

"Aye. As the butterfly – and about as serious. Is it Brindley himself you're intent on seeing?"

"Brindley's dead these fifteen years and more."

"And how long have you been nursing this notion, Mister Sullivan?"

"Three weeks," he replied glumly.

She burst into laughter. "Well – that bangs Banaghan!"

He looked hurt. "But I only thought of it three weeks ago."

"Well – it's still funny. You're like my father. It must be grand altogether to have such fertility of mind – but even more, to have that terrier's will which never lets go. That's what I lack."

"That was never a dificulty with me, Miss Flinders." He gave a boyish grin.

Perhaps he was not lying about his age. Maybe the grime and rags just made him seem old. "There's hope yet, so," she said vaguely. She took a tentative nibble at her hot potato and had to suck air to cool it. "Pardon my manners," she said.

He frowned, still having no idea what she was talking about.

"Have you many other such grand notions?" She asked.

After another of his long silences he said, "I'll show you one more." He rose and stretched. "I'll go gather the necessary apparatus."

Phenomenon . . . apparatus? His conversation promised fresh marvels every minute.

"I'll not be gone long. Sing out if you're troubled by aught."

But the moment he went, she began to realize how tired she was. She almost wished she hadn't spoken – especially when, a short while later, he returned with an armful of reeds and a lump of clay. "I'm about ready to sleep now," she said.

"Champion," he responded absently.

He took the kettle and began filling it with twigs, which he first snapped into tiny pieces; she helped him. Soon it was more than half full.

He replaced the lid and sealed it down with a smear of clay. Then, taking one of the reeds, he cut it between two nodes. With the help of a straight twig, he poked out the pith from its core, turning it into a hollow tube. Then he cut another such length, again between its nodes, which she now helped him to hollow out. Soon they had a dozen tubes, ready for whatever purpose he had in mind.

She could bear the silence no more. "Peashooters!" she said brightly. "We used to make these, my brothers and I. You can also fashion them into little whistles."

He shook his head and placed the kettle at the edge of the fire.

"It'll burn," she warned. "Those twigs'll catch fire."

He winked. Then he wedged one of the reed tubes over the spout, sealing it around the metal with more clay. It almost reached the ground. He placed another tube end-to-end with it, again sealing the junction with a wad of clay. And so on – creating a jointed tube that led from the kettle to a rough tent he had fashioned out of his tarpaulin windbreak, a few yards away. He sealed off the open end with a lump of clay, which he then pierced diagonally, back into the tube, with a twig.

"Your boudoir," he waved a grandiloquent hand at the crude shelter. "Tonight you shall lie in state, illumined as no queen in all the world may yet command."

Thick woodsmoke soon began to issue from the diagonal hole in the clay; one or two of the clay joints were seeping smoke, too. He spat on them and smoothed them over with his fingers.

"If I don't choke first," she said, fanning at the smoke with her hands.

"Just watch!"

He took a burning brand from the fire and, shielding its flame, carried it to her "boudoir." The moment he applied it to the smoke it burst into a bright flame, which danced a quarter-inch or so above the hole in the clay.

"Sweet heaven, how beautiful!" She clapped her hands. "Why it's like those geysers of smoke that come out the end of a log on the fire and that flare up when they catch the flame."

"That's where I recruited the idea."

"But it's brilliant!" She looked at the flame and laughed. "In literal truth. How long does it burn?"

"With that much wood? An hour."

"Why then a very small cauldron would yield light all night! Did you ever tell anyone else about this?"

"I showed Mister Murdock when I was down in Cornwall with Boulton and Watt's. He said he'd build a retort of iron and try heating coals in the same way. But I don't suppose he ever did, or will. And there was M'sieur Lebon, too, in France. He was a conjuror. I assisted him in his tricks for a season. He had some notion of getting up a theatrical show in incandescent gases."

"And did he?"

He stared at the flame dreamily. "Madame Lebon . . . well, she took against me, somehow." He smiled at her, sad rather than truculent.

"What about?" she asked.

"You'll know it yourself soon enough."

"I don't see how?"

When he remained silent she added, "I don't understand you."

He nodded glumly. "That's the beginning. You'll fall out with me entirely before too long."

She laughed. "Little enough you know *me*, Mr Sullivan. The number of people I ever fell out with in all my life (saving the family, to be sure) wouldn't use up those fingers." She held her right hand toward him, spread wide.

He took it as some kind of offering, clasping it in his own, locking his fingers with hers.

The wood-gas flame danced above its blowhole. She held her one free hand over it in token of warmth. "But that's a grand discovery. Are you really indifferent as to whether M. Lebon used it or not?"

He shrugged. "It works. That's all that really interested me."

She withdrew her hand sharply. Only his prediction of it prevented a more open show of her anger.

"Did I tell you one thing about James Brindley?" he asked.

"What?"

He hesitated, as if he wondered whether he dared risk this further confidence. "The man could neither read nor write. Yet he built and supervised hundreds of miles of canals."

"And died rich?"

"I couldn't say. I suppose he must have."

She gave up. Not waiting for the flame to die, she yawned, bade him goodnight, and crawled inside the tent. A moment later he was in there beside her. She turned in surprise but all he wanted was to spread his blanket over her. "I'll do without this," he said.

She squeezed his hand, a half-apology for her earlier brusqueness. He curled up beside the glowing embers and was asleep in moments.

Fondly she stared at him in the dying firelight. He was not like her father at all, really. Her father had a string of ideas, none of which would work; but he threw himself into their achievement, heart, body, and purse. This Matt Sullivan had a string of ideas, all of which were brilliant, yet none of which seemed to interest him once he was sure they'd work. She could just imagine him going up to this Duke of Bridgewater and giving away an idea that would make his grace twice-over the richest man in the North, while Matt would likely be happy with a pat on the back and a purse with a few guineas in it.

What he needed was someone to take him in hand.

Well . . . what he needed first was a good bath and some fresh clothes.

Someone should help him do these things. He wasn't really old. And also he was yet fairly good-looking. Those eyes!

The gurgling of the Frome was soporific.

This trick with the illuminant gases. Marvellous. Gentlemen would surely pay fortunes to have their houses permanently lighted by such means. Perhaps, if she could clean him up and teach him some manners, he and she might wander from one grand house to another; she could sing for their supper and he could build iron retorts and install conducting tubes for the gases. Together, they'd be the wonder of the age.

# CHAPTER FOURTEEN

IN THE EARLIEST LIGHT of dawn the simplest parts of the landscape acquire a strange new life. Stones and bushes waver, grow, dwindle, change shape or colour. For one long magical moment, the entire landscape is peopled with weird, shifting blurs; it is as if all night long they had enjoyed liberty to roam, and this first glimmer of sunlight had caught them roaming still, or in the very act of settling back into their daylight ways.

For Mary, as she stared up and down the valley, these fleeting movements filled the edges of her vision with an army of footpads, runaways, highwaymen. Only when she turned her gaze upon them did they swiftly disguise themselves as a little shrub, the darkening of a hedgerow, a stile, a gap. Yet *someone* was out there. She could hear him, creeping stealthily among the thistles and sow parsley that beset the common and made it such a haven for renegades. And what with everything moving and changing all the time, it was impossible to pin down either the sound or its maker.

She dropped on all fours and crawled back through her makeshift tent, out into the clearing, and over to where Matt Sullivan lay. He was deep asleep by the blackened ruins of last night's fire. It seemed a shame to wake him. The half-light softened the lines of neglect and gave him the look of a young man, with the wisp of a curl falling across his brow. Hesitantly she touched his arm. "Mister Sullivan!" she whispered urgently.

He came awake at once; two sodden holes in the pale of his face marked the opening of his eyes.

"There's someone out there."

He raised his eyebrows questioningly.

"D'you think it's the master of the boat?" she asked. "And his son. Who else would . . . "

"Ssh!" He put his fingertips against the back of her hand. Then, propping himself on one elbow, he strained to catch the sounds of the morning.

A twig cracked.

He sat up. The lithe silence of his movements impressed her. With a wave of one fingertip he motioned her to withdraw behind the cover of the tent. He himself picked up the butt of a half-burned branch and crept away toward the far end of the clearing.

Compared with his stealth the approaching vagabond – or whatever he might be – was clumsiness itself. He made no attempt now to conceal his movements. She, too, picked up a makeshift cudgel, hefting it in her hand as she waited. With the interloper's every footstep her heart beat louder and faster. She felt so congested she could hardly breathe. If he did not show himself soon, she would have to rush out, shouting and flailing at every bush; the suspense was insupportable.

At last, when she could bear it no more and was on the point of bursting forth, she was halted by a loud bellow of laughter from Matt Sullivan. "What did you call the creature? Lucius?"

She rushed out from her hiding place and saw that it was, indeed, the ass, trotting up toward the clearing, a hazy blob of warm grey topped by two dark and definite ears. As soon as he heard her voice, he stopped and gave out a loud bray of delight. Then he broke into a gallop over the last few yards, almost bowling her over in his enthusiasm.

Wildly she flung her arms around his neck and hugged him and kissed him and pulled his ears – and plied him with a catechism of questions and praise: "You clever thing – gave them the slip – and how did you do it – where are they – what's happened to Punch . . . ?"

Matt had meanwhile rekindled the fire, thrusting into its dull, red, barely glowing heart the burned-off ends of branches whose middle sections, last night's good cheer, were now no more than cold, grey ash. Smoke began to curl at once from the tinder-dry wood; soon the leaping flames made fresh night of the dawn.

"What have we for him, the clever fella?" Mary asked. "Have we e'er a little carrot or a potato to give him?"

"He's rich already." Matt pointed at the common land and good grass all about them.

Mary wheedled, cajoled, argued, but to no avail. At the height of it, she halted in mid sentence. Matt, who had been deliberately not looking at her, turned to see why. The question dried in his throat, for there, standing behind her, the tip of a wicked-looking rapier parting the hair of her neck, stood a tall, well-built gentleman.

"Hold still if you value your life!" he said softly, almost as if he feared to be overheard. The fire gleamed on the blade of his sword. "You, fellow!" he told Matt. "Come stand where I may see you better."

Mary, seeing out of the corner of her eye that Matt was preparing to fight, said, "Do as your man wishes. He'll find out soon enough how little we have to part with."

"I want nothing of yours," the stranger said vehemently. "Nor yet of his. Come and stand beside her. I only want what's rightfully mine."

When Matt had joined Mary, the fellow called out, "Crystal! You may come and search now."

"Crystal Coker!" Mary cried. "Then you must be Young Jack Horley." She turned around. "Yes, I recognize you."

"Ho ho! All innocence now, eh, Miss? You weren't so innocent when I saw you yesterday afternoon. You and your hammer."

"You don't look very young," she told him.

"I'm twenty-nine," he protested. "By my whip – what has that to do with the matter!"

"I was just remarking. Can I sit down?" She sat down. To Crystal she added, "If you're seeking the family silver, it's either halfway to Oxford or it's on its way back to Sapperton – depending on whether or not they've apprehended the *Roger* yet."

Matt seated himself, too. Jack Horley was left with his sword tip menacing nothing but the morning air. It wavered uncertainly, then he shouldered the blade.

"Nothing here," Crystal said.

"Well, I never expected they'd keep it about them. They must have buried it."

"I told you," Mary said. "After the fight in the wood we brought the two sacks down to the boat. My companion, Steam Punch, and I were all for taking them straight to Sapperton and claiming the reward off Lord Ferrers. But the master of the boat and his son – whom we'd not met above two or three hours since – they were for melting it down and keeping it. This man here is a witness to it all. He was on the other bank of the canal."

Matt nodded, and kept a watchful eye on the blade.

"Well . . ." The man sniffed, more than half-believing them. "You're not straying out of our sight until we've either confirmed your tale or tracked down our plate." He began to sheathe his sword.

Matt was scandalized. Before Jack could stop him he leaped up, pulled out the blade again, and ran it through the embers. Then he wiped it under the arm of his shirt (to Mary's disgust) and passed it back to its owner. "Rust," he explained.

Young Jack eyed the heavens. "Ecod, I think we've fallen among lunatics," he said to Crystal.

"What next?" she asked; she was looking Matt up and down admiringly.

"What happened to your father, Mr. Horley?" Mary interrupted crossly.

"He's in the lockup still."

"Did you break out? Will they be coming after you?"

He nodded as he sat down. "Everything's gone wrong," he said disconsolately. "It's all so straightforward. We were to borrow back our plate, get married, and then return it – all within the twenty-four hours. Haven't we more right to than him, anyway?"

"Have you?" Mary asked.

"He won it on a horse match, but I saw his jockey drop the bags of lead shot, and I saw Parson Grimes pick them up and slip them back to him after the race was won, just before the weighing."

"Didn't you accuse them?"

"Ferrers is the best marksman in the whole county, and the finest swordsman, too."

Matt's stomach gurgled. He rose and said "Snares."

Young Jack cocked his head toward Matt and asked Mary, "Does he buy all his words retail?"

She leaped to Matt's defence. "And why wouldn't he – when each one is made of gold."

He turned to Matt. "I'll come with you. I'll not see my plate vanish over the hills and far away!"

"No more you will," Mary affirmed. "I'll tend the fire and heat up some potatoes."

Matt looked at her, then at Lucius, and said, "I've counted them."

"And you're guarding me, I suppose." Mary remarked to Crystal once the men had left. "Are you any good in a fight?"

The question took Crystal by surprise. Convention prompted her to say, "For my honour, I suppose."

"I know!" Mary took her up. "I'm always at that game lately, myself. Twice this last month, would you believe it! And me who never had to raise a finger to protect it in all my twenty years! Not to mention being fleeced blind by all and sundry, from booksellers to itinerant Welsh pedlars – and London boatmen worst of all. It's no world for a girl on her own."

"This business with Lord Ferrers is so unfair. Are you Welsh?"

"Let's get a good blaze going. Why does it always get cold just after dawn? Did you ever notice that?" She took a potato from Matt's hoard and threw it to Lucius. "Make it last!" she told the creature. "You'll get no more." Then, to Crystal again, "No, I'm from Ireland. I'm Mary Flinders, by the by – daughter of The Flinders of the Barony of Inchiquin in County Clare." When Crystal looked blank she added, "'Tis three hundred English miles from here and seems like three thousand."

A smile split Crystal's face. "Are you one of those romantic and penniless young Irish ladies of good family, come to find fame and fortune in England?"

Mary had never seen herself in that light but, after a moment's thought she agreed that such was indeed the case. Then she added, "Why – are there many of us?"

They began to gather sticks.

"Well, there were the Gunning sisters," Crystal said. "Everyone's heard of them."

The assertion was so positive that Mary did not feel like confessing she was not of the party. "Ah yes," she said, as if the name had just slipped her mind.

"And this splendid-looking man you're with?" Crystal asked. "Is he . . . er . . . included in your design?"

"He's a genius. A mechanical genius. His name is Matt Sullivan. I couldn't *begin* to tell you all the marvels he can perform. But my only connection with him is that he saved me from drowning when I fell off the *Roger* yesterday, and he gave me shelter last night."

They flung an armful of wood upon the blaze and stood back to watch it catch. Lucius came trotting over for more fodder but

Mary took the remaining potatoes and poked them into the edge of the fire, raking the ashes over them to stop their skins from burning.

"Are you still to be wed today?" Mary asked.

"In a way I'm already married," Crystal answered coyly.

"Does it hurt?" Mary asked.

She was plainly bursting to confide this grand new experience to someone, and Mary could think of a thousand questions beside; but the mere fact of having almost brained Crystal's husband-to-be constituted too slender an acquaintance upon which to venture even one of them.

Crystal, blushing now at the rashness that had forced the confession from her, quickly added, "But we shall make all right today, of course. Or as soon as maybe."

After a silence she went on, "D'you think it was very wrong?"

"I'm sure a wrong must be intentional," Mary replied soothingly. "Or who would 'scape whipping? 'Tis a mere venial slip."

Crystal thought it over and then asked, "Could people slip often, I wonder, and still not *quite* intend to?"

"I'm sure."

"I was thinking, you see . . . if we can't find a minister today."

"God, I'm no theologian. We fight off the men for twenty years then suddenly all virtue's kicking for the other goal. Riddle me that, ye Trinity scholars! A reverend gentleman was once after telling me how you could know a really bad sin. He said, ask yourself: Will it still matter when I'm sixty?"

Crystal laughed and dared to hug Mary's arm. "Oh, you're a grand one to talk with, Miss Flinders. I don't know what's to become of us. I've been ruined with worry. Yet look at you – as well-born as any, I can tell, and probably worse off than either Jack or me, yet you're as blithe as the lark. How do you manage so?"

Mary shook her head and shrugged. "I never thought of it."

Crystal gave her an accusing smile. "It has something to do with this young man – Mr. Matt Sullivan. Confess it, now."

"I confess I'd be most miserable if he hadn't pulled me from the water, dried me out, and fed me." She stooped and turned over the potatoes with swift darts of her fingers. Looking into the fire, she added, "Indeed, I'd likely now be roasting in Purgatory for all those sins that wouldn't have mattered if only I'd lived to sixty."

Crystal tried another tack. "So you're bound for London?"

"Yes." Mary rose and dusted off her hands. "To the household of Lord Tottenham."

"Oh," Crystal seemed startled.

"You know him?" Mary asked.

"Do you?"

"Not in the least. I am very slightly acquainted with one of his household, that's all."

"I am extremely glad to hear it, Miss Flinders."

"You seem to know him, then, Miss Coker?"

"I know *of* him. He's a notorious crony of Lord Ferrers. Each of them is more crooked than the other."

"Oh dear . . . and everything appeared so simple when I left home."

"Well, life's a surprise," Crystal said in a vaguely comforting tone. "And you have a fortunate face."

"What'll you do now?" Mary asked. "If you're on the run, you mayn't linger here."

"If they get the plate back, perhaps we can. Ferrers wouldn't welcome too close an examination of his title to it. Things may be said in a court of law that cannot provoke a challenge of honour."

"But d'you want to stay here?"

"What else is there?"

"Your Jack has a good farm, I suppose?"

"He had, but it's all pledged. There's a fine and a recovery out on it now, even though Jack is the heir of tailzie and provision. I wish I'd known as much before I lost my heart to him."

"You mean you'd follow him now whatever his fortune may be?"

Crystal nodded glumly. After a silence she said, "You must think me foolish indeed."

"I was thinking I've never been in love at all, if that's the way of it."

"You've come a long way to learn as much, then."

There seemed nothing further to add.

Again Crystal started a new subject. "If you don't join Lord Tottenham's household – which I strongly urge you against – what then?"

"Everything I possess except what's on my back – and that greedy ass there – is away with the *Roger*. And poor Punch with it. If I can get back my harp and my books, then I might wander from one gentleman's household to another, singing for my keep and telling them of the amazements I read in a book I bought in Dublin."

"Singing and telling of amazements," Crystal repeated flatly, as if she wouldn't believe it until she heard it on her own lips.

"I know of many amazements," Mary told her enthusiastically. "This is Gloucestershire, isn't it? Tell me, is there a river called the Pever near here?"

"I never heard it mentioned."

"Well, wherever it is, it's in Gloucestershire, and in the year 1773 it suddenly changed course and bore away above ten acres of farmland and everything that grew or stood upon it!"

"Indeed?" Crystal was at a loss to say more.

"I've cogged a hundred such Remarkable Occurrences," Mary assured her. "And could as easily learn up hundreds more. Can you and Master Jack sing in descants? Perhaps we could all travel around together – if you find you may not settle here? And Matt Sullivan could perform his illuminations. Such a jolly band we'd be!"

So infectious was Mary's enthusiasm that, just for a moment, Crystal caught herself wishing this ridiculous, gothick dream were possible. Jack was right – they *had* fallen among lunatics.

"What can Master Jack do?" Mary asked.

"The same as any gentleman. He can ride and shoot and ply his sword – and gamble and drink and wench and swear oaths. Now that he's without land, I suppose he'll end up in some foreign army."

"A life of glory!" Mary said enviously. "There's many of the gentry from Ireland have been forced into that. Papists, of course."

"I wonder are there protestant armies in Europe?"

"Oh lots. Don't worry."

"Worry!" Crystal laughed sarcastically. "Great heavens! It's not what I want for the man. I'd do anything to keep him out of foreign wars."

"But he'd look so fine in uniform. He'd be an officer, naturally. All that gold braid, and his sword . . ."

Lucius pointed his ears and brayed; the men stepped out from behind some bushes about a hundred yards off.

"He looks fine enough to me as he is," Crystal murmured, her eyes fixed on Jack. Then she added politely, "And Mr. Sullivan also, to be sure."

"I believe Mr. Sullivan could turn into a fine old disappointment," Mary responded. "He showed me a marvel last night that could make his fortune – and he simply has no interest in the pursuit of it. He has a way of conveying the heat of a fire – or, rather, the gases that exude from wood and coal when placed upon a fire – he can convey them through tubes, a hundred paces or more if you wish, and set them alight at the end of their journey."

"Mercy! Is he a witch?"

"No no – 'tis all done upon natural principles. I'm sure gentlemen would pay a fortune to have their houses heated and lighted in a manner so convenient and tractable. But now that he's demonstrated the principle of the thing to his own satisfaction, he's lost all interest in its development. He gave away the idea to a French conjuror. A man like that does vex me so!"

Crystal, amazed at her vehemence, said, "And it was but yesterday that you first met him, you say?"

"He has a mind as fertile as the Ganges. He'll articulate a dozen inventions before breakfast – and profit by none of them."

Crystal's tone was as casual as if they were discussing the man in the moon. "Does it not strike you," she asked, "that such genius must need a loving keeper."

# CHAPTER FIFTEEN

THE *ROGER* WAS FOUND lying abandoned at the far end of the newly completed Sapperton Tunnel, the Coates end as canal people call it. Of the master and his son there was no sign, nor of the horse, nor of Steam Punch, nor of Mary's belongings – nor, indeed, of the stolen silver. Mary and Matt went into Sapperton village immediately after breakfast and were brought before the justice to make their depositions. Warrants were taken out for the apprehension of Hal and his father, whose surname, Mary now learned, was Corbett. Sadly she also learned that Young Jack's father, "Old" Jack Horley, had died of a seizure during the night. His daughter had claimed the body and was arranging for it to be brought back to Aston for burial.

Upon promise to keep the clerk of the assize informed of their movements, Matt and Mary, now crown witnesses, were released. No one asked them if they had seen Young Jack, who now had a price on his head. He and Crystal had, in fact, gone into hiding in the Tumbledown woods, near the Coates end of the tunnel; there they were waiting for news.

Matt and Mary returned to the *Roger*, where a frantic warehouse manager was lamenting the breakages caused by Lord Ferrers's agent during the search for his master's silver – and wondering who would pay for them. Also who would deliver the cheeses that would soon begin to rot in the hold?

"As the Corbetts are now felons, or alleged so, the boat will be forfeit to the crown," Mary pointed out.

"But it's not theirs," the manager told her. "It belongs to an Oxford merchant."

Within five minutes, on the man's assurance that this Oxford merchant, a certain Philip Meredith, would be only delighted to have the boat brought to him and its cargo properly discharged upon the way, Mary volunteered for the office and begged Matt, "Would you ever go the length of the tunnel with us – for the legging that's in it?"

As they were about to set off, word came that the Corbetts had been taken. Mary went at once to the clink to discover what had become of Punch – and, of course, her property. But they would say nothing.

She pointed out how foolish they were being. "A clever lawyer might explain away your immediate failure to restore the silver," she told them. "But to take away *my* property after you have contracted before witnesses to convey me to London is so plain and open a felony it would discolour any such explanation and put it quite out of court."

So with ill grace they told her of a little grove above Coates;

there, they swore, they had left Punch ,and all her belongings
except her purse, which they had been unable to find. They spoke
so reluctantly that she was sure they had hidden the silver
thereabouts, too.

Their interview was abruptly closed by the arrival of the
constabulary from Gloucester, to whose gaol the two prisoners
were now consigned.

That voyage through the tunnel, some 250 feet below the
hilltop, was one of the experiences of her life.

"It's like a fairytale castle!" she said as they approached the
magnificent gothic portals that guarded the entrance.

He shook his head. "To me it smells of too much sweat still."

She leaped onto the towpath and persuaded Lucius aboard, just
in the nick of time. Matt stretched himself upon the cabin roof
and prepared to leg the vessel through.

As soon as Mary's eyes had grown accustomed to the dark she
could discern the little pinpoint of the Coates end. It seemed to
move independently in the velvet-black bullseye beyond the
prow. Overhead the light that filtered in from the Sapperton end
picked out the arches of the brickwork; they still appeared so new
that you wondered if the mortar had quite set. In places the rock
was hard enough in itself to need no support. There the steps for
the leggers were cut directly into the stone.

"What's it like?" she asked.

"Walking," he panted. "Uphill. It's the longest tunnel in the
kingdom, you know. Two miles and three furlongs."

Their voices rang and rang again in those confines. The single
candle that guided his feet gave his face a satanic cast when seen
from her vantage near the tiller.

"I'll take my turn if you will," she volunteered.

He laughed.

"D'you think I couldn't?" she pressed.

He kept his peace.

When the dark had quite engulfed them she mused, "There
must be some way of harnessing steam to this caper."

As if he were answering her he said, "This morning –
remember? Young Jack. His sword at our throats?"

"There's no longer need to call him *Young* Jack. Anyway, I
remember."

"Gave me an idea. A tube, see, strapped . . ." He patted his upper arm. "With a dart in it. Compressed spring. Held by a pin on a fine chain attached at the back of your collar. One jerk of your head. Fsssst! Dead!" He laughed. "Good, eh?"

"Wonderful!"

"*Whang!* He'd die amazed."

"We have only your word for it."

"Oh, it'd work all right."

"Since you're never going to make the thing . . ." She sighed.

He stopped legging and sat up. "Are you out of concert with me?" His tone was puzzled.

"Sure it's none of my business. Your life's your own."

He returned to his legging. There was a long, blessed silence, broken only by the lapping of the water and his laboured breathing. She tried to fix every sensation in her memory – or rather the lack of sensation. The near-total dark, the near-total silence, combined with the almost perfect smoothness of their gliding motion over the face of the canal. It produced in her an uncanny sense of bodily withdrawal. If a soul could be liberated from its imprisoning flesh and be let free to wander the earth, the sensation would be very close to this.

"If you could do anything, Matt – possible or impossible – what would it be?"

"Impossible."

"Yes, but what?"

They were now past the halfway mark; the pinpoint of the Coates end had enlarged to a hole through which a flea might crawl.

"I'd polish a slab of stone as smooth as untroubled water."

"What ever for?"

"Sleep on it. No! Lie awake upon it all night through – just to know that I was on the flattest, smoothest, most perfect surface anywhere in the whole of creation."

She laughed in bewilderment. "But why? It would hardly be comfortable."

"Don't you see? Nothing in nature can achieve such a surface. Only man. Perfection lies with man, not in nature. We impose our will upon her. I'd lie there all night and glory in that."

"Nature never yet achieved a goosedown mattress, either. And I know which I'd choose to lie on and glory in man's invention. D'you want me to spell you for a breather?"

He gave a sour grunt – though he yielded his place with some willingness, she noticed. She lay directly upon the warmth that had seeped from his body into the tarred decking of the cabin roof. Clutching her skirts to the back of her thighs for decency's sake, she let him guide her feet for the first few steps. Then he left her and went to the tiller.

For a while she persisted in crimping her skirts tight, but they hampered her so much that at last she just let them fall; what did it matter in this dark, anyway? The labour was hard enough without such an encumbrance; Matt had been sweating when he got down; this freedom of her limbs would keep her cool.

She did not realize that the candle which, from her viewpoint, turned her thighs into two dark shapes, almost lost against the stygian night of the tunnel behind them, turned them, from his viewpoint into a golden vision of enticement. Never had he seen so perfect a pair – firm where her muscles strained, soft where they relaxed . . . slender at her knees, plump around her hips . . . curving inward here, swelling outward there . . . pure and pale as milk in the advancing light of the tunnel mouth, golden, dancing in the flame . . . youthful, lithe, inviting . . .

The wall was approaching; he saw it out of the corner of his eye. He leaned upon the tiller and gently turned the craft back toward midstream. As he stood there, watching her, it suddenly came to him that she was the first woman who ever roused his desire without deliberately provoking it. In fact, it went deeper than that, for this was no simple desire – the kind that might arise and be satisfied within the day. Yet until now that was the only kind he had ever known with women.

The novelty of this new feeling, the demands it implied against his freedom and ease, filled him with disquiet. He was glad that, as soon as they were clear of the tunnel, as soon as they had carried the news to Jack Horley, he'd be away, free of her, northward-bound, headed for home.

They were a furlong short of the mouth when a westbound boat darkened the incoming day. Quickly they swapped back. She was breathless and glowing. Her breast heaved; her eyes sparkled with the pride of her achievement. He searched her face; not a feature would he change, not a curve or a dimple would he wish other than it was. "Get to the tiller," he commanded gruffly. "Keep us as close to the right wall as you may without grazing. There's not above twelve inches of air to divide between the two boats."

"Aye aye, cap'n!" She laughed.

"Way hay, *Roger!*" the other crew hailed them when they came within reading distance. Then, moments later, "Where's the Corbetts?"

"In clink," Matt said guardedly.

"What for?" They were level now, staring curiously at Mary.

"Felony."

"And you didn't get up a gang to break them out?" They were scandalized.

"We're agents of Mr. Philip Meredith of Oxford," Mary told them. "We're just collecting the boat." She hoped they were silently admiring the way she was steering through a gap barely six inches wider than the boat . . . saying to themselves, *Now there's a canal woman!*

"Are they still in Sapperton?" They were dwindling away into the dark.

"If you're quick."

"We'll do what we can," they promised, as if it were a duty they owed the *Roger* as much as the Corbetts.

When they were gone Matt said, "Such recklessness!"

Mary agreed. "The only hanging I ever was at was in Ennis. And one of the condemned was a pickpocket. And while he was kicking and gasping his last – at that very moment, you know – I happened to glance away, and what was the first thing I saw? Only a man picking another man's pocket! God, if hanging doesn't stop them, what will?"

"What stops you?"

"I don't know," she admitted.

"Fear of the wrath to come?"

"I just wouldn't do it. Other people's property has a . . . well, it's like a different colour, a different smell, wouldn't you say?"

He retired into his customary silence.

How far was Manchester from London, she wondered.

# CHAPTER SIXTEEN

THEY MOORED AT the Round House wharf, a little way beyond Tunnel Inn, and went at once to the grove where the Corbetts said they had left Punch, unconscious and possibly dying. There were signs of disturbance in plenty, but of his person (and her property) there were none.

"That means he must be alive," she said. "And he must be well, too, if he could carry off all his things *and* mine."

Matt gave a not-too-hopeful lift of his shoulders.

She stared at the hill under which they had just passed. "He's probably up there now, stealing back to try to find us."

Matt shook his head. "Doubtful. Silver still missing – vagrant Irishman . . ." He pointed toward the horizon.

But she did not believe Punch would abandon her like that, however compelling the motive.

They spent the afternoon checking the cargo manifest and rearranging things – actually playing for time until it was dark enough to go up to Tumbledown woods and bring the ill tidings to the pair who waited there.

"I feel as if I've known you for years and years," she told him.

He grunted.

"Don't you feel it, too?"

He gave a wary nod, as if he suspected a trap.

"Will I call you Matt? You shall call me Mary."

He shrugged.

"If I hadn't met you, I'd be dead," she reminded him.

"No, you wouldn't. You'd be half way to London, learning new songs off Hal Corbett. 'Twas me pointed out the commotion in the spinney up the hill, remember? But for that . . ."

"Ah, don't be spoiling it now, Matt. It's the truth I'm talking, none of your stupid facts."

He laughed. "Come to think of it, I never yet knew an Irishman do otherwise, nor Irishwoman, neither."

"Mock away! There's a poetry in truth, and facts can never hold a candle to it."

Obscure warning bells were ringing in his mind but he gave her a fond smile as he conceded her point.

She underlined it, anyway: "My skin looked black in the tunnel. Out here it's white. That's mere *facts* for you!"

He shivered at the reminder and for the first time he wondered if he would, in truth, be able to part from her.

She laughed. "No one could say the same for *your* skin – and that's another fact."

Her playful belligerence saved the moment for him. He fanned his mild resentment and assured himself he'd be well shot of her.

Their efforts to tidy the vessel had one lucky consequence. In a forward locker they found a horse collar that, with a bit of extra padding, would make it far easier for Lucius to pull the boat.

When all the world was asleep they crept ashore and set off. The moon was just sinking over the ridge of Cowcombe Hill; owls screeched from the woodland verges, and in remote farmyards the dogs barked, and listened, and barked again. In no window did they see even the glimmer of a nightlight. When they reached Tumbledown the moon had gone, but a scattering of ragged, fluffy clouds, like disordered ladies' wigs of a now-antique fashion, caught and held its light with a lambent softness.

Crystal was waiting for them at the fringe of the trees. The moment she saw them she cupped her hands to her lips and gave a whistle like a barn owl. Jack came silently from the dark beneath the trees and joined her. He looked exhausted.

"My father?" he asked in an urgent whisper.

Matt put a finger to his lips, pointed down toward the open pasture, and beckoned them all to follow him there.

Crystal had paid a clandestine visit to her home that day – before the bad news had travelled that far; she had returned with several large bundles of clothing and food. The burden of these they now shared among them.

After a few paces Jack plucked at Mary's sleeve. "Tell me," he begged.

She paused and gave his arm a comforting squeeze.

He slumped. "I felt it so. All day I've felt it."

"The entire populace is amazed at it," Mary said, "and filled with grief for you and your family."

Crystal fell back, slipped her arms about him, and hugged her head to his chest. Mary left the pair of them weeping; she and Matt went down to one of the open pastures to wait. When the others joined them, a few minutes later, they were carrying a brace of hares. "A most extraordinary thing has just happened," Jack said. "One of Lord Ferrers's gamekeepers came up to us – just this minute while we stood up there – came out of nowhere, dropped these at our feet, wished us good luck, and vanished back into the night. What d'you make of that?"

Crystal said, "There's not a decent Gloucestershire man in any parish around who wouldn't gladly see you restored to your lands and property – and wish Ferrers damned into outer darkness."

The words stirred something in Jack. His exhaustion seemed to fall from him. With great solemnity he laid down the hares and all their other baggage and, stretching forth his palm, said, "Friends, give me your hands."

They obeyed. He sealed the stack with his other hand and went on, "By my honour, by my family, by these my friends here gathered, by all that I hold dearest and most sacred, I now pledge my heart, my soul, my life, to the avenging of my father's death, to the restoration of my family's place and wealth, and to the damnation of Ferrers and all his tribe." He stared into their faces, one by one, before adding, "Amen."

"Amen," they chorused.

Mary felt the hair prickle at the nape of her neck. There, indeed, you had that indefinable quality of a gentleman – the chivalric warrior, born to lead. Had she been a soldier she knew she would follow Jack anywhere.

"And now to practicalities," Jack said, in quite a normal voice.

They all sat down, certain, after the gamekeeper's gesture, of their own immediate safety.

"What shall you two do?" he asked.

Mary explained her situation with the *Roger*.

"And you, Mr. Sullivan?"

Matt looked at Mary. "You're going north, surely?" she prompted.

He nodded and repeated, "North."

"And you, squire?" Mary asked. "It won't be safe for you hereabouts."

He pursed his lips unhappily. "No, I must rebuild my fortune elsewhere. In one of the German principalities perhaps? My mother and sisters will be catered to fairly. She has kinsmen in Cirencester. But we must first get to London. I have cousins in Twickenham." He looked across at Mary. "Might we come with you to London, Miss Flinders?"

"If you can pay your passage, sir, you're right welcome. All my wealth and property seems to have vanished off the face of the earth. I'm at the mercy of this Master Meredith in Oxford. Until then . . ."

"How much?" he asked.

"Oh God" – she patted their hamper of food and the two hares – "all I want is the run of my teeth."

"Gladly." He laughed and then, giving the back of his head a diffident scratch, went on, "While in no way desiring to break up this most congenial gathering. I do think we ought to put as much water as possible between ourselves and this part of Gloucestershire. Where is the first lock we shall encounter?"

They all looked at Matt. "You're on the summit pound now," he said. "Twenty miles to the Thames Navigation at Lechlade. It's a fall of a hundred and thirty-aught foot by way of fourteen locks. The first are at Siddington – a flight of four. The keeper might let you through – with a good tale."

"What would he consider a good tale?"

"Shall I walk with you that far?"

"No!" Mary said vehemently, surprising them all. "God, a breeze would deflect you!"

He bridled. "I'll do what I please, madam!"

She stared at him furiously. "It's all talk with you! You'll never make anything of yourself!"

Crystal cleared her throat and laid a gentle hand on Mary's arm.

"Oh, he'd light the world with promises," Mary told her in the same angry tones. "But if he came to a wedding he'd be there at the christening still, so he would."

"And what's it to you?" Matt asked.

She tossed her head and forced herself to be calm again. "Nothing, I'm sure."

After a frosty silence, in which nobody could think of anything to say, he rose. "So," he said. "Good fortune attend you." As he strode away he added over his shoulder, "And I wish Master and Mistress Horley joy of so amiable a companion."

"He can find the words when goaded to it," Jack said.

Crystal nudged Mary. "Go after him."

"Oh he does vex me so."

"I doubt he doubts it! Even so, my dear . . ."

Mary rose and ran downhill over the sheep-nibbled turf. Matt heard her – she could tell by the sudden stiffness of his gait – but he did not pause.

She caught up. "Matt?" she said, taking his arm.

"What?"

"We can't part like this."

"No?"

"Well I can't. Not after all I owe you."

"Nothing."

"I owe you my life."

"So would a dog had I done it for him."

She threw her arms around his neck, swinging from him, forcing him to stop. But when she tried to kiss him on the cheek he broke away angrily and ran off toward the boat. By the time she caught up with him he had shouldered his pack and was making for the horse trail over the hill.

She stood and watched him, forcing the silence to speak for her.

When he was some thirty paces off he turned. "If ever you're in Manchester . . ." he began.

"Yes?"

He spun on his heel and strode off.

A terrible desolation filled her. Every nerve in her body screamed at her to run after him, abandon the boat, her thoughts of London, her quest for fortune. She actually took one step in his direction before all those conflicting claims asserted themselves and held her back. Even then the decision hung in the balance; the breeze off a sparrow's wing could have wafted her onward.

Then the other two approached, and the atmosphere changed, and it was too late. Calmly she untethered Lucius and harnessed him to the towline. "You steer," she called.

She and Lucius strained at the line. The hemp fibres creaked. The boat yielded gracefully and nosed out into mid-canal. But no sooner were they underway than she heard – or half-heard and half-felt – Crystal at her side.

Without a word the woman took her arm.

"What's this?" Mary asked.

"Have tears gone out of fashion over there?"

"Tears?" Mary shrugged. "What have I to do with tears?"

"You know very well."

"For that one? He's impossible. The less I praise him, the less I'll lie."

"You're only saying that."

"I'm only *saying* it. I'm only *thinking* it. If I could tuck it inside a baked potato, I'd be only *eating* it. And if I wasn't yoked with two renegades the likes of you, I'd be only *dreaming* it."

Crystal laughed and hugged her arm the tighter. "Oh Mary Flinders, Mary Flinders, if it's any consolation, I'm sure he feels the loss as sharp as you."

At that Mary burst into tears.

Lucius stopped and looked at her. "Git on!" She kicked out at him, hurting her toes more than his flank.

"Don't worry," Crystal went on when Mary was calm again. "Love always finds a way."

"Would you listen to her!" Mary begged the heavens. "Once and for all now – I would not give a hatful of roasted snow for Matt Sullivan. So let's have an end to it."

"As you wish."

After a silence Mary added, "Anyway, 'twould never have suited."

"True, true. A worse-matched pair never walked the earth." Crystal's agreement provoked another thoughtful silence.

"And for every fish that ever was caught there's a dozen swimming still."

"Aye, his genius was all froth and no body. Better men crowd every turn in London. You'll see."

Lucius plodded on, marking out the minutes with his steady tread.

"I don't even know where Manchester is," Mary said at last.

"Oh, 'tis a most *commercial* village," Crystal told her disdainfully. "You'd surely hate it."

The hedgerows crackled with tiny life. Rabbits in the fields beyond thumped their alarms on the hollow-sounding turf.

"And say what you will, gentility *is* important," Mary added.

"So all the world believes."

"Don't you agree?"

Crystal said nothing.

"Surely?" Mary prompted.

"It was a 'gentleman' robbed us of all we possess – and by means of a debt of so-called honour that proved false. And our only swift redress is by means of a chivalry that would stretch Jack long and cold."

Mary sighed. "But breeding must count for *something*. Otherwise . . ." She could not quite see how to finish the thought, yet she knew precisely what she meant.

After some time they drew near the Siddington lock, the one that Matt had mentioned. "He never did tell us what your lock-keeper beyond might consider a convincing tale," Mary complained.

Lucius's ears twitched. His gait slackened.

"I told him – I said to his face – he was as brilliant as a lighthouse in a bog – and just about as useful to mankind in general."

Crystal stiffened and clutched at Mary's arm. "There's someone there!" she whispered. "A man – standing on the towpath."

Now Mary saw the fellow, too. "Hello?" she called. "Who's that? What's your business at such an hour?"

"Jaysus!" cried a familiar voice. "But that's a woeful shteam out of you, girl!"

Mary dropped Lucius's traces and ran forward, laughing and crying in delight. "Punch!" she called, throwing herself at him and hugging him near to death. "Oh, Punch! Steam Punch!"

# PART THREE

# A RARE OUL' RACE

# CHAPTER SEVENTEEN

I'M COMING, YOU'RE GOING!" The chant rang up the echoing stairwell, striking dread into all who heard it.

"I'm coming, you're going."

The servants stared at one another in terrified paralysis, each challenging someone else to tackle the interloper. One poor valet had the misfortune to be well embarked upon the downward journey as Con Murphy began the ascent; he turned and pressed his face to the wall, as if but yesterday – he was sure of it – a door had opened there. Had there indeed been such a means of escape, and had it led to the vilest pit in the whole of London, he would have taken it singing.

Con passed him by without a glance; there was no profit in a frightened servant. "I'm coming, you're going."

There was one departure from his usual practice: The lump hammer hung loose in his right hand; he made no attempt to smash the occasional banister rod in passing. The reason was simple. Young Jonas Pitman, the target of this mid-morning call, had rented the house from Sir Peregrine Tongye, a close crony of Lord Tottenham and the sort of man who would not be amused at finding his property smashed, even in so noble an enterprise as the collection of a debt of honour.

Perhaps it was this enforced restraint, or perhaps it was that Con had undertaken a surfeit of such calls in recent weeks; at all events, he was beginning to feel a certain flatness to the business. It had been impossible lately to recapture the thrill of that first occasion. He could not now recall the young victim's name but he would never forget the terror in his eyes. Con himself had been nervous, too, never before having dared make so bold with a gentleman. But oh, the bliss of discovering that his fears were matched, overmatched, ten times overmatched! And the power of it, too – in normal circumstances, any of these young coxcombs could have ordered him from pillar to post; but with his lordship's colours in his cap he could make them cower.

Now even these pleasures were dwindling. His reputation went before him. The fear of one of his visitations was so great that his actual irruption upon a household could even appear somewhat of an anticlimax. There was no longer any clash of wills; the surrender was made long before his shadow darkened the threshold, the Jews were engaged, the money borrowed, the inheritance pledged, the expectations mortgaged, the annuity already inscribed . . . it was no more exciting than hunting a dragged kipper nailed to a tree.

If only one of them would show a little spirit, stand up to him . . .

He kicked open the door to what he had been assured was young Jonas Pitman's receiving room but the first thing that faced him was a large half-tester bed, draped in a rich and heavy brocade. Spilled across the counterpane was what he at first took to be a wig, a mass of dark, lustrous tresses; but then it moved, and he saw it was the natural adornment of a young woman. Indeed, at that moment, it was her only adornment.

Con almost forgot himself; he almost spoke a few stammering words of apology. But then a voice, male and peeved, struggled out from somewhere beneath the sheets – beneath the young woman, to be precise – "What the devil?"

"I'm coming . . ." Con began.

"You're not the only one," the man interrupted angrily. "Confound your impudence! Who are you? And who admitted you?"

The woman wriggled until she lay at his side, still face down. She pulled the covers over her.

Jonas Pitman's face was now revealed – youthful but dissolute, handsome though in need of a shave. The eyes were jaded – which was hardly surprising – but they were also cool and watchful, and not the least abashed.

Con was shaken; a surfeit of easy victories had left him

ill-prepared for this. Notwithstanding his wish for a little excitement, a little opposition, its sudden appearance did nothing to restore those early raptures; rather it left him queasily uncertain of the liberties he might now take. "You know full well who I am," he barked with more confidence than he felt.

"Hanged if I do. You're a blackguard, so much is plain. But beyond that . . ."

"Here's my card, so." Con held up his hammer. "I'm sent from my Lord Tottenham on a matter of two thousand guineas."

Pitman closed his eyes and gave a mirthless laugh. "Oh that! You may jump for it – jump the moon for what little good it'll do you."

Matters would have been so different, Con thought, if he had been allowed to smash the banisters in the usual way. The sight of seven or eight of them, fractured, leaning out into the stairwell, always had a most dramatic effect. First the unaccustomed noise brought the young victim out to the stairhead, where he had then perforce to stand and wait, watching Con's slow and remorseless rise, unable to prevent the measured swing of the hammer or to blot out the crash of splintering wood. And then that litany of dread – "I'm coming, you're going!" It was a bold fellow indeed whose courage was not all jelly by the time Con drew level, where his girth and muscle could be measured at close quarters.

Now, brought to an awkward halt in Pitman's doorway, he looked about him, desperate to recover his wonted superiority. Swiftly he crossed the room, away from the bed, toward the window. There he raised the hammer and let it fall on the first delicate object that caught his eye – a small porcelain basket filled with miniature china fruits. The shards flew to every corner of the room; a few were ground deep into the fine mahogany of the cabinet.

He smiled complacently. Slowly, deliberately he began to turn toward his young victim. But before he completed the action it seemed as if the whole world exploded. There was a flash. A loud bang at his right ear was precisely complemented by a vicious thwack at his left as a ball of lead buried itself in the pinewood panelling, only inches away. Moments later his face was enveloped in an acrid cloud of gunpowder smoke. He began to cough.

The woman laughed, a silvery shower that seemed to descend

from on high, far, far above him. Later, when Con recalled those moments of shame, it was that superior laughter which most wounded him. At the time, however, the fear of a much more physical wounding consumed him, for he turned toward the bed and found himself staring down the barrel of a second pistol. The first lay casually upon the counterpane, still lightly reeking.

"This time I shall not aim to miss," Pitman said quietly.

Between his coughing Con drew breath to speak but the other barked, "Hold your tongue." He waved the pistol as if it were an invisible broom that would sweep Con aside. "And get off the carpet! Sir Peregrine can no doubt agree with your master over the loss of a small china ornament, but I doubt he'd take so kindly to a shambles of your bowels upon so fine a Turkey rug." He waited until Con reached the door before he added, "Now, you may tell your master that I hold him an arrant cheat. Tell him beside that my alleged debt to him is a debt of dishonour and I have no intention of paying it. And do not neglect to add that his distinguished name sits upon him like a capstone of fine marble upon a pile of dog turds, encumbering what it cannot possibly ennoble. Tell him there is more, much more, which I would convey to him – and, indeed *should* convey to him had he sent me a man as excellent in brain as you are in brawn – but that I fear your wits will not bear the gravity of it." He smiled. "And now, to borrow a phrase, *I'm* coming, *you're* going!"

The woman laughed again. Pitman turned and threw himself upon her and began at once to behave as if Con had ceased to exist – which is precisely how Con felt as he turned and descended the stair.

All that day he took good care to stay out of his master's way; several times, in chop houses and gambling hells from Seven Dials to Devonshire House, their paths almost crossed, but Con's ear was too acute, and Tottenham himself too taken up with the company, to allow the disaster of a premature meeting. Con wanted his man to be mellow with the casual sport of the day and hot for the evening's more deliberate pleasures before he broke cover.

If only the Flinders girl were here. Ever since he had described the wench to his master, Tottenham had been so hot to meet her. Not a day went by without his asking if she'd arrived yet.

Con finally took the plunge in a coffee house just off Bond

Street; even then he was careful to hide behind a partition until his master's mood was clear.

Tottenham and his friends were enjoying their usual chaff.

"Of all the men I know," one said, "I account Tottenham the happiest."

"Why so?" asked a second.

"Why so? Why so? Why – by universal consent. The true puzzle is *how* so?"

"Yes, Totters!" a third cried out. "How so? What's the secret?"

In the silence that followed, Con could just picture the smile that must slowly be spreading over his master's countenance; certainly when the man spoke that smile was printed on his voice. "No secret at all," he said. "I dare swear any man may learn the art."

"Tell us then."

"Why, it is to be both devout Protestant and ardent Catholic at once."

"Come – here's perversity!"

"Explain, explain!"

"I devoutly *protest* my love of women . . . and am most ardently *catholic* in my choice among 'em!"

The whole coffee house erupted into laughter. Con blessed himself that he had chanced upon this most propitious moment to break his dire news. He was on the point of stepping forward when the first man said, "But in that case he's no different from the rest of us. There's not a man here who does not look upon woman as does a traveller his refuge – namely, a nightly necessity."

"A refuge?" Tottenham echoed. "Ecod, but 'tis an odd sort of refuge where one may stay *up* all night!" Again the house dissolved in laughter.

Once more Con was about to step forth when he was yet again forestalled. "But I protest there is a difference," the third friend pointed out. "You and I, and most living mortals, are but ordinary travellers in such nightly, er, *country*! If the dark o'ertake us and we see no convenient refuge, we give up the quest and return home to our solo and virtuous beds." Coughing and guffawing greeted this assertion. "But Totters is made of altogether different clay. Totters is a dedicated traveller. No fitting refuge being in sight, there's no turning back for him. *He begins to eye old barns and derelict cottages.*"

One of the others caught up the game. "Egad, but that's most true! Why, I have seen him lay forth his charms with quite promiscuous generosity – like any seller of common fancies. Old crones around the parish pump . . . noseless sellers of nosegays in Piccadilly . . . 'tis any port in a storm with him."

"In short," said the first, kicking for goal, "the secret is that all are *one* to his desires . . ."

"And *any one* is all that he desires . . ."

"At *any one time*, withal!" They collapsed in picayune mirth – from which Lord Tottenham's usually prominent laugh was most noticeably absent.

Con then had no choice but to step forth and break his news. His lordship took it ill. He stood. He paced about. He raged. He boxed Con's ears. And the angrier he grew, the greater was the amusement among his companions.

"'Twas the restraint with the hammer, sir . . ." Con tried to explain but was drowned out in the baying of the pack.

"Now this accords with what I have lately heard," one of them asserted in between his guffaws. "Master Pitman has given out that Lord Tottenham's honour is but an old jade, pierced with the thrusts of many a scoundrel's sword."

"Oh, I heard it otherwise," another laughed. "That his honour is a hackney whore – riddled with the shot of every cur in town."

"The Whore, the Pistol, the Sword, and Honour – he has the four points of *your* compass, Totters. Give the devil his due."

Lord Tottenham, seated again, drummed the table angrily with his fingertips. "How do the newspapers survive?" he asked. "When every stray word to one's discredit is brought post-haste by some damned good-natured friend!"

At last the vein of their particular humour petered out and the more general demands of chivalry had to be faced, for none of them doubted but that Tottenham would now have to challenge Jonas Pitman.

"Keeps a brace of loaded pistols at his bedside, eh?" Tottenham asked Con.

The man nodded. "Took them up, cocked the hammer, drew aim, and fired – all while I walked four paces, my lord."

"And missed by a deliberate half-inch."

"Close as a whisker, sir."

"Dick Turpin à la mode," one of the others said. "He'll choose pistols, mark'ee."

Lord Tottenham came to a decision. He rose abruptly and turned to the friend who had spoken last. "You'll second me, Rolle?"

"Be honoured to."

"You may call upon him tomorrow with my challenge, then."

"Where are you going?"

"Home, for an early night of it." He turned to Con. "The pretty little Irish virgin, is she here yet?"

"I have daily hopes of her, sir."

"But she's not here yet?"

"She's upon the road, my lord."

Tottenham scowled. "And so will you be if you don't answer a straight question."

Con bowed his head and muttered, "Not here yet, sir."

His master gave a satisfied nod. "Just as well. I shall pass tomorrow at the pistol range. Bacchus and Venus may wait in the anteroom for a day or two yet – till honour's done."

As he followed his patron home, running in the wake of his carriage, Con marvelled at this strange commodity called *honour*, which fine gentlemen talk of so constantly, and claim so ardently, and dispute so hotly, and die for so readily – though none could touch it, nor see it, nor smell nor taste nor hear it. Tottenham *had* cheated young Pitman. All the world knew it. Yet because none had voiced the thought aloud, his lordship's honour remained intact – until Pitman chose to speak. And now, by maiming or killing the young fellow, Tottenham would mend his honour and go head-high among his peers once more. A strange commodity indeed!

Tottenham must have fought the impending duel a dozen times on that short carriage ride home, for his eyes shone in triumph as he stepped down, his humour quite restored.

"This will be a duel to remember, Murphy, my brave young bully," he said. "No mere 'first blood' will requite so vile a slur. We must shave the trigger to a hair. For this time it must be to the death."

# CHAPTER EIGHTEEN

OLD Q, THEY CALLED HIM – old William Douglas, the Fourth Duke of Queensberry, and the last, too, unless he bucked up and took a wife to get him a legitimate heir. But he was already in his sixty-sixth year, a poor decade in which to break the bachelor habit of a lifetime. Romantic ladies who had led sheltered lives (and there were still a few) sighed that alas it could never be, for in his youth the duke had lost his heart to Miss Frances Pelham (daughter, by the way, of that Honourable Henry Pelham, First Lord of the Treasury, whose death was greeted by George I with, "Now at last I shall have some peace!"). But his grace's "damn'd good-natured friends," as Tottenham would have called them, maintained that his dissolute tastes and habits, which the advancing years had done little to curb, made it unthinkable that he should be coupled with any lady of breeding.

The truth, by long habit, lay somewhere in between. Old Q had enjoyed many a delightful liaison with his female friends and had seen many a disastrous match among his male ones. Moreover, he had turned one of the addictions of his youth – gambling – into a good sound business; together with their graces of Cumberland and Grafton, and lords Clermont, Grosvenor and Barrymore, he had created the modern institutions of the English turf; and almost singlehanded he had gone on to perfect the science of that art. Why disturb so serene a paradise with something so disagreeable, expensive, and demanding as a wife?

On sunny days, and this was such a day, it was his pleasant custom to sit upon the balcony of his boudoir in Piccadilly, at its junction with Park Lane, by the very gate of London, and ogle the pretty girls as they came in fresh from the country. Truth to tell, many of those girls knew no more of the country than the fringe of Hyde Park; born and reared within the sound of Bow Bells, they would go out by the Oxford road, which lay a half-mile to the north of Piccadilly, then trip across the park and re-enter London beneath Old Q's balcony, where they would ogle him back; for, say what you will about Old Q, not even the harshest of his many critics would call him an ungenerous man.

If any young maid took his fancy, he would send his trusty head groom, Jack Radford, to ride after her and bring her back; for this purpose he had built a special staircase, giving direct access between balcony and street. A more conventional admittance of these females to his household, by way of the front door and up the stairs, might later give rise to bothersome claims that they knew his grace upon social terms; eager as he was for them to share the conversation of his *body* he was reluctant for that intimacy to extend to his *person*. It says much for the refinement of Good Society that it is capable of drawing such exquisite distinctions.

"Would you look at that oul' fellow up there!" Mary said to Punch as they paid the final toll of their long journey, at the Hyde Park Gate. "He'll surely know me the next time he sees me."

"He will if you smile back at him like that. You'll have to learn, woman – London people don't behave so."

"What should I do then?"

"Look haughty, look proud, look angry. Give yourself airs. Sneer at all and sundry, whatever chance you get. Then you'll pass for a true Cockney."

They had walked a bare ten paces beyond the house when, in turning back for one last look at the genial old fellow up there, she was almost bowled over by a mounted groom in full livery.

"His grace's compliments, miss," the man said. "An it please you, would you join him upon the balcony?"

"His grace?"

"The Duke of Queensberry."

"Oh really?" She glanced uncertainly at the man upon the balcony, who leered back at her in a most unambiguous way.

Still . . . he was a duke, the highest rank of the nobility. If she was safe with anyone, it must be with such a gentleman.

"On the balcony?" she asked.

Jack Radford nodded encouragingly.

What could be wrong with that – in full view of the world? She turned to Punch. "What d'you think?"

"You know full well what *I* think."

"But a duke! The highest – the very topmost, highest rank of the nobility. Besides, he might know lots of gentlemen with fine houses everywhere in England. He could give me letters of introduction, you see – to places where I could sing and tell my tales of Remarkable Occurrences."

"And you, in return for his gracious kindness, will . . . *what?*" Punch implored the heavens with his eyes, including the groom in the gesture. Jack Radford's long experience was just beginning to warn him that this encounter might not, after all, go quite as Old Q wished.

"I wonder now, does your master know the Duke of Bridgewater?" Mary asked.

The groom was already backing off and preparing a little speech of apology. But too late, for Mary came to a sudden decision and said, "Good man, I have no occasion to avoid this most amiable invitation. Pray present me to your master. I am Miss Mary Flinders, daughter of *The* Flinders of the Barony of Inchiquin in County Clare in the Kingdom of Ireland. I carry letters from the Lord Lieutenant and the Bishop." As she went she turned to Punch and called over his shoulder, "Go and graze Lucius in those fields. See if there's a duckpond where he may drink. I'll be as quick as maybe."

Radford raced back, hitched his mount, and bounded up the stair, eager to convey his forebodings to the duke. But Mary was too quick behind him. He put a warning in his voice and eyebrows as he announced her name.

Old Q did not rise, he merely wafted Mary toward the chair at his side; his twinkling eyes appraised her all this while.

She hesitated so long that the smile faded and he was forced at last into a token gesture of rising from his seat. A mere three inches, a mere half a second, but enough.

"Your grace is most kind." Mary seated herself and folded her hands in her lap.

The groom could not hide his astonishment but Mary did not notice it; she rattled on happily, "What a splendid day. And such a charming view. Oh, is that another park? It looks like any old field when you're down in the street." She indicated the large stretch of open land on the far side of Piccadilly.

"They call it the Green Park," he told her. "You have never been to London before, then, Miss Flinders?"

"Would you look at the sun – it's splitting the trees. I had never left the County of Clare until last month, sir."

"And what brings you here?"

"My feet." She laughed. "I was sent my fare to come to London by ship but I spent it unwisely and so walked here instead – and upon the way have earned my fare twice over."

"A wager, eh! Jove – are you one of these 'peds' – a thousand pounds on John o' Groats to Land's End in four weeks – that sort of caper, eh?" His eyes sparkled like two dark gems. He must once have been a most handsome man, she thought. Even now, with his patrician nose and his strong chin, he was striking. Those eyes seemed to see and understand so much.

Also he had a fine pair of calves still.

"I never thought of that," she said. "No, I brought an abandoned canal boat back to its owner in Oxford for a fee. An Oxford merchant. He gave me twelve pounds for the service. Not entirely ladylike, to be sure, but I'd been robbed of all my money and had no other honourable choice. Does your grace live here?"

Old Q nodded. Within half a minute of meeting Mary he had reached the same conclusion about her as his footman: one of those prickly, spirited little virgins who would be nothing but trouble after her seduction. But her accomplishment as a "ped" – the new craze of the age – was beginning to stir his other instincts. "I wonder now, Miss Flinders – how far would you say you could walk in a day?"

She lifted her skirts a delicate few inches, sufficient to reveal her boot leather. "Now that these fellows are broken in? Why, sir, I believe I might do . . . four English miles each hour . . . eight hours . . . say, thirty miles – in even country."

She was boasting, of course, knowing her words would never be tested.

He nodded appreciatively. "So! What shall we say – a thousand miles in a thousand hours? That should be well within your scope?"

She fanned herself in mock exhaustion. "I'd need good cause for such an undertaking, so I would."

"Forgive me! Forgive me!" He was suddenly all solicitude. "When I sniff a wager on the breeze, I'm quite blinded to all my duty. May I not offer you some refreshment, Miss Flinders? A glass of sherbet, perhaps?"

While his man fetched the cordial the duke went on, "Would, ah, three hundred pounds be cause enough?"

"To walk a thousand miles?"

He misinterpreted her astonishment. "Four hundred then. In a thousand hours, hark'ee. Now how many days is that?" He screwed up his eyes and scratched his brow, pretending not to know.

She answered him almost at once, "Forty-one days. Nearly forty-two."

He was agreeably surprised. "Quick as Cocker! I have misjudged you, Miss Flinders. You are a female of some parts."

She curbed her excitement at the thought of so much money so easily won. But then she began to reflect. Holyhead to London, the journey she had just done – and much of that on the canal rather than on foot – was a mere two hundred and sixty English miles by the parliamentary road. From her home to Dublin had been about a hundred and twenty Irish miles. In round figures, then, the total was not even half of a thousand statute miles – and most of that she had not actually walked. Was she not being just a little rash?

Still – four hundred pounds . . .

"I couldn't walk it at once, sir," she felt obliged to point out. "I mean I have affairs here in London."

"No, no, no – heaven forfend! The wagers would need time to arrange. A good wager is a work of art, you know." His smile suggested they were in some way fellow-artists. "I must avow, Miss Flinders, when I sent my man after you, this is the very last sort of *conversation* I expected we might enjoy together."

The cordial arrived. She sipped it gratefully and took one of the little cakes that accompanied it.

He went on. "And did you imagine that within half a minute of stepping inside this city, you'd receive such an invitation as this?"

"To walk a thousand miles, sir?"

"No! To sit upon a balcony with a duke and take refreshments. Have you ever met a duke before?"

134

"We have only the one in Ireland and I never met him."

"The loss lies on his side, then."

"Why did you send your man after me?" she asked.

Smilingly he stared her out. "You know full well, Miss Flinders."

It was a new gloss for her on the ideals of the nobility.

"The real question," he went on, "is, why did you accept? You're no fool. You must have realized what arrangements I might propose, and I know enough of the tribe of maidens to be quite sure you had no intention of agreeing to them. So what had *you* in mind, eh?"

To say "Curiosity" – which was the truth – would seem to slight him. She answered the first thing that came into her head: "I hoped your grace might give me a letter of introduction."

"Oh? And to whom, pray?"

"Ah . . . to the Duke of Bridgewater."

Old Q laughed. "You'd get no such offer from *him*, I may tell you!"

"Oh, but I have no personal interest there, sir."

"Then why seek an introduction?"

She sighed. What on earth had started this rigmarole? "It's . . . for a friend."

"Aha! Your lover!"

She laughed. "He's nigh-on *forty!*"

*And may the Dear One forgive me,* she thought.

"Hmph!" His lips pressed together until they vanished.

"He works upon the canals – hence the Bridgewater connection, you see."

Old Q eyed her shrewdly and came to a decision. "I say he's your lover – and I shall prove it."

She shrugged. "I don't see how that is possible."

He went on: "I withdraw my offer of three hundred pounds to walk . . ."

"Four," she reminded him.

"Five . . . six . . . what matter? I withdraw it. His grace of Bridgewater lives in Manchester, which is . . . what? A hundred and eighty-aught statute miles? Say, one hundred and ninety . . ."

"Say five days," she said, making a quick calculation – less than forty miles a day . . . it sounded difficult yet it should be possible.

"Four hundred pounds for that, instead. Are you game?"

She did her best to hide her excitement. "And meanwhile, sir, you are laying a fortune in bets on me, in a fair certainty I shall win!"

"We must each strive in this life to increase those things we most desire, little minx. For me it is the company of complaisant wenches and the acquisition of money by inducing others to mistake my certainties for risks. And you? For what do you strive? I suspect it is to further the interests of this almost senile gentleman of forty years. And when you reach Manchester I shall prove it."

His confidence angered her. "If I accept," she said curtly, "it will not be because there is any . . . I mean, not the slightest . . . there's no romantic attachment between me and Matt Sullivan. So if I agreed, it would merely be to show him that I, too, can . . . well, I wish to stir him to action."

"He's the sort of man who needs it, eh?"

"An impossible fellow. Won't speak up for himself. He'd dream out the crack of doom. We parted in such a fire – I lit the whole sky."

"Where is he now?"

"Still camped beside the canal for all I know, mooning his life down and eating off the countryside."

She went on to tell him of their encounter, of Matt's quiet brilliance and learned stupidity . . .

As he listened the old duke realized that Mary herself had no idea of the intensity of her own feelings toward this fellow. Her simplicity moved him in ways he had not felt for years; all desire to tease her evaporated. He rose and gallantly helped her to her feet. "There's my offer, Miss Flinders," he said. "It will require a little time to arrange the wagers. If you're game, return to me here in a day or so." He looked her up and down critically and added, "We shall better the odds if you could whiten your skin, soften your hands in goose-grease, wear exquisite and delicate clothing, and so on. I shall send word if you let my man know your directions."

When she had gone he sat there a long while, ignoring the usual jades below, following Mary with his eyes as she strode out into Green Park. Even after she had gone he sat there, seeing her still in his mind's eye.

# CHAPTER NINETEEN

HALFWAY ALONG PICCADILLY Punch suddenly remembered there was a toll at Tottenham Court, which they would have to pass if they held their intended course across the Duke of Portland's estate to Camden Town. Though Lucius would cost only a halfpenny, Punch resented any outlay upon the creature; so, with all the pride of a provincial newly skilled in London's byways, he led them instead up Bond Street, skirting Lord Grosvenor's lands, until they reached the bushes beyond the Oxford road. There, on the estates of Lord Portman and the Duke of Grafton, he soon lost his way among a maze of paths, fields, ponds, and a meandering brook that kept crossing and recrossing their generally northward route.

"The bloody nobility – you'd think they'd leave London alone!" he complained as he looked about him for landmarks.

And indeed the mixture of ancient common land, fruit gardens, and brand-new building was extraordinary. New streets and squares, which, at one end, looked as if they were in the heart of the city, suddenly gave out, at the other, into fields that Saxons must have tilled.

After skirting a few ponds and traversing the derelict grounds of an ancient manor house they drew near to a high-walled garden from which came the sound of an organ.

"Ah," Punch said with great assurance, "the Marybone Pleasure Garden. This was where Dick Turpin took many a gentleman's purse and many a lady's jewels – and not so long ago, either."

"God send it's safe now," she replied. "Haven't we had enough losses for the one journey."

"One time he sprang from behind the bushes in the pleasure garden and embraced a lady. 'There y'are now, ma'am,' says he, 'you may tell the world Dick Turpin stole naught but a kiss – and went off well contented.'"

The name "pleasure garden" painted in her mind long vistas of garlanded walks, grand pavilions, perfumed arcades, quaint bowers, shady arbours . . . As they strolled on across the hayfields to Camden Town her blood quickened at all the excitements this grand new city surely held in store.

Half an hour later their long journey was at an end. Camden "Town" is an ancient village, well off the beaten track. Travellers for the north country go out of London by the old Roman road through Islington, a mile or more to the east. Those bound for the Midlands take another Roman road, through Edgware and St. Albans, an equal distance to the west. Only local traffic for Hampstead and Gospel Oak comes out by Camden Town.

Light though it may be, it has long since obliterated the village green; only a few ancient oaks, marooned in the middle of the wide, dusty thoroughfare, now hint at the broad grassy mead that used to divide the highway. Other trees, equally ancient, tower over Mother Redcap's, or shade the village smithy, or almost smother the cowkeepers' cottages.

Punch turned to her. "This is your last chance, now. Will you let me have the five guineas to return to your man and I'll tell him you wouldn't come, or . . ."

"But what should I do then?"

"What would any lass of sense do, with seven guineas saved and a duke's offer of good money just to walk where her heart leads anyway?"

Stubbornly she shook her head.

But Con was not in Camden Town that day. At Mother Redcap's the alewife said he had a pair of rooms at Gundry's, a nearby lodging house of a superior character. Gundry himself proved a genial man; forewarned of Mary's expected arrival, he allowed her to leave her belongings in Con's parlour. He also gave stabling and fodder to Lucius. But as to Con's whereabouts, who could ever tell with that one? Perhaps, if she was to inquire at the Rats' Palace, she might hear more to the point. It lay in the rookery of St. Giles, known variously as Little Dublin or the Holy Land, down at the bottom of Tottenham Court Road.

He sat with them and chatted endlessly while they ate. In an offhand way she mentioned her encounter with Old Q; he told her all the London gossip about his grace – and all the other fashionable nobility – things that everyone knew but you'd never see them in the public prints except as cryptic references to *Brutus* or *L--d G--n* (who might be Lord Grafton or Gordon or Gideon or Galen for all you knew). She listened avidly and took it all in. He hadn't a single good word for Lord Tottenham.

An hour later, washed and refreshed, light of all their burdens and even lighter of heart, they set off for London again. Without Lucius they passed free through the toll at Tottenham Court itself, which was now part of the Adam and Eve public house. Opposite stood the Old King's Head, another tavern. Both had been ancient in the days of Good Queen Bess. Apart from a few chimney-sweeps' cottages, no other buildings were at hand.

"Wouldn't you think we were back home?" Mary said. "Two taverns and nothing but green fields all about!"

"At the bottom of this road you'd swear you were back in oul' Dublin," he promised.

Within a quarter of a mile, however, the metropolis began to proclaim itself again; they drew level with some new houses, a whole street of them, running parallel to the road they were on, a little way to the west. "Artists' quarters." Punch resumed his know-all voice. "They live out here for the fresh air and country views."

"Who? What are their names?"

"Sure how would I know?"

"What are those three grand houses beyond?"

"Well, I know one of them is Lord Mansfield's country house. He had to move out there when his town house in Bloomsbury Square was fired by the anti-catholic mobs ten years ago. That was a bad time."

"Were you here then?"

"I've heard tales of it. The soldiers stood about and did nothing until the king himself commanded it."

"Where will you go to hear mass in London, Punch?"

"Oh, things is aisy now," he said; but instinct forced him to look about them before he added, "There's one of the old safe places not half a mile from here, protected by the Spanish ambassador – near the new house that's building for the Duke of

Chandos. That man owns all of this country about us, out as far as . . . God, I don't know – Enfield? 'Tis said he wishes to ride into town from his country house over his own lands all the way. Ten miles or more – whatever it is." He gave an ironic snort. "The ambitions of some men – and here's me would be happy for one small fireproof cottage!"

"And last year's calendar still." She touched his arm in sympathy.

"Aye." He stared at the ground and almost intoned the words, "Were it not for you, girl, those weeks that went past had destroyed me entirely. You're the light that lightens the road, so you are."

She hugged him and wiped away the seed of a tear on his shoulder. "You're a grand, darlin' fella, Punch. When the cut of your grief is healed, you'll find a new happiness. I know it."

They walked on briefly in silence; then, in much brisker tones, he asked, "And you, lass? What'll you settle for?"

"I don't know. I wish I did. I never had such a restlessness inside me before. I never knew the world was like this. I'm the trout who's mad on the mayfly."

Halfway down the road from Tottenham Court the scene changed abruptly. This week, it so happened, was the climax of the Tottenham Fair; and there it was, in all its sudden, raucous glory. It occupied several fields to their left, opposite a quaint sort of modern chapel, which stared across the road in sober, dissenting disapproval.

A drummer was going about announcing that Messrs. Lee, Harper and Petit of Drury Lane were about to begin a performance of the *Ridolto alfresco* in the large tent with the red awning. A rival trumpeted the virtues of Mr. Yates, also of Drury Lane, and his Great Speeches from Shakespeare – in the tent with the golden awning (it was, in fact, a faded sort of dogsick ochre). There was a stuffed mermaid and a living two-headed calf. There was Oliver Cromwell's head, warts and all. Stalls sold sweetmeats, cordials, and recent gallows speeches from Newgate. Come evening there would be a banquet and an exhibition of red fire. A portable organ vied with several little bands, all playing indifferent tunes in different keys. Hucksters shouted, barkers barked, children screamed and laughed, dogs ran about, yapping with borrowed excitement. Mary discerned the unmistakable outlines of a fire balloon, almost concealed among a grove of trees. But when they reached it they found it surrounded by dangerous-looking scaffolds, with men swarming all over it, desperately trying to patch up the damage sustained in yesterday's abortive flight. It would not be ready until tomorrow, they said.

Just then a mournful party came by, pushing a putrefying corpse in a little shell coffin upon a handcart. The woman at the head of the procession begged Mary and Punch for a few pence, just to help bury the poor old fellow – her father. The chapel across the way had refused him the sacrament for want of five shillings.

Mary was about to part with a coin when one of the men jumped down from the scaffolding and ordered the mourners to be off or he'd send for the constable. The woman snarled and spat obscenities – but she made off fast enough when he repeated his threat.

"That's the oldest lay in the world hereabouts," he explained to Mary, to whom he had plainly taken a liking. "What they do, see, is they break into the shed behind the Middlesex Hospital, hard by here, and they steal the surgeons' corpses. Then they go out begging as you saw. And then at the end of the day, having collected ten or fifteen pounds, the more impudent among them go back to the hospital and sell the surgeon his own corpse a second time over!"

His foreman called him back. As he went he turned and said, "If you're still here this evening, we may dance a round or two."

"Everywhere you wander!" Punch said softly to her.

They returned to the fair grounds and were trying to decide between the rival attractions from Drury Lane when they got caught up in the arrival of two boisterous but good-humoured mobs, one from London, the other from the country. At the head of each was a great, strapping woman, a veritable queen bee.

The word soon spread; these were Elizabeth Wilkinson of Clerkenwell and Hannah Hyfield of Newgate Market, who, having had strong words at some recent meeting, had advertised in the papers their intention of settling their honour in a public bout of fisticuffs. Each woman was to clasp a sovereign in either hand. The decision (and the other woman's coin) was to go to the one who held her gold the longest.

"What a strange condition," Mary said.

"It stops them putting their ten commandments on each other," Punch explained, making witch's talons of his own fingernails.

Some way to the north of the fairground was a small hollow. In winter, no doubt, it was a pond; now it created a shallow amphitheatre, ideal for such a bout as this. There was no fixed ring, just a "vinegar" – a man who walked a circle with his hat held before his face and slashed impartially about him with a whip to keep the crowd at bay. Mary and Punch got a point of vantage on the southern side, on a pimple of ground surmounted by an old baytree, whose thick foliage conferred an additional benefit in that it prevented their being jostled or robbed from behind.

"This is a disgrace really," Mary said with glee.

They settled into their impromptu theatre box and she began to look about them – her first sight of a London motley. She had hardly begun to take it in when she saw a familiar figure, indeed, *two* familiar figures. She could hardly believe it.

"Jack!" she cried out. "Jack Horley! Crystal!"

Her voice was lost in the general hubbub, but on the fourth attempt Crystal turned her way and recognized her. She gave a shriek of delight, startling Jack out of his boots; when he saw the cause of it, he added a roar of his own. Then, though they had parted a mere eight hours ago, they were hugging each other and dancing a ringaroses as if they had not met in years.

"I thought you were in Twickenham," Mary said.

Jack shook his head and, lowering his voice, explained: "Not safe there. But we replenished the exchequer, thanks to my cousin's generosity. And now with his help we've found secure if none-too-healthy lodgings with a blackguard of an innkeeper in St. Giles's."

"But that's where *we* were going."

"Crystal and I were just about to eat when we heard of this brawl and it seemed too good to miss. Who's your money on?"

"Oh, I hadn't thought of betting."

"It'll be a close-fought thing by the looks of them."

The two amazons had stepped into the circle and were by now stripped down to their bodices. Their arms were as muscular as any porter's and they strode around like a pair of gamecocks.

Goodnatured boos and jeers greeted their shows of strength. A rash of small betting rings developed all around. "Five to two on Big Bess," shouted one gamester nearby. "Ten to three on Hardarm Hannah," cried another.

These were plainly partisan offers, not the result of cool calculation. "On such bets," Mary asked, "would you get your stake back as well as the odds?"

Punch saw the gleam in her eye and refused to answer; but Jack said of course she would. She slipped Punch two crowns and told him to place one with each. He gazed back at her with a moralist's despair.

"Don't you see?" she told him fiercely. "The one will pay twelve and sixpence, the other, seventeen and fourpence. And the most we can possibly lose is five shillings."

"You'll kiss all ten farewell if the man with the losing book decides to blackleg it over the fields."

"I have the answer," Jack said. "I'll lay a guinea on each. You, Punch, can watch Bess's champion and I'll keep my sights on t'other. We'll sup free and well tonight."

"Jack!" Crystal chided uneasily. "Two guineas?"

He deliberately misunderstood her. "I'd make it five but there's not the class in this motley."

Crystal shook her head at his departing back. "This gambling fever . . . will he ever learn sense?"

"I'm past worrying," Mary answered, hoping to reassure her. "Since I left home, I've learned how easy the money comes and goes. In five weeks I've been twice penniless and twice back in funds, and always from sources I'd never have dreamed of. D'you know – a duke offered me four hundred pounds this morning."

Crystal let out a peal of laughter that turned heads all about them.

"It's true," Mary protested. "You can ask Punch. It was the Duke of Queensberry."

"Aha!" Crystal's expression changed. "Then all the world knows what for!"

"Not for that!" Mary said scornfully. "It was to walk from Piccadilly London to Piccadilly Manchester in five days. For a wager, you see. He'd drum up bets among his acquaintance." Airily she added, "Of course, he tried for the other thing first."

Crystal drew breath and opened her mouth in such a way that Mary felt sure she was going to laugh and come out with some friendly but dismissive remark.

But no sound followed. Instead, Crystal's lips slowly closed again and she grew thoughtful. "How much for . . . er, 'the other thing'?" she asked offhandedly.

"Five hundred guineas," Mary answered in equally careless tones. God, wasn't it just like trying on new bonnets! Two days ago, she'd never have dared traduce a duke in such terms.

Crystal shook her head and gave out a vaguely moralistic sigh. "You refused, of course?"

"Of course."

A moment later Crystal asked, "What's he like close to?"

Mary, remembering something Gundry had told her, said, "Oh, his daily bath in milk and crushed almonds has kept his skin pretty fine."

"I don't believe it," Crystal laughed. "This is all your blarney."

"Well, you may go and ask the public milk sellers around May Fair. There's not a household within half a mile of that end of Piccadilly will buy milk off them – for fear of where it might have been first."

Crystal chuckled and hugged her arm. "And you not six hours in London – milk and almonds, indeed!"

"I'll bring you with me next time. I shall probably go back to tell his grace I accept the walking challenge."

Crystal seemed indifferent to the suggestion.

"Don't tell Punch," Mary added quickly. "He was just bursting with advice. I don't like people to tell me what's wise and what's not."

"*Nor* I," Crystal agreed eagerly. "If I do accompany you – if I find time, that is – we won't tell Jack, either, eh? It'll be just *entre nous.*"

A great huzza went up; the fight was about to begin. A gentleman in an old-fashioned three-corner hat, more respectable than the one Old Q had been wearing, had been pressed to serve as referee. He made both women walk one final circuit of the ring, hands open, to show a guinea gummed by sweat into each spreadeagled palm. Then with no more ado he shouted, "Box on!"

The cheering began: "Go at her, Bess!" and "Kill, Hannah, kill!" Punters and partisans filled the air with their cries.

"Bring out the burgundy! We want blood!"

A wag cried, "Milk'll do me!"

The vinegar lashed out with all his might. "Hats off, hats off!" was everywhere. Wigs were knocked aside. It was: "Show us a tooth!" and "Show us a dozen!"

The two huge women flailed at each other with little science and even less thought for their stamina, until at last they were too winded to go on. Both had drawn blood but their cheeks were so red with exertion it hardly showed.

Then a lucky punch – or an accidental one, anyway – from Bess caught Hannah's front teeth and knocked the upper pair clean out. Bess hopped round the ring, clutching her skinned knuckles and whimpering; it was during this manoeuvre that she dropped one of her guineas. Hannah, bent double and trying to cough up one of her incisors, was surprised to be tapped on the shoulder and be told that she had won the point.

From the next "Box on!" the fight was in deadly earnest. Mary, who had joined the crowd in carnival spirit, was now too sickened to watch further. She turned from the spectacle and sought the easiest way out. Crystal was a mere two paces behind. But the rest of the crowd thronged forward, filling their wake as fast as the two women were let through. "Oh my, don't this just beat Walsingham's hanging!" one eager little Cockney cried.

"What was Walsingham's hanging?" Mary asked when they had at last burst free.

"Oh did you not hear about that?" Crystal told her. "It was pitiable. I'll wager most of this mob was there, too." And she went on to tell the tale of it.

Walsingham was a poor out-of-work clerk who had tried to commit suicide by slitting his own throat, but misguided friends saved him and stitched him up. Then someone peached and he was tried before the city aldermen, who sentenced him to hang for his crime. But when he was hoisted upon the gallows the stitches in his throat parted and he was able to breathe through his wound. The hangman had to scrape up a handful of clay and block his opened windpipe with it before he would die. "Yet that was all he'd desired in the first place," Crystal concluded.

Mary shivered at the tale. " 'Tis death and indifference all about us. And how blithe we are that move among it!"

# CHAPTER TWENTY

THE ST. GILES'S ROOKERY is the world on its head. Here unsafe is safe, fair becomes foul, vice assumes virtue. Here freedom itself is a kind of arrest, for those who would enjoy its liberties must confine themselves to its maze of vile lanes and narrow courts, where the Bow Street Runners venture in vain.

In vain but not in peril. Indeed, there will be a smile on every corner and cheery cries of "Hello, Bill!" and "Hey there, Charlie Keep-peace!" – cries that will carry to the chimneypots. And suddenly all those myriad little courtyards, which are accessible only through someone's private cellar, will throng with the masters and apprentices of crime – the whole canting crew, from rufflers to kinching morts, jarkmen to delles. And devil a thief will the thieftakers take.

In all that sanctuary of sin there is no finer haven than the Rats' Palace in Ivy Street, an ill-favoured impasse that leads felons to fortune and all to damnation. Looking at the city map you might suppose you could go directly into Ivy Street at its open end; but the map cannot show Stunning Joe, the Gay Bulldog, who lets pass no bum bailiff, no writ server – nor plucked pigeons bent on revenge.

It was Stunning Joe who sprang out and barred the way of the four revellers, flush with their winnings on the bareknuckle ladies. But when he heard that two of them were guests of Canting Corley, landlord of the Rats' Palace, and that Mary was the doxy of Lump Hammer Murphy, and Steam Punch her pal, he waved them on like royalties.

"My *pal*," Mary said with a laugh, taking Punch's arm. "What might that mean?"

"Whatever you think yourself. In my own view, a pal is one who'd tell Con Murphy that his 'doxy' took one look at this stinking village of the damned and suddenly remembered an urgent engagement at the far end of Piccadilly."

"Ah, go on with you!" She tossed her head. "We're safe enough together. The place looks dead anyway."

"Ivy Street is for the aristocracy, the league of canting gentlemen. But just let you go round the corner there, where it's fifty beds to a house and fourpence a night for a half-bed or threepence for a straw crib . . . you'd see visions to put the Earl of Hell in a fright."

Crystal overheard this and clutched Jack's arm.

"That's why we're safe here," he told her.

"While the money lasts," she answered glumly.

"The hue and cry will die down soon and then we can make our way to Dover. Cheer up! We were poor at breakfast, rich at dinner, and now at supper we're richer still."

"Something always turns up." Mary tipped in her crumb of comfort.

Jack caught the light of despair in Punch's eye. "What ails?" he asked.

"You and this one." He nodded toward Mary. "I never met such a brace of hopefuls. You'd have drained all Ireland in the Deluge."

"I wish someone'd drain you of your thin blood," Mary told him, "and put back a stouter heart."

Canting Corley himself let them into his palace. His outward demeanour was obsequious but it would not have deceived a babe. To cross his threshold was to step back down the centuries to an age of barbarism. The benches and tables were set upon rough-hewn treetrunks buried in the ground; the wood was black from generations of smoke and snuff and spilled liquor. The same colour also masked the one beam and the boards of the low ceiling. Two of the windows still had panes of horn, which Mary had read of but never seen; the rest were all of cheap glass bosses. Every light was narrow and short; what little illumination fell upon them in the pinched alleyway had then to struggle through the grime of years. A candle in each opening would have doubled the light and yet still leave dark the chamber. It was several minutes before any of them even noticed the casks of ale and porter set on trestles all down one wall.

"What'll it be?" asked their host. "I have some fine Geneva gin, new in this day, guaranteed to lay you out for twopence. Straws free. Or I'm just about to broach a firkin of Burrell's Imperial Stingo, which many a Jack Tar has sworn to me will bring him back to London dock from halfway round the world."

". . . to lie in St. Giles's gutters and be relieved of every stitch and penny!" Jack added. "No, master, we'll eat before we sup. What's your best in that line now?"

The answer came without hesitation: "An alderman in chains, your honours. That's a right old St. Giles's feast now. The lord mayor hisself wouldn't dine on better, which I know for a fact, having a nephew as works in the Mansion House kitchens."

They hesitated, not knowing what "an alderman in chains" might be. He misunderstood and added. "A shilling a nob, seeing as I've already taken the greatest liking to your honours. Or eighteen pence and you may sup yourselves blind. Can't say fairer now, can I?"

They all looked at Jack. "Try anything once," he said.

They played cribbage and supped small beer until the meal was ready. The tavern filled up with rogues of every kind. The men among them ran appreciative eyes over the two women, noted Punch's muscle and Jack's sword, and let discretion rule. Their females were a great surprise, not to say disappointment, to Mary, who, being brought up on the imagery of moralistic prints, knew that women of the criminal fraternity were boozy, blowsy doxies in verminous rags, creatures with eyepatches and pox-mined features and brown-stumped or black-gapped teeth. Yet here were young delles and grand dames who, but for the want of some small elegance in their clothing or coiffeur, could have passed in any society ballroom.

The alderman in chains proved to be a great turkey wrapped about with strings of sausages and roasted to a fine succulence. The four of them took their places around one end of the table and tucked in heartily.

"I've not had such a feast in years." Mary spoke to no one in particular but her remark was taken up by a well-turned-out and sweetly perfumed young female near by. "You're where the fishing's always easy, darlin'," she said.

Over the next five minutes, in a confession that would have been frank if it had been in plain English rather than some obscure canting lingo, she made it clear that every man and woman there, saving the four newcomers, lived by crime. She herself "stripped lush kiddeys out on a spree."

"Didn't you understand about this place?" Jack asked Mary.

"One or two, I thought. But *everyone!*"

A man sitting opposite, who had so far kept his peace – and a menacing, watchful sort of peace it was, too – now spoke. "In every age," he said, "there are fools with money and ingenious men and women without. The test of a civilized commonwealth is this: How swiftly may said wealth pass from the fools to the wise? For gold left in the hands of fools is the greatest danger to the common good." He waved his hand toward the company in general and concluded, "Why, I venture to swear that these fine people have taught the wayward sons of the rich more good sense and more useful knowledge than all the Latin masters who ever lived and wrote. They have cleansed the commonwealth of more dangers than all the militia, the constabulary, and the watch in combination."

"You give crime its credentials, sir," Jack said. "May we know your name?" He introduced himself and the other three.

At the name Horley the man's eyebrows rose. "Here I am called Crackmans," he said. "No lord, no mister, no handle. Plain Crackmans, the hedge. You, if I mistake me not, are of that ancient family lately robbed of all you owned by a lord of recent creation – not a year's journey from Gloucester? Then you know full well what I mean. My lord Ferrers is that species of thief who may attend the king's levée. He is the legitimate robber while you, who took no more than your due, must skulk here and consort with us – the mere bobtail of so eminent a villain."

Jack's face darkened and his hand edged toward his sword. "Do you imply, sir, that my father, God rest him, was the fool with the wealth?"

"Was he the wise man then? But more to the point, will you confirm that imputed lineage by playing the undoubted fool now? If so, then you are the most foolish fool in this" – he looked contemptuously around – "this ship of fools."

There was anger among those who overheard the sneer, but Crackmans stared them down. "Most of them will hang in chains before their necks are very much older."

Jack, impressed by the man's command, cooled his anger and asked, "Are you implying, sir, that I might have legal remedies?"

"I imply naught, but I assert this: There are legal ways to turn wise men into fools. And if a wise fool has wealth – however acquired – then the law has its cranes of parchment, its grapples of ink, its stevedores in wigs, and its dockside bummarees in ermine – all of whom will eagerly ferry it into bond for you. The lawyers will hang all the world in chains ere they touch one of their own!"

Curiously, although he spoke the words in answer to Jack's inquiry, it was to Crystal that he addressed them.

All evening the patrons of the house came and went – went empty and came back with sacks full of fine clothing, kerchiefs, watches by the score, love lockets, jewelry, and purses newly emptied of their gold. These were pored over by Canting Corley, who offered prices between a fourth and a third part of their worth, which bargains were entered in a book kept by Corley but signed by both parties. The price agreed, the fruits of the crime were dropped through a trapdoor into the cellar.

Everyone brought their booty to the landlord and the bargains all went down in the same little book. Mary noted that if the prices grew keen, Corley would glance out the corner of his eye at Crackmans, whose merest nod or shake would determine his answer.

Crackmans, seeing that she had noticed the exchange, said, "I do it for mere charity, Miss Flinders. Can you imagine the likes of these poor creatures taking a watch for sale to Ludgate? They'd be ketched and duffed before they could say it in guineas."

"Charity!" Mary scoffed. The man made her flesh to crawl. Honest rogues she could tolerate but not this "gentleman's" sophistries.

"It's not all profit, my dear. Even commissioners of gaol delivery need the oil of angels."

"You're very candid with us, sir," Jack said angrily. He was annoyed at the way the fellow kept ogling Crystal.

"Perhaps I foresee a grand future for you all. Or" – he lowered his voice and spoke as if in jest – "perhaps I see none at all."

Some fiddlers came in and a woman with a tambourine. Her

suggestive dance was on the point of becoming lewd when Crackmans, with a meaningful nod toward the four strangers, threw her a threepenny piece; the others, as at a signal, tossed their coppers, too, grumbling as they did so. But soon their disappointments were forgotten as they clasped hands and waists and began to caper and whirl about the floor to the insistence of the music.

Mary forced a reluctant Punch to squire her but it was a country dance and so she soon got a turn with everyone, young and old, drunk or sober, sweet of breath or stinking. The rounds brought her back to Punch.

"Still time," he said. "Look about you – this is Con Murphy's world. You have no business here. Will I tell him you went to see the duke?"

She shook her head. " 'Twas I took his money, so I'll hand it back."

After the next change she faced Jack for a stately galliarde, or what would have been stately but for the general tipsiness of the company. "I have no great liking for this Crackmans," he said.

"In all this company you're not alone. Yet I think he's no man to cross."

"Why does he keep staring at Crystal? Look at them, heads-together now – what's he telling her?"

"Doubt anything but her loyalty, Jack. That girl'd go through Hell and Connaught for you."

Some time after midnight, when the celebration was at its height and the gangs coming "home" with their loot as fast as the trapdoor could open and close, in walked Con Murphy.

It could have been the king himself, for though he was but a worm to Lord Tottenham, here he was royalty. Even Crackmans rose, somewhat nonchalantly, and offered him a seat. But Con just stood there, letting his eye rove around the company.

Mary had the image of a fit young yard bull brought suddenly from a dark stall. She stifled an impulse to cry out, knowing he was seeking her, excited at the stir his entry had caused. He had not changed a bit, or where he had, it was for the better. The linen shirt was now of silk, open at the chest. The canvas trews were now tight pantaloons that modelled every curve and sinew. His red hair was more luxuriant still. His face, but for that scar, unmarked, youthful, vigorous . . . handsome.

She had forgotten just how handsome he was; now her heart turned over to see it. Unable to check herself she took one step toward him.

He stayed his ground but held wide his arms, forcing her to close all the distance that separated them. While she kissed his neck and cheek and intoxicated herself in the strong, dangerous smell of him, he grinned over her shoulder at the company, as a circus rider might say, "Look – no hands!"

Unseen in a far, dark corner, Punch watched and despaired.

## CHAPTER TWENTY-ONE

THEY DANCED TILL FIVE. Con was lionized by all. But when the glory of his first entry had waned, Mary began to sense that his popularity was no greater than his last fight. He was the latest "go." One defeat and the glister would tarnish; two, and the go would be gone.

*Indeed and why not?* she thought. *What else had the fellow to offer?* Already she was vexed with herself for being so attracted to him earlier.

At last the fiddles wilted, the night's loot was stowed, the bargain book closed, Crackmans departed. Punch had slipped away, unnoticed by anyone. Jack and Crystal retired above, her eyes full of smoke and slumber, his with argument.

"To Gundry's lodging house?" Mary asked Con as they stepped from air that was putrid into that which was merely foul. She was relieved to hear him say, "Not I. His lordship has a young puppy to put out of its misery this morning, and I'm to help him."

"Young puppy?"

"Aye, at dawn. In the Field of the Forty Footsteps."

Strange were the ways of this London aristocracy.

In Monmouth Street they saw a merry gang of bucks. The object of their laughter was a young gentleman, stripped to his shirt – fleeced, no doubt, in Drury Lane.

"What are they doing to him?" she asked.

"They call it the Squire of Alsatia's prick dance."

As they drew closer she saw why. The game was to form a circle around the fellow and then the buck behind him would give him a little prick with his sword. When he spun round, the one now behind, who had earlier been in front, did the same . . . and so it went on, with whatever buck happened to be behind him supplying the "music" for the dance.

"'Tis the band that always plays a little sharp," Con said.

By the light of a link torch she saw the bloodspots all over the fellow's shirt; with sudden poignance it recalled Matt Sullivan for her. "I don't like that," she said. "Hurry up – where are we going?"

"I told you. To his lordship's house in Swallow Street."

"How long will they torment that poor fellow?"

"Till he has the sense to drop."

"He's a gentleman and so are the others. I don't understand this London."

"'Tis the richest, randiest, rantingest city in all the world," he answered contentedly. "And has served me well."

For a man who was supposed to be welcoming his future bride, Con was being decidedly offhand. "Are you not pleased to see me, sweet?" she asked to test him.

"Of course I am. Didn't I send you the money?"

"Ah!" she laughed happily. "I can give that back, for I earned twice as much upon the way."

"The devil!" He turned and gripped her arm fiercely. "Have you sold your . . . what have you done?"

"Let go! You're hurting me." She writhed but could not get out of his grasp. "Con!" She wished she could see his face.

"Answer me! What have you done upon the way?"

"I told you. Will you let go before I roar."

He relaxed his grip until it no longer hurt. "How did you earn it?"

"I bought a dress in a fine shop in Dublin, which was a fault for I had only the passage money left. So I played my harp and sang some of the old songs on the voyage and earned our bed and board that night, and more. So then I did the same each night and recruited my fortune again. But wasn't it all fecked off me by a little Welsh hoor in Gloucester. So then Steam Punch and I got a help on the way from a canal man, but he was taken up by the constabulary, and so I brought the boat on to Oxford myself and the merchant paid me the draft of it, which was twelve pounds, and that's what I have and will gladly give you back your five."

He relaxed and laughed. "Ah, Mary, Mary! You're the grandest girl and I'm the fool for doubting you. Crackmans is right – you're worth a thousand of any other doxy in that room."

Her anger went. "Is that what he said?"

"It is so."

"Con?"

"What?"

She sighed. "Nothing." Why *had* he brought her here to London? "Nothing," she repeated on a dying fall.

They walked on in silence. "Nothing" described it perfectly. Not love. Not hate. Just . . . emptiness. Nothing.

He said, "I'm fighting Sterling Jim Bacon next week. We could be wed after that."

He spoke as if he were reading the words from a book, as if he barely understood their meaning. She gave his arm a perfunctory squeeze, which he took as answer enough.

In the servants' hall at Lord Tottenham's house they had porridge and whey, kidneys, bacon, chops and eggs, saffron buns and honey.

"You live like a lord himself," Mary said proudly.

"Aye, and you shall live like a lady!" He laughed, as if he had just made a joke.

A carriage drew up outside. Con leaped to his feet. "That's me engaged."

"And what am I to do?"

"Come out now and stand casual by me. And if his lordship speaks to you – be pleasant with him."

She followed him outside. "What d'you mean?" she asked. "Of course I'll be pleasant with him."

"You know full well what I mean. 'Twill do us no harm if you're *good* to him."

He stood upon the foot pavement, close to the bottom of the

steps that led up to the grand front entrance, and began pointing out her directions back to Gundry's. His manner was awkward and he kept turning her to face the steps, in which position she could not follow the directions he was also trying to give her. And when he had finished, he began all over again. He kept looking up toward the front door. At last it opened, much to his relief, though there was terror in his voice as he whispered, "Here's his lordship now. Remember – be good to him."

But she barely heard him for by the dawn light she saw the most handsome young man she had ever set eyes on – tall, pale, slim, dark-eyed, magnificent – a lord to his gloved fingertips, if ever one walked the earth. He paused at the top step. "Ho! What's this?" he asked. "The prime article! Here at last, eh?"

"Indeed, my lord." Con was grinning like a puppydog. "And just in time."

"You may well say so!" His master laughed as he walked down the steps. "Has she a name?"

Mary curtseyed, "Mary Flinders, an it please you, sir. Daughter of *The* . . ."

"*An* it please me? And it do! Bang up! Where is she bound?" Although he spoke of her as a third person, he continued to gaze directly into her face. His dark, piercing eyes threw Mary in a turmoil. A remote voice, hardly her own, said, "To Camden Town, sir."

He smiled and walked to his carriage. His movements were lithe, graceful – and in some way predatory; a hunting cat had just such a walk. He knew precisely what effect he had upon her. "Then we shall lighten your way by half, my dear." With mock gallantry he offered to hand her up inside.

"This is Lord Rolle." Tottenham, climbing in behind her, indicated a shadowy figure already seated. " 'Morning, Rolle. Here's Miss Flinders at long last."

"Your servant," the other muttered.

They set off at a trot; Con jogged alongside.

"I'm the daughter of The Flinders of the Barony of Inchiquin in County Clare," Mary added.

Tottenham frowned. As her eyes grew accustomed to the gloom she saw that a degree of uncertainty had crept into his stare. "But I was led to believe you lived on some . . ." He broke off and glowered angrily at Con, still trotting faithfully beside the carriage. Then, turning to her again, he asked, "And how does your father, Miss Flinders?"

"Fair, my lord, I thank you. Between legacies, you know."

Lord Rolle began to laugh. Tottenham stared furiously at him – which only served to increase the man's mirth.

The suspicions that Mary had been struggling to suppress for several hours could no longer be held in check. "Lord Tottenham," she snapped coldly, "You will oblige me by stopping this coach. I shall alight here."

Tottenham's discomfiture deepened. He began to flounder among the conventional sentiments. "Miss Flinders . . . ah . . . I most humbly crave your pardon." There was, needless to say, neither humility nor craving in his voice; in a sharper tone he added, "It is becoming quite clear that the Murphy creature has misled me – grossly misled me – both as to your character and your family."

"I can't think how, sir, for he knows so little of either."

His lordship, recovering something of his poise, eyed her speculatively. "And yet you have come here to marry him – or so I understand?"

She could see he did not believe it; he was merely testing her response to the notion. "There was never the slightest question of that, my lord. He sent me five guineas, all . . ."

"Seven, surely?"

"Five, on my honour, and all unasked – of which I made grateful use and will now repay. And the quicker the better, I'm thinking, for, indeed, I begin to misthink his true purpose in fetching me here to London."

She stared directly into those sublime eyes, forcing him to look away. In a voice barely audible above the rumble of the wheels he murmured, "I promise you, I'll have the flesh off his ribs when he's won the match." He faced her suddenly and said, "Stay?"

She felt her will beginning to dissolve.

"Please?" he added.

"I don't understand what you may mean by 'stay,' sir."

He smiled. "I have some small business to attend to here in the fields. Most tiresome, but there it is. When I have done, I shall be most deeply obliged if you would return and breakfast with me."

"I have already done that, Lord Tottenham. Beneath your roof, anyway."

"I mean where I may see you – and converse with you. It was cruel of you to hide yourself away."

She knew she was going to agree but she didn't want him to know.

"Perhaps your day is already crammed with engagements?" he suggested.

"I shan't want to eat again."

"Then I offer you coffee and counsel. Never breathed a maid who needed it more."

She watched him go; that same feline grace, and the same overpowering menace. She did not like him. She could see that everything Gundry had said of him was probably true. Yet there was something about him that stirred her out of all proportion. It was an immediate, visceral feeling, outside her control. If he were near, that side of her flesh seemed to tingle with some preternatural awareness of him – like warmth yet not warm. Nevertheless, as he went off on his mysterious business, she allowed him no assurance he would find her there on his return.

Then, after a few minutes in the carriage alone, she thought she might as well watch them put this puppy out of its misery – some new sport, perhaps? She descended from the carriage and immediately recognized the place as the field beyond where the balloon had been tethered yesterday, beside the common where the Tottenham Fair was held. And indeed among the trees she caught glimpses of the tents and banners, limp in the morning dew.

"Where's this Field of the Forty Footsteps?" she asked the groom.

He sook his head and sucked a missing tooth. "No place for a female, miss."

"Why not?"

"Two brothers fought there, long ago. Dreadful affair. Shocking. Hacked each other to shreds. They sent for stretchers but had to gather them up in sacks." He drew a deep breath and added portentously, "And wheresoever their feet dinted the turf, the mark is there still. They won't never go away. The Duke of Bedford had it all ploughed over, but when the grass grew back – why there was the Forty Footsteps, plain as a pox and twice so deep."

"But why has his lordship come to such a place?"

The man frowned. "Don't you know?"

She shook her head.

"To fight a duel, of course."

He said more but Mary did not hear. She was already running as fast as her feet could carry her in the direction she had seen Rolle and Tottenham take.

"Miss!" he called after, angry at being unable to leave the horses.

"He could be killed!" she shouted back.

At the edge of a clearing Con sprang from among the bushes and barred her path. "You?" he said in surprise.

"You never told me it was a duel." She tried desperately to see over his shoulder.

"I did. Anyway what's it to you?"

"Is it over?"

"Pretty near."

She evaded him then and ran on toward the field of honour, nearly twisting an ankle in several of the hollows for which the dismal place was named; the battling brothers must have been two giants. She arrived to find Tottenham standing, swaying slightly, bleeding from his left arm and side, towering over a prostrate and apparently lifeless opponent – a fair young man bleeding profusely from his thigh. Two crimsoned rapiers lay near by.

But she had eyes only for Tottenham. "Are you hurt? Is it bad?"

Still staring down at his victim he held his arm out for her inspection. "He should have chosen pistols," he said evenly.

The blood was pulsing out of his arm.

"That must be stemmed," she said, and without hesitating she raised her skirt and peeled off a stocking. She straightened; their eyes met; for a second or two he was speechless. Then he took the stocking from her and pressed it to his cheek. "A moment ago it was so shapely," he murmured.

"A gentleman would not have noticed."

"The gentleman is bleeding to death."

She snatched the stocking from him and bound his arm tightly, using his cane as a tourniquet. The pulsing of the blood was stilled. "Have you sent for the surgeon?" she asked.

The young man's valet and his second came running up with a

litter. "There's a surgeon in Red Lion Square," Tottenham told her. "They'll bear him there."

"I mean you! You should see a surgeon."

"I hope he dies," he murmured as they bore the body away.

"That's disgraceful!"

"He swindled me out of a great deal of money. That's the disgrace."

"To stand so close to your Maker with such harsh judgment on your lips."

Tottenham turned to her again. "You truly mean that!"

"Indeed, I do."

He seemed chastened, or perhaps it was his weakness, now that the stir of battle was past. "Bear me home," he said. "I haven't forgotten my promise of breakfast."

Con lifted him in his arms, as easily as a feather bolster.

"Damn breakfast," Rolle said, pushing himself between Mary and Tottenham. "We've got to get you all stitched up and on the Dover road within the hour. Pitman's dead or I'm a Dutchman. You must lie low for a month or two."

But Tottenham laughed. "I'll see Queensberry. He'll arrange something. God's wounds, what are patrons for if they can't arrange a little protection – eh, Murphy, me old Lump Hammer!"

He maintained his cheer all the way home but as Con carried him up the steps the loss of blood finally told upon him and he passed out. When his door opened, he recovered sufficiently to turn and beckon Mary. He gripped her wrist with surprising strength and, though his eyes were shut and he appeared unconscious, he held her all the way to his bedchamber. Moments later the surgeon was there. He put setons in the wound, to prevent the scar from healing hard over any lingering infection, and said with bland confidence, "He'll live." As they were all about to withdraw, Tottenham opened his eyes and croaked, "Miss Flinders?"

Mary returned to the bedside.

"You won't go?"

"I shan't leave London."

"I mean this room. Don't leave this room."

"If you wish it, sir."

He sighed contentedly. "Then I will sleep."

She called Con back to drag a divan to the bedside. "He has a

159

great liking for you," Con said happily. "It will do us no harm when we're wed. Be good to him now."

She shuddered as she shut the door on him. In less than twelve hours she had fallen slightly in and entirely out of love with Con. What had she ever seen in him?

For a while she sat watching Lord Tottenham. His features in sleep lost all their menace. He became approachable, almost a baby.

It was safe to sleep; she had not slept since coming to London. She closed her eyes. The world flew around her but it was not the everyday world of things you could touch and lean on and smell. Feelings were in there, too – half-thoughts, strange wishes, unfamiliar desires – and they merged and flowed into one another like strands of foam upon a heaving wave. There were people, too, who shared that same fleeting presence, merging into one another. It was a cycle that gave her no rest: People became things became desires became people again. In the end they all became Lord Tottenham; he was like pepper in her veins.

She must have slept long, however fitfully, for one moment the room was bright with the morning sun and the next they were calling for tapers and she was bursting. Her nose led her to the privy, which was a curtained alcove beneath the main stair. When she returned, Lord Tottenham was stirring. They brought him beef broth and blood pudding, which he asked Mary to feed him. He joked with her between spoonfuls.

"You could well do this yourself," she told him when she saw how easily he moved and heard the firmness in his voice.

"And deprive you of the pleasure? If you were a cat, you'd be purring now."

"Hah! You have that many airs, my lord, you'll vanish on the first good wind."

He stared at her with a kind of sad, accusing gaze until he forced her to an unwilling smile. "That's better," he said. "A little peep of honesty – like the breaking of the sun from behind a cloud. What d'ye think of honesty, Miss Flinders? May I help you to become the first female since creation who ever tried it?"

The unwilling smile became an even less willing laugh as she tipped the last spoon of broth between his lips. They were so perfectly chiselled, those lips, she wanted more than anything to lean down and kiss them.

"Where shall we start? With the Murphy? Can you be honest with me about him?"

She shook her head. "The thought of him makes me squirm. I shall give him back his five pounds and be free of him."

Tottenham chuckled. "In that case, you're free of him now. The money was never his."

Her eyes narrowed. "You? Did you give it him?"

"It's not my day for honesty – but yours. Tell me – d'you like me?"

She pulled a dubious face. "Why did you kill that poor young fellow?"

"Oh? Is he dead for sure?"

"Half-kill him, then. I don't know."

He relaxed. "That's *dis*honest. You know well that whatever I might answer, it would have not the slightest effect on your feelings about me."

She remained silent.

He took a bite of the blood pudding, which was not to his taste though he persevered. "Am I as bad as the world has painted me?"

"Sure what do I know?"

"Would you marry me?"

"God no!" she blurted out.

"Nor I you!" He laughed until the pain in his arm tweaked him back to sobriety. "Good – we now have a vast estate of common ground between us: We would not be yoked together! What does that leave, eh? If not the parson's mousetrap – what's left to share?"

"You should rest your arm."

"Your honesty would be a better medicine, Miss Flinders."

She shrugged awkwardly. If only he would make definite suggestions, she could turn them down. But he was too clever for that.

He said, "You could stand up, turn about, walk to that doorway, pass through it, and never see me again. Will you do that?"

"I might. And then again I mightn't. It all depends."

"Upon what?"

"Upon whether you can hold your whisht and stop bleating such moonshine."

He wiped the last crumb of the pudding into his kerchief.

He swallowed a mouthful of claret, which wet his lips and left them sparkling. Then he said, "You still haven't answered my question, Miss Flinders."

"Why should you care to hear my opinion, my lord? If it accords with your purpose, you'll use it, or *ab*use it. If not, you'll mock it with clever sentiments."

He laughed uncomfortably. "What a shrewd young observer you are. I'll flay that cur Murphy. He'd dine with Venus and come home praising naught but her ale. Tell me about yourself, your people. Truly, I wish to hear it."

It was impossible, of course, here in this elegant London house with its silk-hung walls, to convey the long meagreness of life along the austere, rock-domed fringes of County Clare, especially to one who had probably never handled a pitchfork nor seen a sod of turf in all his gilded days. But then Mary was never one to shun a task on the trifling grounds that it was impossible; at the end, when she had told him all she could think of, the admiration in his eye held no taint of condescension.

"And you, my lord," she prompted. "Tell me something of yourself?"

"Breeding!" he marvelled, still lost in admiration of her. "Breeding will out, no matter what. You have lived the life of the meanest peasant, Miss Flinders, and yet your breeding is untarnished. It is all true! I sensed it at once – and so did Rolle." He closed his eyes and sank back contented.

"It's not fair if you tell me nothing of yourself," she complained.

"I, too, should be like you," he murmured. "If, through some misfortune, I lost all my inheritance, I should go to our estate in Virginia and farm it . . . with a mere handful of slaves and hardly any servants. I should be on the land from dawn to dusk. Just like you. Breeding will out!"

His voice sank from a murmur to a whisper. Thinking him more than three-fourths asleep already, she reached forward and straightened his covers. "I'd as liefer talk to my own back teeth," she commented aloud.

His hand shot out and trapped her by the wrist. He was nowhere near asleep. "Kiss me once and I'll leave you in peace," he begged.

"You may kiss the back of your . . . neck," she replied.

His grip relaxed until it was a mere caress, sending a thrill through every part of her. She bent over him then. He smiled but did not move. Her lips sought his. The beat of her heart shook the whole bed. At last they touched. His good arm encircled her and they seemed to melt into one being.

Even then she knew she did not love him. This was not love but some wild, wayward disorder of her passions. With this man she knew she would find not one moment's happiness. He was pain, betrayal, a mockery of all that was tender and true. But all her knowledge, sure as it was, lay powerless before this new addiction of her senses.

# CHAPTER TWENTY-TWO

DESPERATE TAILORS and harnessmakers were kept waiting for days in the Duke of Queensberry's outer rooms; so were the sellers of fans, silk stockings, and other trinkets with which his grace liked to thank the ladies who flitted through his life (and which he thus purchased by the gross). But Mary and Lord Tottenham were granted immediate entrée.

She was feeling especially grand tonight, for, though she still lodged at Gundry's and held no place in Tottenham's household, his lordship's valet had rummaged through half a dozen wardrobes and assembled for her as dainty an ensemble as any lady in London might wear: a flowing white gown of the finest silk and a garland of glazed flowers, all scarlet and gold, in place of a bonnet. It was not the very latest mode, perhaps. All the female clothing in that bachelor establishment had been abandoned by, or snatched back from, a succession of young jades who, in Tottenham's view, no longer pleased but who, in their own view, were no longer able to please his somewhat experimental taste in venery.

Queensberry was delighted to see her – a response that was noted with carefully hidden surprise by Lord Tottenham, to whom Mary had related only the bare outline of his grace's proposal. The duke called for more candles and paced about her as if she were some new and precious piece of sculpture.

"Perfect!" he kept saying. "Perfect! Oh you have doubled our odds." He put his hand to her cheek, which she had whitened as he had commanded, and said with tenderness, "But you must not use this whiting too often, you know. My aunt, Duchess Catherine, the old dowager, died of it, God rest her. The white lead is insidious to the blood. She used it every day."

Tottenham laughed sarcastically. "Set fear of death in the ring against female fashion, your grace, and fashion wins at the first blow."

The duke scowled. "You're in no favour here, Tottenham."

The other smiled and answered evenly, "Favour or not, I may still be of service."

"I've nothing for you."

"That would be a pity, your grace." There was a peremptory edge to the reply; it was a veiled threat.

Queensberry spoke to a footman. "Search about for Colonel Elliott and Mister Darberry. Try White's and Almack's first. Say I have the female ped for their perusal."

"Give out my name, too," Mary added.

Tottenham almost had a fit that she should presume to qualify the commands of a duke to his own servant. Even Queensberry, tolerant as he was toward her, grew angry. "How now, miss?" he said sharply.

"Well, your grace – 'the Female Ped'! How does that ring? A good match for Hardarm Hannah and Battling Bess, I'd say. But 'Miss Flinders' now – wouldn't you think twice before you gave her a fan, for fear she'd puff herself away?"

Queensberry roared with laughter. "By Jubilee, but the maid's right! Tottenham – hey? Ain't she right?" He nodded to the footman. "Say she is Miss Flinders, the *lady* ped."

When the man had gone, the duke began a more critical survey. "Egad, now you set me to think on it, there is still something not quite the lady . . ."

"Jewelry?" Tottenham suggested.

Queensberry stabbed a finger at him. "You have it!" He turned to a second footman. "Tell Harkness he is to open the vault and bring the dowager's jewelry, all the lesser pieces."

The 'lesser pieces' filled several boxes; they must have been worth tens of thousands of pounds. Mary could not imagine a household in which such value might simply lie in a vault for years, doing nothing, earning nothing. She saw that Tottenham, too, was agog as the duke upturned several boxes over the polished table and scrabbled among the treasure they spilled; it would need pounds of beeswax and elbowgrease to remove the scratches he did not even notice he was making. Could a person ever *become* like that, Mary wondered. She doubted it. What they said about the nobility was true – one had to be born to it.

While they waited for the betting gentlemen to appear they had a high old time trying on one 'trinket' after another. The choice was not easy; this one was too old fashioned, that was simply lost, or did not match her eyes, her hair, the shape of her face . . . another made her too grand, or too old, or too Spanish. In the end they settled upon a discreet pair of earrings, set with amethyst and diamonds, two dainty rings of sapphire and diamonds, and a velvet mask, as if for a masked ball, spangled with brilliants and chastely edged with tropical feathers. This last was Mary's choice, on the grounds that it would add to the mystery.

"By thunder, that's it!" the duke cried excitedly. "We have our story now – Miss Flinders is a young lady of breeding whose family has fallen upon hard times! Like the Gunning girls before they were presented at court. So, rather than part with her few simple jewels, she is undertaking this pedestrian adventure in a desperate attempt to revive their fortunes and rescue her poor, aged father from gaol! Desperate" – he winked – "and probably forlorn. My, my, Miss Flinders – if you haven't trebled our odds at a stroke!"

Mary hid her amusement at the duke's belief that this tale was fiction from end to end.

Tottenham, seeing how his patron's humour was restored, took the chance to remind him that certain decisions were now pressing. The duke became serious again but his anger did not revive. "Will the young fellow – what's his name?"

"Pitman."

"Will he die?"

"They say he'll more likely live – if he escapes the gangrene."

"Hmph! Still, you had better lie low. We'll think of something. The post of Chief of Ulster Constables – they give it some different name up there, but that's the position – it happens to be vacant at the moment. I suppose I could persuade his majesty . . . on the other hand, there is an office I held when I was Earl of March and Ruglen. I hold it still, I believe. I could resign that to you – for a consideration."

Tottenham cleared his throat. "May one ask . . .?" he said tentatively.

"Oh – Vice Admiral of Scotland. It's five thousand a year. Yours for twenty."

"And it carries the same immunity from arrest?"

"While parliament sits – long enough for you."

"Vice Admiral, eh?" Tottenham mused. "One needn't actually *go* to Scotland?"

"Good God, no!"

"But still – twenty thousand!"

The duke grinned. "Beggars must be no choosers."

Beggar! If he had been slapped across the face the young aristocrat could not have been more angry. Mary, admiring her jewelry and mask in the glass, saw him look about in frustration. Their eyes met. His hardened.

He crossed the room, grasped her roughly by the shoulders and, walking behind, thrust her toward the duke. "Ten and the maid," he offered.

Queensberry's lip curled in a sneer. "You puppy! She's not yours to bargain away."

"Is she not?" Tottenham's voice was insistent and low. "Tell him!"

She shook her head at the duke and said, "It is his humour, your grace." But Tottenham's hands upon her, his breath at the back of her neck – the very touch and nearness of him – all had their effect. And Queensberry saw it, saw her shiver, read the desperation in her eyes . . .

Never in her life had she seen a disappointment so sudden, so great, so plain. Indeed, it was more than disappointment; it was the pity and terror of his advancing years; it was sorrow for a youth he had lost past all redeeming. Once perhaps, he too had been able to fine-tune a woman's flesh as Tottenham now tuned hers. Had he forgotten it – remembered the fact but forgotten its overwhelming power until he faced it now in her despair?

She saw the veils of withdrawal fall before his eyes. That strange, unlikely comradeship which had sprung up so naturally between them from the first, perplexing them both, died in that instant. He had no further interest in her, save as the object of his wager. She felt more alone – indeed, she *was* more alone – than at any time since leaving Poulaphuca.

All this she saw and understood upon an instant.

"'Tis only his humour," she repeated, lacklustre.

Old Q emerged from his sadness, businesslike again. "Twenty," he said crisply. "Take it or leave it."

Tottenham cast her aside as if she were a cloak he had just shrugged off. He stepped beyond her and continued to argue with the duke.

Watching the young nobleman's movements, listening to his voice, she fell to wondering what that canker of destructiveness within him was. Wherein did it lie? How might she core it out of him and restore him to the nobility that must surely lie buried somewhere beneath that cynical and dissolute façade?

She caught sight of herself in the glass. What before had seemed attractive was now tawdry. The beauty it conferred was like this whiting on her face; it leached an insidious poison inwards.

The duke would not budge from his twenty thousand. Tottenham's fury mounted, but at last he had to agree. Colonel Elliott and Mister Darberry were announced. Mary was so amazed at the sudden parade of affable geniality from both Tottenham and Queensberry that she almost forgot to mask her face.

In the next five minutes she learned how a prize heifer in a show ring must feel. Her feet, dainty in her silken slippers, were inspected minutely. She was made to strut this way and that. They quizzed her as to her family and antecedents – to which she replied truthfully in every particular except as to the dates on which the various lands were lost. Queensberry, who supposed she was inventing it all, was full of admiration; yet that was still a thousand miles from the affection he had earlier shown.

"You have surely licked the Blarney Stone, Miss Flinders," the colonel said, as if he grudged her a win of some kind.

"Indeed I have not, sir. I was never in County Cork in my life."

"You were dipped in the Shannon then," Mr. Darberry added.

"I was closer to it than a whisker," she allowed.

"What say ye now, gentlemen?" Queensberry pressed. "Your six hundred to my two, Piccadilly to Piccadilly in four full days?"

They gazed at her, pursed their lips, drew dubious breath.

The time limit suddenly registered with Mary. "Surely your grace means five full days?" she said.

Grinning wickedly he shook his head. "Couldn't get decent odds at five, my dear. Four makes it a real contest."

She gulped. "It most certainly does."

The duke turned to his victims – his other victims, for Mary now included herself in that category. "It means she must walk over forty-five miles a day, gentlemen. Look at her! D'ye see even twenty in such a frame? What – twenty? D'ye see *ten?*"

Mary, committed by now to her part, sucked gently at her cheeks, seeking to appear haggard and frail. It caused her lip to tremble slightly. The colonel saw it and his eyes filled with pity. He turned to Queensberry and said, "By Jove, you're on!"

She knew he had spoken not out of a conviction that the odds were fair but rather to end her humiliation (as it must have seemed to him). She felt like the worst kind of deceiver – yet what had she done wrong? Suddenly she wanted more than anything to be shot of them all, even Tottenham. Yes – to finish with Tottenham, bid farewell to the duke . . . to be on the road to Manchester, to see Matt Sullivan again. For all his neglect of his person there was nonetheless something clean about Matt.

The duke was saying to the colonel, "You have an equerry? Or someone you may spare to invigilate her upon the way?"

"Invigilate?" Mary asked.

"Of course." They all faced her. "Both sides will follow you with scrutineers to be sure you walk every step of the way. I thought you understood that, my dear."

"I have a subaltern who needs a change of air," the colonel said. "And you, Duke?"

He smiled, not at the colonel but at Mary. This was his revenge for the hurt she had done him, wittingly or no. "Yes, Colonel. I, too, have someone who needs be quit of London for a season."

# CHAPTER TWENTY-THREE

IT TOOK A FURTHER TWO DAYS to organize the Pic-to-Pic Stakes, as Mary's pedestrian steeplechase came to be called. The fever ran high through all the gentlemen's clubs; two whole pages in the wagers book at White's were taken up with bets on this one event. A certain Mr. Rowley offered a spectacular double: fifteen to one that Mary would complete her walk in time *and* that his own father, who was ailing, would be dead before then. At Almack's they opened a special book.

Mary divided her time between Camden Town and Old Q's house in Piccadilly. She slept with her feet wrapped in lint soaked with spirits, and several times a day she rubbed oxfat into the leather of her boots. She was to wear her dainty shoes for the first five miles of the journey, to better the odds among last-minute gamblers simple enough to imagine she would wear them all the way.

It was a life of near-deceit, of lying by implication, but she tolerated it for its central purpose: to put the best part of two hundred English miles as quickly as possible between herself and this unscrupulous circle – and to give her enough funds never to retrace her path to disillusion.

She saw nothing of Con, who was now, in any case, in strict training for the Sterling Jim Bacon fight. On the few occasions they met he kept alive the fiction of their engagement, telling her to "be good" to Lord Tottenham as it would stand them both in fine stead for the future. She saw then that his idea of a "future" was to be perpetually beholden to some lordly patron, always currying his goodwill, abiding his kicks, bowing beneath his spite, gratefully snatching up whatever crumbs of favour he might deign to let fall.

Lord Tottenham himself found it prudent to leave town that same night he took her to see Old Q. He would have to stay clear of London until his place as Vice Admiral for Scotland was gazetted. He was, as the duke had intimated, to be one of the scrutineers of the Pic-to-Pic. He would begin that task at St. Albans, which she ought to reach by noon of the first day.

For the other side, Colonel Elliott had selected a young ensign in his own regiment, the Honourable Artillery Company, a Richard Page, of the pike and musket detachment. He was to ride in a coach, but a furlong behind, so as not to distract her. The same coach carried her clothing, a raincape, victuals, an umbrella, and the two books she could not be parted from: *The Amazing Tablet of Memory* and *Moll Flanders*.

On the eve of her departure she made a final call on the duke. Halfway down Piccadilly she met Crystal.

"Oh, these so-called 'gentlemen' of London!" she complained, waving her hands as if shooing off flies.

"Why stand about here then?"

"Oh . . . well." Crystal gave a weak laugh. "I wasn't. I didn't . . . I mean, I just happened to be here and happened to see you. But mercy, now I think on't – you did promise to introduce me to Old Q."

Mary, though she had only the vaguest recollection of the engagement, linked arms with her and chatted happily all the way to Park Lane. Jack had gone to Tilbury to arrange passage to France.

Out of Tottenham's company Mary's robust personality soon reasserted itself. Old Q warmed to her once again, gave her an exquisite ivory fan and a pair of silk stockings, showed her off almost skittishly to his acquaintance, as if she were a new mistress. She complained about this when at last the company had gone. "To gain the notoriety without the gold that makes it bearable is hard," she said angrily, meaning to ask him to undo what he had done next time he met those gentlemen.

But he leaped in at once and offered her fifty guineas for the favour that would justify the notoriety she had already earned. Mary was about to protest when she remembered how worldly and offhand she had been on this topic with Crystal – who was sitting there, listening agog.

She swallowed her annoyance and with an inconsequential laugh said, "That makes me a quare old mixture so. I have feet worth four hundred guineas . . ."

"Pounds," the duke interrupted.

Mary shrugged. "Feet worth four hundred and an immortal soul worth fifty!"

"Why then, egad, name your price!"

"Not for a thousand guineas, your grace – and well you know it."

"Do I really?" The duke went to an oak chest that stood against the wall. Taking a key from his fob pocket he unlocked it and drew forth an enormous leather purse. "I wonder now – have you ever *seen* a thousand guineas?" Casually he upended the purse over the table. "My winnings on Amaranthe at Newmarket. Just happen to have it by me."

It was a monstrous pile, a gleaming pile, a mouthwatering, sinful, glistering pile; three times more than many a hardworking man or woman might earn in a lifetime. Mary's tongue went dry; she had no idea why she continued to shake her head and say no. It was not just the money she was risking; she thought also of the offence she must be giving Old Q.

Crystal let out a gasp. The duke glanced briefly toward her and smiled. There was a strange pride in him. Suddenly Mary understood that, far from taking her refusal as an insult, he thought it magnificent; in some way she had redeemed herself for the hurt she had unwittingly caused him the other night; she had earned back that intangible commitment from him – which might yet prove more valuable than all this gold.

"So, egad!" he said, leaving the money lying on the table. "If you won't go to *my* bed you must to your own. I suppose you know by now that you carry more than ten times that pile to Manchester."

Just before she and Crystal took their leave, he opened a drawer in his bureau and fished out a travelling clock with an alarum bell, which he gave her without comment; also several sheets of paper. "I had one of my scribblers copy this out of a vade-mecum for you – the shortest, flattest way to Manchester. I have a levée to attend in the morning, so I shall not be on hand to witness your departure, I fear."

"But your grace will be in Manchester at my arrival?"

"Doomsday itself would not prevent me." He spoke with a special relish, as if he had a further surprise in store.

At the street door Crystal suddenly said, "Oh dear, I need to go."

"We can use the bushes in the park," Mary told her.

But she said she would be afraid of footpads, and Mary should walk on home.

Mary stood her ground.

"I have another idea for a wager," Crystal explained. "I want to tell his grace."

"No, Crystal. Don't go back."

"Fifty guineas would pay a lawyer."

Mary shook her head.

Crystal lowered her eyes; her voice fell almost to a whisper. "Five hundred would see our claims through the House of Lords itself."

"There must be another way."

Still with lowered eyes Crystal turned again to the duke's door.

"Listen!" Mary urged.

"It's no use," Crystal told her. "Ten thousand bishops could bar my way yet all I'd see is my darling Jack, stretched on some foreign field of war with carrion crows for his shroud." She shivered. "Just go, Mary, dear. Then you needn't ever say whether I returned to his grace or not."

Mary turned on her heel and stalked angrily away.

A little way up the street she found Steam Punch waiting for her. "Lord, man, are you to be at my heels for the rest of my life?" she snapped. Then, instantly regretting her unkindness, she went on, "Ah, pay me no heed, dear friend. I'm annoyed at Crystal, who is being the perfect fool. Have you waited long?"

"I hear of work on the Grand Trunk," he said.

"That's north, isn't it? Manchester way? We may share the road. I'm sure that's allowed."

He cleared his throat. "I thought I'd go by the navigations, the way we came. See if your man Sullivan is still a-stargazing and a-woolgathering at the country's pleasure. And if he is, sure I'll kick him every other shtep of the way to Manchester."

She threw her arms about him and kissed him on the neck and ears. "God, what have I ever done to deserve such a friend as you?"

Embarrassed, he unpeeled her and they resumed their homeward walk.

"Would you do one other small tiny little favoureen of a favour for me?" she asked.

He knew at once what she was about to beg, for he answered: "Sure anything, me darlin' one – except bring that damned ass with me."

She laughed and jumped upon him, forcing him to pickaback her up the street. "Please?" she murmured coaxingly in his ear. "I have to do near forty-five miles each day and he'd break my heart so he would."

Before they reached Bond Street he had yielded.

Next morning at seven, Old Q's open-top sociable drew up outside her lodgings. It created quite a stir. The single letter Q surmounted by a ducal coronet – the device that had earned the duke his nickname – was famous throughout the city. She felt like a royalty as she was driven into town. At the bottom of the Tottenham Court Road it seemed that the whole of St. Giles's had turned out to see her go by; the lucky delle who would earn so much so easily – and all of it legal. She searched among them for Jack and Crystal, or Canting Corley, Stunning Joe, Crackmans . . . but identifications were impossible in that sea of faces.

From criminal London into artisan London, down Crown Street and into Leicester Fields, again they were out to see her pass, the plucky maid who would restore her family fortunes – a dilemma they understood in their very bones. When the carriage paused to let a herd of fat cattle pass on their way to Smithfield, a matron dashed out from the crowd and pressed a hot pasty into her hands, wrapped in paper. "God be with you, my pretty," she cried. "My John shall manage without his meat for once."

And so through fashionable London, the whole length of Piccadilly, where she remembered to look demure and chastened, responding with shy mortification to the applause from every balcony and upper window. Even the Duke of Devonshire and Georgiana his duchess, London's foremost hostess, were at their window to see her go by. The pathos of her tale and the fortunes that hung upon her success or failure had, in one way or another, touched every heart and purse in town. But the greatest surprise of all was to see Crystal waving to her from

Old Q's balcony – and with Jack at her side! The duke himself, as he had forewarned her last night, was at Buckingham House.

There was no ceremony. She came under starter's orders at once, to leave when the tollgate clock struck eight. Her scrutineer, Richard Page, was presented to her. In the stiffest possible manner he explained that she was not to run – nor hop nor skip – but to walk, heel-and-toe, each step of the way. If forced to run, by a downpour of rain or a runaway horse, for instance, she was to go back and resume her walk from that point. "And if you take a wrong turn," he added . . .

"Oh I shan't do that." She flourished the sheets of paper copied from the vade mecum. "I have so many useful *pages* by me!"

He seemed incapable of smiling; she thought him a desperate young prig and was glad he'd always be a furlong behind her.

The clock began to strike eight and the starter signalled her to be off. "Go on! Go on!" urged those onlookers who had money riding on her back. But she saw Crystal threading her way among the crowd and waited. Jack was some yards in her wake. The two women embraced each other warmly. "I see Jack there," Mary said. "You got home without *mishap* then? No need to . . ."

"Come on now!" people cried.

Crystal grinned. "I just came to wish you luck." Jack joined them and gave her arm a friendly, painful squeeze. By now the crowd was going mad with impatience.

"You'll do it, I'm sure," Crystal went on. "Or I hope you will, for I've bet my every last shilling on it." She spoke these words directly to Jack and laughed at the shock in his eyes.

*So that's to be the tale!* Mary thought sadly. "Well, I must be off," she said.

Half the gamblers in the crowd considered her insouciant delay to be a great sign of confidence and offered last-minute bets on her; the other half considered it overconfidence and accepted.

In Park Lane, near Seymour Place, she saw a familiar figure running among the bushes, boxing at the leaves and pulling ferocious punches on the treetrunks. "Con!" she called out.

Without breaking his stride he veered in her direction and kept pace with her, almost running on the spot. He was scarlet with his exertions and the sweat was running down in rivers. He was conscientious, give him that.

"That's you away then," he said breathlessly.

"I'm bound away, yes. I hope you gain all you wish, Con dear."

"You have a grand day for it. Have you food and money?"

"I have all I need. 'Tis all carried in the coach behind me."

"God be with you, then." He bounded a stride or two away from her and then returned. "You'll meet his lordship?"

"This noon at Saint Albans."

He winked cheerily. "Be good to him. He's not that bad a fellow once you know him. And if it does *you* no good, 'twill do *us* no harm."

*Poor Con!* she thought. He'd keep up his threadbare imposture until his master ordered him to desist. You couldn't help pitying a man like that. He might kill you at his master's command, yet there was no real harm in him. She was glad to know they would probably never meet again, yet she thought about him with a certain maternal affection all the way to Tyburn Turnpike, which was a good half-mile. There she met her first choice of roads. This was the dismal spot where, until a few years ago, felons had been hanged by the score. For most of that time "the nevergreen tree of Tyburn" had stood far out in open country; but now the city had encroached. A new house already stood upon the actual gallows site in Connaught Place; luxuriant grass and weeds had reclaimed the tenancy denied them by thousands of trampling feet all down the centuries.

The fingerboards pointing out the two roads – west to Oxford, north to Edgware and St. Albans – made her choice easy, but she consulted her script as a matter of principle. Mr. Page's carriage was just passing through the Tyburn toll and turning into the Edgware road when she reached the present fringe of London. From here to St. Albans, twenty miles distant, was nothing but open fields, coppice and common, and small villages – Paddington, Kilburn, Edgware, Elstree, and Radlett . . . They were all set out in her script.

She had had neither time nor good enough candles to read the pages last night. Now, having nothing better to do while she walked, she studied them carefully, which was easy enough when the road lay smooth and straight before her. The duke's "scribbler" had copied it all down slavishly. She had expected no more than a utilitarian list of towns and villages and a careful marking of every fork, junction, and side road, plus perhaps the accumulated mileages from London and to Manchester. Such a list did, indeed, occupy a column down the centre of each page. But upon its left and right hung a most detailed "tourist" of the passing scene. Thus at Kilburn, she learned, she would tread near Belsize House, the home of H. Wright Esq. "The mansion," it said, "is a handsome, new structure, standing in a delightful park, which is approached from the Hampstead road by a noble avenue of trees."

Casting her eye down the page she saw that every gentleman's house, great or small, was listed at the appropriate point beside the road – as if she might take morning chocolate with Dennis O'Kelly Esq. of Canons Park in Edgware and converse with him about his celebrated horse Eclipse (it was all noted down by the scribe) or cry in for early luncheon and a dish of tea with Mr. Phillimore, at Kendal Hall near Radlett, and quiz him on his studies of Homer.

More practically, the crossing of every little river and stream was recorded, and whether the bridge were of wood or stone. Here and there the scribe had noted "Cornfields" or "a Mighty Rock." There were more cryptic markings, too, such as "Obelisk" or "Noble Vista" or "Folly." She was reassured to find her way set out in such minute detail; it also showed how seriously the duke took his gambling. When he said his profession was to turn the flimsy doubts of others into his certainties, he spoke plain truth; he left nothing to chance that might as easily be secured. She tucked the papers in her pocketbook and strode out in good heart.

At Brent Bridge she was grateful at last to unbuckle her dainty shoes and put on her sturdy walking boots instead. She was a quarter of an hour late – but she'd make better time now she was on the open road and was properly shod. "Let's hope this fine weather lasts," she said to Page.

"Chatter, chatter!" he replied frostily.

She grinned at him. "Is this a punishment for you, then?"

He gave a snort, there was fury in his eyes, but he said nothing. Before she set off again he consulted his watch and made an entry in a book.

"What's that?" she asked.

He looked about, as if seeking some cause not to respond. At length he said curtly, "I'm to keep a particular log of every single occurrence."

At that moment his horse did one of the two things for which horses are notorious. She looked him in the eye and said, "Scribble scribble, sir. Don't let me hinder you!"

He *almost* smiled.

*I'll have you camping in the palm of my hand before we reach Manchester*, she promised herself.

The next hour she made up the shortfall, reaching the Hertfordshire border at the eleventh milestone; but the pace had been stiff and she doubted she could keep it up. She slackened off a little, yet she reached the sixteenth milepost, near Colney, exactly at the allotted hour of eleven. She began to relax; but the worry of not being able to make the pace was soon replaced by another – that of taking the wrong turning. It was already plain to her that the timetable allowed little or nothing for going astray.

Noon found her at a temporary pause outside the church of St. Stephen, on the hill overlooking the valley of the Ver, with the little town of St. Albans rising steeply beyond. The carriageway turned sharply to her right but she could see traces of an old track going directly ahead across the fields, through what looked like ancient earthworks. The tourist said this was the site of the Roman city of Verulamium. Her way from London – and its continuation for the next fifteen miles beyond St. Albans – was the old Roman road called Watling Street. So, in theory at least (and assuming that the earthworks did, indeed, represent Verulamium and not some scholar's romantic fancy), she ought at this point to be able to strike across the fields and pick up Watling Street again on the far side. In fact, she could see a very Roman-looking road about a mile away to the northwest.

But would it be signposted? And then again, if this was Verulamium, might there not be half a dozen Roman roads radiating away from it?

Also, to be sure, there was the meeting up with Lord Tottenham. She thought of asking Mr. Page to go in and collect him, but felt certain he'd refuse.

His carriage drew level with her at that moment. "Giving up?" he asked with a chill little smile.

She flounced off down the hill but at the bottom, although there was a bridge over the river, the track vanished into a mire of marshy ground. She could just about see a way across it for herself, to the steep hill that led up into the town, but Mr. Page was going to have to find some other access. She leaped from tussock to tussock until she reached the orchards below the abbey. There she turned and looked back, to see Page asking directions of an angler. The last she saw of him he was driving westward up the valley on the far bank of the Ver.

*I could run and he'd never know it,* she thought.

But no one could run up the hill that now faced her. She arrived exhausted at the crossroads at the top. She had determined to head straight out of the town, leaving word of her passing with everyone she met – in short, putting the onus on Lord Tottenham. But before she reached the end of George Street she felt a tug on that invisible thread which seemed to bind her to that man, and she knew – win or lose this venture – she would have to find him before she went on.

It cost her more than an hour. In the end she traced him to an inn on the Hatfield road, in the very opposite direction to her own road out of the town. He was in as foul a mood as she had ever seen; she knew then that he had come out along this particular road deliberately to spite her, as if he blamed her for his present situation. "Have a drink," he snarled.

But she had slaked her thirst at one of the other taverns. "You've cost me time enough," she replied. "I'm bound away again. You may fulfil your duty or no, as it please you."

He sprang to the door and caught her by the wrist. "I said drink."

Her independence withered; she followed him to the counter and sipped from a glass he had already filled, awaiting her arrival. She had to finish it to the dregs before he would let her go; he answered none of her conversation.

He refused her a lift in the saddle behind him back to the crossroads, even though it would have been within the rules. When she arrived there, on foot, she knew it had been a mistake to take the second drink on an empty stomach. She went to the gutter and induced what Steam Punch once called "Joseph's yawn" – the yawn of many colours. It put his lordship in a paroxysm of anger but she was past caring.

Just round the corner, back in George Street, they found Page waiting for them; he too was in a fury. "Where've you been?" he demanded. "You're supposed to stick to the carriage road."

"I did so!" She fished out her pasty – the one the woman had given her in London – and pointed to the fingerboard at the crossroads; the hill up which she had walked was clearly posted *London*.

He scowled. "I saw you leaping over the marsh," he said. "I have made a note of it. Leaping is not walking."

Tottenham turned upon her and asked in a scandalized voice if this were true.

She gave a weary sigh. "I know both you fine gentlemen are as pleased with your part in this affair as a fiddler in the rain. Can you not vent your spleen upon each other and leave me in peace? Or d'you lack an introduction?"

"We already know each other," Tottenham said sharply. "But see here – *did* you leap across the marsh? If so, I think we must declare this race lost here and now."

Page stared at him in astonishment.

Mary answered with weary anger: "I undertook to go as a pedestrian from London to Manchester. Upon encountering a marsh I did what any pedestrian would do – I leaped from tussock to tussock the way it wouldn't wet me. If that was wrong, I'll be disqualified in Manchester, but come all hell against me, I mean to get there. You may keep up or lag behind or go howling astray as you please." She walked off, stuffing the last of the pasty in her mouth.

"Dash it, Tottenham," Page said behind her, "it's for me to raise the objections. Your part is to counter 'em."

The sound of their squabbling faded on the afternoon air.

Before she was a mile out of town – and full eight miles behind her timetable – she began to suspect that the pasty had been poisoned. At first she thought it was the drink Lord Tottenham had forced her to gulp down, for the pain in her belly had come upon her before she had taken a bite. But she had got rid of the drink and still the pain was there – ten times worse. She wondered she could stand, let alone walk.

Of course the pasty was poisoned! That woman had been in the pay of someone who had bet against her and wanted to make sure of winning. What a fool she had been to trust anyone when so many thousands of pounds depended on it.

When she reached the top of the next hill, a further mile from town, the pain was so intense she had to squat in the verge and press her stomach to try to still it. The men must have thought this was a natural pause for they held off a discreet distance.

Then she got rid of the pie the way she had the drink. She crouched low amid the straggling hedgerow; from a distance it must have seemed like a fall.

## CHAPTER TWENTY-FOUR

THE MEN SAW IT and hastened toward her. Tottenham said at once, "This walk is clearly too much for you, Miss Flinders. I beg you to withdraw."

"I must go on," she told him. "I'm miles behind already."

It was Page who helped her to her feet; he, too, was worried out of his shell of pride. "I second that, Miss Flinders," he said. "It was a brave try but to persist now would be sheer folly."

"No. I have to go on."

"I'm sure a public subscription would make good your family's loss," he told her. "The general tenderness toward you . . ."

"Could easily lose its way inside an acorn shell if your attitude of this morning is any sort of a guide. Anyway, what of the duke? I have an obligation there, too."

Tottenham gave a curt laugh. "He won't notice. Believe me, the man's worth a million."

Page nodded in agreement, though he clearly thought it odd of Tottenham to speak so harshly of his patron.

His lordship took her arm but she slipped hastily from his grasp. "It's nothing so serious. I was poisoned, but not enough to . . ."

"Poisoned!" Tottenham was filled with alarm.

"A woman in London gave me a pasty. She must have been paid by . . ."

"Ah! That!" he said. "I mean . . . I didn't know about that."

"I hope you were not going on to impute this poisoning to Colonel Elliott, Miss Flinders?" Page's frostiness was returning.

"Of course not, Mr. Page. I'm told several hundred have wagered against me. It could be any one of them."

She took a hesitant step, endured a moment of dizziness, and then went to her hamper to see what she might find in the way of wholesome food. She was pleased to discover that Old Q's housekeeper had put in several pots of honey.

Its effect over the next hour was to make her a lifelong devotee of the stuff. The cramps in her belly returned briefly once or twice but the pain was never disabling; she gritted her teeth and kept up her stride even though the sweat broke out all over her. In the shivering bouts of weakness that followed she found a fingerful of honey an astounding tonic. By midafternoon, though she had made up none of the lost miles, she had sacrificed no further ground. She was then at the village of Market Street – and feeling mightily glad that the Romans had had the sense to find a valley through the Dunstable beacons, whose rolling, wooded slopes rose on both sides. Even so, the road had gradients enough to slow her down. The rises, though brief, were punishing, and the downhill slopes were no compensation, for they jarred her heels if she kept up her full thirty-inch stride. There was an art to this walking business – as she was rapidly learning.

For the first few miles after her spasm Tottenham had ridden beside her, constantly asking after her condition. He was plainly concerned for her and kept begging her to consider Page's proposal to raise a fund and pay off her father's debts.

"God, hasn't that been tried!" she protested. "A score of times. Within the year he's back in quare street – and in gaol again soon after."

"A charitable fund could be arranged to pay income only," he countered. "The capital could be placed beyond his reach."

But she shook her head and strode relentlessly on. "I'll not let down Old Q."

He reined about and cantered away in a huff to rejoin Mr. Page, but his kindly concern for her welfare put fresh vigour into her pace.

By the time she reached Dunstable, having covered thirty-three of her allotted forty-six miles, the evening was well drawn on. She had finished the honey – and had slaked the thirst it gave her with a gulp or two from every wayside pump. She decided it was time to pause and take something more substantial. Her long tramp from Ireland had taught her the value of a full belly. "A half-hour at a good table is worth five upon the road," Punch used to say.

The Saracen's Head looked inviting. She chose a roast pullet, because it was ready to serve, and asked them to bring it out into the garden. They refused unless she paid first. When she said that two gentlemen were following with her money, a farmer who had been drinking quietly at the other end of the bar piped up, "You're that ped-woman – Pic-to-Pic Mary! 'Twas in the Lunnon papers."

Word spread through the town and she soon had an admiring circle around her out in the orchard. Everyone wanted to talk to her; she got tired of being told she was late. The land was overstocked in mathematical genius. Still, they were an open-hearted lot. The innkeeper, seeing what trade he was doing in bystanders, refused her payment, and householders and stall-keepers on her uphill way out of town pressed on her more pies and pots of jam and comfits than she could eat in a month. One old soldier advised her to take salt each night against the cramp.

At the mention of the word she began to worry. There was indeed a desperate unwillingness in the muscles of her legs, a tight, hard sort of pain not at all unlike a cramp. She still had almost twelve miles to go to make up her first day's timetable. Even at her best rate she would hardly make it before nine, perhaps not before ten. If this ache in her limbs grew worse, she doubted she'd make it at all.

Should she therefore say sufficient unto this day? Stop at the next inn? Take the rest she had surely earned and rely on an early start tomorrow to make up the lost miles? *Yes!* said the siren voices. *No*, said wiser counsel. Twelve hours a day at four miles an hour would leave four hours to spare out of the allotted forty-eight. It would be folly of the rankest kind to fritter two of them away before half a day had run.

Yet all the way downhill into the valley beyond Dunstable, then up again to Katehill, then down again to Hockliffe, those siren cries grew evermore insistent. Indeed, at Hockliffe her head was so swimming with fatigue tht she almost forgot to turn off toward Woburn. She went full twenty paces beyond the fingerpost before the name registered with her and some dimly aware little corner of her mind recalled seeing it in the duke's guide – which she now consulted. She grudged every one of those twenty retraced steps. The gentlemen were far behind but she made sure they saw her taking the right-hand fork.

The hill out of the village was almost the last straw, though she was at least safely on the Woburn road. She no longer looked for an inn, nor even a cottage where she might purchase a night's sleep upon the floor; not even a barn. The very hedgerows looked enticing, a dry ditch as welcome as a feather bed. The only thing in her favour was the cool of the evening and the gentle glow of the westering sun. But for that she would have collapsed where she was. Even so, when she reached Woburn, though it was four miles short of her ambitions for that day, her feet refused to carry her past the Royal Oak. She slumped into a rustic seat beside the door and waited for the gentlemen to arrive – and waited . . . and waited . . .

Eventually she asked a man on horseback if he had seen anything of them. He replied that a coach with a gentleman in it and a rider beside had turned off toward the abbey, the Duke of Bedford's country seat, which was just over a mile away. In her exhaustion she had walked straight past without noticing the grand house at all.

Anger fought her exhaustion, but lost. Since Dunstable she had kept a guinea in her pocketbook, so she got the landlord to send to the abbey for her trunk; meanwhile he asked her what she might care to eat. The London papers obviously made less mark here than they had ten miles back down the road. In Woburn she was no constellation.

"A plate of loose meat," she told him. "Whatever you have that's handy. And a quart of ale."

She was served a grand sirloin roast atop a fierce mound of potatoes and greens. She remembered the soldier's advice and doused it liberally with salt, which gave her the thirst to finish the ale in no time. Tom Elphick, the landlord, watched with astonishment as the meal disappeared. "No need to ask if you relish it," he commented.

"God, it's that good you could follow it with your fingers," she agreed. "What have you in the style of a pudding now?"

A generous portion of spotted dick went to join the beef, and in the same short order.

"We have a coach party benighted here with a broken wheel," Elphick warned her apologetically. "It's four or five to a bed this night, I fear."

She shook her head. "May I ask who is up betimes in this house?"

"Bessie's up first, ma'am, for the kitchen fire and the breakfast. She's up at five."

"Then you may shake me out a little straw somewhere quiet and be sure she rouses me early. My alarum clock is at the abbey. She could set me out three eggs, a kidney or two, some bacon, sausage . . ."

He laughed. "I know! Whatever's nearest to hand!"

At that moment the lad returned from the abbey, without her trunk but with a note to say that his grace desired the pleasure of her company to supper – and that there was a bed for her beneath his roof. One of the abbey coaches stood at the door. She went out and said to the coachman, "You may thank his grace from me with humble courtesy and say I mean him no disrespect but it would take two footmen just to hold up these eyelids. Also the Duke of Queensberry would eat me a mile off if he heard I took this wager so lightly." As an afterthought she called out, "And you may convey to Lord Tottenham that I mean to be on my way tomorrow at five or soon after. And he may do his duty or not as it pleases him."

The rules were that she could set her own times; if the men did not keep to them, it was no penalty to her.

Tom Elphick listened to all this wide-eyed. Then, deeply apologetic and calling her "your grace" every step of the way, led her to his own chamber and even had clean sheets put on the bed. She was asleep before her head touched the bolster. "Be sure I'm woken at dawn," were her last words.

"'Tis the Duchess of Queensberry for sure," Tom Elphick told the rest of his company when he returned below.

Some said there was no such person and it was notorious that Old Q, like their own, much younger duke, was a bachelor. But Tom had the conclusive argument: Who else but another duchess would refuse the Duke of Bedford's invitation without hesitation – and send such a peremptory afterthought to Viscount Tottenham. "No, i'faith, our 'Miss Flinders' is a duchess at least – an eccentric duchess out walking for a wager."

The man in person brought in her breakfast next day, using all the silver the house could muster. He drew back her curtains as if he himself had just engineered the dawn sky they disclosed. "As your grace commanded," he said.

The night's rest seemed to have nothing for her fatigue; even to stir in the bed was a torture. But as she sat up and drew on her shawl, the movement brought some kind of anaesthetic and her condition improved from the impossible to the merely awful. "Why d'you call me 'your grace'?" she asked. "I'm no duchess."

Elphick laughed. "Quite so, ma'am. Quite so. Enough said. You may lead a horse to water but a nod's as good as a wink, eh?" And he winked – not at her but vaguely, at the room in general, drawing his whole establishment into her supposed conspiracy.

Still, if the delusion brought her a breakfast of this size and splendour, she'd give it every scope. Elphick, waiting on her like a footman, cleared his throat and raised a finger toward her tray. "There's a billy-dew from the abbey, ma'am. Perhaps it escaped your notice?"

It had indeed. A note from his grace of Bedford. Mr. Page, it said, had explained the signification of her walk to Manchester and its importance to Queensberry. He quite understood her desire to sleep rather than sup and would impute no discourtesy to her on that score. If she succeeded in her aim, she could count him among her many grateful admirers for – with Mr. Page's advice – he had placed twenty guineas upon her against Lord Tottenham's thirty. She must stay at the abbey on her return to London.

The note had a pretty crest; she kept it in case she might one day start a scrapbook.

But why was Tottenham betting against her? Hedging, perhaps? Yes, that was surely it.

The hour was a few minutes short of six when she bade farewell to her host and assured him of her warmest recommendation. It was all she could do to stop him bowing backwards before her all the way to Woburn Sands. Of Tottenham and Page there was no sign.

The peace of the countryside was profound. It delighted her to think that this early start might even give her a few miles in hand by nightfall. But the ache in her limbs was intense. Her veins seemed filled with acid and the muscles beneath her buttocks, the ones that twitched at the start of each pace, were two rods of fire. Even her back ached though she carried nothing; she made windmills of her arms but neither exertion nor change of position brought relief.

Yet within two or three miles, by the time she passed through a still-slumbering Woburn Sands, the pain had come to seem normal; at least it was no longer an obsession. There was even a kind of narcotic drowsiness about it. Her awareness of her own movement became remote, disjointed. In one of the newly harvested fields to her right she thought she saw Tottenham, cantering his horse. She called out but the man rode on regardless – probably a farmer or hunt servant out for exercise. Before the hour was up she reached Wavendon, her goal of yesternight.

Here she found the first error in the vade-mecum. The fingerpost showed her road, the one to Newport Pagnell, as going off to the left; but the vade-mecum made no mention of such a turn. At every other deviation a meticulously drawn hand with outstretched index finger had pointed right or left; but here it was missing.

However, the parish sign was unequivocal: Newport Pagnell was five miles distant down the road to her left. She had covered two of those miles when she came to a fork that was not marked at all in her papers. Fortunately there was a cottage nearby – more of a small villa, in fact – with signs of movement at the curtains. As she went up the path she heard a man and a woman indoors, shouting at each other. Before she could knock, the door was opened by a small, belligerent, unshaven gentleman in a nightshirt. "D'you write from dictation?" he asked Mary angrily.

"When I'm not in a hurry to reach Manchester by Saturday."

"Never mind all that," he barked. "Answer the question."

"I will if you answer me one first. Which of those two roads goes to Newport Pagnell?"

"Roads don't go anywhere," he said primly. "You can't catch me so easily."

She gave up in despair and turned on her heel.

"Wait!" he cried. "Why d'you wish to go to Newport Pagnell?"

She explained as briefly as she could.

"Well you've come the wrong way," he told her. "Should have gone straight on at Wavendon."

"But the fingerpost . . ."

"Never trust them. Villages are full of mendicant louts with no better amusement than to divert the fingerposts."

She sighed and turned to face the way she had come. But a crafty look came into his eye. "If you'll take down some dictation for me . . ."

"We don't need any dictation today, thank you!" a woman's voice shouted from within.

He ignored it. ". . . I'll run you back there on my horse. Save you twenty minutes and a quantity of shoe leather. How anyone could mistake this miserable lane for the king's highway is beyond me!"

"I did wonder," she admitted.

But he had already vanished indoors, shouting, "Come on, come on! We haven't long, you know!"

"No dictation today!" the woman repeated when she saw Mary. She was in her thirties, a few years younger than the man. She wore a mob cap and clutched a blanket about her.

The little villa was crammed with enough furniture to grace a country house – which is no doubt what it once had done. Here, however, its only effect was to impede ordinary movement about the room. Little tables were piled upon big ones, and chairs upon them, and books or vases upon them. Chests marked Best Linen, Quotidian Linen, Servants' Linen, lurked in the shadows beneath. There was not a free yard in any direction. You could tell the length of the human arm by the circular margins where at least a year of dust met at least a year of waxing.

The man gave Mary a sheaf of paper and a pen; he proffered an inkwell.

"Must I write standing?" Mary asked, dipping her pen.

"If it helps – by all means. Set down this: *Mrs. Pinchpenny says I may have a carriage and four the moment our fortunes are restored.*"

She scribbled away while he watched complacently. "Who is 'I'?" she asked.

"Who *am* I," he corrected. "I have no idea, but it hardly matters. Just do as you're told and you'll be away the quicker."

The woman interrupted, "Set down this, too: *Mr. Spendthrift will never restore our fortune!*"

"That's an opinion," the man snapped. "What you said was a promise. There is a difference between a promise and an opinion, but I'd hardly expect *you* to . . ."

Again the woman interrupted. "Set down that it is *my* opinion, that it is Parson Woddis's opinion, that Lady Snelling is of the same persuasion, that my father and mother . . ."

"Your father and mother!" he crowed scornfully. "Where, pray, did they learn it, ma'am? At the bottom of a bottle, I make no doubt!"

"Set that down, too," the woman said excitedly. "He traduced my father and mother. Omit none of this. You are my witness as well as his."

Mary scribbled furiously, thinking that the less she interrupted the sooner they would be done and the quicker she'd be taken back to the highway.

The argument raged on for ten minutes. He was, in turn, Mr. Neerdowell, Lord Lackleather, Master Puff, Squire Curry-Favour, the Laird of Windybreeks . . . while she became Mistress Snivel, Lady Whine, Millstone Moll, and Duchesse Despair. The burden of their quarrel was that they had once owned lands and money; he believed they would rise again, she was sure they would not. By way of proof she pointed to three dead orange trees, miniatures, of course, in tubs near one of the windows. "Can't deceive an orange tree," she said. "They know a gentleman's house, and they know the house of an impostor."

The joy of proving each other wrong – and having every word of it noted and signed by a witness – was all that now kept them alive. In some way the Duke of Bedford was instrumental in their loss. From the venom they heaped upon him Mary guessed that the poor man had actually tried to help them; at all events, he seemed to be their chief hope of a rise in the world.

All this Mary had to summarize and witness and date. Then, fearing she might never get away, she said casually, "With your permission, I'll put in a good word for you with his grace."

If she had fired a cannon she could not pave produced a greater effect.

"You!" the woman said with unbelieving scorn.

"Sure I know him quite well. Didn't he send me a note this very breakfast?" She drew forth the paper and waved it briefly before them – long enough for the crest, the date, and the informal signature to register.

The wife's demeanour changed at once. "Miles, my dearest," she said, all sudden sweetness. "You must hurry Miss Errmerr back to the highway as quick as you can. This could be the start of everything all over again! All over again!" As she spoke she wafted a hand toward the door, releasing her clutch on the blanket. It fell, to reveal that she was, in fact, naked as Eve. Nothing surprised Mary any more.

She passed her record of the matrimonial argument to the man, who read it carefully. "Pretty good," he said. "You've left out one or two things but I've forgotten them already myself."

He carried it into the next room, where, to Mary's great surprise, he opened the lid of an ornate coffin that spanned two low tables and placed it reverently within. His wife, blanketed once more, squeezed among the furniture and came to stand by Mary. "Blasphemy," she murmured, watching her husband closely.

"In what way?" Mary asked.

"He doesn't trust the Recording Angel. I'm sure it's a deadly sin, aren't you?"

A few minutes later Mary was hanging on for dear life behind Miles-my-dearest (the only genuine name she had for him) as he galloped back toward the main road. When they arrived and he set her down she could contain her curiosity no longer. "Why do you not trust the Recording Angel?" she asked.

He looked at her in surprise. "Do *you?*"

She shrugged. "I don't consider it my place either to trust or distrust that fellow."

"More fool you, then. Good day t'ye." He rode off as if his anger were the most righteous thing about him.

It was eight o'clock. She could have stayed in bed another hour and trusted the vade-mecum. Of Tottenham and Page there was still no sign.

She set her face northward and resumed her walk. Why, she wondered, did all those sweet and tender feelings of courtship wither when transplanted to the realms of matrimony? Why was rancour so plentiful in that land?

## CHAPTER TWENTY-FIVE

THAT DAY TURNED INTO one long sleepwalking nightmare for Mary. The muscles of her calves and thighs burned. Her ankles swelled and she had to loosen her laces; but that simply caused the bootleather to chafe, so she had to tighten them again. With the swelling came weakness; she had to watch her way with care, in case some small pebble or sunbaked wheel rut might twist her foot from under her. The fine weather turned overcast and oppressive, conjuring sweat out of the driest skin until the whole world longed for one good thunderstorm to clear the air.

Through sheer stubborn determination she kept up the required pace, arriving at Northampton just after noon and Market Harborough around five; she was well set to reach Leicester, her goal for the second night, by eight. She would then be just ninety-eight miles from London, with "only" eighty-four to go.

Every few hours, wherever there was a cooling stream in which to lave her tortured feet, she stopped for brief refreshment. To her companions it seemed impossible she could continue in this fashion. Lord Tottenham grew increasingly angry at her self-torment, her refusal to admit defeat. He promised to pay her the four hundred pounds himself if she'd but give up the contest.

She refused. "It's a matter of honour."

"Five hundred then."

Yet, as Tottenham grew more glacial, Page softened toward her, not into actual warmth but as far as a sort of wary admiration. He plainly did not like his aristocratic companion one bit. When Tottenham rode off and came back with an apple dipped in toffee for her, Page intercepted it and, declaring it would give her the colic, threw it to Lord Tottenham's horse instead. His lordship then had a monstrous fight to retrieve the sweetmeat before the creature could swallow it, complaining that the sugar would ruin its wind. And again at another resting place, when Tottenham brought her a tankard of ale from a nearby inn, Page, pretending to assist her, jostled the tankard and spilled some of its contents – and then he upset the rest of it in trying to mop up. From his truculent smile Mary saw it had been deliberate.

It was almost as if the two men were fighting over her, absurd as the notion might be. Certainly Page seemed unwilling to leave her in the unattended company of the other.

But as evening drew on and they reached Oadby, a few miles short of Leicester, Tottenham's horse had the misfortune to cast a shoe. He called out the smith, who then had to rekindle his shoeing forge; the business was quite obviously going to delay him half an hour at the least. He wanted Mary to stop for the night and depart an hour earlier the following morning but she refused and pressed on.

While the forge was yet in sight, Page hung back, as was his habit. But no sooner were they round the first bend than he came trotting up and drew level with her. "Will it distract you if I haul alongside for a while, Miss Flinders?" he asked.

She shook her head wearily. "I'm past distraction. I can think of one thing only – or three-in-one: a quart of ale, a baron of beef, and a mattress of goosedown."

There was no laugh of sympathy – no beating about the bush at all with him. "I must take this opportunity to caution you against Lord Tottenham," he said.

"Oh, really?"

"He is determined you shall lose this wager."

"Has he said as much?"

"His every action speaks it for him – surely you've noticed? Pray tell me, has he any cause to dislike his patron, the duke?"

Mary thought back to the evening the three of them had

met – that vague and veiled threat which Tottenham had managed to imply. "I don't know what may unite them, Mr. Page, nor what prompts his grace's patronage. I know he has demanded twenty thousand pounds for this Scotch place he has sold Lord Tottenham, but . . ."

"There you have it!" Page interrupted. "Tottenham has bet heavily against you – and thus against his grace, too – as a way, I suppose, of recouping that outlay." He frowned at her. "Keep walking, Miss! If I am the cause of your stopping, I must withdraw again."

She resumed her stride. "D'you mean . . . recoup *all* of it? Surely not?"

"Oh, I know Tottenham's not rich. But he has enormous expectations. All the Jews in town would fight for the privilege of lining his pockets. So he could place bets up to twenty thou' with no effort whatever."

There was the sound of a horseman behind. She glanced over her shoulder but it was not Tottenham. "You should be careful what you say about him," she told the young man. "He'll call you out. He's famous for it."

"Too famous!" Page laughed. "The days in which Tottenham may foist those tricks upon any gentleman in London are long past. Only gullible little pigeons from the country fall for it now. Indeed, young Pitman's the last of *them*, I dare swear. Tottenham's quite mad, you know."

After a pause, she said, "Even so, I'm sure you're mistaken. I can't believe he means me actual *harm*."

"Can't or don't wish to?"

She lengthened her stride. "You are impertinent, Mr. Page."

"He rose very early this morning – to be out on the road ahead of you. Some mischief that failed."

"He was out in the fields for a ride. In fact, I met him."

Page was unabashed. "Oh? An odd pastime for a man about to spend the whole day in the saddle! I supposed he might be out to divert fingerposts. I noticed the one in Wavendon was turned this morning."

"If such were his purpose, the village idiots had saved him the labour. I do not like this tittle-tattle Mr. Page. It is more worthy of the nursery than the world of gentility." As an afterthought she said, "But this explains your childish tricks with the toffee apple and the ale he brought me."

"We shall see," he replied evenly. "If at any time before we reach Manchester, your food should taste excessively of salt . . ." He let the rest hang.

"What then?"

"Then I am right." After a further pause, he added, "But I wonder if you will have the courage to tell me? Or will you merely swallow the mouthful and try not to pull a face?"

"This is absurd," she told him crossly. "You had better withdraw to your distance before Tottenham rejoins us."

Alone again, she pondered his warning. Circumstantially it hung together, and yet she could not credit that Tottenham would be so ignoble.

Page had not been there when Tottenham himself had seemed at death's door; Page had not glimpsed the mute plea in his eyes, which had said, "I need you." Page had not felt the grip of his hand. Page could not measure that particular lightning which passed between them whenever their eyes met. Tottenham might play Satan himself to the world at large – but never to her. She would not believe otherwise of him. He might slight her, even hurt her, but he'd never do her actual harm.

That second night they stopped at the Bell in Leicester; over supper she took pains to show that none of Page's poison had worked. In fact, she was now quite certain Page was playing his own devious game; he had more cause than Tottenham to wish her the loser.

Curiously, though, her beer *did* have an extremely salty taste.

Next morning she was again away before either of them, though Page's breakfast was carried up to him as she left. She glanced back at the inn and saw him watching her from his window; what poisonous tale was he plotting now? Tottenham's curtains were still drawn tight.

The day was a little easier. The weather continued overcast and heavy but the pain in her limbs responded almost at once to fresh exercise. It was as if they had ceased to be connected to her; she seemed to float upon their action rather than to cause it. The only sensation was the jarring of each step, which came to her through bone rather than flesh. She felt as if she could stick pins into her muscles without the slightest hurt.

It was a good hour before the two gentlemen caught up with her, upon the way through Mountsorrel, where startling hills of red granite rise to the forests of Charnwood and join the Derbyshire peaks. Here there were several punishing slopes, but the road always chose the gentlest of them and she learned to content herself with that.

Lord Tottenham, looking ghastly from his revels, told her she was mad and sinful to persist in this folly. Why would she not take his offer of five hundred pounds and rely on the fund that Page had proposed? She told him how honoured and pleased she was that he felt so solicitous of her wellbeing; she wished she might do something to ease the pain of his wounds – though he had made no complaint of it. Brusquely he reined about and rejoined Page at his customary station behind her.

At Cavendish Bridge she stopped to bathe her feet in the Trent and take a bite of food. Tottenham was still out of sorts so she tried to cheer him up. "Did you know," she said, "that sailcloth was not introduced into England until 1599?"

Tottenham gave a contemptuous snort. Page nodded toward the far bank. "That's Derbyshire over there."

"How many counties have I been in?" she asked Tottenham – who pretended not to hear.

Page listed them for her: "Middlesex, Herts, Bucks, Beds, Northants, Leicestershire . . . only Derbyshire and Cheshire to go!"

"Are we somewhere near Staffordshire? Did you know that salt mines were discovered there in 1670? I wonder who built them originally?"

"Why this fascination with history?"

She wished it were Tottenham, not Page, who was showing the interest. "Nothing," she explained. "It's just that I've reached the letter S in my *Amazing Tablet of Memory*. Sailcloth and salt . . . and . . . things." Her voice tailed off.

"On the subject of salt . . ." He smiled, leaving the rest of the sentence hanging.

She ignored him. Tottenham ignored her. But Page never for one moment ignored Tottenham.

The land hereabouts was so flat she made record time. The harvest was in full swing. Men with scythes bestrode the fields like giants, while strapping country girls, their arms crimsoned with stubble pricks, followed them and built the shocks.

She did not stop at Derby; indeed, her way in through St. Peters and out by Fryars Gate skirted the very edge of the town, which she traversed in under five minutes. A short way beyond, at Mackworth, the weather broke at last. Huge drops of warm rain fell in torrents. The baked mud refused to soak up the water, which lay in sheets across the highway, driving her to the uneven grass at the verge, where it was impossible to maintain her pace. At first she tried to shelter beneath her umbrella but the squalls plucked at it so fiercely she was impeded even further. The oilskin clothing turned into a sweat-box within minutes. Finally she threw it all back in the coach and accepted gratefully the stream of cleansing, cooling water from above.

But at Langley the clouds rolled by, leaving her in the glare of the full evening sun. Her sodden clothing became unbearably steamy and she had to stop the coach and change. For the next two hours the mixture of squally summer rain and broiling sunshine continued. She had to use the umbrella despite its inconvenience. And thus, by eight that evening, exactly in keeping with her timetable, she came to Ashbourne, at the heart of the beautiful Dovedale country. She was one hundred and forty miles from London, with forty-two to go. She had gained a two-hour advantage over her timetable, but there was hilly country ahead.

Once again they supped hugely and she went directly to her chamber. Shortly before midnight a monstrous thunderstorm passed across the county. High above the wind-tossed clouds there was almost continual sheet lightning, which produced a muted rumble like the traffic on London cobblestones, and an eery, flickering illumination in which the room was hardly ever dark. There was also fork lightning, whose brilliance hurt the eyes and whose deafening thunderclaps were almost instantaneous. They shook the very timbers of the inn and rattled the pitcher in the washbasin by the bed.

The air was so oppressive she had no covering but a linen sheet. She thrust her head beneath the pillow and tried to sleep again. The storm had awoken her from a particularly pleasant dream in which she had discovered that old fairy-tale standby, a pair of ten-league boots. The sensation of striding effortlessly from hilltop to hilltop was sweet beyond bearing.

But a huge clap of thunder, so close it must surely have taken off half the roof, suddenly made her sit bolt upright. In the silence that followed a voice said, "Be calm, little heart. Do not fret."

The voice was Tottenham's but the tenderness was not. The disjunction made her wonder whether she were awake or dreaming still. Then she turned and saw the man himself, seated at her bedside. She reached forward hesitantly and touched him, half fearful that her fingers would pass right through the image. But he was real enough. He was also fully clothed. She became aware of her nakedness and clutched the sheet about her.

In that same infinitely tender voice he said, "No."

Just the one word.

For some reason it calmed all her fears, so that when he reached forward and with the tip of his finger hooked the sheet from her grasp, she let it fall, let him look where he would.

Not all the illumination in the room came from the lightning; he had brought a candle with him. It stood on the floor beside the chair in which he sat. He stooped and picked it up, placing it between them, on the low bedside table. His eyes were embers in that dark. His face, starkly lit from beneath by the warm light but with its shadows continually overlaid in the cold electric brilliance from beyond, flickered strangely between humanity and sculpture, hot and cool, satanic and saintly.

Her own mood, too, hovered uncertainly between apprehension and joy. She sat there, fleshed in the warm rays of his candle, marbled by the light from heaven, and awaited his pleasure.

For long moments he stared at her, until her exhausted muscles rebelled and she fell back upon the pillow. Then he reached forward and touched her shoulder, massaged it gently with his fingertips. The most delicious sensations ran through her body; she longed for him to touch her breast like that, even moved herself halfway to make it happen. But his hand moved with her. "You are like no other woman in the world," he said.

His gentle voice was drowned in a thunderclap, yet somehow she heard every syllable.

"Why are you so tender with me when we are alone – and so beastly in company?"

"Am I?"

"You know you are."

He lowered his eyes. "I'm ashamed of my feelings."

She thought of telling him he should be more ashamed of his behaviour but some female instinct forbade it, made her put her hands behind her head, made her ask instead, "How does shame enter into it?"

He looked briefly at her and then away, even more decisively. "Not ashamed," he whispered. "Frightened."

"Frightened!" Astonishment sprang from her pose.

"Don't you understand?"

She shook her head.

He gave a hollow laugh. "Love is no freedom. I fear your tyranny."

She lay half-up on one elbow, leaning toward him. "But I am not in the least bit tyrannical."

"Not you, but your body." He shook his head angrily. "Not your body! Your *person*. Your very being. Your existence."

"This is all imagination . . ."

"No!" He smashed a fist into an open palm. Then, taking a grip on himself, he peered into her eyes and asked, "Is there no one in your life – has there never been anyone – of whom you think with rage, and yet cannot help *but* think? One whose image rises in your mind's eye and prompts your mind's talons to rend it to a shambles?"

His gaze seemed to pierce her; she looked away.

He said, "I see that there is. Now perhaps you understand why I fear to yield to you?"

She gave a single ironic laugh. "*You* yield to *me!*"

He leaned forward and raised the sheet to cover her. "Oh, I know you would yield to me. And I know what you would yield: everything but your heart."

Angrily she threw the sheet off again, this time to her knees. "Words! All you know is words!"

"But if you would yield your heart . . ."

"Yes?"

"Then, by way of token, yield me this race."

"You mean lose it deliberately?"

He nodded and rose, taking up the candle. "Then and only then shall I know I may safely risk myself with you."

She reached forward and caught his sleeve. "One kiss before you go?" she begged.

He shook his head. His smile was the smile of a more familiar Lord Tottenham. There were two more storms that night. Between them and her tears she enjoyed little sleep.

# CHAPTER TWENTY-SIX

SHE WAS AN HOUR LATE the following morning, though, alas, she did not realize it until she reached Buxton, where the Assembly Room clock struck noon as she passed. Old Q's clock, by contrast, stood at the quarter after eleven. This travelling timepiece had until then been so reliable that at first she supposed the Buxton clock to be fast; but Page soon disabused her of the idea. His chronometer, which he had set to the second when they left London, showed that it was, in fact, a quarter *past* midday. The Buxton clock was fifteen minutes behind the hour at London Bridge.

"You might have woken me," she grumbled, though she knew the rules forbade it. "One of you could have had a fit of sneezes outside my door."

This discovery so angered her that she mistakenly took the Tidewell road out of town instead of the planned route through Shallcross. By the time she discovered the error her two-hour advantage had been lost; indeed, it cost her a further hour to regain the right way, which led back through Buxton, where the clock read ten past three. She ought by now to be halfway to Stockport. The omens were not good.

At four, on the steep hill that winds up to Fernilee, she came within an ace of twisting her ankle. Some swift instinct caught her in the nick of disaster and made her accept the fall. Her elbow took the brunt of it – and a most painful brunt it was. But at least her ankle had suffered no more than a twinge of discomfort. Her eyes met Tottenham's; he no longer pleaded – he challenged.

As she stood at the top, gathering her breath, she looked back the way she had come and saw a fine coach just about to begin the ascent.

"Here comes Old Q or I'm a Dutchman," Lord Tottenham said.

It was indeed the duke – and Colonel Elliott and Mr. Darberry, too. Both gentlemen were grinning hugely, but Old Q's face was dark as thunder. "How now, Miss Flinders!" he cried as they drew near. "We had hoped to pass you out at Stockport."

"Speak for yourself, Duke!" the colonel said happily as they came to a halt. "I'm pleased enough to find her here."

"Your grace's clock let me down," Mary tried to explain.

"Twiddle-twaddle!" he shouted. "That old timekeeper will go a year for the loss of half a minute." He consulted his carriage clock and brightened. "Still – if you take no sleep, you have the best part of fifteen and a half hours ahead of you. Even at one mile an hour you should manage it."

Everyone looked at her, expecting her assurance that it would be no difficulty. She wondered why the words stuck in her throat. It was more than mere anger at his behaviour; had part of her already decided to give Lord Tottenham the proof he sought? She glanced at him. He had noted her silence and was delighted, though he took care to conceal it from his patron.

The duke grew angry again. "Well, I had thought to offer you some alfresco refreshment, Miss Flinders, but, seeing your condition, I think we'll drive on." He nodded to his coachman, who stirred up the four greys to a smart trot.

As they receded the duke turned and shouted, "If you're not there by eight tomorrow morning, young woman, then find some mountain path where this coach cannot pursue you!"

Furious, Mary sat upon a milestone, folded her arms, and stared at the hills all round.

Silence returned, broken only by the liquid chatter of a skylark.

"The arrogance!" she said.

Page laughed.

She turned on him. "Yes, I did not look to you for any feeling, sir."

"Quite the contrary, Miss Flinders," he replied. "I laughed for delight at the sheer innocence of your outburst. Surely you realize that, by ducal standards, Old Q is the soul of good nature? Does your *Amazing Tablet of Memory* not mention the Proud Duke of Somerset?"

She tossed her head angrily and said, "Probably!" – unwilling to admit that her book might omit any fact in the entire history of the world.

"When the Proud Duke rode down to Petworth, he sent riders ahead to clear the fields and lanes of common men, so that no mere peasant eye should gaze upon his glory. In his own house the servants had to turn and face the wall if he walked by."

Tottenham, seeing how Mary's curiosity was piqued by these revelations – and seeing her anger begin to dissipate – interrupted. "You'd best step lively," he said. "You'll only enrage the duke to no good purpose."

"Oh!" she cried, looking him directly in the eye. "If I had *purpose!*"

"What then?" he asked.

"Then you should see what you would see." She rose, infinitely weary, and resumed her torture. A short while later, Tottenham remembered some business he wished to discuss with the duke and rode off after him.

No sooner had he vanished over the lip of the hill than Page said, "I don't suppose that fellow could have gained access to the clock Old Q lent you?"

"If he had the opportunity, then so did you," she rejoined tartly.

"Are you taking your fill of salt?" he asked.

"What is this obsession with salt, Mr. Page?"

"Yes, perhaps it is time I explained: On our second day, when he went to fetch you that ale – the tankard I deliberately spilled, you recall? – he had hardly gone within when he returned and took a snuffbox from his saddle pouch."

"But he doesn't take snuff."

"Exactly, miss. A palpable hit, egad! What's more, this so-called 'snuff,' far from being black or brown, bore the strongest resemblance to the whiting ladies use upon their complexions. So I later took the liberty of exchanging it for salt. Now may I repeat my question?"

She kept silent. There had to be an innocent explanation.

"You answer me nonetheless," he said complacently as he halted the carriage to let her draw ahead.

Surely Tottenham would never do anything to harm her?

A few miles farther on, where the road wound down into the valley once more, she had an encounter that brought her speculation to an end – both in the immediate sense that it set her life in danger, and, more generally, in that it put Tottenham's character beyond all reasonable doubt. For there, just before the crossroads at Whaley Bridge, she encountered a stray bull.

It was a Leicester Longhorn, one of the fiercest breeds. A glance through the hedgerow at the empty field showed it had not been running with cows, otherwise it might even so have been docile. It stood in the middle of the road, about a hundred and fifty yards away, and waited, head low. She looked behind her but Page was not yet in view.

Running was the worst thing she might do. In any case, there was nowhere to run. The hedges were too high to leap and too dense to scramble through. About fifty yards ahead there was a gap among the thorns. With a little luck, if she did nothing to antagonize it meanwhile, she might reach the spot and hurl herself to safety. She was surprised at how little fear – how little anything – she felt. These last days, and especially the night just gone, had drained her of emotion.

When there remained but twenty yards she suddenly heard the thunder of the carriage behind her. Page had seen the situation and had whipped his horse to a runaway gallop. "Way!" he yelled. "Give way!"

She leaped for the verge just in time as the carriage thundered by. Page was standing on the driving board, brandishing a pistol; she glimpsed a second, tucked in his belt. The bull snorted, tossed its horns, pawed the dust. She waited for the shots, but none came; he was trying to get as close as possible before he risked his aim.

At last the bull charged. A shot rang out but by then it was too late. The horse panicked and shied to one side; the bullet must have gone wide. Those wicked horns caught the horse in the neck and shoulder, lifting it bodily off the ground. Its scream was almost human.

The carriage, impelled onward by its own momentum, was

twisted like a plaything. It did not simply spill its occupant upon the road, it dashed him. Mary's stout traveller's trunk saved his life for it rolled until it settled immediately before him; thus when the vehicle broke from its shafts, shattered its axle, and went spinning sideways, over and over down the road, the trunk took the force of the crash, and the next rebound of the splintered vehicle scored the road a full two yards beyond him. She waited for him to move but he lay there, apparently dead.

By now the bull had extricated itself from the horse, which struggled in the throes of death. By chance, its flying hooves dealt the bull a mighty blow on the shoulder. It gave out one vast bellow of pain and turned upon the horse. It was a contest between brute stupidity and the random tremors of death. Kicks that would have killed a man were traded for a goring that would have finished off an elephant. At the end of it the horse lay almost in two, still twitching.

The bull pawed and tossed his horns for a long time before it seemed ready to acknowledge its victory. Yet, by that paradox which attends all violence, victory was itself a defeat – for the bloodlust aroused by those last, pathetic twitchings of life was immediately cheated by the peace of death.

Then her blood curdled. Page, stirring in his unconsciousness, caught the creature's attention. It gave a strange, gurgling cough and made a lunge up the bank from the ditch toward the road.

There was no time for thought; she could easily have leaped through the gap by now but she could not abandon the unconscious young man. Boldly she stepped out into the highway and shouted at the bull: "Shoo!" Even at the time, when those insane eyes turned and fixed themselves upon her, it had a comic aspect.

Page had carried a brace of pistols, yet she had heard but one shot. It was her only chance to save him – to find that second pistol and finish off the bull – she who had never fired a weapon in her life!

The bull was still undecided between her and the body on the ground. Committed now, she walked toward it, crying "Ghittaaaaan!" and "Heooooouw!" as if herding cows at home. It unnerved the bull. Then suddenly she had the inspiration to open and close her umbrella as she advanced.

The creature had never seen anything like it. Once or twice it tossed its horns experimentally in reply but she held her course and went on pumping the umbrella for all she was worth.

It pawed menacingly at the ground and twitched its tail. And, incredibly, it backed away!

Still she came on. By now there was an iron band closing around her chest. Her vision narrowed to one tunnel of light with the bull at its centre; around the edge flew a writhing of darkness — the oblivion impatient to claim her.

The animal gave out a bellow, but the end of it was strangled in another gurgle. It was an utterly *un*bovine sound; even the bull was startled by it.

She had at first intended to edge past the monster, keeping her panting umbrella between them, but now some instinct told her to go on walking directly at it — an instinct encouraged by the glint of uncertainty in its eye and the continuing backward steps.

Now all her vision had dwindled, beyond mere blackness, to that small central universe where stood the bull. Even her own body seemed to evaporate into the void. The pointed tip of her umbrella touched its nose. She prodded sharply and opened it with all the ferocity at her command.

With a movement she had never seen before, except in young lambs or puppies at play, it gave a frolicsome backward leap; a ton or more of muscle being frolicsome is a rival to Poseidon and she felt the ground shudder beneath the onslaught.

She risked one more prod but then a shout of, "Miss Flinders!" distracted her.

She turned. Page had regained his wits and was leaning on one elbow, a pistol — the undischarged pistol, she hoped — in his free hand. But it was quivering like an aspen.

"Fire!" she yelled desperately.

The bull, no longer perplexed by the umbrella, took its chance and lunged toward her but it slipped in the soft mud of the verge and fell to its knees. At last she had the wit to turn and run. Why did Page not shoot?

She made it to the other verge before the bull reached the highway. There, in mud no firmer than that which had gained her those vital seconds, she fell and lost them — lost everything. She lay there, watching the bull size her up, knowing these must be the last moments of her life.

Almost arrogantly it began to walk toward her.

*Matt!* The word popped into her mind. There was no image of him there, nor thought of him either. Just the name — the enormous comfort of his name.

When the bull was halfway across the road Page fired. She saw the dust fly as the bullet bounced harmlessly between its legs. She stared at it calmly, quite ready to die.

Yet the bull had ceased to move. It turned its face aside, almost as if it had forgotten why it was here at all. Suddenly, as if an invisible poleaxe had fallen from the sky, it keeled over and died. Actually, it did not so much keel over as forward. The very tip of its horn came to rest on Mary's right foot — with a hundred pounds of dead bone and muscle behind it.

The worst thing was not the pain — there was curiously little of that — but the certain knowledge that, as far as the wager was concerned, Manchester might as well be on the far side of the moon.

## CHAPTER TWENTY-SEVEN

PAGE'S SHADOW FELL across her. "But I missed!" His voice was all bewilderment.

Mary was shivering like a moth, but whether from delayed fear or from a pain that she had yet to feel she could not say. She tried to extract her foot from beneath the dead bull's horn but found it too heavy. In fact, it required all the young ensign's strength to lift the head. Its one wild, skyward eye was full of disbelief. Flies began to settle.

"Would you kindly unlace my boot?" she asked when her foot was free. Her voice fluttered all over the scale.

His eyes were filled with admiration. "I never thought to see the like of that!"

"Careful!" There was a stab of pain in her ankle.

As gingerly as he could, tweaking the lace an inch at a time, he continued to work at her boot. "What ever possessed you?"

"I couldn't see any other way. When he'd slaughtered the horse he was going to murder you. It's all right. You can go a little harder."

But he stopped altogether. "You mean you did it to save me?"

She nodded. "I know there's little love lost between . . ."

"You . . . and a *parasol*, against this leviathan! But . . . Jove! That was certain death."

"It was not," she said stoutly and then winced at a twinge from her ankle. "I had him flummoxed until you called out."

"And then? What were you going to do then?"

"Edge over to where you lay and try to find the other pistol. I only heard the one shot."

"Well, by heavens, Miss Flinders – one platoon like you and England would need no army."

"England has whole *regiments* like me, Mr. Page. Isn't Ireland your army's nursery?"

His nod conceded the point. "I think the creature took one look at you and yielded up the ghost. My bullet certainly went wide."

"The second one, yes. But I believe your first shot got him. 'Twas only the rage and madness kept him going. Would you just give a little hint of a tug at my heel there?"

She gritted her teeth against the expected pain but none came. "A bit more," she told him. "God, I think we're in luck."

"Luck you call it!" Slowly he removed her boot.

Her ankle was swollen like a bladder. After various experiments they established that a pull on the heel – as when taking off her boots – caused only slight discomfort. Pressure in the other direction was mildly painful. Worst of all was a sideways touch against the ankle.

"That means it's not broken," she said.

He asked, "D'you know about these things?"

"No. I've just decided it from personal experience. Lord, but I'm thirsty suddenly."

He rooted among their scattered effects and found the canteen undamaged. "A real battlefield scene, what!" he said as he held it to her lips.

The cool, grateful water eased her trembling and left her

feeling more than half-recovered. Perhaps this wasn't the disaster it had seemed.

At that moment a couple of field lads came running up. Page sent them on into Whaley Bridge to call out a doctor and rent a hack and chaise.

"Let's not be hasty," Mary told him.

"You need have no worries about the wager, Miss Flinders. In circumstances like these it'll either be washed out or it'll be judged on the time and distance covered. And as for you, well, when word of this gets about, a subscription in town will raise a thousand overnight, I make no doubt. If I possessed as much, I'd put it up myself."

A farmer came galloping down the road. "Is anyone hurted?" he cried. "I'll have you know that bull cost me a hundred guineas." At the sight of the creature he started to wail, not very convincingly.

While he and Page argued points of law and custom, Mary struggled to her feet. She could just about bear the pain of hobbling on tiptoe, at least as far as the wreckage of the carriage. The smashed shaft looked just the sort of thing she needed – almost six feet long and with the iron hitching eye in firm wood a foot or so below its splintered end. Most of the traces were still on the mangled corpse of the horse but a few straps lay among the debris. From them she fashioned a couple of loops, one for her armpit, one for her hand – turning the whole into a sort of crutch.

"What madness is this!" Page broke off his argument and came over to her.

"There's a petticoat in the top of my trunk, if you'd be so kind?"

"You're surely not thinking of continuing?"

"We've still not settled who's going to compensate me," the farmer pointed out.

"There'll be no need for your adjudications and subscriptions," she told Page. "I'm not having all the labour of those days past just 'washed out' by your committees. So are you going to get that petticoat or must I complain you hindered me?"

He gave a hopeless shrug and went over to her trunk.

She smiled at the farmer. "It's not so bad."

"Bad? It's a bloody disaster – my prize bull shot to death on the king's highway . . ."

"He died of a broken heart," she told him.

With the petticoat to cushion the edges of the straps she fashioned an adequate crutch. She borrowed a knife from Page and hacked off the leather side to her boot where it would touch her bruised ankle. Then she pulled it on, but laced only the first three holes. A few experimental steps satisfied her that the crutch could take sufficient pressure off the joint to enable her to continue the remaining sixteen miles to Manchester. It was then ten past five; she had just under fifteen hours in which to do it.

"Why?" Page asked her despairingly.

"Because no one – no one – should be permitted to succeed by such means as that." She nodded toward the bull.

For a moment he was puzzled. Then, aghast, he said, "Tottenham?"

"Do you doubt it?"

He gave out a whistle and his eyebrows rose yet higher. "Not now that you say it. Yet I'm astounded it's *you* who . . ."

"Well, there's no time for that now," she cut him off before he could make more of it.

He became businesslike again. "If you do resume the walk and lose it, there'll be no going back and adjudicating from this position, you realize? Once you walk down that road in earnest, the race is on again and all the original conditions apply."

"Then I'm already wasting precious time." She left him to continue the negotiations with the farmer, hire a new coach, and arrange for the debris to be cleared. In Whaley Bridge she met the doctor, who looked at her ankle and said it should be "set in plaister."

"Is it broken?" she asked.

He hesitated and then said, "Yes." But she could see he was guessing.

"I'll have it set at Manchester, so," she agreed.

He shook his head at her folly.

At the edge of the village she saw a carpenter easing a window sash. For sixpence he trimmed the broken end of the shaft and mortised in a crosspiece; he also put a dowel lower down, where her hand could grip it. The trick with the leather strap and rolled-up petticoat had not really worked.

It lost her half an hour but she reckoned it worth it. Now, with the properly fashioned crutch, she noted the sixteenth milestone to Manchester, and the length of its shadow, and set off at the briskest pace she thought she might be able to sustain. By her reckoning, and by the sun, she took just over half an hour to reach the fifteenth milestone.

Two miles an hour . . . say, eight hours to go . . . she'd be in Piccadilly with five or six hours to spare. She decided then to vary her route, just in case Tottenham got word of her continuing the race and came back. He must now be so desperate he'd do anything to stop her.

Page caught up with her at a nameless little hamlet just before Disley. She explained her intention, with which he at once agreed. Her vade-mecum directed her through Hazel Grove and Stockport, a road that veered from west to north. If she could find an alternative road, one that went north first and then turned west, it might prove no greater in distance. She sought the advice of an old woman sitting in a doorway peeling medlars. The crone replied she knew of *no* road to Manchester, had never been there in her life, had no desire to go there, thought Manchester people the scum of the earth, and had no great opinion of anyone who sought their society.

An elderly man standing behind her in a torn smock silently pointed out the road they sought and gave her a warm, reassuring nod.

"And you're no gentleman," the woman called after Page. "Leaving a poor cripple girl like that to walk!"

By repeated asking of the way they negotiated the lanes around Marple and onward to Comstall and Romilley without mishap. There, it being eight of the evening, they paused for supper at a likely looking inn. The landlord ran his eye over her original vade-mecum and quickly furnished her with a substitute – minus the tourist gloss on gentlemen's houses. It led, as she hoped, northward by Bredbury and Denton, where it turned and ran west for two or three miles before it rejoined her original road on the very outskirts of Manchester, at Ardwick Green.

All would have gone well if they had not met a know-all on the winding, hilly road into the country – why didn't she take the next lane to her left and follow it down across the valley of the Tame to Reddish and there ask her way to Gorton, which was but a mile or two from Ardwick Green? It would cut five or six miles off her proposed walk. She thanked him and accepted the advice. The pain in her ankle was becoming continuous.

By daylight they could no doubt have done it, but as night fell they came to a junction of no fewer than six lanes at the very bottom of the valley. They realized they were lost.

"This must be Rome," she said.

"Shall I unhitch the mare and ride on?" Page suggested.

"Even if you found the way, would you be sure of returning to this place again in the dark?"

"What about going back and sticking to the main road?"

"We've lost too much time already. Could *you* retrace our steps with absolute assurance in this blackness? I think our only course is to wait here and ask the first passer-by."

He agreed gloomily. "Except that we might wait a month in a place like this. The weeds are knee high."

"Have you a flint? We could at least light one of the gig lamps."

After a great deal of trouble he got the lamp going. By the light of it she checked her clock against his chronometer and set the alarum for five the following morning. "And that's to assume no one comes by and that we're no more than ten miles from Piccadilly," she commented.

He unhitched the horse and left it hobbled to graze the hedge-row and verges. When he returned he found her spreading a blanket beneath the coach. "We'll be out of the rain there," she told him.

"We?" He was shocked.

"Who else?"

"But see here . . . I mean, I could not possibly pass the night alone with you."

"Don't you think that's for me to say?" She held the lamp up between them. "Which of us isn't to be trusted?"

"That's hardly the point," he said stiffly. "I shall sleep in one of the fields over there."

"Is that wise?" she asked. "If any passer-by attacks you, I and my umbrella shan't be on hand to give you our protection."

He laughed, much against his will. "Well," he conceded. "No one must ever hear of it. I shall kindle a fire and sit up till dawn."

She lay beneath the carriage, snug under the coachman's coat her brother had given her. He sat by the fire, feeding it with sticks as it died. They talked far into the night – of their childhood, their homes and family, of life . . . their hopes . . . the future.

A shower of rain passed over. "Do come in under here," she told him.

But he would not.

"This honour is a strange commodity," she mused. "Those who should possess it in the greatest measure – I mean our dukes and lords – seem as foreign to it as baboons. Yet here's a plain mister all set to catch a chill from a positive surfeit of the same!"

She thought he might laugh at the jibe but he looked at her sharply and said, "So you have little opinion of our *betters*, Miss Flinders?"

"Bettors is all they are!"

Even at that he did not laugh. There was a deep bitterness in his tone as he said, "Our aristocracy has cast its nobility into pawn these many years. They can think of nothing but gold, place, pride, gold, self-aggrandisement, frivolity, and gold."

The vehemence of his outburst took her by surprise. But the effect on him was as if he had confessed a great burden off his conscience. He relaxed at last and added with a chuckle, "Still – let them enjoy it while they may. 'Twill not endure much longer."

"What may you mean by that?"

"Can you not feel it yourself, Miss Flinders – the twin cankers of crime and disaffection that are eating out the heart of Old England? The mob rules everywhere. The common people go cheated of their most elementary needs – why, there is a bread riot somewhere or other almost daily. It surely cannot be long before, like our kinsfolk in America, we rise and throw off these ancient yokes of privilege and despotism?"

"And you an officer!" she said, amazed.

He smiled. "You suppose that casts me among them?"

"Are there many who feel like you?"

He became wary. "Never mind that. Perhaps you disagree?"

"A month since, I most surely would have. But what I've seen those recent days – seen and heard – and found myself compelled to endure and connive at . . . I cannot *but* agree. Oh, I have doubled my few years since I set foot in Holyhead, Mr. Page."

It came on to rain in earnest.

He stuck it out manfully beneath her umbrella but eddies of wind still carried the raindrops to him; then he heeded her twentieth entreaty to stop being such a stiff-necked eejit and come in where it was dry. Even so he bumped his head in trying to remain seated upright. She persuaded him to lie on the blanket beside her. He placed his sword between them and lay there shivering. Angered at his stupidity, she pushed the sword aside and rearranged the greatcoat to cover them both.

"Just because of my republican sentiments," he explained, "I should not want you to think me incapable of acting the gentleman."

She laughed. " 'When Adam delved and Eve span – who was then the gentleman?' Oh hard – I must get some sleep. I'm worn to a ravelling."

"Be assured you are safe with me," he told her.

His insistence upon his own chastity was becoming quite as alarming as his silence on it might have been. "Of course I'm safe," she answered soothingly. "That business of growing up I mentioned just now? Well, Mr. Page, I achieved half of it in your good company, so doesn't that make us like brother and sister?"

He turned to her then and kissed her on the cheek. "Oh, Miss Flinders, in me you have the most devoted brother, until the day I die."

Then not even the ache in her ankle could keep her from sleep.

When the alarum rang next morning he was gone – but only as far as the Tame, where he was shaving by the light of the dawn. The river meandered three miles for every one it progressed; she found a nearby bank where she could perform her ablutions in privacy. Mercifully, her ankle had stopped aching. She thought the swelling had gone down, too. When Page saw it he agreed.

"You were up early," she told him.

"A trick one learns on Tower Guard. You're pretty cool, Miss Flinders. I supposed you'd be off at once."

"A trick one learns upon life's highway, Mr. Page. A half-hour at a good table is worth five upon the road."

They breakfasted on the last of the cold pie and conserves she had been given by the good citizens of Dunstable – it seemed like weeks ago. Most of that food had been handed out to beggars upon the way, of whom, as Page had said last night, there were plenty.

"Well, little brother," she joked, rising to begin the final stages of her walk, "I think that must be my road." It was, in fact, the only one of the six lanes that reached the top of the hill to their west, even though its immediate direction from the grand junction she had dubbed "Rome" was, in fact, northeasterly. "You'll catch the horse and follow on?"

His hug was more than brotherly, though he called her "little sister," after the jesting fashion she had set.

"I'll take the clock," she told him. "Just in case. I believe I've plenty of time but one never knows." She set the alarum for the hour of eight.

"Wouldn't you set it for a quarter-to?" he asked.

"And give myself fifteen minutes of purgatory?"

He shrugged, not quite accepting her logic. Then he brightened. "Talking of purgatory, the duke must be out of his mind with worry."

They parted on a republican laugh.

There was no one about but she kept the sun at her back and set her course north by west; and so, by lane and bridleway, shepherd's path and crooked stile, she limped her slow and painful progress to Gorton. There a man driving a herd of dairy cows told her it was a straight road to Ardwick Green.

She asked how far it might be.

He thought it little above two miles.

And from Ardwick Green to Piccadilly?

That could not be above a mile.

She looked at her clock and her heart sank. It was five past seven. Even if the man's estimates were accurate, she could hardly cover three miles in less than an hour; and if he were out in his reckoning, by as little as half a mile, she had no hope at all. She set off as if the Earl of Hell were at her one good heel.

Those last miles were worse than the whole journey put together. The sweat poured from her, partly induced by her exertions, partly by the pain – for she was now reckless of anything beyond the need to win.

Poplar Grove farm came and went; now her only landmark was what she took to be – *hoped* to be – the steeple of the church at Ardwick Green. As she drew near, her clock told her she had fifteen minutes to go.

A mile in fifteen minutes? It was impossible.

At the green itself some kind of fair seemed to be in progress. Her way was barred by a large crowd, all with their backs to her, watching a procession – at least, she assumed there must be a procession for she could not see one inch of road.

"Let me pass, please," she called out, frantic at even a moment's delay.

No one paid her the slightest heed.

"Please!" she almost screamed.

A woman turned round, looked her up and down, and said, "You're not the only cripple in the world."

"I'm not a cripple at all!" Mary yelled at her. "I have a wager to get to Piccadilly by eight."

The woman laughed harshly. "Then you're in quite the fashion!"

"But you don't understand," Mary pleaded.

"What's your name?" a man asked.

"Mary Flinders. For the love of Christ . . .!"

"Anyone can say that – just to get a place in front," another woman commented. "Mary Flinders is coming through Stockport, as all the world knows."

She could not believe it – all these folk were waiting to see her pass by! Inspiration struck. "Will you look at this!" she shouted, holding forth the duke's clock with its unmistakable Q surmounted by a ducal coronet. "This is the clock his grace gave me to time the race by. I am Mary Flinders! If you do not let me through, I shall tell him of your obstruction and . . ."

But they were already parting, shouting, "Way there! Make way! 'Tis Pic-to-Pic Moll."

"You've come by the wrong road," one of the men told her reproachfully as she squeezed by. He pointed at her crippled foot. "*And* you've gone and lost the race. That's all about it."

"At least I'll not die of sympathy," she snapped back.

But when she gained the highway a great roar went up and she found a clear way before her. She looked at her clock. Ten minutes left! It really was hopeless.

Down Ardwick street she hobbled, to the bridge over the Medlock, then up the slope to Bank Top and down again to a little brook. All the way they cheered her: "Go it, lass! Thou can do it yet!" Children skipped and danced at her side. She'd have given all her winnings just to swap ankles with one of them for the next five minutes; the money mattered nothing to her now. It was just to win, to get there before the minute-hand sliced off the hour.

"How far to Piccadilly?" she panted.

They all answered at once and she heard nothing. The world was beginning to swim around her.

"Is that it yonder?" Unthinkingly she raised the crutch to point at the rise ahead. Her ankle could not take her weight and she went bowling in the dust.

A man came out to help her but she screamed at him to leave her be; she had to complete the walk without assistance. He handed her the clock and said, "Only half a mile, luv."

She glanced at the time – two minutes to go. The fastest runner in the world might just manage it.

And yet the people cheered. "Go on, go on, go on!"

Perhaps there was some point to it: If the race were indeed lost, then there was honour in losing by ten minutes rather than fifty – which was the pace her tortured body would now prefer.

At the bend in the road, just a furlong ahead, she saw a streak of white across the paving. It must be the finishing line, the entrance to Piccadilly. The road there was full of gentlemen, all jumping up and down like children and cheering her on. All but one, and that was Tottenham. He stood there, calm, aloof, certain she would cheat Old Q at the last.

And then her alarum clock rang.

The race was lost.

She stopped and leaned upon her crutch, closing her eyes with relief. Let Tottenham believe what he wished. No need for further struggle.

But the crowd pressed around and screamed at her to go on. How *could* she give up now and fie on her and shame on her . . .

She surrendered her will to theirs. On wave after wave of their idiotic cheers she let herself be carried forward, up the alpine slope of Shooters Brow, on, on, on . . . toward that wall of gentry, that infinitely distant white line. Far beneath her, way down there among the horsedung and rubbish, one boot filled with lead followed another filled with fire, and somehow, though she had lost all sense of connection with those distant parts of her, she was enabled to lurch forward one more pace.

"Left!" cried the crowd, and "Right!" and "Left!" and "Right!"

They took their time from her – about a pace every two seconds. Somewhere in the distance a rifle band was playing an impossible march.

Among the faces ahead she was now able to make out others that she knew the duke . . . Mr. Page . . .

Mr. Page?

How could that be?

He must have gone about and come ahead of her while she was crossing the fields at . . . names deserted her.

Where was she? What town was that?

Why was she stumbling down the road like this?

Oh look! The Duke of Bridgewater!

No! The other one.

Bedford?

No – Thing. The Duke of Thing!

She couldn't find him. All the faces were foreign. Faces in dreams. This must all be a dream.

She'd wake up in a moment and find the bull's horns piercing her heart . . .

At last she saw the white tape beneath her and she collapsed upon it.

But it took about ten minutes to fall and during that time her lucidity returned.

She remembered the wagers and Hyde Park and Lord Tottenham at St. Albans and an idiotic quarrel between a man and his wife and the thunderstorm and lightning and salty ale and the clock in Buxton and the duke's anger and her own and the bull and Mr. Page sitting stubbornly in the rain and . . .

And above all she remembered she had lost the duke's wager.

## CHAPTER TWENTY-EIGHT

THE MOB WAS HUSHED to silence. Was the girl dying? Was she dead? Had her indomitable will overplayed that valiant heart? Old Q, lips trembling, bent low and listened.

"She breathes!" he said.

The murmur ran through the company. "She breathes! She lives!" But still the silence hung upon them.

And then the bells! First, from far-off Oxford Street, St. Peter sang out in high tenor: One . . . two . . . three . . . St. Paul, a moderate baritone, answered him from Turner Square: . . . two . . . three . . . four . . . Nearer still and hurrying to catch up, St. James joined in his descant: . . . four . . . five . . . six . . . Then booming over all, the stolid, basso chimes of the infirmary clock, not a hundred yards away: . . . six . . . seven . . . *eight*! For all their lack of synchrony, their theme was one grand unison: The hour was eight of the clock.

Again the crowd went wild: She lived. She breathed. And she had beat the clock!

Mary came round as they were lifting her onto the litter. The first thing she saw was Old Q – and, immediately over his shoulder, hanging above the pawnbroker's on the corner of Chatham Street, a clock with its hands coming up to eight.

The duke, seeing her look of impossible hope, followed her eye. He turned back, shaking his head sadly. "Ah my poor child, it is slow, I fear. You have failed me."

But everyone else laughed and grinned at her and patted her arm until she was forced to conclude that somehow, by some magic yet to be explained, she had won.

"Your grace's clock . . ." she began.

". . . was accurate," he cut in, still with that doleful accusation; but then, unable to maintain the jest a moment longer, he burst out laughing and said, " 'Twas accurate to *London* time!"

"London time . . .?"

". . . is twelve minutes in advance of Manchester – being the more easterly. In short – *I* have won, Miss Flinders! You walked it inside four days and I have won!"

"And Lord Tottenham? Where is he?"

The duke's face darkened. "The devil take him!"

"But he was here." Her eyes fell on Mr. Page, who was shaking his head. "I just wanted to see his face." The world trembled all about her; the motion of the litter was giddying. She lay back and closed her eyes, all cares banished. Moments later she was asleep once more.

Old Q had arranged for them to stay with Mr. Brian Trueman of Hart Hill; Trueman was a crony of his youth, in the days before he inherited the dukedom, when he had been Earl of March and Ruglen. Mary was sleepily introduced to him as they bore her indoors but had no memory of it when she awoke full twenty-four hours later. Her ankle was now a peacock blue and twice its customary size, but the surgeon said it was naught but a bad bruise and all it needed was strapping.

She was the queen bee in that house. All week long, and all the following week, too, there were dinners and supper-balls in her honour; the entire quality of Lancashire was eager to meet Pic-to-Pic Moll and congratulate her on having restored the family fortunes. She was reluctant to say that she hadn't as yet enjoyed the sniff of a single guinea; everyone assumed the duke had rewarded her handsomely – for handsome indeed had been his own profit.

He had made fifteen hundred clear on his various wagers, even after allowance for the promised four hundred to her; Trueman had made a hundred and fifty. Tottenham had made five hundred on his open bets, but rumour said he had lost a great deal more on the secret bets he took against her.

"Where is he?" she asked the duke for the hundredth time; they were taking a limping turn about the grounds before lunch.

Old Q, who until then had merely barked or snorted at the mention of the man, now said, "He's waddled – until he can face his creditors. He's a lame duck, my dear."

"Will he be back in London?"

The duke laughed harshly. "I doubt it! He failed to cough me up my twenty thou', so he's not confirmed in the Scotch place and has forfeited my protection." He glanced shrewdly at her. "Disappointed, eh?"

She shook her head. "Not in the way your grace implies. I wanted to see his face when I won."

Old Q raised an eyebrow, sucked a tooth. "Why on earth did he do it, egad? Such an uncommon foolish thing!"

She hesitated before she said, "You remember the evening he brought me to you? How he made an offer of me in place of ten thousand?"

"Yes, why did you not cry out against it?"

"That was a great triumph for him. Rash, foolish, truculent – aye – and yet a triumph. He hoped to repeat the trick here on an even grander scale."

The duke digested this before he said, "Then he must have been very sure of himself. It's unlike Tottenham to take such a risk . . . except on what he would consider an absolute certainty."

It was not true, of course. Tottenham lived for such risks. It was the duke himself who moved only from certainty to certainty. She realized the man was working the conversation round to a point where he might quiz her loyalty directly; so to head him off she laughed and said, "I wonder where he learned *that* trick!"

But the wily old dog was not deflected. "Did you lead him to think it such a certainty, I wonder?"

The question, but even more the tone in which it was asked, revealed to her what a lonely, selfish dog he was. Any other man would have sugared those words with some slight interest in her, as a person in her own right; but not Old Q. He might be prey to the occasional softness; if someone served him well, he could even be generous – and not just in a mercenary way but in his spirit, too. Yet these were the mere outer ramparts of his invested soul – defences to be sacrificed when the pressure was on. The creature at their heart, the essential aristocrat, asked only one sort of question of each passing novelty as it swam into his ken (and, she now realized, a passing novelty is all she was to him): "Is it for me or against me? Can I trust it? Will it serve my purpose, bend to my will, augment my position?"

That was what his question meant. Not: "How interesting that Tottenham judged you so badly – tell me what happened between you!" But "Is it yourself, Mary Flinders, the reed that dips with every wind? Or is it Tottenham losing his power of judgment? Which of you must I discard?"

Page was right.

She chose her answer carefully: "When Folly would entice my Lord Tottenham, she needs more patience than bait."

He laughed delightedly. "Well said, little jade! You have a fine-honed wit when it needs."

"And talking of patience . . ." she continued.

He grinned and led her to a slight eminence at the western end of the garden; marble steps wound their way up to an Italian gazebo where they sat awhile. At length he pointed vaguely to the west and said, "Worsley Old Hall lies some five miles yonder." He turned and studied her keenly. "The home of his grace of Bridgewater, you know."

"Ah."

"Does the fact interest you?"

She shrugged.

"Here's another then. When we first met at my house in London, you were in the company of a giant of a fellow and a . . ."

"Steam Punch!" Her heart began to race.

". . . and a long-eared ass. It is lately reported that the same two creatures are at large in Manchester, the one praying, the other braying, to be told your whereabouts."

His tongue lingered jestingly on his lip. She knew she was somehow playing his game but she could not stop herself from asking, "Only the two of them?"

"Ha!" he pounced. "She does not say, 'Oh how pleasant, I must go greet my two old friends at once' – no, no, no! None of that! All she wants to know is whether there's a *third* member of the party. Now who, I wonder, might this trinitarian be?"

She rose and limped toward the entrance portico. "By your grace's leave, I must go and see them directly."

"Come back!" he laughed. "You would go in vain, for they are here already!"

She spun around, radiant in her joy. "They? All three of them?"

He nodded. "Steam Punch . . . Lucius, the Golden Ass . . ."

"And Matt Sullivan!"

"Ah, sweet nymph! Would that *I* might stir such colour!"

They recrossed the lawn, she hopping with impatience, he pretending to a greater age than yet afflicted him, while he led her round by the rose garden and laundry yard to the stables. There the first sight to greet her eyes was Punch lying on the cobbles, fast asleep in the morning sun.

She called out his name; from the open stable door came a wheezy bray that could be none other's than Lucius. Punch leaped to his feet and came awake at the same instant. Much to his embarrassment, Mary threw her arms around him and hugged him and kissed his neck and laughed and tried to tell him a hundred of her adventures in two sentences. His discomfiture was ended when Lucius poked his soft, blunt nose over the half-open door.

There was another orgy of reunion before she casually asked Punch if he'd met any old friends upon the way.

Punch looked all about them in bewilderment. "God, wasn't he here when I dropped off? I never knew such a fellow. He'd go to Cork by way of the German Ocean."

Old Q tugged at her sleeve and with silent amusement pointed toward the roof.

And up there on the ridge she saw the unmistakable outline of Matt Sullivan; he was leaning against the cupola, staring at the weather vane, deep in thought.

Trueman himself entered the stable yard at that moment. He followed their gaze, saw Matt, and called out, "You're wasting your time, Sullivan. That dashed thing has never worked properly."

"Upside down," Matt said.

Trueman laughed as he joined the others. "Upside down, eh?" he said to them. "I expect he's right. I've only lived here fifty-odd years. Ellis, my head stable lad, he's only been here seventy. And not one of us ever thought to look." He raised his voice and called up to Matt, "Can you rearrange it fitly?"

Matt looked down and noticed Mary. For her the rest of the universe ceased to exist. "Hey oop then, lass," he said.

She nodded, unable to say a word.

He turned to Trueman and asked if there were a shoeing forge nearby.

"Right beneath your feet."

He nodded in satisfaction, then, balancing with the practised ease of a tumbler, walked the ridgetiles to the gable end. Mary ran evenly with him up the yard and held the ladder as he descended. To her dismay she saw he was still in the identical shirt he had worn at Sapperton, though more recent dirt disguised the earlier grime. "You promised me you'd wash this when you got to Manchester," she murmured reproachfully when he was near enough.

He stared back at her icily.

"Oh Matt!" she coaxed, but then the others came up and she could say no more.

"Well now's the time," Old Q said to Mary. "In London I promised to prove something to you. I wonder if you remember?"

"I'd be heartily obliged if your grace would speak of it elsewhere and upon some other occasion," she said frantically.

"Nonsense – no time or place like the present, egad! I have prepared within – in the bureau which Mr. Trueman has kindly requisitioned to me – I have prepared two packets. One bears a bill of exchange for four hundred pounds, payable at sight in favour of Miss Mary Flinders. The other contains a letter from me to His Grace the Duke of Bridgewater, commending to him in the strongest terms one Matthew Sullivan, man of most excelling genius."

Mary stared miserably at Matt.

He glared back in disbelief. "Who asked you?" he demanded.

Old Q barked one word more *"Choose!"*


## CHAPTER TWENTY-NINE


MARY MADE HER CHOICE. Matt turned on his heel in anger and went to kindle the shoeing forge.

Trueman then remembered his original reason for coming out – he had bad news from London for Old Q; the two friends walked off up the stable yard.

Mary looked at Punch and nodded toward the forge, raising her eyebrows inquiringly.

He shrugged. "Sure he's not the only rabbit in Connemara. The mould that made him made an army beside."

From within the workshop Matt called to Punch, asking him to run up the ladder and bring down the vane, which would lift off quite easily.

She went into the gloom of the forge and found him puffing at some tinder. "Why be angry?" she asked.

He did not stop.

"You are angry."

"I'm short of breath for speechifying."

"I thought it would please you. Anyway, it wasn't my idea, it was Old Q's."

"Make up your mind." He stooped and blew again at the tinder, though by now it was well enough alight to thrive in the harsher blast of the bellows.

She put her foot to the treadle and gave the bellows a gentle pump. The flame swelled, and though it was not enough to endanger him, he leaped back with an oath as if she had blinded him. Then began a great feast of outrage.

She laughed and pumped the bellows in earnest. "I used to have a wooden doll could act with more conviction."

He subsided and said grumpily, "You want to be more careful." He put his foot beside hers and tried to shove her aside. But she bumped him away with her hip and told him to get on with building his fire.

She made several more attempts at conversation but he refused to answer. The warmth of the day and the heat of the fire soon had him sweating. He took off his shirt.

Laughing in triumph, she snatched it up and ran out into the yard. Matt followed her for a few paces but saw how undignified the struggle would be, even if (or especially if) he won.

In looking behind her she almost bowled over the duke. He steadied her, glanced at the shirt, then at her fine dress, and smiled. It brought home to her the dilemma she was now in.

Mary Flinders, daughter of *The* Flinders of the Barony of Inchiquin in County Clare, guest of Brian Trueman Esquire of Hart Hill, could not possibly stand in her host's stable yard, doing the washing of an itinerant navigator. She looked over toward the drying yard, where Jenny the laundrymaid was hanging out the linen.

"It's your day for choices, Miss Flinders!" Old Q said.

His amusement stiffened her. "'Tis the same one, your grace," she replied and marched over to a rainwater butt, where she began a vigorous laundering of the offending shirt. It was disgusting beyond tolerance. "Jenny!" she cried. "Bring soap!" When the maid came, Mary yielded up the office to her and rejoined Old Q, who said coolly, "More a gesture than a choice."

Punch came striding down the yard, bearing the vane like a

brand. Trueman followed him into the forge to watch the work progress.

"You go at life like your mad bull," the duke went on when they were alone once more. "And never a care for the dividend."

She nodded, chastened. "I misjudged him. What should I do?"

"Come back to London with me. The whole world is avid to meet you. I'll have you presented at court. You'd transform the entire Season." When she said nothing he added, "You don't belong here."

"I mean what to do about me and Matt?"

"Do nothing. He has no need of you, neither friend nor wife nor help. That's what he's telling you now."

From the forge came a mighty hammering.

"He's just working off his anger," she said.

Old Q gave a mirthless chuckle. "You are resolute, I am stubborn, he is damned pig-headed – isn't that the way of it?"

She nodded and made a small gesture at a smile. "How do I mend matters, Duke? You understand people so well."

"Matt Sullivan requires no great art. You rode him at a fence and he refused – that's all." When he saw she did not grasp his point he added, "Well – how does one ride an unwilling horse at a high fence?"

"God, I don't know. In Ireland there's no such creature."

He laughed, this time with humour. "Then you must learn an English art. *All* our mounts are unwilling – so we either defeat 'em, or we eat 'em."

She suddenly recalled what Trueman had said, about having bad news, and asked if it were a bereavement.

"In a way, yes," he sighed.

Before she could question him any further Matt emerged into the sunlight, triumphantly holding the modified vane. He plunged it into the water butt, where it hissed and spat at the turgid liquor, the distillation of his own shirt, which was now hanging on a bush in the garden. Mary looked at his half-naked body in frank admiration. He saw the glance – and tried to seem nonchalant.

Then, still determinedly impassive, he greased the rewelded plate and went up on the roof, where he reseated the vane as it ought to have been seated in the first place. The moment he let go, an obliging zephyr spun it gently this way and that. The onlookers cheered. Matt attempted a theatrical bow and almost killed himself by overbalancing. Mary gave a scream and ran forward to catch him. He edged his way back most gingerly to the ladder.

Once again she held it for his descent.

"That was foolish," he told her gruffly. "If I'd fell, I'd have killed you."

"I'd have done the same for a dog," she told him, equally shortly, and went to join the others.

The duke was explaining his bad news as Matt came up:

Some time ago he had noticed a journeyman coachbuilder called Sam Davison who used to trundle carriagewheels from various wheelwrights' premises to his own workshop in Long Acre. Sam had become pretty adept at the sport and the duke had brought out his famous Jean-Moyse stopwatch and timed him over various distances. Then, while standing one day in his own mews with a group of gentlemen friends, waiting to look over some horseflesh, he drew their attention to a loose carriagewheel that just "happened" to be leaning against a wall. Out of the ensuing discussion he engineered an argument as to whether the bowling of such a wheel assisted or retarded the runner's speed. The duke hotly maintained the former – so hotly that he induced the others to bet against him. There was a waiter at Betty's cakeshop in St. James's, also famed for his prowess at running. The duke had also timed him, on the sly. The form of the bet was that Sam Davison, "bowling that very wheel," would run a furlong down Piccadilly faster than the waiter.

"Unfortunately," Old Q concluded, "it now seems I was too clever for my own good. 'That very wheel' was six inches shorter in its diameter than the wheel young Sam was bowling when I timed him. And now it is found that he can in no way bowl the smaller wheel as fast as the larger. My opponents are holding me to the letter of my words, so it would appear that I have lost my bet." He sighed. "Eight hundred guineas!" He looked at Mary with jocular hopefulness. "What about a walk back to London in *three* days, little jade?"

He swept her and Trueman indoors for luncheon. During the meal a footman came in with a message from the head groom to say that the two navigators were removing sundry wheels from the carriages. Trueman rose angrily but the duke, guessing what they were at, promised to make good any damage. After the meal they hastened back outside, expecting to find Matt and Steam Punch bowling wheels like children at a fair. But they were nowhere to be seen; and Lucius, too, had gone.

They did not return until evening, when the whole house was roused by the hammering of wedge keys as the wheels were restored to their axles. The duke ran out of doors, closely followed by Mary and Trueman.

Mary was disgusted to see that the shirt she had washed at such a risk to her reputation was as filthy as before – though at least the dirt was "new."

"Well?" the duke asked impatiently. Matt's smile revealed he had the answer; he drew breath to speak but Mary cried, "No!" and sprang forward to clap her hand over his mouth. "The secret must be worth . . . what shall we say – four hundred guineas?"

Old Q was livid. "You ate that cake, miss!" His words were almost a scream. "Not a crumb is left."

Matt peeled her hand gently from his mouth and gave it a reassuring kiss that sent a shiver through her.

The duke saw it and grew angrier yet – the more so because his own position was so feeble. He stormed off up the yard, but before he reached the gate he turned and they saw that he was all smiles again. "Two hundred," he offered genially, returning to them with the air of the most reasonable man in all the world. "A quarter of the stake."

Matt looked hesitantly at Mary, who said "At the risk of seeming *resolute*, your grace, I must humbly submit that if you win, you're eight hundred richer. Lose and you're eight hundred poorer. So there's twice eight hundred in it. Never mind the stake, let us consider what's *at* stake."

"Oh, you shall learn what's at stake, miss," the duke promised. "And right soon." with a curt gesture he conceded her demand; he was smiling with everything but his eyes.

Matt had taken five of Mr. Trueman's wheels for his experiments; two still lay against the coach-house door, one great, one small. The first he now proceeded to bowl up and down the stable yard.

"Crack my ribs if he's not a fair rival to Sam Davison!" the duke marvelled.

Matt then took the smaller wheel and tried to bowl that, too, but with nothing like the same velocity.

"You have it!" Old Q called out. "There's the rub! Now what's your answer, eh? The thing's impossible."

Taking up the little wheel Matt led them around to the other side of the house, where there was a slightly sunken walk between two raised parterres, each fringed with a paving of smooth stone.

He looked at Trueman and raised an eyebrow.

"Bowl away, good fellow, if there's salvation in it."

Standing in the sunken walk Matt lifted the wheel and set it on the paving. Its top was now waist-high, exactly the height of the larger wheel on level ground. He then bowled it the length of the parterre with as much ease and speed as he had shown with its big brother.

Old Q laughed and clapped hands; then he remembered the rest of the bargain and said disgustedly, "Four hundred pounds for *that!*"

"Guineas," Mary reminded him.

"And am I to build a parterre down Piccadilly?"

"Planks," was all Matt answered.

"The answer is obvious now it's pointed out," Trueman cut in. "May I ask how it came to you?"

Matt shrugged, grinned, looked uncertainly at the horizon.

The duke clapped him on the back. "Ah well, you're a stout fellow, Sullivan. I'm not saying I wouldn't tire of you inside a week" – he glanced at Mary as he spoke – "but you've saved my wager for me. No doubt of that. You shall have your draft for four hundred guineas." And, with a nod that included all but Mary, he strode indoors.

Trueman followed him. Punch gathered up the wheel and carried it back to the yard.

Matt nodded toward the door through which the duke had disappeared. "You've cast off a good friend there," he told Mary.

"And what have I gained, Matt? Has it been worthwhile?"

He turned and looked at her. His eyes filled with tenderness and he raised a hand to her cheek. "You're too good for me, lass. And all the world can see it but thee."

Filthy though his fingers were, she clutched them to her and said, "You know *nothing* of the world. Nor yet did I when first

226

we met – or I'd not have gone one step more toward London. There's as much greatness in you, Matt, as there is meanness in all their grandeur."

He shook his head and said, "Er . . . the duke's letter to Dux?"

"What of it?"

"Buy it off you for four hundred?"

She was about to refuse when she realized its importance to him. She took it from her pocketbook and handed it over.

"Now I've earned it," he said.

A footman came out with the duke's bill of exchange on a salver. Matt studied it before handing it to her. "That looks in order."

She passed the paper back, saying, "You must endorse it to me." She asked the footman to fetch ink and a pen.

While they waited, Matt began to pace about uneasily, shaking his hand as if it were wet. She asked him what was the matter.

"I've put out a sinew in this arm," he said crossly. "I can't seem to catch it back right."

He was still the world's worst actor but this time she did not tell him so. When the servant brought the implements to Matt she intercepted him and, taking up the pen, wrote "Please make payable at sight to Mary Flinders." An inch or so below, she added the date.

Taking a chance, she handed it to him, saying, "I hope you have sinew enough to set your autograph name between my two scrawls."

He wrote with the unwieldy pen, with his darting tongue, with his pursed lips, with his knotted brow, with his flaring nostrils, with his laboured breath, and with every other muscle in his body, too – a concert of pains that took a full minute to orchestrate. But there it was at last every letter legible and in its right place.

The footman withdrew. She waved the paper in the evening breeze to dry. "One day," she said, "that signature will command greater respect in the banks than the one on the other side, for all its nobility."

He smiled. "Such fond fancies!"

They were interrupted by a most embarrassed Brian Trueman, who stammered his apologies but begged to inform her that his grace required him to let her know she was no longer welcome under his roof. "I must apologize for him – though he's my friend," he concluded shamefacedly.

For a moment she was too stunned to speak.

"I am at your service, Miss Flinders," he added, "to convey you to my neighbour, James Pearson, who I know would be both delighted and honoured . . ."

She recovered her voice. "If there be any difference between an infant and a duke," she said, "it is that the infant *knows* it is but a child."

"Egad, there's truth in that," Trueman allowed, "though he's my friend."

"And all for four hundred guineas – when I have just won him thousands!"

Trueman's misery deepened. "He is among my oldest, dearest friends, Miss Flinders – yet all you say is true."

"And then to go and put *your* honour to such a test, Mr. Trueman!" Mary clicked her tongue.

The poor man was now too miserable to say a word.

"Though he *is* your friend," she concluded.

He nodded morosely; any moment she thought he'd burst into tears. "Well, well, well!" she said more briskly. "You may tell your most noble friend that such petty spite is not worth the trumpeting to the world at large. You are kind, Mr. Trueman, to wish to convey me to Mr. Pearson's, but I think it were *un*kind to put your neighbour's honour to so severe a test. Is he not also your friend! And where should you then turn if he, too, should prove . . . well, no matter, no matter. Enough of that. But pray tell me this much – are your stables also closed to me? If we are all to bring our friends into the reckoning, I have finer ones out there, I think."

He wrung his hands, visibly withering in the fire of her scorn. "Dear me, dear me! I tried to argue with his grace, but no man may prevail against him when this black mood is down."

"Come sir," she said more plainly, "may I or may I not sleep in your stables?"

He threw up his arms in a gesture of reluctant hopelessness. "He would be beside himself with fury."

"How so?"

"Do you not see? If you banished yourself there, it would be no mere trumpet for his spite, 'twould be a whole military band – for the servants would talk of it from this to Christmas."

She laughed harshly. "Then I can think of no more fitting means of intelligence for one whose intelligence has proved so mean!"

Trueman gave a miserable little laugh. "What to say? What to tell him?"

"Should he recover before he returns to London, you may tell him that though my grudge be as huge as high Olympus, my soul has proved too mean to bear its weight. Therefore I have abandoned it somewhere upon the highway."

He pressed her hands between his before returning indoors.

In the deepening twilight she and Matt walked over the lawn to the gazebo. "You've a wit as nimble as king salmon," he said.

She leaned her head against his shoulder. "I'm obliged to return to London, Matt. I have . . . certain unfinished business there. But I'll come back here, to you, as soon as I can."

"Nay," he said. "Stay there! You were born to shine."

"And so were you."

He shook his head. "I can't settle to it. I have this . . ." He could not find the word.

"Idleness?" she teased.

But he took her seriously. "'Tis no idleness, love. There's days when I've got to lie in the sun, or in the rain, and . . . just think. I can't explain it. I just need to think."

"What about?"

"Everything."

After a pause she said, "There's no other woman, is there, Matt? You're not simply being kind to me?"

He gave a brief, ironic laugh. "There's been too many."

"Oh?" The news surprised her. "What do *I* lack, then?"

"You? You're more than all of them set together. You're the champion lass of the world."

Even in her delight she had to ask, "Have there truly been so many?"

He gave his head an ambiguous tilt. "Funny thing. I'd not cross the road to court one of them."

"But?"

"Well, I didn't need to. That's where all the trouble lies."

She took a risk. "You'll need to with me, Matt, me darlin'.

When I return, 'twould mortify me to find you dreaming in a tent beside the Bridgewater Canal."

She had gone a little too far. He turned from her, his jaw set tight.

She tried another line. "If I hadn't clapped my hand to your lips, would you just have given Old Q your idea for nothing?"

He made no reply.

"And now, with Dux, will you do the same? Give him your ideas for nothing?"

Still he was silent.

"Well, Matt, I'll not pester you. I'll leave you to make the arrangements and show me how clever you are when I return. Just you be assured, though – I shall return."

He relaxed; the inquisition was over. Tomorrow could answer for tomorrow. Gently he began to caress her.

## CHAPTER THIRTY

TOTTENHAM WAS IN FRANCE. No, Tottenham was in America. Tottenham had been seen in St. Giles's . . . also at his favourite Bond Street coffee house . . . in a whacking academy in Monmouth Street . . . on the Dover Road . . . at Holyhead. In short, Tottenham had vanished so thoroughly off the face of the earth that everyone saw him everywhere and all at once.

Mary thought it wise to remain in Manchester until her ankle mended fully. Old Q, however, returned to London the day after his ill-tempered banishment of her – which was a full week earlier than he had intended. He blamed the preparations for the great wheel race in Piccadilly, but Trueman told her it was a tender conscience that drove him in such haste.

Page went back to his regiment, but with promises of organizing a subscription on behalf of her father.

Of course, Silent Sullivan, the world's greatest communicator, sent no word to Mary of his audience with Dux; she heard it all from Steam Punch. It seemed that Matt's "jug & kettle" system (as she called it) to save and reuse one fourth portion of the water in a lock would serve Dux close to home. His mines at Worsley now had more than thirty miles of canal underground, penetrating to almost every level of the coalface. Every ton raised through locks to the surface displaced at least a ton of water downward through that same cascade – all of which had to be pumped up again. So each gallon reused was a gallon that did not have to be raised. Matt was appointed to supervise the adaptation of one lock; if it was successful, work on the rest would follow.

Punch himself was the ganger on the job. "Sure, I'll keep an eye on the fellow for you," he promised her. "Though what made you pick such a rod for your back, colleen, Lord alone knows."

"Why d'you say so?"

"Oh God, he's the goat that knows but one way down the mountain, and that's up!"

"Will he come and see me?"

"He knows you're too far above him. You'll go to London and forget him. He says you'll be a duchess yourself yet."

"Such an eejit! I'll go and see him, so."

But Punch shook his head cannily. "Let the fella prove himself with this first lock now – which is as certain as rain. After that he'll be made engineer-in-charge, and my bones say he'll be another man then. He'd look at you more square if you follow."

In a way it was the same advice as Old Q had given.

With everyone else gone away, she ought to have been the loneliest woman in the land. In fact, she never knew such bustle and fun. She stayed at the Duke of Bridgewater's – the inn, not the Old Hall. She could have had the pick of twenty private houses, but that would have slighted the other nineteen; hence the neutral choice of a public house instead. In any case, she was hardly ever there. She was still the catch of the northern season and was out to a ball or a supper on most nights of the week. Forty guineas went on new gowns alone.

She had half a dozen serious proposals of marriage and several times that many for a less permanent arrangement. The Marchioness of Pendlebury wanted her as a companion. Countess Semple desired to take her on a ladylike version of the Grand Tour. Signior Valldoro offered to rewrite his operettas to suit her voice and range if she would but join his company. And there were at least four theatres where, experienced or no, she could walk, or limp, into the leading role overnight.

One budding author wrote a dramatic version of her journey: *The Tribulations of Pic-to-Pic Moll*. It was all there, from the touching moment when the king himself kissed her hand at the starting line, through the episode with the rabid dog, and the nightly attempted violations of her maidenhead, the romantic interlude with the Minstrel Gipsy, the proposal by the mysterious Masked Baron, and the stately dance she and Old Q performed as they crossed the finishing line together . . . he had omitted nothing. When she turned down his offer to play the lead, this fiction did not languish unseen in the scribbler's garret but appeared on the streets the following morning as a penny broadsheet, complete with a "likeness" that left her safe to go about, unremarked by those few citizens who did not actually know her by sight.

At Lady Grey de Wilton's ball in Heaton House, toward the end of her sojourn in the city, Dux himself created a sensation by appearing in public for the first time in many a long memory. Even more astonishing, his sole purpose was to meet a *woman*, this Mary Flinders. He was duly presented to her.

Though now advanced in years, well into his fifties, he was still in full vigour, a powerful, thick-set man, ill at ease in such gay society. She imagined him far more at home sitting a half-bred hunter on the bank of some canal, a crust and cheese in one hand, a foaming tankard in the other, and a knotty navigational problem before him. Within moments of meeting him she knew how well he and Matt must have got on.

He was even more negligent of his dress than Matt – a proper Captain Queernabs in an old-fashioned cardinal cloak; indeed, he was so dishevelled he could only have been one of two things – either a filthy old tramping man who had accidentally strayed indoors and was being tolerated by some charitable eccentricity of the hostess, or a duke.

For some reason he seemed fascinated by her and the tales he had heard. He asked her especially about her family and home in Ireland; and, in her cheerful, artless way, she told him everything.

"You are not at all as I had imagined you, Miss Flinders," he said.

"Dear heavens, your grace, is my reputation so coloured, then?"

"Quite the contrary. It is so whited one thought only of the sepulchre."

"How people do love to exaggerate!"

"But what really impresses me – now that I have met you – is your interest in young Sullivan. He is no great talker, is he!"

"No babbling brook," she agreed.

Dux eyed her shrewdly. "And as to you, I imagine you could take your pick of a dozen fine gentlemen now?"

She gave a scornful laugh. "I am this season's butterfly, sir. This is my one summer. But Matt Sullivan will be a constellation down the years."

He pulled a face. "You are too hard on yourself, young lady. But you are right as to Sullivan. Hark'ee – it is not possible we should converse here like rational beings. May I prevail upon your time so far as to invite you to take a dish of tea at the Old Hall tomorrow afternoon?"

She hesitated, not because she doubted him, still less because she was insensible of the honour, but because she did not want Matt to see her in such grand company; it would only confirm him in his "you're too fine for me" nonsense. Not that she supposed Matt might be invited, but the risks of being seen by him, either coming or going, or strolling in the grounds, were obvious.

Dux misinterpreted her hesitation. "My niece, the Honourable Miss Rowena Carmody, will also be there," he added.

"And Matt Sullivan need never hear of it?"

"Ah!" He understood then, and, smiling, shook his head. Then with a grave bow, long out of fashion (and in his case, long out of practice, too), he added, "I shall send my carriage for you."

Later she asked Lady Hanbury, one of the other guests, whether Dux had ever been married. Then she was told the sad tale of how, thirty years ago, he had been engaged to the young and newly widowed Duchess of Hamilton, who, as Elizabeth Gunning, had been one of the four "Beautiful Gunnings", daughters of a bankrupt Irish squireen who had come to London and secured the patronage of the Duchess of Bedford.

"Perhaps you know the family?" Lady Hanbury asked.

This time Mary had enough courage to shake her head and admit, "Only the name, your ladyship."

"Ah – those were wild times," the other said nostalgically. "The Gunnings had to break into their own house and steal back their furniture at dead of night to get it away from the bailiffs, you know? And those four girls were so beautiful! When they were presented at court the nobility stood on the tables to see them. I've known a street choked with a throng of several hundred – just to see Elizabeth get into her chair of a morning. And as to the theatre! If it were known any of them would attend that night, why the place would be filled a half-hour early instead of one hour late."

All four sisters had married well, but Dux had taken against one of them, Lady Coventry, and he told Elizabeth he would expect her to sever all relations once she was his duchess. She naturally refused, severed all relations with *him*, and married the Duke of Argyll instead. Dux had retired to Worsley and had never gone out in society again – "except on rare occasions like tonight." Lady Hanbury smiled at her. "He came to see you, of course."

"Oh I doubt that, your ladyship!"

"Then you're the only one here who does. He loathes all women now. You won't find a single female servant at the Old Hall."

"He mentioned one female," Mary told her. "His niece. A Miss Rowena . . ."

"Carmody?" Lady Hanbury's eyes lit up. She turned to a neighbour and tapped her peremptorily on the arm with her fan. "My dear Dodo – you'll never guess – but here's a thing! They've sent the little Carmody girl to languish with Dux!"

"Poor creature!" Dodo laughed with hearty malice and then added, "Serves her right!"

Lady Hanbury turned back to Mary. "Still," she said, taking up her earlier theme, "the poor old duke cannot be granite through-and-through. I suppose the similarities between you and the Gunnings were too great for him to ignore." She tapped Mary's arm with her fan. "When you return to London, my dear, you must find a patroness to present you at court. You'll be a duchess yet, I make no doubt whatever."

"You are most kind," Mary answered awkwardly. She was beginning to dislike those beautiful Irish Gunnings and the precedent they had set; and this society was utterly moonstruck on precedents.

"Yes," Lady Hanbury affirmed, "I shall write to Lady Charles Douglas. She cordially detests Old Q, who is her husband's kinsman, and would simply love to present you, if for no other reason than to spite him." She glanced at Mary. "Why do you smile, child?"

"I was just wondering how society would shift without all its hatreds and intrigues."

"Oh la! We'd fall apart, to be sure."

The following afternoon, punctually at four, Mary stepped from the Duke of Bridgewater's carriage, mounted his steps, and paused briefly to look about her. Never had she seen an establishment that so plainly said *bachelor*. There was not a flower in sight. The "garden" was all fruit bushes, pheasant covert, and jumps for horses; everything in this man's life had to justify itself, earn its place. They said he had bought tons of marble statuary in his youth, in Rome, while on the Grand Tour – and all of it still lay in its original crates in his cellar.

When she stepped inside, the overwhelming impression was of paintings. They covered every wall, some no bigger than a slice of bread, others large enough to accommodate the very battles they memorialized. She was taken to a room with high windows that let directly out into the utilitarian garden. A young woman of about her own age rose and introduced herself as Miss Carmody. "His grace has decided to entertain us on the bank of his beloved canal, which is more beautiful to him than the Nile. It is certainly every bit as muddy. But you have no parasol? Never mind, I have several."

Her hair was black, lustrous, and curly, hanging in enviably natural ringlets below her shoulders. She was very *à la mode*; her loose, flowing dress, being gathered up beneath her bosoms, left little else to look at and nothing to imagine. Her large, dark eyes had a liquid intensity. And, like a liquid, they were never still but watched Mary's every move with all the darting severity of a bird. There was something birdlike, predatory, about her altogether. For no reason she could lay a finger on, Mary formed the impression that Miss Carmody had, indeed, been sent to languish in this house as some kind of punishment; certainly there can have been little pleasure for her in such an establishment, managed entirely on masculine lines by an unwashed old misogynist like Dux, who could talk of nothing but canals.

"His grace is fond of art," Mary said by way of conversation as they went outdoors.

"Oh they only *look* like paintings," Miss Carmody said.

"Are they fakes?"

"No. They are investments."

They passed a blackcurrant bush, laden with fruit and covered with a net against the birds. The girl lifted the net, wrenched off a small branch, and hurled it to the edge of the lawn. Then she glanced at Mary to see how she responded to this vandalism; there was a truculent challenge in her eye.

A thrush descended on the branch and began to peck furiously at the fruit.

"Aren't they God's creatures, too?" Mary said.

This genial tolerance did not please Miss Carmody. "You've been having a high time of it, Miss Flinders," she said coolly.

"Oh I'll be glad when it's over. If I'd imagined for one moment it would create such excitement . . ."

"But why else do it?" Miss Carmody's surprise and curiosity were genuine; she was easily knocked off her high horse.

"Ah, 'twas a bit of a cod, really. Then Old Q put about that tale about restoring the family fortunes and . . ."

"You mean it's not true? Is your father not in debtor's gaol?" The notion that Mary had practised a gigantic imposture on society seemed to thrill her.

"Oh no, that's true enough. But he's more than happy there as long as we can send him in good victuals. Besides, the whole family's glad to have him where he's safe. But Old Q didn't think he'd get good odds on such a tale."

"So what do you really want, Miss Flinders?"

Without hesitation Mary answered, "Never to see my name in the journals again."

"Not even be presented at court?"

"Oh! Lady Hanbury's talking of that. Sure I don't know how to stop her."

Miss Carmody had great difficulty grappling with the notion that any kind of a life was possible that did not begin with a presentation at court – still less that a woman who had the choice might choose *not* to be presented. "I'd never have thought of that," she murmured admiringly.

"What d'you mean?"

"I mean on my own. But if you've not been presented at court, there's nothing they can do to you, is there? They can't marry you off . . . nor parade you up and down in the selling stakes . . . my dear, it's utterly brilliant!"

Mary had no idea what she was talking about but was happy to let her ramble on. They crossed the Booths Bank road and wandered on across the moor, toward the canal. At length Miss Carmody said, "Of course, Dux *has* to take an interest in me, but what about you? Why did he break the habit of years to seek you out the other night – and at the Wilton Egertons of all places!"

"I have no idea," Mary replied.

But Rowena Carmody was answered soon enough. They came upon Dux sitting in the middle of a large patch of daisies – garden escapes rather than wildflowers. "See these?" he called out. "Returned home from Newmarket once – won a small fortune off your friend Old Q, I remember – found my gardener had filled a whole bed with *flowers!*" He spoke the word with disgust. "Knocked all the heads off with my stick and told him to root them out. Often wondered where he threw them." He pointed toward his feet. "Only just noticed."

Now that they were close Mary saw he had trampled and broken many of them. Matt, she thought, would never do that, despite his other distressing similarities to this not-very-attractive man.

As if he read the name in her mind, Dux began at once to talk of Matt. He wanted Mary to describe how she had met him, what had been her first impression, what Matt had talked about, what made her realize he had special qualities that raised him above other men.

Mary had no desire to talk of such things in front of Miss Carmody, whom she regarded as a dangerous child in a woman's body, but Dux was insistent and bit by bit he drew the whole story from her.

And then, her purpose being served, the man lost all interest in her. He went on talking – about his beloved canals, of course – but she had the feeling that, had he been alone, he would have spoken the same words to a sleeping dog. When their tea was over, he bade her the curtest farewell and went off to his mines, which were only half a mile down the canal bank. Leaving the footmen to clear up, Rowena took Mary's arm impulsively and swept her homewards.

"This Matt Sullivan," she said. "He sounds an utter paragon. I long to meet him for I don't believe any man could be so perfect."

PART FOUR

ON THE ANVIL

# CHAPTER THIRTY-ONE

N HER WAY SOUTH, Mary at last took up the postponed invitation from the Duke of Bedford to stay at Woburn Abbey. If he, too, proved childish, he could hardly outshine Old Q . . . or if dirty, then Dux would surely outdim him . . . or arrogant, or selfish, or overweening proud, why then she had already met his peers in all those lines, too. Like him or hate him, the one thing she could not afford was to offend him by driving on past Woburn.

The word *abbey* conjured in her mind some gloomy gothic pile, crumbling in the clutch of ivy and steeped in the cold and damp of several hundred winters. But this ducal seat confounded all such expectations. On her original journey north she had been too exhausted to turn aside, a mile or so short of the village, and admire what was in fact, after Blenheim, the finest and almost the newest house in the land – more splendid by far than any of the royal homes. Now, as the carriage bowled up the Grand Drive, winding its way through park and farmland, among prettily contrived lakes and watercourses, she gained her first view of that stately palace and found it quite breathtaking.

When she had mentioned to people in Manchester that she had begged postponement of an invitation from his grace, they told her she must be mad; the man had the most inflated opinion of his own importance; she should now abandon all hope of favour from *that* quarter. Mary had to keep producing the duke's letter to convince them otherwise.

On her arrival at the Abbey's magnificent entrance, that same scrap of paper worked its familiar magic. She was cordially received by the household steward, who kept her waiting no more than a minute or two before he showed her to her chamber.

The interior was even more stupendous than the approach had led her to expect. She had seen some gracious houses since coming to England but this outsplendoured them all. Furniture, plate, porcelain, paintings – all were of the finest in workmanship, the most exquisite in taste, the most lavish in conception, and no doubt the costliest in the world. She ascended among them, lost in awe.

Her guide was surprised she had no maid but said he would arrange for one to attend her. Without putting it in so many words, the fellow managed to let her know that few commoners beneath the rank of cabinet minister had ever slept in the house, and those that did were usually granted no more than a palliasse in a corridor.

Actually, a corridor might have been preferable, she thought. Her chamber overlooked a quadrangle between two wings of the house; on the fourth side, opposite her window, they were demolishing an ancient chapel – perhaps the sole surviving building of the original abbey – to complete the vast, open-square plan of the house and create a new state entrance. The splendid portals by which she had been admitted would soon be no more than the back door. But at the moment, everything was wreathed in dust.

The maid, Temperance by name (but not by her breath), proved to be an old woman who had in earlier years served the fourth duke's second duchess. Fragments of gossip, passed on to Mary in Manchester when she said she would pay this call on her way south, ran through her mind as she let the beery old creature prepare her for dinner, which, in that household, was at six. The dowager duchess, who was still alive and somewhere beneath this very roof, was the grandmother of the present duke. Neither of her sons had outlived their father. What had someone said about her at the coronation of George III? She looked like an orange-peach, half-red and half-yellow. She was a granddaughter of the Duke of . . . something. Marlborough, was it? Or had that been her husband's first duchess, Lady Diana Spencer? And wasn't one of the daughters married to the present Duke of Marlborough?

Mary sighed. All these threads of alliance became so tangled.

And in the end, what did they signify? Yet everyone treated them as if they were matters of life and death, and not to know them was considered worse than a banishment to the colonies.

How impossible it would be simply to "go into society"! All those things you had to know without ever being told – who's allied to whom; and who's Whig and who Tory; and all those buried scandals; and the hatreds cloaked in smiles and protestations of "Your most devoted, most humble, most obedient . . . *et cetera*."

"How many will be seated to dinner?" she asked the maid.

"His grace supposes there'll be just the twain of ye," the woman replied with a superior, I-know-better smile.

"Who else, then?" Mary pressed.

"'Tis my opinion that when word gets to *her*, she'll join ye, milady."

"To the dowager duchess, you mean?"

"No! The other one. Mistress Parsons."

The snippets of remembered gossip took on firmer outlines in her memory: "Two cats glowering at each other across the courtyard, each in her own wing of the Abbey . . . one a forebear to the duke, the other to half London.' Who had told her that? No matter. The duke had this notorious mistress, who was always referred to as "anybody's Mrs. Nancy Parsons." Bedford was her third duke for she had already obliged their graces of Grafton and Dorset. One wit had called her "Ermine Street," partly after the old Roman road that led directly to *Bed*fordshire – and partly for the number of noble lords whose fur-lined cloaks had hung in her parlour.

This was no stately home but a stately hornets' nest.

The toilette complete, the old maid led Mary down to the grandest dining room she had ever seen; surely several hundred could have been seated there and still have the freedom of their elbows. The table was laid for two; but it was not the duke who waited to greet her, it was another woman. She was – she could only be – Mary considered her carefully – yes, she must be the dowager duchess.

She looked somewhat younger than her seventy-odd years but with all that paint and powder it was hard to tell; in any case, she was clearly much too old to be anyone's mistress. Her wig was of a most antique style.

Mary gave the deepest curtsey and said, "Mary Flinders, your grace."

The other laughed and raised her swiftly. "Three inches will do me, my dear. I'm plain Lady Maynard." She inspected Mary minutely, like a butcher at mart. "The dress is your own, I take it?" she asked at last.

"Eh?" Mary said. "I mean, I beg your ladyship's pardon?"

"Well . . . a borrowed carriage . . . no maid to serve you?" She smiled knowingly. "Astute that. Very." Seeing Mary's puzzlement she added, "When Mrs. Bellamy, the actress, waited upon the old Duchess of Queensberry to solicit her patronage for her benefit night, she came by chair in a silk dress. Of course, the duchess wouldn't even admit her. Not at home! Not at home!" She laughed warmly and then, almost as an aside, added, "But she gave her five hundred pounds two days later, when she called on foot and in cottons!"

"I'm afraid his grace will find me surpassing dull," Mary said. "I don't understand this invitation. What can Lord Tottenham and Mr. Page have told him?"

Lady Maynard gave out a rich peal of disbelieving laughter before she returned to her own line of conversation. "Don't mention the Duchess of Queensberry here, by the way," she warned. "Have you heard of the orange-peach?"

"Oh, was *she* the one who said that!"

The other nodded. "Dreadful old woman. Tongue as rough as Devon cider! When ladies called whom she did not like which was most of 'em, she'd take them for a stroll into her farmyard and sit on a dungheap – and, of course, they'd have to oblige her and seat themselves, too."

Mary laughed at the scene. "I'm sure I should have done no such thing."

Lady Maynard looked at her shrewdly and said, "No, I don't suppose you would."

Mary wondered – should she ask this very kindly, informative lady about "anybody's Mrs. Parsons?"

The other relaxed visibly. "I can see I jumped to certain false conclusions about you, my dear. I thought you were another Miss Gunning, or even an Elizabeth Chudleigh!" Seeing Mary's puzzled frown she explained, "I supposed you had come to England intent on capitalizing the fortune on which you sit." She touched Mary's blushing cheek. "And believe me it *would* be a fortune, too."

"I can't think why you should have supposed such a thing, Lady Maynard," Mary answered awkwardly.

The other sniffed. "Can't you? Old Q is the fourth richest man in the kingdom. Bridgewater's the third. Our lord and master" – she gestured vaguely at the ceiling – "is the second. Ask him for a letter of recommendation to Marlborough and you'll have reached the first. All in one season! Not a bad canter for so lackadaisical a filly, wouldn't you say!"

Mary drew breath to explain but her mind's ear leaped ahead and heard her own protesting tones, so querulous, so despairing of belief. By way of reply she said, "I've heard of the Gunning girls, of course, but who is Elizabeth Chudleigh?"

"Was!" Lady Maynard smiled. "She died last year. Hers is another name not to mention in this house, by the by. She, too, was an adventuress. Daughter of the governor of Chelsea Hospital, no fortune beyond her face and figure. Learned the wiles of Venus between fifteen and twenty. Got took up by the Earl of Bath, who found her a place at Court. A more drunken, dissolute, lewd-tongued woman never lived. Dressed next door to nakedness. Foul oaths were all her rhetoric. Men loved her, of course, as they always do! She'd have been Duchess of Hamilton if the duke hadn't been packed off on the Grand Tour the day after he proposed to her. (He was the one who later married Elizabeth Gunning, by the way, when she was dowager Duchess of Argyll.) The old king, George the Second, made no secret of his love. The Duke of Ancaster . . . and Lord Hervey . . . they were like flies to her stinking meat. But the reason you are not to mention her name here is that she married our hostess's cousin, the Duke of Kingston – having conveniently 'forgotten' she was already married in secret to Hervey! You must remember the scandal? Are you so young? Aiee!"

Mary cleared her throat. "By 'our hostess' I suppose you mean Mrs. Nancy Parsons?"

Lady Maynard frowned and then gave an odd little laugh. "No – I mean her grace of Bedford. The dowager." Her tongue lingered thoughtfully on her lower lip before she added, "Tell me, what do you know of this other lady – this Mrs. Nancy Parsons?"

"Well, I've never met her, of course . . ."

"But" – her eyes twinkled encouragingly – "you must have heard things?"

Not knowing how thick this Lady Maynard might be with the duke's mistress, Mary said noncommittally, "Oh, to be sure . . . all the scandal that any fool might believe."

"Most of it true, I'll warrant. What, for instance? Don't be shy. Remember – I belong to that age which required an Elizabeth Chudleigh before it could be shocked."

Hesitantly Mary said, "One lady told me she is commonly referred to as 'anybody's Mrs. Nancy Parsons'."

An astonishing change came over Lady Maynard. Her paint-white face went even whiter; her nostrils stiffened; her eyes turned black and large; and she suddenly screamed at the top of her voice, "It is a lie! It is a most damnable lie! And I'll thank *you* . . ."

Her fury was interrupted by a shout of male laughter from the door. "Hoist with your own petard, my lady!"

Both women turned to see a remarkably handsome young man, no more than twenty-five years of age, standing at the threshold. He was clearly waiting for their acknowledgment. Lady Maynard gave a deep, royal curtsey; Mary swiftly followed suit.

"Please!" he said as he joined them, raising Mary with a kiss of her hand. "Miss Flinders, I presume? Your most obedient." He bowed as for a queen.

He had thick, curly, dark hair and a roundish, almost cherubic face with intensely observant eyes. His nose was fashioned with that Roman bend which comes out in the Russells every few generations; and his lips, though full and sensuous, revealed none of the coarseness that tales of his arrogance and profligacy had led her to expect. In short, she found Francis, Fifth Duke of Bedford, a disconcertingly attractive young fellow, utterly different from "her" other dukes.

She sought for mockery in his gesture but felt none. "Your grace has been so generous and patient. Please accept my renewed assurance that only my own dire situation prevented me from . . ."

"Yes yes yes. I remember all that." He smiled and, still holding her hand, assisted her to the table.

He looked at the two place settings, then at Lady Maynard,

and said, "You must be dining elsewhere, *anybody's Mrs. Nancy Parsons!*"

Angrily, defiantly, the woman seated herself in Mary's place, to the duke's right. Mary turned pale as the understanding dawned. The duke saw it and said, "Calm yourself, my dear. She provoked you to it. I heard her myself." He raised his voice and commanded, "Set two extra places at the other end of the table."

He directed the orders at no one in particular but the butler and a dozen footmen scurried to obey. To Lady Maynard he said, "The duchess will join you, ma'am, I make no doubt."

No sooner were the two new settings laid than Lady Maynard marched the eighty paces or so that separated the two ends of the table, swept up as much plate and glass as she could carry and bore it all back again. The duke's eyes blazed his fury. He glanced at Mary to see how she was responding; she, desperate not to be the cause of any disturbance, said the first thing that came into her head, which was, "Isn't it fine enough for an alfresco feast? 'Clare to God, that sun would put a fire out of joint still."

For a moment his anger swelled; she thought he was about to vent it all on her but he broke into sudden laughter and told her she had the answer – they'd put the food in a hamper and take it on his barge upon the lake.

Though he spoke only to her, the arrangements were immediately put in hand. Taking her by the arm, he led her out to the lawns on the western side of the house, where they sauntered down through the deerpark to the water's edge. Lady Maynard, shod only in cotton slippers, could not immediately follow. By the time her outdoor shoes had been carried to her along all those miles of corridors, the young couple were afloat.

Anyone else bent on an open-air *soupé intime* would have put the hamper in the boat, dismissed every servant, and rowed off into the evening. But dukes are different. No duke, and certainly not this Bedford, could go about town without his army of outriders, his walking footmen, his running dogs, and his auxiliary coach; so, too, now upon his own lake at the heart of his own estate. Though there was no one to impress but himself and an already dangerously impressed Mary, he kept up the airs and graces that were as natural to his grace as air itself.

The boat was a gilded barge with padded seats and silken cushions; an ornate Chinese table, set with a full service in gold

and crystal, stood beneath a gaily striped canvas awning deco-
rated with the family crest and its motto, *Che sarà sarà*. It was
flanked by two smaller barges, laden with servants and food; a
fourth vessel, a common rowing boat, lay several chains offshore,
connected by a stout manilla line to the ducal barge. In all there must
have been three dozen servants – oarsmen, footmen, chefs, and a
rather queasy-looking butler – in attendance upon this simple
picnic. Most impressive of all – the entire production was organized
within a few minutes of their arrival by the shore.

The duke indicated vaguely the direction he wished to take,
and the oarsmen did their best to comply. After the initial service
of chilled melon, which Mary had never tasted before, the
footmen withdrew and their barges pulled a respectful distance
away. Thereafter, when the duke wanted anything, he simply
raised a finger (a gesture so slight that Mary missed it the first
time or two) and the attendant barges closed in and the deck
swarmed with minions, food, wine . . . whatever he might lack.

And all this while, on the distant shore, stalked Lady Maynard,
a dark speck of fury and, no doubt, of hunger too by now. From
time to time the duke noticed her. "Who can measure their
minds?" he asked with a sigh. "Do *you* understand her?"

Mary, supposing the question to be ironic, laughed.

Here at last, she decided, was a *real* duke. Young, handsome,
supremely at ease, spending money merely by breathing,
surrounding himself as a matter of course with the very finest of
everything . . . to Mary he seemed a demigod. Her heart began to
race. When people had prophesied she'd be a duchess yet, no such
ducal image had leaped before her eye.

She realized why he had been so quick to accept her suggestion
of this alfresco feast. She had intended nothing more than a
simple repast on a rug spread out upon the lawns; but his mind's
eye had leaped at once to this more-than-royal barge, with its
awnings, and its silken cushions, its curtained alcove at the stern.

She glanced toward it now, all pink and gold in the evening
sun. Perhaps he had fallen in love with her at sight. Borrowing
the imagery as she fancied it must have flickered in *his* mind's eye,
she saw herself lying there beside him, watched his hands
straying over her dress, fondling a button, a hook, a strap, easing
the silk from her, peeling her like a fruit. In that vision she did not
protest . . .

*Che sarà sarà.*

All through the meal he talked only of mundane things – her home and family, the gay time she had enjoyed in Manchester, and the fund organized by Mr. Page to clear her father's debts, to which it seemed all London was now eagerly contributing. She barely listened; for while he talked he flirted with his eyes; they spoke his real conversation. She watched his hands as they gestured, strong yet exquisite, with those long, slender fingers.

At last the meal was done. With a knowing smile he rose and held out his hand. Their touch was electric. Her heart was now so boisterous she could scarcely breathe. He led her beneath the awning. She sprawled among the cushions and closed her eyes. She was dimly aware that outside there must be at least three dozen menservants, all looking on, all knowing exactly what was about to happen, yet they and their world were now so remote from hers that they ceased to matter.

Through her eyelids she was conscious of a sudden darkening; the duke's head must be close above hers. "Mmmmm," she murmured encouragingly.

"Here, don't go to sleep on me," he chided.

She chuckled silently at the very thought.

Then he lay beside her, propped up on one elbow, and began to speak of agricultural improvements.

For a moment she supposed he was teasing, but then he drew aside the curtains to point out the new sheep-shearing and exhibition house he had built on the home farm. She sat up, blinking at the influx of light, and saw to her dismay that they were close inshore. Footmen sprang aboard and, folding the damask tablecloths, spread them over the shoulders of two gardeners who stood up to their thighs in the water, ready to carry their master and his new mistress (as they must now suppose) to the bank. Lady Maynard, unable to cross the little river that fed the lake, had gone upstream to the footbridge and was now bearing down upon them.

The duke led Mary to a pretty little wooded knoll and began to point out the other parts of his farm, describing all the improvements he was making. At first, Mary listened with but half an ear. Yet soon, almost against her will, she found herself becoming absorbed. Farming – though of a very different kind – had, after all, been her entire life until a few short months ago.

"We who seek to subdue Nature-in-the-raw," the duke said, "do we not also learn from her that there is a wonderful wholeness to all of life? Even that most artificial creation, human society, cannot escape her sway, Miss Flinders. Today's seedling is tomorrow's oak; today's commoner, tomorrow's duke. We look out at such a scene" – he waved his hand before them, completely ignoring Lady Maynard, who was by now toiling very close – "and we say, 'This is as 'twas in my father's time. All's well.' But all is not well, Miss Flinders! The seedlings plot revolution. The very blades of grass breathe sedition all about us."

"Ah – the agriculture of despair!" Lady Maynard said, saving Mary the duty of a comment (which she would have been hard put to make – for all she could think of was how lush these pastures were and what would they not give for such grass at home). Her ladyship had relaxed into a grin the moment she heard the nature of their conversation.

Mary looked to see how his grace took this chiding. There was an ambiguous glint in the man's eye – a certain contemptuous tolerance was clear enough, but there was something else, darker, less easily named.

He turned to Mary and continued in the mildest vein, "Human society, too, has its docks and thistles, which will thrive in whatsoever soil and climate, and despite our best forays with scythe and mattock."

"It also has its lumps of turd," Lady Maynard put in jovially, as if fully supporting him, "which have no power to fertilize till they have faded even from memory."

The duke's smile, directed at Mary, was acid-sweet. "You must not suppose, Miss Flinders, that we all practise so *crude* a husbandry here."

Mary saw a chance at last to extricate herself from their urbane quarrel. "Primitive husbandry is all we know in the barony of the Burren, sir. There, such grass as this would be revolutionary and seditious, indeed, for it would make the tenant a hundred times richer than his landlord."

"Ah!" Gratefully he took the line she offered. "Had you but will enough and time, Miss Flinders, I have the sovereign cure-all for such ignorance."

And leaving a disgruntled Lady Maynard, who had not even

recovered her breath, to bring up the rear, he hastened Mary back to the Abbey.

From the moment of their meeting she had puzzled over his character; at times he seemed so mature and knowing, at others almost childishly petulant. It reminded her of something but she could not think what. Now, hastening across the park, trying to keep up with him, it suddenly struck her that he was very like Rowena Carmody.

A disturbing image rose before her mind's eye: Miss Carmody's pretty tresses, Miss Carmody's bright eyes, Miss Carmody's ample bosom, so generously available to the world's inspection . . .

Alarmed, Mary wondered what on earth could have possessed her to leave Matt on his own back there, and with such a fuze burning up at the Old Hall? At once she decided that tomorrow, the moment she had taken her leave of the duke and Woburn, she would return directly to Manchester.

Arrived at the Abbey, they went at once to the library.

"People talk of manufactures," the duke said scornfully, "of steam and power without limit, but I say poppycock! Such things may create enough wealth to delight a Quaker – that I grant you. But true wealth is in the land. The gold they forge in the Royal Mint is but a token of the true gold we harvest here, season after season."

He loaded down a string of footmen with volumes of every size and all upon the subject of agricultural science. Then, so pleased was he with her aptitude and interest, he led her to the very door of her chamber. Yet again he abandoned his mistress to pant and sweat in their wake.

He ordered Temperance to bring candles throughout the night, for as long as Mary desired to read. "What would I not give," he murmured, running his hands lovingly over the spines of the books, "to be *you*, Miss Flinders – to be on the threshold of this wonderland for the very first time!"

As he left, closing the door behind him, Lady Maynard must have arrived. Mary heard her breathless, aged voice cry out several times, as though it were a sentry challenge, the one word: "*Naughty!*"

Hoping to bid her goodnight, to close the day in amity, Mary ran to the door. Duke and mistress were walking away down the passage.

"Yes!" her ladyship was telling him sternly. "His disgraceful grace was *naughty* this evening."

He laughed; there was an odd excitement in his eye as he asked, "Naughty? Was I really? Was I *very* naughty?"

"Indeed," she replied grimly. "His grace deserves a most thorough whipping!"

The duke laughed and his step became, if anything, more jaunty yet.

As they vanished round the corner Mary realized that the world was wrong. She was not "anybody's Mrs. Nancy Parsons". She was Mrs. Nancy Parsons' *anybody*.

# CHAPTER THIRTY-TWO

AT THE LAST MINUTE Matt Sullivan had just managed to stuff his great fists into his pockets; the only other place for them was the Duke of Bridgewater's jaw. The man was an extinct volcano – an eruption of novel ideas in his youth, dead as a doornail now. Oh, he'd employ Matt to fiddle around, make the odd little improvement, but on any larger subject his mind was as closed as a banker's vault.

"The trouble with you, Sullivan," Dux said, "is a great want of evenness in your labour. You scatter new contrivances like some demented Vulcan. You just . . . wander about my estate improving things without a by-your-leave. Which, let me assure you, you would not get!"

Matt stared back, speechless at the man's ingratitude.

"Well?" Dux roared.

Matt shrugged.

"Did I ask for an automaton to scare off the birds? Did I – eh?"

Matt stared at the horizon.

"Did I ask for horse jumps that re-erect themselves?"

"Your grace's niece . . ." Matt began.

". . . is neither owner nor heiress of this estate. She is not even of the blood! She counts for less than the worms – at least they are good bait for the fish."

Matt was silent once more. Dux returned to his catechism: "And did I ask for gates that open and close themselves? You've done every urchin for miles out of his pennies. What's next, eh? The groomless-horseless-whipless carriage, no doubt! If you have your way, I shall keep a hundred servants in idleness while my entire estate whirs and clicks and grinds about me at the insistence of wind, water, and gravity."

Goaded almost beyond endurance, Matt said, "Well now, a horseless carriage is no idle fancy, your grace. I have, in fact, seen such an engine in France. What they do, you see, is . . ."

The duke made a choking sound, turned on his heel, and stormed off. "You stick to the job for which you were hired, man – save ten thousand pounds of water on each use of the locks in Worsley mine."

"But I've *done* that," Matt yelled after him. "All they need is building."

Dux turned around in triumph. "Exactly! At last there's one point on which we may both agree: All they need is building. Go thou and do it!" He stalked off toward the Hall.

Rowena Carmody slipped out from behind the barberry where she had concealed herself the moment they heard Dux approaching. "Oh my dear," she said tenderly. "If only I had his money! You should invent and invent till your brains ran dry."

He kept his eyes fixed on the archway through which the duke had passed. She watched the angry twitching of the muscles at his temple. A strange pity filled her. How easy it would be to fall in love with him, rough and common though he was. She took a hold of herself.

He turned at last and looked at her. "I wish all things were possible," he sighed. Where had he heard that before? It sounded like something Mary might have said.

She gave a dry little laugh. What an uncanny knack this almost wordless man had for getting directly to the heart of the matter! Her discontent was precisely that – she wanted all things to be possible. She wanted to enjoy the advantages of society – the gossip, the intrigues, the ballrooms, the fun, the ready flow of wealth; but she also wanted to avoid its fetters – the calculated alliance, the settlement, the pin money, the unspoken bargain, the narrow circle.

In brief, she wanted to be so firmly established in society that she could flout its every rule.

In briefer, she wanted her cake and eat it.

In briefest, she wanted to be a duke!

If only there were such things as duchesses-in-their-own-right. But peeresses of that kind went out in the Middle Ages. Those must have been the days for a woman.

"I'm sure all things *are* possible," she said wistfully. "It's not time we need, so much as ingenuity."

He said nothing.

"A penny for your thoughts?" she asked.

Still he remained silent.

"A guinea, then?"

He looked away and shivered; but that was all the move he made. She came closer, brushing her whole self against him. The perfume of her body, untainted by soap, was heady.

He swallowed.

She murmured, "Why do we fashion so contorted a maze out of a thoroughfare so broad, so ancient, so well-travelled?"

Then, quite abruptly, she broke free of him. He expected the usual barrage of no-we-mustn'ts and oh-this-is-wrongs – the age-old anvil on which the elemental iron of male need is forged into penitential shackles – but all she said, as she skipped away, was, "Come to my window tonight." A few more skips and she turned again. "If you don't, I shall come to yours – and that'll be the end of *you*."

At that same moment Mary, having reached the place where the bull had almost killed her, told Mr. Trueman's coachman to halt awhile. On her way south she had taken a different road so this was the first time she had seen it since that almost-fatal day. She walked about, marvelling that so few traces remained of so stirring an event. There was the gore in the mud where the creature had slipped; now it was matted with new velvety tips of young grass. And here lay the ashes of the fire in which they had burned what was not worth salvaging of the carriage; already the heap was pierced in several places by new fronds of dock leaves. Beyond that she could find nothing.

Even if she had died, it would look no different. If you require a monument, don't look about you!

A passing horseman, travelling in her direction, paused and asked her if she needed assistance.

She laughed. "You're six weeks too late, sir."

She explained as she climbed back into her carriage. His interest was roused and he plied her with questions, falling in beside her as the journey resumed. The carriage hood was down, so conversation was easy. Finding her lively and agreeable, he asked if she had any objection to their sharing the way for a while.

"You are not a highwayman?" she inquired.

"No indeed. I am, in fact, a civil engineer. Thomas Croxley, your humble servant."

She raised her eyebrows, never having heard the term. "Civil, eh? I hope the attribute is catching, sir, so that we may soon be surrounded with civil butchers, civil innkeepers, and even civil bailiffs."

He laughed. "It is what we have determined to call ourselves – as distinct from military engineers, you see. We construct bridges, harbours, canals – that sort of thing."

Naturally, her ears pricked up at the word canals. She said, "You probably know his grace of Bridgewater?"

He was so astonished that even his horse stopped. "I do indeed, Miss Flinders." He spurred forward and drew level again. "More than that – my sole purpose in coming to Manchester is to call upon his grace at the first opportunity. What fortune! Do I take it that you are familiar with the duke? I don't suppose . . . might I make to bold as to ask . . . ?"

Sensing an undeserved respectfulness in him, she quickly said, "Oh, not that he and I are on social terms – I mean, I wouldn't claim that – well – not really."

"Oh . . . ah?" he glanced at her uncertainly. "Forgive me."

"Well . . . oh, it's so complicated."

"Not at all. I quite understand. Don't embarrass yourself further, please. Such is life!" He laughed awkwardly. "Who shall cast the first stone, what!"

"It's just that, well, you remember the walk I mentioned? When I was telling you about the bull?"

"The wager?"

"Yes. Well, my fee, you see . . . I mean, the Duke of Queensberry promised . . ."

"Another duke!" He gave a knowing smile. "I suppose you and he are also, ahem – 'not on social terms'?"

"Yes. No. Well, in a way. But never mind that. Queensberry stood fair to win several thousand pounds in wagers on my ped race, and I was to get four hundred if I managed it within the four days." His eyes went wide in surprise but she pressed on, "However, when I arrived . . ."

"In time?"

"You may say so – didn't the hand of the clock graze me as I passed! Anyway, Old Q offered me a letter of introduction to Bridgewater instead."

"Instead of four hundred pounds? Egad, but you must have had great hopes of old Dux. Did nobody tell you . . ."

"No, no – the introduction wasn't for me, it was for Matt Sullivan."

This time Croxley almost fell off his horse. "*Who?*"

"Matt Sullivan!"

"Ye gods, but this is witchcraft!"

"You know him also?" Well, I suppose, being in the canal trade . . ."

"No – much closer than that: I was thinking of Matt Sullivan not half an hour since."

"Sure there's no witchcraft in that. Wasn't I thinking of him, too. The fool speaks the master's thoughts, that's all."

Croxley recovered himself and, clearing his throat, asked, "In view of your earlier, and may I say extremely frank confessions, Miss Flinders, would it be impertinent to ask . . . ?"

"I mean to marry him," she said bluntly. "He's working for the duke, so we share a common destination, you and I."

She watched closely for the engineer's response. His mind was obviously seething with questions, all too personal to venture on so fleeting an acquaintance. At last he nodded. "Good. The fellow needs someone to manage him. I hope you know what you're taking on? Is your family descended from Sisyphus, by any chance?"

She laughed. "Oh, if I roll *this* stone to the hilltop, my Matt will devise some way to prevent its thundering down again – unless, of course, he's quarrelled with Dux and wandered farther afield, which wouldn't surprise me at all."

"I see you know the man well, Miss Flinders. May I ask how you met?"

"I was about to inquire the same of you – and why he was on your mind, Mr. Croxley."

"The canal on which I am presently engaged, the Rugely & Coalbrookdale, has reached an impasse that admits of no easy solution. I was thinking that if one man could provide an answer, that man is Matt Sullivan. But I despaired of finding him. For all I knew he had vanished off the face of the earth. The second-best man would be old Dux – hence my journey." He went on to relate the incident with the stonemasons and the arch. She remembered Matt's telling her the same tale, during those hours of waiting at the Coates end of Sapperton Tunnel. She interrupted: "So you were the man who said he used the cosine of the angle to scale down each course!"

He raised his eyebrows. "And what, pray, do you know of cosines, Miss Flinders?"

"A sight more than Matt Sullivan, I may tell you!"

He frowned. "I beg leave to doubt that. I grant you there's some mystery about the fellow – why a finished engineer should hire himself out as . . ."

Mary suddenly took one of the great gambles of her life. "The only mystery about Matt Sullivan," she said, "is how a man who can neither read nor write can outshine a whole dictionary of engineering, civil or military. Mr. Croxley, will you tie your horse behind and sit within? I want to talk to you about Matt Sullivan. And the future."

He glanced uncertainly about him. "The future?"

"Your future. My future. And – unless we've both mistaken our man – the future of canals and roads and bridges and, if it doesn't sound too fierce altogether . . . the future of civil engineering in this fair land."

# CHAPTER THIRTY-THREE

SHE WAS SO IMPATIENT to see her Matt again that, having returned the carriage to Brian Trueman and enjoyed a light supper with him, she made her excuses and set off immediately for the little grace-and-favour cottage with which his grace had favoured Matt. Apparently the same impatience had moved Croxley, for he stood there, too, in the moonlight, hammering at the door.

"Not a drinking man, is he?" he asked when he saw her approaching.

She shook her head and, bolder than he, raised the latch to let them in. "It's *his* place and no mistake," she said, surveying the chaos that even night could not hide. "Matt!"

There was no answer.

A figure darkened the doorway. From somewhere beyond came the braying of an ass.

"Steam Punch!" she called out in delight, running to him and throwing her arms impetuously around his great frame.

"Sure it's been all of eight days!" he said dismissively.

Lucius pushed his way indoors. He gave her a loving bite and snickered. She dealt his neck several hard slaps. "Ah g'wan ya great babby!" Then turning to Punch she asked, "Where's Matt?"

"Throwing sand at the gale. Though he thinks he's building the pyramids, of course."

Her heart sank. "Is Miss Carmody in it?"

"Who else?"

"Oh God, I knew it."

"When I said you should leave him here, sure I hadn't the pick of a notion that one was about the house. Will I bring you to the Hall? Your man's not long gone."

She gave his arm a squeeze. "You come, too, Mr. Croxley," she said as she passed.

He shook his head in amazement. "The words may be English," he told her, "but it's a different language all the same."

She rounded on him, laughing: "Your first Irish bull, Mr. Croxley – 'different all the same'!"

They set off for the Old Hall. When they crossed the Brooks Bank road Mary said, "Ah yes, I recognize the way now."

"Visiting the duke, is he?" Croxley asked.

Mary put a gloss on it for him. "Poaching his rabbits more likely. That's just the sort of thing would appeal to him."

They approached a paddock. Punch trod on plank that stood an inch or so proud of the road surface. The gate clicked and swung open under his weight.

"Oh, be sure he's passed this way," Mary said as the gate swung to behind them.

The paddock was set about with horse jumps. Croxley examined one of them curiously and then gave it an experimental push. It fell over, then, after a pause, righted itself once more.

"It's like following an elephant over a desert," he said. He was in raptures and kept repeating, "Oh, but he's my man!" at every new wonder.

When they reached the edge of the great lawn Punch suddenly put out a hand to stop them. At first she saw no cause but then he pointed to the gap that opened upon the stable yard; through it a length of ladder was being cautiously extruded.

"Burglars?" he suggested in a whisper.

She said nothing. A large bedroom window up on the first floor was open.

"Gad, it's Sullivan himself!" Croxley said. "I'd know that walk anywhere."

"Proprietor of the universe," Mary murmured.

They watched Matt carry the ladder along the edge of the flowerless flower bed and lean it gingerly against the wall of the house, immediately below the open window.

"Quick!" She gave Croxley and Punch a push. "You two stay ahead of me."

The engineer was about to argue but when he saw her stoop and gather her skirts to the top of her thighs he turned in embarrassment and ran across the lawn beside Punch, as swiftly and silently as he could; she was close behind them.

Matt was halfway up the ladder by the time they arrived; he turned and froze in the very attitude of guilt.

"A fine evening, Matt," Mary said. "If this is one of your experiments, Mr. Croxley and I can save you the trouble."

"Croxley?" Matt echoed in bewilderment. "Mr. Croxley – the engineer?"

"Indeed, Sullivan. How d'ee do?"

"*Civil* engineer!" Mary, relieved to discover they had arrived in time, was now resolved to torment him to the last ounce of the situation. "And he's just the man to tell you that you'll find the ladder safest when the cosine of its angle with the ground is around a half."

Croxley began to laugh so hugely and with so much doubling of his back and slapping of his thighs that he failed to see Rowena Carmody's face make a brief appearance at the head of the ladder.

Matt also missed it. But Mary did not.

"Eh?" Matt responded angrily.

"About sixty degrees." Croxley was still half-choked with laughter. "Forgive me, dear fellow. It'd take too long to explain but the young lady is quite right."

"Why?" Matt asked grumpily. "Why both of you? And here?"

"We met quite by chance upon the way. I have encountered some trouble with a tunnel on the Rugely & Coalbrookdale and I was on my way to consult with his grace when . . ."

"Trouble?" Matt was immediately interested.

". . . when your betrothed" – he turned and included Mary – "informed me that you were to be found here, too. I could not have wished . . ."

"Betrothed!" Matt stared angrily down at her.

"Just listen to the problem, will you," she told him.

Matt turned to Punch. "You're a grand old pal."

"We spoke of it once," Croxley continued doggedly. "I don't know whether you remember it – the Cannock Tunnel?"

"Too narrow," Matt said immediately.

"Exactly. Delays of four and five hours are quite common.

They can only grow worse. We'll lose all our trade to the Birmingham & Fazeley when it opens soon."

Matt was now thoroughly at ease again. He turned to face them and, leaning against the ladder, said, "Double the tunnel?"

"That's what the fools are proposing to do. I was hoping for better advice hereabouts."

"How much would it cost, doubling the tunnel?" Mary asked quickly.

There was a commotion in the room above. An angry roar, like a fanfare, announced the appearance of Dux's face at the window.

"What in the name of all damnation . . . ?" He looked at the ladder, at Matt, at the group on the lawn below, before turning to his niece, who now stood at his side.

"Trouble at Cannock Tunnel, your grace," Matt said conversationally.

"Up to all your old tricks, eh, Miss?" Dux growled at Rowena. "I can see exactly what was planned *here*." Then to Matt he said, "Cannock Tunnel, eh? On the Rugely & Coalbrookdale. Well, I told them so." He looked down at the lawn. "Dammit – is that Croxley there?"

The engineer bowed. "Your grace's most humble and obedient."

"What's this trouble you're in?"

Croxley explained.

"You were about to say how much the doubling would cost," Mary reminded him.

"Miss Flinders?" Dux asked. "Thought *you* were in London. Don't you know they've raised over a thousand pounds for you?"

"*How* much?" Mary asked in surprise.

Croxley, thinking she was prompting him again, said, "It would be several thousand pounds – possibly as much as four."

"Egad!" Dux said. "I heard 'twas but one. You'll be quite the heiress, Miss Flinders." He lost interest and turned to Croxley. "I suppose they will have to double? Madness! They wouldn't listen to me, of course."

They all looked at Matt.

"Must be other ways," he said uncomfortably.

"For the right price!" Mary was quick to insist.

Matt said, "Four hundred pounds!"

"No!" Mary rounded on him before Croxley could say Done! "That's the only sum you can think of, isn't it!"

He was taken aback by her fury.

She turned to the engineer. "A halfpenny a ton."

Croxley winced. Dux (seeing that the canal was not his) laughed heartily. "She has you, by Jupiter! Boxed and skewered! Your own fault! Your own fault!"

The man shook his head. "But the total rate is only a penny a ton."

"Per mile," she reminded him.

"Perhaps you're not aware that the entire canal is only twenty-five miles. You're asking a fiftieth share of the venturers' income."

She looked up at Dux and raised her eyebrows. His smile told her nothing.

She beckoned Matt. He descended quickly, thinking she wished to confer with him privately; but when he reached the ground he was surprised to see her spring upon the ladder and run up to the window. "What should I do, sir?" she asked the duke in a whisper. Then, seeing Rowena in the shadows, she added at a more conversational level, "Good evening, Miss Carmody. I trust this night air does not settle too heavily on your chest?"

Dux, whose navigational enthusiasm had led him to forget his niece entirely, said, "I haven't forgotten, miss." To Mary he murmured, "What'll you do when you haven't me to consult?"

She shrugged. "Leap in the dark."

"Then do it now. Trust your instinct."

Disconsolately she returned to the lawn, where she said to Croxley, as if it were the seal on her defeat, "A halfpenny a ton, then."

"There must be a limit, too."

"Very well, it shall be limited to twenty years from the date on which your trouble is at an end."

He nodded dourly. "Well at least I have something to put before the directors." He turned to Matt. "Could I also give them the merest sketch of your answer?"

"When I've thought of it," was the cheerful reply.

Dux's voice was equally bright. "Have no fear, Croxley. He'll furnish you twenty answers by dawn – and twenty more by tomorrow's sunset. Your difficulty will be to choose among them."

None of them knew how to take their leave in so bizarre a situation. Dux made it easier when he said, "Well, my friends, I'd invite you all within to drink a bumper on this bargain, but . . . duty calls."

He spoke the final words in so ominous a tone that Rowena repeated weakly, "Duty, sir?"

"Yes!" He rounded on her. "I suppose I must now scour the hedgerows for the young miscreant I'll surely find hiding there."

"Young miscreant, uncle?" Her bewilderment was, of course, quite genuine.

"D'you take me for a fool?" he roared. "Isn't it plain as moonlight you intended to elope yet again! Who is it this time, I wonder?" He wafted his arm toward Matt. "And I suppose if Sullivan here hadn't been poaching my grounds and come across your ladder, you'd be halfway to Liverpool by now."

# CHAPTER THIRTY-FOUR

HUMAN MUSCLES are useless," Croxley explained as they walked back in the moonlight. "And there's no towpath for a draft horse. Ergo, it has to be steam."

Matt sniffed.

"You don't agree?" Croxley pressed.

He shook his head. "Too much power, too widely spaced."

"D'you think so?"

"In Cornwall. The best Boulton and Watt. Only six cycles a minute."

The engineer sighed and then slumped, as if only the air had sustained him. "Yes, I agree. That's what had me defeated. I had hoped you might find some way around those objections." He gave a self-mocking laugh. "I even thought of using steam to pump water through the tunnel – to create a current, you see?"

Matt stopped and stared at him. "Well!" he said excitedly. They had reached the canal bank. "We could do that here." He stooped and touched the surface of the water. "That's the exact level at Knot's Mill in Manchester. No locks, see."

He turned expectantly to Croxley, whose idea it had been – though the fellow was only just beginning to realize it. "I see!" he said. "Drain the mines into it at this end and let the barges float . . ."

"Unmanned," Matt pointed out.

"Yes, unmanned, all the way to Manchester. No locks! Also there's what – a forty-foot drop down to the River Irwell at the other end? Why, Dux could burn his coal here and sell its motive power thirty miles away!" He turned eagerly to Mary but the sight of her cool eye staring back at him accusingly brought swift sobriety. "Ah." He cleared his throat. "But, ahem – Cannock. It's no answer there. If not steam, what then?"

Matt tapped his forehead.

Croxley went on: "Possibly . . . horses? I considered that, too. The only way I could devise was a giant windlass at each end with a single rope stretched taut between them, the full length of the tunnel. You'd have a horse-whim at each end, too, connected to the windlass by a crank. The rope would shunt back-and-forth, back-and-forth, like a double-acting piston. You'd get power in both directions, see? The fellow in the barge would just grab the rope when it was moving the way he wanted to go."

Matt shook his head.

"I know what you're thinking," Croxley said. "Too much stretch. Wet days, dry days . . . you'd go mad with the adjustments. And slippage. Even a chain . . ."

Once again Matt shook his head.

"Yes," the engineer sighed, "I abandoned that idea, too."

They finished the journey back to the cottage in silence – Matt's silence. At the threshold, he clapped the engineer on the shoulder. "Take heart, man."

"Tomorrow?" Croxley asked hopefully.

After he had gone Mary said, "But you'll tell him nothing until there's a legal agreement, eh?"

"Oh, but I trust him."

She saw the deliberate provocation and refused the challenge. Punch caught her eye and was suddenly galvanized into taking his leave.

The other two strolled after him as far as the water's edge.

"Angry?" Matt asked when they were alone.

"Have you candles beyond?" She nodded toward the cottage. "Or one of your fire-conducting tubes?"

He shook his head and smiled at the memory.

"We'll stay out in the moonlight, so. I wish to see your face."

"Why did you come back?" he asked.

"To prevent the sort of folly we almost saw tonight. Great gods and little fishes, man – what were you at?"

He turned and walked away. "Her fault."

"Oh no, Matt. *That* fault needs two backs and four hands to its making. The one thing it can manage without is brains."

"D'you own me, now?"

"I do not. But I do love you. And I'll tell you this – it's far stronger than owning."

The confession halted him in his tracks, allowing her to catch up without haste. She walked directly into his embrace and snuggled up to him – then she raised her head in surprise and said accusingly, "You've taken soap to your skin!"

"More fool I!"

There was not one atom of pretence in Matt. He led her among the rushes and laid her down. The moon was at its zenith, almost painful in its brilliance. He lay beside her and took her head between his hands. There were sudden stars in her veins. From the tip of her scalp to the ends of her toes, the flesh of her tingled.

"Oh Matt!" She wriggled herself hard against him. "Oh, my darling, darling boy!"

He undressed her, running his eyes, his fingers, his lips over her nakedness, turning her to jelly. Wherever he touched her he seemed to create new nerves in her flesh. His caress started fires that ran wild through all her body. He kissed her lips and the soles of her feet burned; their knees touched and her whole frame shivered. And when he had finished, almost without pause, he began again. The first time had hurt her a little; the second time, though, she discovered why people would risk their reputations and even their souls for a taste of such joy.

"I never guessed," she told him. She was so full of the discovery she felt like busting. How could a few weak sinews – literally a handful – contain such ecstasy? And where did it conceal itself between times? "I never guessed."

He said nothing.

"Matt?"

"I never did such a thing before."

She dug him with a disbelieving thumb.

"Truly. Oh, I've been through the pauper's gate to paradise – too often. But . . . never *that*."

Her arms stole about him again. She nuzzled his earlobe with her lips. "What was the difference?" she asked in a whisper.

"You."

She shivered with rekindled longing.

"It's a love poem," he said.

"What is?"

"Listen: . . . . . . . *You* . . . ." His lips brushed hers. "That's all the love poem I'll ever need."

At that she dissolved into tears. And kissed him. And gave herself to him, every last fibre, all to him . . . and so slept fitfully till dawn.

Chill and stiff, they hastened back into their clothes.

After a makeshift breakfast she said, "Do you really, really, really love me, Matt?"

He smiled at her.

"Aren't you going to tell me?"

Still his only answer was a smile. Then he took her hand and led her away down the canal bank. Within a few minutes they came to the Worsley mine smithy. The blacksmith himself stood at the door, hot from some exertion and gasping gratefully at the fresh, cool air. He was a shambling, grinning bear of a Cornishman called Fred Chigwidden. "What's this-yur then, boy?" he asked.

"Over the anvil, Fred," Matt said. "The old way. Fitty like."

Fred smiled. "Proper job. Proper job."

"Name of Matt. Name of Mary."

"Matt and Mary." As he repeated each name he stared deep into their eyes, almost as if he feared to confuse the two names unless he fixed them in his mind with such deliberate care.

"Matt . . . and . . . Mary. An em and an em – now that couldn't be better. Royal, that is. An em and an em."

He threw a couple of offcuts of boilerplate into his furnace. "Pump away," he said. "We'll do this-yur fitty like."

Pure, bright sparks danced and vanished in the gloom of that grimy shop as the pair of them, hands on hands, pumped at the bellows. Fred meanwhile sharpened his steel chisel at the whetstone.

"What is all this?" Mary asked. She guessed, of course, but she wanted it in words, out there between them.

"Your answer," was all he'd say.

She watched spellbound as the smith deftly chiselled a letter M out of the glowing sheet. It was still cherry red as he finished. He lifted it in his tongs and quenched it in a water butt, where it spat and sizzled until it was just warm enough to dry itself while he brought it to her; cool enough to hold.

"Mary?" he said.

She nodded.

"Take this, maid, and secrete it about you."

She slipped it inside her bodice.

He repeated the process, fashioning a second M out of the other sheet. This, too, he quenched and gave to Matt, who hid it inside his shirt.

Chigwidden, now seeming more like priest than smith, pointed to a spot in front of his anvil, at the same time nodding toward Mary. She came and stood where he indicated.

"You are Mary?"

"I am so."

"Have you token of your name, Mary?"

She brought out the iron initial, which he inspected solemnly, as if he had never seen it before.

"Do you choose any one man above all other men in our company, whether of high or low estate, whether rich or poor, whether fair or foul?"

"I do so."

"And will you keep yourself as his woman and his alone, through all absence and privation, through tribulation and duress, through trials and shadows, to succour him and bear his childer, until death shall quench those mortal fires we here unite?"

"I will so."

"Then I charge you – name that man."

"His name is Matthew, known as Matt."

"Step forward Matt. You are Matt?"

"I am. Here is the token of my name."

"Do you choose Mary above all others of high or low estate, or rich or poor, or hale or ill, or fair or foul?"

"I do."

"Are you well resolved to keep yourself as her man and her man only, through her travails and your temptations, to nurture her and all your childer, and comfort their perplexity, until death shall quench those mortal fires we here unite?"

"I am so resolved."

Reverently he placed the two Ms back into the furnace. Then he took up two pairs of long-handled tongs and gave one to each. Mary soon understood they were to hold their initials in the glowing coals while he pumped them back to white heat once more.

When they had reached that condition he beckoned them toward the anvil. Matt knew of old what to do; Chigwidden guided her hand until the glowing M was head to toe with Matt's – making, in effect, two triangles united at their tips.

"Matt and Mary," the smith intoned as he hammered at the metal. "Mary and Matt."

He went on repeating the names until the two initials were welded; while they still glowed, he took up his own tongs and, turning the single workpiece this way and that, skilfully hammered the rough edges back into the main mass until all was smooth again.

Mary's scalp tingled when she saw what they had done. Matt took a couple of paces and stood facing her, smiling genially. "Now that's a wedding," he said.

Through her tears she could only nod.

In a conversational voice, quite unlike his priestly intonations, Fred told her, "This next part now, backalong the years, folk belonged to do this with the iron still hot. You could tell a man or woman, married over the anvil, by the scars on the wrists, see."

He plunged the united symbol into the water and brought it to them dry and warm, as before. Matt, still standing facing her, now inserted his right hand up to the wrist into one of the triangles. "You too," he told her.

"Does it hurt?" she asked.

He leaned forward and kissed her tenderly. "No more than any other kind of marriage."

# CHAPTER THIRTY-FIVE

I ONLY MARRIED YOU," Matt teased, "so as to get this blasted cottage cleaned out."

"Tempt me not!" She gave him a playful punch. "I considered it and then I decided no. It'd make it too much like home. This isn't our home. I don't want to live here. I don't want us to be beholden to Dux for anything, especially for the very roof over our heads. I just want to leave here as soon as we can."

He was pleased. "I'm a wandering man myself," he said.

That wasn't quite what Mary meant but she decided to break him to it by gentle degrees.

Dux proved difficult. His bonhomie of the other night had quite evaporated – no doubt because of his failure to catch the suspected lover lurking in the hedgerows. Now he insisted Matt should stay. True, there was no formal contract between them, but an agreement was an agreement.

"What's it to me if the Rugely & Coalbrookdale haven't the sense to heed my advice?" he asked Croxley.

He wanted Matt to give the engineer as many useful suggestions as his fertile brain could manage and then return to the improvements at Worsley pit. "You may take the morning off," he said magnanimously. "I won't grudge that."

It was a dispirited pair of men who returned to the cottage.

Dux's suggestion infuriated Mary; she was adamant on one point: Matt was giving no more free advice.

"I'd not be missed," Matt told her bitterly. "Punch and the lads can manage."

"Then let's just up and leave him," Mary suggested. "We came on the wind, we may go on a breeze."

"You'd need another trade first," Croxley warned. "There's not a mile of inland water where that man's word does not run." He smashed his fist into the palm of his hand. "It's so short sighted. The Rugely & Coalbrookdale intersects with both the Grand Trunk and the Stafford & Worcestershire. Dux has principal shareholdings in both of them, and their traffic is bound to suffer unless we can overcome this difficulty."

"Did you tell him that?"

"There comes a point beyond which there's no talking to a duke."

She could hardly quarrel with that.

The same afternoon Mary took care to be on the canal bank as Dux went by on his habitual walk to his beloved pits. She dropped him a curtsey. He paused. "I wish you'd go up to the Old Hall, young woman, and have a word with my niece."

"What has she been saying, sir?"

"Nothing. She seems to have taken the Sullivan oath of silence."

"Oh." Mary was surprised. "From all I hear of your grace's great regard for our sex, I would have thought that a most satisfactory outcome."

She feared she had played the wrong chord. His eyes went wide in shock, then glared in anger. He ceased to breathe. For a moment they were locked thus; but then something in her expression must have pinched out the burning fuze, for his mouth twisted to a reluctant grin and his breath finally burst out in a reluctant laugh. "If you aren't the most impertinent minx!" he said. "What d'you mean by it?"

"Is it not true?"

"And if it is? Has a duke no privilege left?"

She pointed to Lucius, contentedly grazing among the wild-flowers. "If you came upon that creature there with his leg caught in a mooring line, kicking and kicking – thinking the rope was out to harm him – kicking till the flesh was raw, I mean – could your grace possibly walk on, saying, 'Even the ass has his privileges'? For my life *I* could not."

His smile faded. Their eyes locked. She braved it out, though his stare was terrible; she knew he was waiting for her to yield. He was on that knife edge she had glimpsed more than once in Lord Tottenham, between tenderness and cruelty.

Tenderness won. "You think that of me, do you?" he said. "An old donkey who kicks at bonds that chafe."

She shrugged.

"Walk with me." His words were oddly pitched between command and request. He held out his arm. She would have preferred the upwind side of him but she accepted the offer without flinching.

"*She* was also an Irish girl. I suppose you know the tale?"

"The barest facts – her sister had a certain notoriety. You forbade their intercourse and she refused you. And that was the end of it all."

"You don't understand it. I can tell by your tone." He shook his head, as if to clear it. "But what's here, ecod? I have not spoken of it from that day to this."

"There are so many things I cannot understand," she said, before he could vanish back into his shell. "Old Q told me he had never married because all women are whores . . ."

"And who than he should know it better!"

"Precisely, sir. He can waste his life in the most degraded practices, but his duchess must be pure as snow."

Dux sniffed. "I hold no brief for that old reprobate, but he's right in one thing, hark'ee. A duke may spread his seed where he will and no harm to his line. All he does is enhance the common stock. But the same is not true of his duchess. She hangs her bastards on his escutcheon – and 'scapes the bend sinister by it." In milder tones he added, "Of course, if the blood means naught to you, it hardly matters."

"Isn't that a fierce sort of philosophy altogether?" she said. "Hasn't the pursuit of it cost you the greatest happiness a person can know?"

He chuckled and patted her arm. "You speak from the depths of your honeymoon stupor." Feeling her start he added, "You don't imagine people keep word of such things from me, eh?

Well, believe me, the wrath is yet to come. I could lead you on a Grand Tour of a hundred marriages, all within ten miles of where we stand, and prove to your entire dismay that I've had the best of it. A dead wife is the best meat a man may relish."

Taking another enormous risk she leaned her head against his arm and said, "I think that's the saddest note I ever heard man sing."

He jerked his shoulder, pushing her away; yet there was an odd gentleness in the action. "You almost make me believe in things I know to be impossible, Madame Sullivan. I suppose you were lying in wait for me, hoping to use these strange powers of yours to make me release your husband from his obligations here?"

"There'd be no shame in that, sure?"

"What reasons had you in mind to advance? Or was it to be a salty petition?"

"I may assure you upon one point – I had no intention of broaching the subject that has now been broached. I hope your grace believes me. I have no idea how that came upon us."

"Nor I. You're a dangerous woman to have about the premises, Madame. And so that is why – to put you out of your suspense – that is why I shall let your husband go. You are more dangerous than all the Gunning girls together. The only power they had was their beauty." Almost as an afterthought he added, "Beauty alone would never move me now."

# CHAPTER THIRTY-SIX

CROXLEY LEFT MANCHESTER a couple of days in advance of them. They travelled down the Grand Trunk to Rugely, about twenty miles north of Birmingham.

"Did we have to bring yon creature?" Matt asked with a sour nod at Lucius.

"You should be glad of it," she told him. "'Yon creature' is a token of my fidelity – any ass that saves my life has a place beside me while I yet live."

The rich, rolling farmland of Cheshire and Stafford recalled her conversation with the Duke of Bedford. Now she told Matt of that remarkable evening at Woburn Abbey. "D'you think it's true?" she asked. "That the only sure and permanent wealth lies in the land?"

"Dux wouldn't agree," he answered.

"No. Nor would the canting crews of St. Giles's. I'm sure they believe the only sure and permanent wealth is to be found in the purses of fools."

"And Old Q would say the same."

"Yes, but all the money they gain . . . they don't actually *make* it, do they. Well, some of them in St. Giles's do, but they're hanged for their pains. If you think about it, the only place where *new* wealth is actually created is when someone puts one grain of corn in the soil and in due season harvests thirty or more. If you could follow each golden guinea back to its true origin, it wouldn't be the mint where it was coined, it would be out here, in these fields all about us."

"Ergo? – as Croxley says – "

She raised an appreciative eyebrow. "You learn fast, my love. Ergo, while you are solving the problem of the Cannock Tunnel, I must beg your consent to go onward to London and see about this fund which people have kindly subscribed. Not before time, I may say – they must all think me disgracefully neglectful."

"What'll you do with it?"

"I must obviously apply it to the release of my father. But what then? That's the real question. If I leave him at liberty over there, it will all start again."

"Settle them here, instead?"

She drew a deep breath and replied, "You must be the one to determine that, my darling. I was thinking that if we could purchase a goodly farm somewhere, in countryside such as this . . ."

"Us! Settle?" The idea seemed to shock him.

"Oh, I don't imagine *you'll* ever settle. I'm quite resigned to living like the sailor's wife. But if you had some nestle to call your own – somewhere to invest all those vast royalties and receipts you're about to earn . . .?"

". . . and settle your parents there, too?"

"Well . . . keep a cool and jaded eye upon them. People have been so kind, and I know I must sound the purest ingrate, but – honestly – I wish they hadn't. Some things are best left alone. It's true my mother's life is hard, but she makes it harder than it need be. She could have a comfortable little dame school if she wished. It's her choice not to. And as to my father – oh, what may I say of him? You'll see it for yourself soon enough. Although, come to think of it . . ." She looked pensively at Matt. "I wonder? Am I just adding brushwood to the flames – or will I be fighting fire with fire?"

"What's the difference?"

"Two sides of the one coin, my dear."

"You'd best go to London," he agreed, fearing that the conversation was about to turn into a close dissection of his own character.

They left what little luggage they had at the Shrewsbury Arms in Rugeley. Croxley joined them for lunch and then took them directly to Cannock Tunnel.

"Did you see Brindley's magnificent aqueduct as you came into town?" he asked. "A noble structure! Now there was an engineer! The amazing thing, d'ye know, was that he could neither read nor write."

"Is that a fact?" Matt said distantly.

Mary winked at Croxley, who said no more upon the subject – except obliquely, when, faced at last with his own tunnel at Cannock, he commented that it was "in no way a noble structure."

The landscape was wilder than any through which they had passed on the journey south – a mixture of highland moor and forest. "Good-for-nothing country," Matt said.

"Good enough for coal, by heaven!" Croxley interjected. "And that's more than half our trouble." He waved toward a line of coal barges, waiting impatiently to squeeze through the corset of the tunnel. "Nor," he went on, "are the return barges empty. Coal is money and money is investment. And great houses. And fancy goods. So there you see them – laden with mine machinery, roadstone, fine porcelain, parts for carriages . . . all passing up the canal in perfect balance with the coal that has paid for them."

Mary rounded off the point: "And all have to negotiate that one narrow tunnel."

"What remedies have you tried so far?" Matt asked. He plucked an ear of wild barley and pushed it in at his cuff – the old childhood game of mousey-climb-my-sleeve.

Croxley pointed to a barge laden with mining equipment, among which were some large pulleys of the kind used on uphill railways to allow the horse to work on the level beyond the hillcrest while the waggon climbs the slope. "I had some notion of using those fellows, one at each end of the tunnel, to make an endless loop."

Matt sucked dubiously at his teeth.

"Yes, of course, with your genius you see the problem at once," Croxley said. "The tension would vary too much. How would we stop it slipping off? Well, I thought we could put a third pulley in, free to move sideways and kept taut by a heavy weight in a waggon on a short length of sloping railway. D'you see?"

Still Matt shook his head.

"Quite, quite!" the engineer hastened to agree. "The resistance to motion would be prodigal! Three horses could scarce manage. I wish I were as quick to see the objections as you! Unfortunately, I've already acquired the rope. Several miles of it, indeed. Can you conceive of any other machinery?"

Matt pulled the mousey-mousey ear of barley from the region of his armpit and held it up. "Yes," he said. Then, passing it to a bewildered Croxley and giving him an encouraging thump that almost dislocated the poor fellow's shoulder, he added, "We can use the rope meanwhile, though."

"Now?"

"This minute."

With no more ado he arranged for the rope to be stretched between two teams, each comprising four great draft horses, so that a mile of it was in the tunnel and the second mile beyond. At the midpoint, right by the tunnel mouth, he directed a barge to be attached by its own towline. Then the team at the far end walked forward at a pretty slow pace, drawing the barge into the tunnel. The pace was slow enough for the next barge to be poled up to the point where it, too, could bend its towline around the moving rope . . . and so on, barge after barge, with the horses straining ever harder as the burden increased. All this while the idle team at the back end of the rope was walking toward the tunnel, keeping their end something between fully slack and taut. When they reached the mouth of it, the whole process was reversed, with the idle team becoming the hauliers.

After a few runs for practice they found they could haul four barges through the tunnel each time. Only the first barge would be positively hauled to the very end. The rest drifted the last few fathoms under their own momentum while the teams were being reversed. They also tied cork floats to the line so as to keep it clear of the bottom mud, whose drag almost doubled the resistance of the boats.

With the help of flares they worked all night and cleared the jam by dawn. After that there were rarely more than four barges needing to use the tunnel at any given moment.

Croxley was delighted. "But this is all the answer we need, man," he said.

Mary, who had quietly counted the barges, said, "That's over six hundred pence since last night."

The engineer gave a disbelieving whistle.

Matt laughed. "Equal to a cow and calf. Look for the herd while you're back from London." To the engineer he said, "Now let's be about the *real* solution."

Mary would have preferred to continue to London by canal, but the journey by post chaise was a mere day and a half, and – as she said at their sorrowful parting – the sooner gone, the sooner back.

She was away for more than a month, during which time the last of summer gave way to a bright, golden autumn. Matt worked at the tunnel night and day, sleeping only on trips to the ironfounder's or when he was held up by the labour (or lack of it) of others. He first set some eighteen hundred iron brackets in the western wall, just above the gunwale height of a barge. Upon them he fixed a miniature railway that ran the full length of the wall; its gauge was a mere six inches. Between the two rails, resting on well-greased rollers, was a third rail, which he called the haulage rod – a long, jointed chain of flat iron rods whose upper surface was slotted with regular teeth, cut oversquare, like dovetails. This haulage rod was connected by a crank to a two-horse whim at each end of the tunnel. There was thus a horse-powered stroke forward, about four feet in length, followed by a horse-powered return stroke, four feet back again. The horses walked an endless circle about their whims. Matt's ingenuity was perfectly shown in the way he arranged matters so that the two teams could never pull against each other.

When the rod reached the limit of its forward slide, at either end, it tripped a ratchet that disconnected it from the whim. At precisely that same moment, the other end reached the limit of its backward slide – whereupon it tripped a ratchet that connected it to the whim at that end . . . and so on, back and forth all day.

Each barge was rigidly connected to a miniature waggon that ran upon the rails. This waggon, three foot long and barely one foot high, also contained a ratchet, which was flipped one way to go through the tunnel from north to south, the other way to go south to north. As a result, the single haulage rod could pull a barge in either direction.

A barge would move forward on its horse-powered stroke and then free-float under its own momentum, with the ratchet going clickety-clickety-click, while the horses at the other end pulled the rod back to its origin.

There were four waggons, so up to four barges could use the tunnel in one direction at any one time. And a waggon could be sent back empty if no barge happened to be waiting for it. The haulage rod consisted of over five thousand identical cast-iron segments. They would not last very long, of course, but casting was the only way to make so large a quantity in so short a time. Even before they were installed, though, the ironmasters were already forging the longer-lasting rods that would replace them as they broke. The directors of the canal company were appalled at the size of the bill, which was not far short of a thousand pounds – until Croxley reminded them that the estimate for doubling the tunnel had been more than four times as much.

"Are you going to patent it?" the engineer asked when they had finished cheering the first barge to emerge on the inauguration run.

"I'm not fussed all that much," Matt answered casually. "I've already thought of a better way. But there's a satisfaction beyond all price in solving such a riddle, don't you think?"

"If you do it as easily as that – aye. Mrs. Sullivan will be pleased. D'you know what tonnage has passed since you began?"

Matt chuckled. "That'll be her first question."

"Well, it means at least sixty-three pounds to you."

He whistled. "She's to thank for that."

"Indeed. There can be few couples in all the land who make such perfect partners. You're a second Brindley!"

Matt appeared not to have heard.

Quietly Croxley repeated the assertion, but in quite a different tone: "You *are* a second Brindley, aren't you, old fellow."

Matt nodded hesitantly, still not looking at him.

"You'll have the leisure for schooling now," the engineer pointed out. "And the fee."

"Flat things on a page," Matt said awkwardly, "flummox me. Real things – quite another matter."

"What about figures? Numbers?"

Matt shook his head. "If you was to say sixty-three . . . I'd like as not write the three before the six. North, south, east, and west – it's all one to me on paper."

"How fortunate you are, then, to have a wife who seems to know more of mathematics than many a man. How came she by that skill, I wonder? Have you asked her?"

"Her father – he was told by a priest, a Roman priest – 'learning in the mind of a woman is a trophy on the walls of Hell.' He was enraged! First time he ever found himself in agreement with a papist. She told me he changed his opinion on the very same instant. Her mathematical education began that evening." He gave the other a shrewd glance. "Still – you may know your cosines, you and she, yet who was it discovered the way of reducing the courses in a skew arch, eh?"

Croxley nodded the concession. "But you'll allow me this," he went on. "When we put your idea to the test and found it worked, I wrote at once to several of my friends, all civil engineers. The sketch I did for them was very rough – because to make the same sketch half a dozen times and make it fine would be a most tedious transaction. But I could afford to make it rough and still be understood because in my text I said that the reduction was in proportion to the cosine of the angle toward the springing line of the arch. There you see the power of it! With those simple words, together with the crudest of sketches, an engineer in Russia could make one half of the arch, and another in Scotland the rest. Bring them together and they'd match to perfection."

"And cost a fortune!" Matt deliberately refused to see the point. Then, casually, he nodded toward the canal bank, where not a single barge was waiting. "I'll wager that's a sight you never thought to see, eh?"

A few days later, Mary returned. Her joy – and her pride in Matt – knew no bounds. But her first question was, as he had predicted, "Have you been counting the tonnage?"

"All duly recorded, love. Cheat me and they cheat theirselves." He closed his eyes and shook his head as if he still couldn't believe it. "Two quids a day!"

"First thing we'll do is get you a new shirt," she told him crossly. "What do you do with them?"

He had taken lodgings in Rugely – not that he had spent more than a few hours there during the entire time she had been away. The autumn was now well established and she was glad of the fire that brightened the hearth.

The moment they were alone he lifted her in his arms and carried her to the bed. "I took a bath not a week since," he told her virtuously.

But she struggled out of his grasp. "One more will do no harm to either of us. You may soap my back and then hop in yourself after me."

The landlady's son brought the bath in before the fire and the maid filled it.

Matt could not wait. Her back was only half soaped when he tore off his clothes – quite literally in the case of that offending shirt – and climbed in behind her.

"Here now just you stop this!" She giggled delightedly as he lifted her into his embrace.

Hours later, dry but still not dressed, they lay side by side in the firelight, teaching each other all over again the caresses that gave them the most particular pleasure.

"I think I'd have gone mad, lass," he said, "if I'd not met thee."

"You keep too much inside you."

He laughed at the unintentional innuendo. "Not this evening!"

"You know what I mean," she said crossly.

He was serious again. "There's two people I can talk to. Thee and Croxley. I've had some rare chats with him."

"And Punch."

"Aye, but he's not here, is he."

"Don't be so literal."

They began to dress. "Talking of absent friends," he said, "did you meet anyone as knew us?"

She had, in fact, met Crystal and Jack but she had no stomach to talk of that encounter just yet. She pretended to think he meant upon the journey. "Not on the way up. I went up by post chaise, remember? But there were several on the way back – I came down by canal." She gave him their names and passed on their greetings.

Over supper she said, "If you could find a way, Matt, of combining the speed of the post chaise with the comfort of the canal, you'd have the whole travelling world at your feet."

She intended the remark as no more than a pipe dream but it produced the sort of gleam in his eye that she was beginning to know rather well. "You can already do it?" she asked excitedly.

The promise lingered in his eyes but all he said was, "Tell me now – what happened in London?"

She gave him the bare bones of it. Old Q had won his race down Piccadilly, between the waiter and the bowler of carriage-wheels; so pleased was he with the outcome, he had renewed his friendship and given her fifty pounds to seal it.

"Good of him," Matt said.

"Yes and no. He also said I was to let him know if we have a clever notion for a wager. So his fifty pounds may be no more than prudent investment. I was also pounced upon by the Dowager Duchess of Bedford – the orange-peach – who very kindly offered me the same service she'd performed for the Gunning girls – presentation at court, etcetera. I could hardly refuse. She'd have been mortally offended. And anyway, there were half a dozen other grand ladies all waiting to step into her shoes."

His face fell. "You mean . . .?"

She laughed. "Yes!" You've just bathed and bedded a wench that's well and truly out in society – where to be *out* is to be *in!*"

He toyed with his food.

"What's the matter?" she asked.

Each word was unwilling. "I knew it really. That's where you belong. In society. I'm only holding you back."

She wanted to hit him. She wanted to laugh . . . to cry. "Would you ever listen while I tell you about society." She drew breath and paused to consider how best to make him see it. At last she said, "There's one place where I'm quite certain the Bible is wrong. Remember where God takes Moses up Mount Pisgah and shows him the Promised Land, all flowing with milk and honey? That's the part. I don't believe it. There's no such land. There never is. It's a Hebrew dream. What Moses actually saw from the Pisgah heights was desert and yet more desert. If it flowed with anything it flowed with sand and flies and scorpions. And what he actually said to God was, "Why have you shown me these things, O Lord? Was I not happier with my dreams?' That's what really happened."

"And what did God reply?"

"He said, 'Now indeed Moses your childhood is behind you, for at last you understand that only the Wandering Tribes may keep their dreams.' I don't suppose the knowledge was any true comfort to Moses, though." A faraway look crept into her eyes.

Matt saw that something had happened to her in London. That old madcap sparkle had gone out of her. He was afraid to ask.

When his silence penetrated her reverie she relaxed and smiled. Reaching across the table, she squeezed his hand. "Oh, that's what I missed most – the holy quiet of your company."

"Yet you came back the slow way, by canal?"

She did not immediately respond. She stared at him intently, watching for his smallest reaction, as she said, "When I left here, I thought there was just me to consider. What were sixteen hours of boneshaking hell beside the knowledge that I'd be back here with you all the sooner? But . . . listen, I'm still not certain now, it may all be a false alarm, but better safe than sorry – I *think* there's two of us – and one whom the boneshaking might harm." And she laid a gentle hand, its fingers spread in a great protective curl, across her belly.

# CHAPTER THIRTY-SEVEN

SHE AWOKE the following morning to learn that Matt had already left. "Did he say where he was going?" she asked the landlady.

"Not a word, missis." The raised eyebrows added, *Surely you know him by now?*

Thinking he could only be out at the tunnel, she cadged a ride on one of the boats. The skipper told her he was honoured; to every passer-by he introduced her proudly as the wife of the masterman who had saved the canal.

"Well, Mrs. Sullivan," Croxley said, "and wasn't I right to go seeking your man?"

She wondered had he been arguing the point with his directors. "I'm overwhelmed," she replied. "The deference our dukes demand by the accident of birth is given to Matt by right of achievement."

"Well said! No man ever walked with mind so nimble. He sees everything in a flash. Why, with the tilt of one eyebrow he conveys a whole chapter of mechanics."

Such a gush of adulation disquieted her. It was understandable that others might have questioned Croxley's judgement in consulting a taciturn, secretive, and unschooled labourer – and equally understandable that he now wished to cry up "his" discovery; but this was altogether too much. She pondered carefully before she replied: "We must be sparing of our . . . oh, how may I put this?" She smiled. "Let me just say I believe my husband is in no danger of *under*esteeming himself, Mr. Croxley."

The man seemed disposed to accept the caution, but then, after thinking the matter over, he replied, "It is not his self-esteem, Mrs. Sullivan, it is his silence, which is at once his strength and his weakness. Did you know that he and Dux came almost to blows?"

"Sure that's no surprise – but I fail to see the connection."

"Oh, there is every connection, believe me. Another man would out with an oath and be done. The storm would blow over. But your husband nourishes the impeachment within him, where it festers until it must erupt."

It was a point she had not considered, but as soon as Croxley made it, she felt he was right. She said, "He already seems a little cured, even in these few weeks while I was away. He was ever too solitary before. But now he has you to talk to . . ."

"And you, ma'am."

"*Some*times," she said with sarcastic emphasis. "This morning he forgot the office and I awoke to find him gone. Where is he, by the way?"

"Oh?" There was an evasive gleam in his eye. "Not with you in Rugely?"

She fixed him with an accusing stare. "Come now – something's afoot."

He looked away and scratched his chin. "You'll have to ask him, ma'am. I'm permitted to say nothing."

She returned to their lodgings and spent the rest of the day at composing a letter home – a task that had defeated her several times on her journey back from London, despite its many easy hours over tranquil waters.

As far as her parents were concerned she was a simple young lady from a remote corner of Ireland who had left home three or four months ago to travel to London and, with the aid of letters of introduction, seek her fortune. What would they make of a letter filled with her adventures with the Duke of Queensberry, the Duke of Bridgewater, and the Duke and Dowager Duchess of Bedford – not to mention Lord Tottenham and half the nobility and gentry of the North? How could she say that within a month of her arrival there were plays about her on the stage, and broadsheets to celebrate her fame . . . that she had been presented to King George and that grand ladies had climbed on tables and windowsills in the room to see it . . . and, oh yes, finally, she was now living in humble lodgings, engaged in a pagan marriage to an illiterate mechanical whose present whereabouts were a mystery.

And by the way, Dearest Father and Mother, I, who had no more than four pounds when last you saw me (and all of them borrowed), am now privileged to inform you that I am possessed of nineteen hundred pounds for your support!

The floor was strewn with discarded efforts before she would admit defeat. In the end, all she wrote was:

My Dear Parents: Such Adventures that have befallen me you'd never believe. If Word of them has reach'd the Dublin journals, and thence to Co. Clare, I beg you afford no credence to the most part of it. What is Truth Ye shall hear when we meet, and it is of that Meeting alone which I now write.

I am Well, and indeed may say I was never Better. I am Wed not to Ignatius Murphy nor to Lord Tottenham, nor, indeed, to any of that Tribe, but to a most Darling and Ingenious Man by the name of Matt Sullivan, a Civill Engineer who is consulted on all the most Important Canals in the land – even by the Duke of Bridgewater. I vow my dear Father's eyes kindle at this Intelligence! There is more. My own Matt is most Impatient to become acquainted with Ye both and on that ac. I send, by my good Brother William, a note for 250l. with the which he is to discharge all Debt and purchase my Father's Liberty. The remainder Ye are to apply to your wardbrobe and Passage to Bristol, from where, do Ye but mention my Husband's name, Ye will gain free and untrubbled passage by Navigation and Canal to this town of Rugely:-
– Where Ye are awaited with Duty and Eagerness by,
yr. Humble and Ever-Affec. dr.

Even then she hesitated to send it; only when she heard the collector's cry from the next street did she take her courage in her hands, seal the letter, and bring it down to him.

Matt did not return until well after dusk. She threw her arms about him and hugged him for dear life. After a while his hands stole down and began to raise her skirts.

"Would you ever stop!" she laughed.

But he was not to be denied. Hastily, over the edge of the bed, not even removing their clothes, they rediscovered paradise.

"I was thinking of that all day," he told her as he recovered his breath. "You, too, I'll wager?"

"I was thinking of you," she allowed, "but in somewhat different mode – mainly I was thinking, *Where on earth is the man?*"

"Here at last." He pulled a contrite face.

"You're a husband now, Matt. You can no longer restrict your communion to yourself and the skylarks."

"Sorry."

"And didn't I feel the eejit of four kingdoms when Lord Amplehush called by and I couldn't tell him if you were north, south, east, nor west."

He put his hands over his head, as if sheltering from a bombardment, and asked, "What did he want?"

"Only they want to give you a gold medal!"

"To me?" His delighted face emerged from behind his arms. "Have you got it? Did he leave it here?"

She raised her hands briefly in baffled resignation. "I give up!"

"What was it for? Did he say?"

"It was for silence, what else?"

"For science?"

"No – *silence*! Oh God, it was for gullibility, man – there's no gold medal, nor any such person as Lord Amplehush."

The barb of her wit stung him not at all; he saw her story as nothing but a childish deception. He was short with her all during supper. She again asked him where he had been but now he refused to tell her.

Later, however, with a full stomach, and good ale seeping into his veins, and a warm fire, and a long evening ahead, he began once more to grow amorous. That was when she fetched out chalks and a slate.

"What's here?" His eyes were shocked.

"Time to begin your mathematical education." She looked at him and laughed.

"What's funny?"

She shook her head. "I was reminded of something that happened when I dined with the Duke of Bedford – but that tale will keep. Take up a chalk now."

"Mathematical education!" he said disgustedly. "I don't need your cosines and things.'

"You may never use them, Matt, but you're going to move increasingly among people to whom they are as natural as nails. Don't you think you should at least understand what trigometry and suchlike can do?"

Grudgingly he admitted it – but the hour that followed was stiff with resentment.

And then there came one of those magic moments, a flash of experience that you can look back on all your life and say, "That was when things changed." She was showing him how to plot the sine of an angle, and as the points began to form the familiar, rather beautiful 'sine wave,' she felt him grow tense with excitement. It so surprised her, after his earlier resistance, that she paused.

"Go on!" he urged.

When the wave was complete he let out the breath he had been holding. Then he made her sponge it out and draw it again, to prove it had not been some artistic sleight of hand – that those dull columns of numbers in her *Book of Tables* really did conceal this most beautiful shape.

After that there was no holding him. He took the book and drew the curves for himself, for he could read numbers even if he sometimes muddled their writing. He marvelled that elegant parabolas should emerge so easily from simple lists of figures.

It fascinated her that abstract numbers – the black and white symbols on a page – continued to baffle him; but the curves he derived from them became the material of an almost continuous explosion of further ideas – notions that would never have occurred to her no matter how much she applied herself to it. Mostly his ideas took the form of questions:

If you could instantaneously freeze the surface of a pond, would the waves upon it be sine waves?

If you put a pencil at the bottom of a pendulum and dragged a sheet of paper past it at an even rate, would that also draw a sine wave?

Ditto with a pencil at the top of the beam of a Cornish engine?

If you let a piece of string hang slack between two points, did it form a parabola – a curve derived from the table of cosines? If so, could you use it as a handy, on-the-spot aid to determine the courses of his famous skew arch – by tying knots at fixed intervals and taking your levels from them?

Again and again he sought to work these new discoveries into his actual experience, to give them roots of metal and stone – the very stuff of engineering.

The list grew and grew. His excitement was the nearest thing she had ever seen to drunkenness in a man who was cold sober. At length she had to remind him of the way he had wanted to spend the evening when she had first brought out the chalks and slate. Even then, although he took to the exercises of love with his customary vigour, there was something suspiciously mechanical in his movement.

Beyond a doubt, she thought wryly, he was bobbing up and down on a sine wave.


# CHAPTER THIRTY-EIGHT


THE FOLLOWING DAY, when she again asked him where he had been, he said, "I'll take you there."

They hired a fly and went over the hills to Sandwell, a few miles northeast of Birmingham. There they alighted and walked down the slope to Smethwick Hall, to the bank of what looked like a canal.

"It is a canal," he assured her. "One of Brindley's as a matter of fact."

"But why is it all . . . I mean, it hardly looks used."

"It isn't. It's abandoned."

"An abandoned canal!" Mary said, as if the two words flatly contradicted each other.

"If I had my way, England would be littered with such waters." He went on to explain that, out of sight at the bottom of the hill, a bold, deep, new cut by John Smeaton had "ironed out" a section of Brindley's meandering follow-the-contour route – and incidentally cut out six locks.

"So why have you brought me here?" she asked.

"I've been working on an idea you gave me."

"Me!"

"Come and I'll show you."

As they walked along the greening towpath, he explained that while constructing the Cannock Tunnel engine, he had been trying to work out what gearing to put between the horse-whim and the haulage rod; too little and the horses would be over-strained; too much and they'd use more energy going round the whim than in hauling the load itself.

"We dragged empty barges up and down the canal at different speeds, see? Measure the stretch of the rope. Afterwards – static weight – same stretch – tells you the pulling force of the horse. Compare it with the speed. Anyway, there was this massive horse – Poseidon. Managed to get up a canter. And old Joe Scrimshire, driver, said as the beast had an easier time of it at that than at the trot or walk. Didn't believe him. Of course. Made him do it again. And then I spotted it."

"Spotted what?"

He gave a confidential nod. "Watch."

Floating in the now-undisturbed waters of Brindley's old cut was a miniature barge, about four foot long and carved from a solid baulk of timber. At its prow was a ring of iron, to which was fastened a length of cord, the other end being tied to a mooring post on the bank.

Matt unhitched this line and set out along the towpath, dragging the model behind him as a youngster might pull a toy. "Watch the waterline," he told her.

His walk turned into a trot, then a run. She kept level with the model, taking his footfall as a guide.

"There!" he said and gradually slowed to a halt. "See it?"

"I heard it. It made a different note – the gurgling of the water."

He thought for a moment. "Aye, it would," he said. "Never thought of that. Watch again – and tell us why."

He ran back, towing the model over the same stretch of water. This time, when he cried "There!" she saw it.

"It didn't sit *in* the canal like an ordinary barge. It more-or-less sat *on* it. Almost on top of the water."

He slapped her heartily on the back, bringing tears to her eyes. "That's it, lass! Exactly as with Poseidon."

"It's very interesting, darling," she said dubiously.

"Don't you see it? The notion was yours – as I said."

She shook her head.

"It was," he reaffirmed. "You said about the comfort of canals and the speed of the mails." He nodded at the model. "There you have it."

"But how . . . I mean, you couldn't expect a horse to run a hundred miles towing a barge at those speeds . . . could you? Not even a pair of horses . . . or three or four."

Grinning, he shook his head. "A fresh team every few miles! Eh? Twelve mile an hour. Easy. Even stopping for locks. And if the locks were always in our favour . . ."

"*Our* favour?"

He prodded the model with his toe, making it bob up and down, as if in agreement. "You're looking at our fortune and our future, lass. Not like Dux's boats, Warrington to Manchester for a shilling. They're no more than plain cargo barges with extra rooms for people. No! Something new." He drew in a dramatic breath, a rare gesture for him. "The Sullivan Express!"

"No! The *Silent Sullivans!*"

Her matching excitement loosened his tongue still further, as if he had half-expected her to pour scorn on the idea. "Aye – you could step aboard her, here in Birmingham, at nine of the evening. Retire. Comfortable bed. Awaken at Castle Field, Manchester – or Parliament Street, Liverpool – at nine of the following morning. Return that night. Three trips a week each way. Ten shilling the single journey!"

"More," she said. It was the most exciting idea she had ever heard. "Do they serve victuals on Dux's boats?"

"There's tables. Bring your own."

"Sure we could go one better. Had we but a little galley, and meals half-prepared ashore before setting out, couldn't we serve a royal feast. That would bring in even more money. Twelve shillings the journey. Even fifteen?"

"Aye! Aye! Breakfast too, why not? And good wines and spirits. A floating inn!"

"A water palace." She held his arm, giddy with excitement. "And I could sing to my harp. Oh when can we start?"

He gave her a crafty, sidelong look. "There's more."

"What?"

"The mails. This fly boat could carry the mails."

She tested the idea. "Would it be as fast as the post chaise?"

He shook his head; but then he pointed at the water. "How often will you see that under ten foot of snow? Once or twice in a long life. Or mired to the axles? Never. They hardly ever freeze, what with the traffic that's on them. Reliability, see. When the difference is eight hours by land or twelve by water, the reliability will tell."

While she was absorbing this he added, "A patent for carrying the mails . . . that's better nor a civil pension."

The thought sobered her. "The coaching faction would slit our throats first."

"Still . . ."

"Well!" She brightened. "I'll tell you one thing – we'll never run from a good fight. What's our next step?"

"Build the barge."

"Build it? Can't we adapt one?"

He shook his head. "They're made for carrying roadstone, coal, see?" His stretched fingers showed the thickness of their timbers. He closed them to less than half the distance. "That'll do us. No stormy waves. No rocky coastlines. Think of one of Old Q's thoroughbreds compared to Poseidon." His eyes gleamed as he said, "She must look like a flier!"

"Will *you* build it?"

He nodded and stared down at his hands. "*Our* secret – while we're ready to launch her."

"But Matt – have you ever built any sort of a vessel in your life?"

"No."

His tone implied that he saw no difficulty. After some thought she went on, "I think we ought to tell Dux."

He scratched his chin.

"I know you and that one don't pull in tandem, but even so, he's no man to offend."

Matt looked away toward the horizon.

"God love us," she persisted. "He controls the waters we'd hope to ply upon."

"The law says a canal company can't refuse . . ."

"The law! Listen, Matt – if I've learned but one fact since I stepped off the mailboat at Holyhead, it's this: The English law is there to say what happens when there's no duke in it to say otherwise. The law does not regulate the behaviour of dukes. We *must* tell Dux."

Still he would not agree – nor disagree either.

She threw up her hands and walked off. "God send respite from stubborn, silent men!"

He joined her, cheerful at not being forced to a commitment. "Talking of the nobility – had you word of Lord Tottenham in London?"

"They say he's in France. And Con Murphy with him. I expect it's the truth, too. That's where Lord Rolle was for sending him before he appealed to Old Q. You see what I mean by the power of a duke?"

"And what of Jack and Crystal Horley? They've wedded?"

"They have so. They were in secure lodgings in St. Giles's but she couldn't abide the company there – not that I'd blame her for that. So she found a different kind of protection – oh Matt, it's awful – and now they live in Mayfair, in a grand house in South Audley Street."

Matt looked quizzical.

"She has become a most *popular* young lady. D'you not follow?"

"You mean . . . ?"

"Yes – she's *anybody's* Mrs. Crystal Horley."

"Nay." He stopped, scandalized at this news. "I can't see Jack allowing it."

"That's the worst part of all. Crystal games a lot, you see, at cards. And the gentlemen – her gentlemen – force the game to make it appear she wins. So Jack goes about praising her skill at the table, when all the time it's . . . the other thing. But he knows the truth – of that I'm sure."

After a pause Matt said, "Remember that night in the field? Above Sapperton Tunnel – that oath he took?"

"Oh stop! Listen Matt while I tell you – the things I've learned about so-called gentlemen since that evening!"

"I've never thought much about them, one way or t'other. But that was a grand oath of Jack's. I'd have followed him to the four corners after I heard that."

"In the days of chivalry perhaps it still had meaning. But from the behaviour I've witnessed, just in these few months, I don't see how the English 'gentleman' can outlive this century. Perhaps Mr. Page is right – sweep it all away!"

Matt resumed their walk. After a short silence Mary went on, "I can't fathom Crystal. When we first came to London and it was a question of Jack's going to fight in some protestant army in Europe to restore their fortunes, and she told me she'd do anything to keep him out of such danger – well, I never for one moment imagined that!" In bitter tone she added, "I blame myself as much as anyone."

"Why?"

"Don't ask who introduced her to Old Q – which, of course, is where it all began. Now she has a whole league of gentlemen about her. 'My stable of thoroughbred stallions,' she calls them. At first I thought she was just being bold, to brazen out the matter. But it's the truth. She says men are fools to pay so well for what she would gladly yield unbought. God save the mark!"

"I still can't believe Jack really does know."

"His pretended ignorance rings as fine as the oath he took that night. God, he'd cut the head out of any man who spoke the truth of Crystal. He spends his time – and her earnings – in high living. London has ruined him."

A broad, sloping field lay between them and Smeaton's new cut. They crossed it in silence. As they approached the towpath he said, "We must seek new lodgings hereabouts." He pointed toward a likely looking farmhouse. When they were halfway there he suddenly said, "We'll do more for the cause of revolution than a hundred of your Mr. Pages. The *Silent Sullivans* will be a revolution all their own."

# CHAPTER THIRTY-NINE

MUCH TO MARY'S DISQUIET they did not let Dux know what was afoot. Instead, Matt rented a barn at that farm above the new cut, near Spring Grove, and there he and an old boatbuilder, who was as sparing of words as Matt himself, began to construct the first of the *Silent Sullivans*.

And from those new lodgings she sent word to Croxley that if her parents arrived in Rugely, they were to be redirected down to Birmingham. They also passed word among the canal folk.

The engineer's curiosity was naturally stirred and he himself turned up on their doorstep the following week. Matt was reluctant to show him the boat – or the ribs of it, which was all there was to show. But, after enjoining the man to secrecy with oaths that were almost Masonic, he relented. Even then he would say nothing as to its purpose.

This ritual surprised Mary; from the way Croxley had behaved on the day she had gone seeking Matt at Cannock, she assumed he knew all about it. Later, he fished Mary for more, saying, "It's like no canal boat I've ever seen."

For loyalty's sake she held her tongue, though she longed to tell him everything and ask his opinion.

"I hope it *is* for a canal," he went on. "Those ribs are too frail for the sea."

She thought it no disloyalty to say, "At least I may set your mind at rest on that score."

"I'm vastly pleased to hear it, ma'am. We canal people suppose our present situation to be a marvel but I assure you, ten years hence we shall look back in scorn at our present complacency.

Last year, you know, but one single canal was authorized in parliament, at a capital of ninety thousand. One canal in the whole of the kingdom. But this year . . . guess how many?"

"Double?" Mary suggested. "Thrice?"

"Sevenfold! Yes! Seven new canals will be authorized by the end of this year. When they're completed, they'll double the number of companies we have at present – and more than double the mileage. And the combined capital of those seven is three-quarters of a million pounds! But even that is only the beginning. Next year, there'll be more still. In short, ma'am, this would be no time to turn your backs on the business."

"Where does so much unfettered money come from?" Mary asked. She had seen at first hand the wealth of a few exceptionally rich men – the three richest in the land after the Duke of Marlborough, if Lady Maynard was to be believed – but such wealth was mostly bound up in estates and houses and merchant vessels and the like; it could not provide more than a tiny pick of such vast loose capital.

Croxley laughed. "That's the most amazing thing of all. When Dux and Brindley were building their first little canal, he couldn't cash a note, not at any discount, within a hundred miles of Manchester. He had to trot round his estate on a little pony – can you imagine Dux doing this? – he trotted round collecting every little ten-shilling debt he was owed. And that's how he paid for his canal. And now – only thirty-odd years later? Now they must disguise their subscription meetings as funerals or society balls, or hold them on the tops of Welsh mountains, for fear of being overrun by subscribers. If Dux was to promote a canal from here to the North Pole, shares would be at a thousand per cent premium within the week."

"But that still doesn't say where the money's coming from. I mean, if they hold a meeting – no matter where – and sixty thousand is subscribed in the course of two hours, where has it all come from? The subscribers must have withdrawn that money from somewhere else. But where? What other enterprise has lost it?"

"Ah!" He pinched his lips between his fingers and made small popping noises while he considered his answer. "In a manner of speaking," he said at last, "the money, as such, is not actually raised at the meeting. I mean, the directors don't walk away with bags of actual gold. All they have is the subscriber's promise to pay his share of the venture if called upon to do so."

"But why should they not call upon him to pay his share? How else do they get the money for the survey . . . and all the labour and materials for the construction?"

"Oh, he'll pay some of it, of course. Perhaps each subscriber, will pay five pounds of every twenty-five-pound share. And that would be enough to survey the line and build a part of it. And then it can happen that the profit on that part of the canal alone is enough to fund the rest, without any further call upon the subscribers."

Mary shook her head in amazement. "Isn't it what people always say – there is but one seed for money and that's money itself."

Croxley grinned. "Not necessarily, ma'am. There's a lot of subscribers could never pay their calls. They rely on the fact that – the way things are – a twenty-five-pound share could rise to a hundred, five hundred . . . a thousand pounds." Seeing her jaw drop he nodded vehemently and pointed to the new cut at the foot of the hill. "Where d'you suppose the money came from to pay for Smeaton's work down there? The profit is enormous. You couldn't get a twenty-five-pound share in the Birmingham & Wolverhampton today for under a thousand. So, to return to the point, you could subscribe for twice as many shares as you can truly afford and, if they do no more than double in value – which would be very poor performance for a canal share, I may say – you may then sell half, and the half you retain will have cost you nothing. I hope I'm not giving you ideas now!"

Her scalp tingled with excitement. "I thought society was mad with the fever of gambling, but sure it's everywhere. Is there any branch of commerce, or any other human activity, where gambling's not the rule?"

He raised his hands, much as to say, 'I know of none such.'

"If all that is true," she went on, "then the five pounds that brought me from my home to London – I could have subscribed a twenty-five-pound share in the Birmingham & Wolverhampton with it, paid up the five, and then sold it for a thousand?"

"Indeed you could."

Still it seemed incomprehensible to her. "Sell it for a real thousand?" she asked. "Real sovereigns in my hand?"

"Real, real gold."

"But then *that* money has to come from somewhere. It's not just promises on paper."

He nodded a concession. "I suppose you could say it comes from the future, Mrs. Sullivan. It'll be repaid out of receipts from the trade upon the canal waters. A penny a ton . . . twopence a ton . . . it soon mounts up. As, indeed, you are already discovering for yourself." He nodded thoughtfully. "I'd never seen it in that light before, but that's where it comes from: the traffic of the next half-century and more. You and Mr. Sullivan hold a tiny little mortgage on coal that lies yet unmined, on pots that are still virgin clay in the fields, on grain that stands twenty seasons from the grain in those barges down there." He turned to her. "Had you considered it?"

"Indeed and I had not."

"And how does it strike you?"

"I have a book above, filled with amazements, but doesn't that bang them all!"

## CHAPTER FORTY

HER PARENTS ARRIVED on a raw day that November. They had never been a demonstrative family; their greetings, though warm at heart, were cool upon the surface. From the moment they stepped off the barge, Mrs. Flinders was the dominant figure, as brisk as the day; her husband – The Flinders of the Barony of Inchiquin in County Clare, and now looking every inch of that elevation – was a benign patriarch who, when he was not withdrawn into some grand reverie of a notion (which could happen between one footfall and the next), beamed with a generalized if impractical goodwill at all the world.

They were to stay at the farm for the moment. The farmhouse was large and most of the family had fledged and flown, so there was room enough for all.

"Had you an agreeable voyage?" Mary asked as they stood on the canal bank, waiting for the baggage to be uncovered.

Her mother sniffed. "The Flinders has conceived a grand notion for ameliorating the comfort of . . ."

"All it needs, you see," her father interrupted eagerly, "is to lay a great chain upon the seabed from Cork to Bristol. Then fit windmills in place of sails and she could haul into the teeth of any wind. And the fiercer, the better. It does away with navigation and tacking at one stroke, d'ye see?"

"You're still the oul' lighthouse in a bog," Mary told him affectionately.

"Rust," Matt murmured.

"Aha!" The older man's eye gleamed as he turned upon his son-in-law. "The chain, you see, is to be passed through a bath of tannin oil upon the vessel before it is returned to the seabed. A sovereign cure for the rust is your tannin oil."

Matt laughed, put an arm about his shoulder, and bore him off to the barn.

"And then there were two," Mrs. Flinders said half to herself as her eyes followed them up across the field. "It was never thus in my father's time."

"Come away in," Mary told her. "We have much to discuss while they reinvent the world."

But Mrs. Flinders would not move until she had supervised the unloading of their baggage. While she handed out the commands, prodding the air and ground with her umbrella, she told Mary of *such* an agreeable man they had met upon the way. He knew Matt slightly, or so he claimed, and was most interested to hear all the news of his affairs. Mary listened with half an ear. The canal world was full of people who knew Matt.

"He is a cousin of the McGrotty's at the forge in Ennistimon," Mrs. Flinders added.

The name meant nothing to Mary.

Mrs. Flinders had made lavish and excellent use of the money her daughter had sent. She seemed ten years younger, and Mary realized that the dour, withdrawn personality she had known in all those years, was no more natural to her than the poverty that had nurtured it. The woman was now in her true element, bright and sharp, keeping the world up to its mark with the tip of her umbrella and the point of her tongue.

While they walked up the lane, with the little ice pools groaning and cracking underfoot, Mary recounted her adventures – a story that continued as they stood before the fire indoors, rubbing life back into their knuckles; and there was yet more to tell as they withdrew above to unpack all those new clothes and put them to air after their long, watery journey. She kept her drama as matter-of-fact as possible – no easy feat when its heroes were a pride of obsessive dukes entirely caught up in their greed or lust, their hauteur, their grudges . . . when the minor cast included a band of jovial outlaws who in popular prints would be called "desperate," though they were no such thing . . . when the walk-on parts were strangers whose eccentricities bordered on madness (not to mention King George himself in that capacity – or incapacity) . . . and finally with villains in the form of a bull and a nobleman whose behaviour had passed over that border.

And through it all, Mrs. Flinders listened with a calm that only augmented Mary's surprise. Her mother's questions seemed almost random; some had a point, others none: What was the colour of the bull? Had Lord Tottenham a sister? Why did she, Mary, never think of marrying Mr. Page? Were the king's teeth all sound? Had Matt any money of his own? Yet even the most sensible of these queries was more in the nature of a verbal lubricant to the tale, rather than a genuine request for enlightenment.

At last Mary drew her story to its close. She had told everything, including the fact that she was with child, which by now was certain.

After that delight had been shared Mary waited for some more general response; but all her mother said, or sighed, was, "It takes so *many* generations to make a gentleman."

In a tone that invited little argument, and got none, Mary responded, "Matt is the most of a gentleman I know." For good measure she added, "And the next-most is a republican revolutionary who'd see every lord in the land served an oyster and an artichoke for breakfast."

Actually, she thought to herself, Mr. Page wasn't the next-most; that honour fell to Punch.

That night she asked Matt, "Why shouldn't old Punch come and work for us? And him so handy with the horses."

Matt gave a non-committal shake of the head; his mind was all on the *Silent Sullivan*.

"Or with the steering, then. Couldn't he take the helm? He's delicate at that, too. If, after the baby's born, I'm to play my part in the family business – below in the galley, say – I'd want someone I could put a face on in the dark up there."

He shrugged. "I'd given it no thought."

"Hah – isn't *that* the truth!"

He was surprised.

"I'll tell you something else to which you've 'given no thought,'" she went on. "How are we to commend our service to the populace? How are people to hear of it? Have we handbills printed? Or placards to post in the assembly rooms?"

After a guilty silence he said, "Aye – I see."

There was a pause in which she ought to have said "Good," but didn't.

"How you put up with me . . ." he offered with an apologetic chuckle, three-quarters genuine.

"I have a better idea than handbills and posted placards," she said, "though we'll need them, too. But remember what I told you about Old Q – if we thought of any good subjects for a wager?"

He raised his eyebrows enthusiastically; already he had caught the drift of her idea.

"I believe there's many a booby would wager highly that no party of forty gentlemen might dine in Birmingham, move no farther than twenty paces from their table, and find themselves, within twelve hours, in Manchester."

Matt laughed in delight.

"Sure, even if they worked out that canals were in it," she went on, "for what coach can carry forty men, not to mention a dining saloon? – they'd never believe the twelve hours."

He grew more thoughtful and asked where they'd get forty gentlemen all wanting to go from Birmingham to Manchester.

"But isn't that the whole purpose of our vessel?"

"On her first run, I mean."

Inspiration came to her aid: "We'll take the first forty names in the wagers book. The minute they see the lines of the *Silent Sullivan* they'll know they've lost, so we'll at least give them a royal banquet and I'll sing the grandest airs. And thus all their lives they may boast they were there the night Matt Sullivan abolished the statute mile. And wouldn't all the world get to hear of it then?"

"Will you write to Old Q or go in person?"

"God, I ought to go and see him." She sighed. "But a letter will have to do. I must urgently seek out a farm, somewhere by the canal between this and Manchester, and settle the oul' wans there."

"Send them to seek out the place for you," he suggested, "while you're in London."

"Why?"

"A pension is a sour pie. If they found the place, the occasion to grumble would be less."

She threw her arms about him happily. "You're no fool on your day, Matt me darlin'. It would be better if I saw Old Q rather than wrote. He's sure to have ten thousand questions – the caution that's in him – and it would take an unconscionable time to satisfy him through the mails."

She had other business in London too – business she had set in train on her previous visit. Mr. Page, the honorary secretary of the appeal fund, had arranged for his attorneys to draw up a deed appointing Mary the trustee of the moneys. At her own request there were stringent limits on the enterprises in which she might invest – no canals for the total insulation of Ireland! She might buy ready-broken-in farmland to the full extent of the fund – no vineyards in the Burren. She might invest up to one-third in proven canals or in enterprises whose income derived chiefly from the trade upon them. And no part of the capital was to be spent on day-to-day living, other than that which had already been sent for her father's discharge and their journey to England. Thus not all his pleas or blandishments would be able to pry one penny out of her for his "bog lighthouses."

What with one thing and another it was almost December before she set out – with promises to be back before Christmas. The new fast route to London, opened within the last few months, started, paradoxically, by heading northwest toward

Fazeley; but there the Coventry Canal led south to the Oxford, and thus to the Thames Navigation, whose waters she was now beginning to think of as a second home. The journey took five days by ordinary barge but there were usually one or two lighter fly-boats that could clip a day or more off the journey, making it only a day slower than the coach in winter. These were regular barges with part of their cargo space converted into general cabins for passengers. They went at ordinary speeds but paid a higher tariff (and, of course, charged a premium fare) to secure priority at the locks.

As luck would have it, such a fly came south through Fazeley not ten minutes after her arrival. She could be in London by Wednesday and leave again on the following Monday. Her father was right – what a wonderful age to live in, to be sure!

In the ladies' cabin there were two doughty matrons playing cribbage and discussing in considerable detail (some of it rather coarse) the virtues and drawbacks of the men in their own circle of friends. After a cheerful smile of welcome they paid Mary not the slightest attention. When Mary learned that Mr. Belevedere "could dangle a pair of riding boots from it without a hint of a droop," she decided that, cold though the day might be, she'd arrive in better health if she took one of the journals out on deck.

She was by now thoroughly in love with the canals. True, the newest additions cut unsightly scars through the countryside, but within very few seasons the raw earth settled beneath a new mantle of green and then the navigations began to look as if they had been there since Eden. When the locks had acquired a scrape or two and strands of verdant weed began to trail down into the murk, it was extraordinary how *established* all the machinery seemed. The silence was the other blessing, the silence and the smoothness of the ride. The coaches would give you a headache in ten minutes. In the summer you sweltered or choked in dust; in winter you could freeze or perish with the wet. And, summer or winter, the rumble of the wheels with their iron tyres was a torment. But here, drifting over the sylvan waters, the only consistent sound was the trotting of the horses and the liquid gurgle beneath the bows – interrupted for variety by an "Ahoy there, Jacko!" and a "Way-hay, Cap'n!" as barge passed barge. Sometimes, when the crews were well acquainted, there would be facetious cries of "Bang, bang – your watch!" or "I kept the box warm whilst you were abroad!" Along the canals, surliness was the exception; upon the highway, it was the rule.

There was an amazing amount of traffic over the new cut to Oxford. Every mile they passed out at least one and often two or three other barges, who naturally yielded priority to them; and coming the other way – well, it was like a commercial armada! On earlier voyages she had taken the scene for granted but now, with Croxley's words in mind, she cast a more observant, knowing eye. She noticed an astonishing amount of lime. It couldn't all be for building, surely? Then she remembered how the Duke of Bedford had praised lime as a fertilizer – how it could double and treble the yields of some soils. A single barge could carry more than a pack-horse team might fetch in a month. It was almost too frightening to think about. These English Midland farms were already fertile beyond belief by the standards of her own native farmland; but what if their fertility was doubled, and more? The income would be only fierce – and that would mean new, grander houses and new, grander things to put in 'em – and yet more goods upon the canals and yet more money into circulation . . .

She had a sudden vision of the whole nation forging ahead in an upward spiral of prosperity. Everything had been waiting these decades past – perhaps centuries – for the canals to connect them together: the lime kilns to the fields, the crops to their markets, the money of the nobility to the enterprise of men like Matt and Croxley, prosperous towns to country villages that until now had been rich in nothing but nursing mothers. All had been stultified for lack of these narrow, connecting threads of water and the cheerful men who plied their craft upon them. But now – could the process be stopped even if men wished it?

And why should any man wish it? Surely within two or three generations, pauperism would be abolished and beggary reduced to doleful memory?

With such thoughts in her mind she turned to her papers. It was a cold day, but sunny. In the lee of the ladies' cabin, with the sun full upon her, it felt almost like summer. But she had hardly settled to her reading when a shadow fell across the page.

She looked up to see a man preparing to seat himself upon the gunwale. He smiled at her. He was of a like age with Matt, a labouring man but dressed in his Sunday suit. His smile was not the tenderest sight for he was lacking several teeth, and those that remained were brown from tobacco. "Mrs. Sullivan, ma'am?" he asked.

She nodded warily. He had started his journey, like her, in Birmingham – in fact, at Ladywood, just half a mile below Spring Green. She had caught his eye a couple of times on the haul to Fazeley, but on each occasion he had looked hastily away.

"Are we acquainted?" she asked.

"I'm an old mate of your husband's ma'am. Aaron M'Grotty's the name. May I sit and pass the journey awhile?" He waved his fuming clay pipe. "Have you an objection to this?"


# CHAPTER FORTY-ONE


THE *SILENT SULLIVAN* drew day by day nearer to completion. Matt had one cardinal rule for her construction: *If it weighs more than a pound and we can't think of three combined purposes for it – then leave it so until we can.* Every shelf served double as a brace and triple as a cross tie. Without the bunks and partitions, her sides would have collapsed at the very launching. Her decking, which would never have to bear the weight of a cargo, was of thin larch cross-plies bedded in tar, to save the weight of more traditional oak; it, too, served to equalize the pressure upon the sides. The housing was of lapped cedar . . . in short, she was a canal boat built with all the lightweight skills of a swift and fragile phaeton. Her displacement, unladen, would be a third of any other canal boat of similar size. His helper, Noah Jimson, who had begun the enterprise on a high note of skepticism, ended it filled with pride. "She'll fly like the rising swan," was now his opinion.

Matt was less happy. As the euphoria of his great discovery

began to dissipate, it was replaced by painful calculation that ought to have been made at the outset. The trouble was, he was illiterate with large numbers and relied on instinctive guesses that so rarely let him down. And Mary, for her part, simply trusted those instincts.

He now realized that to voyage from Birmingham to Manchester in twelve hours was something of an impossibility, to say the least. There was a choice of two routes, one heading northwestward through Wolverhampton, the other going northeast to Fazeley, the canal upon which Mary had begun her journey to London. From either point both waterways then converged, meeting at Hay Wood on the Grand Trunk – and not a mile of a difference between the pair of them. The total journey was just short of one hundred and fourteen miles. At twelve miles an hour (*if* he could achieve that), it should be possible. But, as he was now beginning to realize, he had somewhat underestimated the delays due to the locks, of which there were more than ninety via Wolverhampton and almost eighty by Fazeley.

Obviously Fazeley was the better route. But even if someone rode ahead to each lock and made sure all was ready, it would still take around five minutes each time. Five minutes doesn't sound long – until you multiply it by eighty or so; and then it comes to around seven hours! On top of that there were the tunnels; he'd completely overlooked them. Harecastle, a mile and three-quarters long, took an hour and a half to leg through, and Preston Brook would add a further forty minutes. Perhaps a special team of leggers could cut that total to under two hours, seeing the lightness of the vessel – but it still left only three hours to cover the remaining hundred-odd miles. Thirty-five miles an hour? Not even a stage fly on good roads could do that.

Birmingham to Manchester in twenty-four hours would be enough of a challenge. In twelve, it was a sheer, utter, absolute, damnable impossibility. He had sent Mary down to London to drum up wagers on a certain failure. How to get in touch with her? If only he could write! But the only people he'd trust at dictation were Mary's parents, and they were somewhere between Rugeley and Stoke, looking for a goodly farm. If he breathed a word of his doubts to anyone else, it would be spread throughout the Midlands, the bets would pour in, and Old Q's losses would be huge.

He made tentative inquiries about the emigrant ships.

More practically, he racked his brains far into the night, seeking even the most lunatic answers to this impossible challenge. One was actually not so idiotic. They could start at Aston, a suburb of Birmingham, and still claim to be within the town. That would eliminate eleven of the locks on the Fazeley route, bringing the number down to "only" sixty-seven.

Tantalizingly enough, a fair number of those locks were in close flights – at Curdworth, for instance, a few miles from the start, there was a downward flight of eleven inside a mile; at Kidsgrove, another eleven; and at Sandbach, only a mile or so farther north, there was a flight of eight. Matt was not the first to wish that some giand hand could pluck a boat from the canal at the start of such a watery staircase and transport it smoothly to the other end; but none had ever wished it more fervently.

Then one night in a dream the answer came to him. He awoke in ecstasy but it did not survive the first pinprick of dawn, for his dream answer was to build a huge caisson, or hollow cylinder of stone, at the foot of the flight; he could lead the vessel into it and then flood the tube with water from the upper pound, which would raise it the full vertical distance in one smooth lift. The idea was not entirely novel. Indeed, something of the sort was already done on a lesser scale in some of the lifts at the Worsley mines. But, of course, it would cost ten thousand times more than they could possibly hope to win.

Alas, dreams are so powerful that even the memory of them can colour the whole day; the euphoria of this "perfect" solution would not leave him. Time and again his heart leaped up in gladness that his problems were over, only to sink again with the waking knowledge that such was far from being the case.

Yet he felt sure there was an answer there somewhere. It was the idea of the tube . . . something about a tube . . . All day he cudgelled his brains. Toward evening it stole upon him, and with such insidious gentleness that, at first, he did not recognize it for the answer at all.

And then it was so blindingly obvious he could have hanged himself for failing to see it all along.

The finishing of the *Silent Sullivan* was now literally that: finishing – shaving, sanding, filling, caulking, painting, and varnishing. So, leaving Noah to do what he did best, Matt went to Curdsworth, to Kidsgrove, and to Sandbach, where he began to set in train the necessary arrangements. And then, for good measure, he solved the problems of Harecastle and Preston Brook tunnels, too.

Next he went to the ironworks at Coalbrookdale.

And finally he swallowed his pride and went to see Dux.

Mary returned to Birmingham that same week. When Matt came home, Steam Punch was with him – but he was sent off almost at once to walk back to Manchester, stopping at the farms and stables along the way, arranging the horse stages.

Mary, though pleased to see Punch again, had little occasion to show it, being by then beside herself with worry. "I'd no idea where you'd gone," she told Matt. "I even made inquiries as to the emigrant ships."

He laughed scornfully. "Me? Emigrate?"

"Not you – us! We've got to do something, Matt. We're ruined if we stay."

He smiled a tolerant, superior smile, which she took for the vacant grin of idiocy. "You know that from here to Castle Field is a hundred and fourteen miles?" she asked earnestly.

"Aye."

"And even going by Fazeley, there's still seventy-eight locks?"

"And the tunnels, love. Don't forget them – four thousand one hundred and nineteen yards without towpath."

Her eyes narrowed. "You *know* then!"

He grinned.

She hurled herself upon him, beating his chest with her fists. "Oh God, you'd raise the furies. You know we're beaten! You know we've as much hope of getting to Manchester in twelve hours as a cat in a kennels."

He nodded calmly. "Let us hope the whole world agrees."

His assurance dented hers; she looked at him with a wild, impossible hope in her eye. "How?" she asked, hardly daring above a whisper. "Steam? A full head of sail? How?"

"I'll show you."

"No, tell me!"

"Very well." He drew a deep breath. "Water" – he spoke with judicial solemnity – "is a liquid."

She waited for more, and then said, "Is that all?"

He nodded. "It's very easy to forget that fact. Is Old Q coming?"

Her exasperation returned. "Old Q rode over to the Lea Navigation and spent half an hour talking to some narrow-boatmen. He came back offering a thousand to one against us."

Matt's eyes lit up. "Write at once – tell him he's on for fifty guineas."

"Fifty!" She was incredulous.

"It's all we have left. I had to pledge the rest."

The following day he took her over to the iron foundries and showed her his answer to the problem. It was a much calmer Mary who returned to their lodgings. There she wrote at once to Old Q, saying she would gladly wager fifty at his odds . . . or, if he lacked the stomach of his convictions, she'd come down to even money . . . or, best of all, she'd pass him her private assurance that Matt had, once again, done the impossible. So if he, Old Q, would back her in secret (for a star-i'-the-eye female could get better odds than an astute old professional like himself), she'd go in with him for a quarter of the winnings.

He replied with an offer of a fifth, provided she told him something of Matt's solution.

She answered: "The more who know, the poorer the odds."

He accepted at that, but imposed a limit of three thousand pounds. He hadn't become the third richest man in the country by foolish speculation, she thought!

The news spread like melted butter that this lunatic woman was going about the Midlands laying small bets – a pound here, five pounds there – that within the next twelvemonth a party of twenty gentlemen would travel by canal boat from Birmingham to dine in Manchester inside twelve hours without assistance of on-board steam or sail! It was too good to be true, especially when the type of vessel in which this feat was to be accomplished would soon be available for inspection every Saturday and Sunday, at her moorings at the top of Holborn Hill in Aston. And even more so when, on every other day of the week she would be flying along the canals to Manchester, at twice the speed of the regular boats, and with all the locks in her favour – and still proving it required the full, rounded day to complete the journey.

Dear God – wasn't it in the company's own timetable which the stupid woman was handing out to anyone who even so much as glanced her way? Every Sunday and Wednesday, at nine in the evening, the *Silent Sullivan* would be leaving Holborn Hill, arriving in Stoke near half-past seven the following morning. And at eight, she'd move onward to Manchester, arriving by eight-thirty that night – twenty-three and a half hours after leaving Birmingham. So how were they going to cut that time in half? The *Silent Sullivan*, indeed – there'd be silence in the Sullivan marriage when it came to honouring all those wagers!

One or two takers had the wit to stipulate that the vessel would not leave the water.

"Are you afraid she might fly?" Mary joked.

"With that man of yours you'd never be sure," was their answer.

When she cheerfully accepted the condition, there was a fevered scramble to place bets with her before the men with the sanity arrived at her gate. She shortened the odds to eight-to-one on, and still they pressed their wagers upon her. And when Launching Day drew near – a crisp, bright day in early February – every approach to the canal was thronged with the curious, the gloating, the smug, all come to spend their winnings in advance.

The vessel was launched on Smeaton's new level, of course, not Brindley's old abandoned summit, where Matt had first demonstrated to Mary the technique of "skimming" a boat. The previous day the *Silent Sullivan*, shrouded tight until not one copper nail was showing, had been carefully hauled onto a set of six bogies and lowered down the hillside on wooden railways. The ease of the operation gave qualms to one or two of the gamblers . . . suppose she could bypass the locks in that fashion? But then they reminded themselves that "the vessel shall not leave the waters of the navigation during the journey." So there could be no tricks with railways.

The Flinders of the Barony of Inchiquin in County Clare did the honours, wetting her bows with a mixed pint of ale, half from Birmingham, the rest from Manchester. No one needed reminding, he said, of the amazing prosperity the canals had brought to England in general and to this part of the country in particular. When the Duke of Bridgewater had built his pioneering waterway, people would rather have played ducks and drakes with a guinea than invest it with him; but now you couldn't hold a public meeting of any kind, not even a wedding party, without the bursting-in of would-be investors convinced it was a secret meeting of shareholders arranging a new issue.

And all this had happened in thirty short years! What would the next thirty bring? No man could know that. But here and there they could glimpse the shape of it – those with eyes to see. For some lucky few, like those present on this day, it was revealed in every last detail . . .

At which abrupt moment he gave a signal and the two proud boatbuilders drew away the shrouds to reveal the wonder of the new age, the *Silent Sullivan*, the sleek and lovely phæton of the waters.

There was a silence you could bounce rocks off, and then a cheer that raised heaven. Swiftly, smoothly the lines payed out through the snatch blocks and she completed the last three feet of her journey into the waters. Like the shell of an empty egg, she hardly dinted the surface.

Then came the moment for which (without knowing it) they had all been waiting. For weeks now gentlemen connected with the canals – and that included almost every man of substance throughout the Black Country – had been studying the new timetable and telling one another it simply was not pososible for a boat of this size to average eight miles an hour over twenty-four hours. True, now that they had seen her lines, both in and out of the water, their confidence was shaken; but even so . . . eight miles an hour!

Matt invited a couple of dozen ladies and gentlemen aboard and then hitched up four matched greys, hired for the occasion. They were spirited creatures, full of oats and muscle – altogether different from the usual bag-o-bones nags that were daily flogged to death on these same towpaths. When Steam Punch, who sat mounted on the lead horse, cried "Hup!" the team almost wrenched the towing eye out of the gunwale. Mary, standing securely on the bank and peering into the cabin windows, could see the shock in the eyes of the party aboard as the vessel was seemingly plucked from beneath them; then the laughter as they thrilled to the speed.

Before they had gone twenty paces they were into an easy canter and looking for a gallop. There was an incredulous gasp from the crowd as the vessel lifted almost out of the water and began to skim upon its surface. The horses almost fell into the gallop at that. The first lock of the Aston flight was less than a mile away, so they had not far to go before they would have to slow down, but in those few furlongs they must have set new standards of speed upon water. Furious arguments broke out among the crowd, where dedicated gamblers with stopwatches had timed her over the course; the bank was thick with men pacing out the lengths they had marked in their minds; one could not hear oneself think for cries of:

"That's never a *yard*, man – step out, step out!"

"Damme, I've lost my mark – was it this bush or that?"

"Stand aside ma'am, if you please, there's a man here a-measuring!"

One group swore she had touched twenty-eight and two-thirds of a mile per hour; another said it could not have been above eleven, despite the impression of speed. "The horses were mostly galloping on the spot," they declared. In general, though, the concensus lay between fifteen and twenty miles to the hour.

Worried frowns were everywhere. Notebooks were fetched out or borrowed from ladies. Little ivory pencils flashed at their calculations. Results were compared, the calculations redone . . . and the frowns began to ease again. Even at twenty miles an hour, the locks and tunnels would defeat the Sullivans; for they would consume at least nine of the permitted twelve hours of the journey.

The following evening, with a full complement of gentlemen aboard, with Matt at the helm and Punch on the lead horse, the *Silent Sullivan* began the first of her scheduled journeys to Stoke, for which the fare was fourteen shillings, and onward to Manchester for an additional fifteen. Dinner was half-a-crown, breakfast a shilling. She returned full, too, and repeated the double journey, full again both ways, during the next five days. Their first week of operation, after paying the inns that provided the on-board meals and the farmers and liveries that furnished the horses – and, of course, the canal dues for privileged right of passage – their clear profit was little short of one hundred pounds.

"Did I not always maintain it?" the Flinders chortled. "The future is with the canals! Was that not my constant song, my dear?"

"For ever and a day," his wife confirmed.

# CHAPTER FORTY-TWO

THE CLOSER TO HELL, the sublimer the view," Mrs. Flinders chanted.

"Ah, pay her no heed, daughter," said The Flinders. "Keep your eyes closed until I tell you now."

"What about Matt? He should close his eyes, too."

"Sure he passes it by four times a week. There's no surprise left in it for him."

"It's not fair. I tell you what – I'll turn and face backwards, so. Otherwise the movement of the boat unsettles me." She opened her eyes and found herself staring straight into Matt's, which were worried. "It's nothing," she assured him. "Only the movement in the locks. On the levels I'm fine."

He was only partly soothed. "If you weren't so stubborn . . ."

"I'm determined this child of ours shall be born in our own farm on our own land now. No more of your lodgings, thank you."

"Any old roof is still a roof."

"Talking of roofs," The Flinders intervened cautiously, "this one at Summerley Farm does need the smallest bit of attention now."

The valley behind them narrowed downward past the villages of Stone and Little Stoke. "There's seven locks there in under a mile," she told Matt.

He winked knowingly.

As they rounded the bend a furlong or so beyond the third and topmost lock of the Meaford flight, The Flinders gave a triumphant cry of, "At last!"

She turned and saw ahead of them a broad valley, verdant even now in winter, rising steeply within a few miles to the North Stafford Hills. There, beneath an eternal pall of soot and smoke, stood the five Potteries: Stoke, Hanley, Etruria, Burslem, and Newcastle – the industrial "hell" to which her mother had referred. Here in the valley, though, upwind on the prevailing south-westerlies, all was rural tranquillity, clean and arcadian. To the west, beyond the meandering Trent, was a magnificent palace, finer by far than Sandon and Ingestre and the other stately homes they had passed that day.

"Why, it's like the king's house in London," she said.

Her father nodded, pleased at her quickness of observation. "It is built to the same plan," he told her. "Trentham Hall, seat of the new Marquis of Stafford – Earl Gower as was."

"Aha – our vendor himself! Are those his gardens? But they go on for miles – I never saw such grounds, not even at Woburn." Her eye quartered the landscape, noting the shrubbery, the varieties of trees. "Is his agent a good man of business?" she added. "Or will he take us through all four kingdoms before he sells?"

"He seemed eager enough."

Her mother snorted. "Sure he couldn't believe his luck. That's poor land between the two waters. You could set it down beside Poulaphuca and none would mark the difference."

"Houl' your whisht, woman," her husband said. "Hasn't it ten times the heart of any land in the Burren?"

"And if it has?" she asked amiably. "Wouldn't that still leave it poor?"

Mary took careful note of the canalside herbage and kept her own counsel. Her eye caught that of Punch, silent at the helm; he gave her a cheeky wink, full of ambiguous amusement.

At the Trentham lock the keeper was surprised to have the *Silent Sullivan* coming through on a Saturday. "No one saw fit to tell me," he grumbled to Matt, whom he knew quite well by now.

"Private run," Matt assured him.

"To Summerley Farm," Mary explained. "There's no hurry today."

The man recognized the two older folk from their earlier visits – the "two mad Irish gentry." Now at last he connected them with Matt. "So *this* is your son-in-law!" he said. Then, with a conspiratorial glance over his shoulder, he lowered his voice and added, "Don't buy it. That's my advice to ye."

"Why, here's a change of tune!" Mrs. Flinders said.

"Why not?" Mary interrupted.

"Oh, the land is sour. And the soil is thin."

"The grass looks well enough."

"There's a little frost," he agreed. "I grant you that. The northern hills are a grand shelter. But any grass looks good in winter."

"What's wrong with it in summer then?"

He pulled a face. " 'Tis thin-shanked stuff – like you'd see up on the peat moors." His finger raked north and eastward, along the line of the hills.

She smiled, as if his words had confirmed some private conclusion of her own. Then he, perhaps feeling he had been somewhat unpatriotic about his native soil, nodded toward the ornamental gardens around the Hall and said, "But it'll grow the grandest rhododendrons. Come May, and you'd travel all Europe to see the likes of those."

"There's no laurel, I notice," Mary said. "Nor Irish arbutus. Nor laurustinus."

The man shrugged noncommittally and pulled a what-have-we-here face at Matt.

When they had left the lock behind, Matt raised his eyebrows at her. "It means the soil is acidulated," she told him.

"Bad?"

"Terrible. But fear not – the answer is beneath our very feet." He frowned.

She laughed, enjoying his excluded bewilderment. "Meaning, my darling, that there are very few games only one may play!"

"There!" cried her father when they had negotiated a few gentle bends. "Summerley Farm!"

She raised her hands to her cheeks and gave a gasp of pleasure, for there before them stood one of the most beautiful farmhouses she had ever seen. It was an Elizabethan half-timbered dwelling nestling in a grove of cedars, facing south, and with a neglected stretch of park running away westward to the banks of the Trent.

"As I warned," he said guardedly, "it is not in the best of repair . . ."

"It was the family seat back in the days of Sir Richard Leveson," her mother interrupted, implying by her tone that even if the old pile were roofless and crumbling, such a lineage would nevertheless render it more habitable than the hideous, modernistic palace on the farther bank of the river.

There was a winding hole just ahead – a circular enlargement of the canal where any boat up to seventy-two feet, the longest permitted to ply on the Grand Trunk, could turn about. They availed of it and moored on the western towpath, facing the way they had come.

Matt helped Mary ashore with fastidious care. "I'm all right," she said with a tetchiness she regretted but could not prevent. She hated any suggestion that her pregnancy was an affliction or disability – especially now, when, so near to term, it was plainly both those things.

Mrs. Flinders smiled to herself. She had rarely felt for Mary those bonds of affection that are supposed to unite parents and children. The girl had often seemed no more to her than a cheerful, obliging stranger who, slightly to the surprise of both, happened to be sharing her life for a season. But from the moment she learned her daughter was with child that missing bond had started to form. Mary's life, Mary's future, Mary's hopes – these began to obsess her. She was filled with strange emotions, so new to her she still did not know how to cope. Sometimes she would be over-responsive, too fussy, too meticulous, too protective. She knew it, of course, and could feel the annoyance it provoked in her daughter, and yet she could not curb herself. Then at other times those elements in her make-up which would sooner return to their old, cool, easy cohabitation made her offhand . . . even neglectful. She longed to find some middle way between these wild swings of mood, but it eluded her still.

Her only constancy was her concern for the girl. Some part of her was always vigilant, always knew where Mary was. At this moment, for instance, strolling over the fields toward the beautiful old ruin of a farmhouse (and one could not, in all honesty, call it anything else), with the cold easterly breeze sweeping across the valley from behind them, her right cheek and ear – the side toward Mary – almost glowed with the awareness of her presence there.

"Will you stop your fashing," Mary was saying to Matt,

pulling her arm from his grasp. Then immediately she took his arm and hugged it to her.

A ruined balustrade enclosing a once-fine terrace now blocked their path; its pierced-stone openwork used to spell out a Latin inscription, but now only the name RICARDUS LEVESON was properly legible. "There was a nunnery here in olden times," Mrs. Flinders said. "It was given to the Levesons at the dissolution."

"Like Woburn to the Russells," Mary mused. "Those were the days to be of the king's party." She instantly regretted the observation for she had forgotten that those were also the days in which the Flinderses had been given their lands at Inchiquin.

The roof of the old Elizabethan hall had once been tiled, but except for a small area at the far end, it had long ago fallen in, to be replaced by humble thatch, which, in its turn, was now yielding to the ancient precept that "what goes up must come down." Here and there it had been replaced with tarwashed sailcloth, weighted down with half-dressed stone.

Now that they were close enough to see the dilapidation of the place, Mary halted in amazement, staring first at it and then at her parents. Only people whose last home was a Burren farmhouse would see any merit in such a rough pile of stone and brick. "Are you both sure this is what you really want?" she asked.

"The *construction* is sound enough," her father said, as if that quality could somehow be separated from the house itself. "And with modern ways of building, you know . . ." He lacked the courage to complete the sentence.

Matt had already gone indoors.

"If it could be restored to its former glory . . ." her mother said vaguely. Her eyes strayed toward the "modern monstrosity" over the river but she, too, did not complete her thought aloud.

Mary suddenly understood what had brought this rare agreement between the two of them. Her mother saw it as a cheap return to yesteryear: This house, duly restored, would far outshine the old Flinders castle at Inchiquin, which had been slighted by Cromwell's men and never restored. To her father, by contrast, it was a chance to teach a gang of long-mouldered Tudor builders how they ought to have gone about their business. To this conflicted unity she could now add a reason of her own: the land. She had not the slightest doubt but that it was potentially far more valuable than its asking price. As soon as it was theirs, they could build a wharf by the winding hole down on the canal. Then night soil from the Potteries could be got for the asking, as much as the land could take. And lime, too, could be brought in by the bargeful. If she could not raise the value of these acres sixfold before the turn of the century, she wouldn't deserve her own footprints.

Matt returned, shaking his head. "Guess why it's so cheap," he said.

"But is it past repair?" Mary asked.

He gave a noncommittal shrug. "D'you know why they always built the upper parts of the house so as to overhang the ground floor?" he asked.

"No – unless it was to keep the rain off the foundations."

"Come and I'll show you." He took her hand and led her indoors.

She saw at once what he meant; so much plaster had fallen away that the structure was completely revealed. In a modern house there would be stout joists every foot or so, upon which the upstairs floorboards would be laid. But here only two beams spanned the entire room. The floorboards had to carry their own weight plus that of any furniture standing upon them, so the builders had used the weight of the upstairs wall as a kind of counterbalance. Over the years the timber had yielded to these opposing forces until it now appeared like nothing so much as the surface of an ocean frozen during a heavy swell.

"You'd be dizzy just going to bed," Mary said.

"We can take all the floors out," her father explained eagerly, "and replace them along modern lines."

Matt shook his head. "You'd lose the counterbalance."

"Ah but we can put columns outside to support the overhang, you see."

"Doric columns and Tudor timbering!" his wife sneered. "And a Gothick campanile, no doubt? Or a Hindoo east wing?"

Mary came to a decision. "Is it absolutely beyond repair?" she asked Matt.

"No!" answered her parents in their unwonted and slightly bewildered unison.

With a reluctant sigh Matt said, "Cheaper to demolish and rebuild." As if offering a sop he told his father-in-law, "Lots of useful stone and timber."

316

"But it *could* be rebuilt?" Mary insisted. "To look exactly as it did in its glory?"

He nodded, but his eyes added, "If you were daft enough to try."

"Then we'll rebuild so," she said. The restoration would, she knew, delight her mother; and the direction of the labourers would keep her father out of mischief for years. And with Matt around to curb his wilder fancies, no great harm could come of it – surely? "Is any part of it whatsoever in habitable condition?" she added.

Mrs. Flinders pointed to the farther end of the house, the only part where the original tiles were still intact. "There are four rooms down there."

"Five," her husband corrected.

"The fifth is yours, so."

"Then we're agreed," Mary said. "Our search is at an end."

Matt, as usual, said nothing.

"All that's left to do, then," she concluded, "is to chide Lord Stafford's agent for this outrageous price he's asking."

# CHAPTER FORTY-THREE

Not married!" Mrs. Flinders shrieked. "That's an outrage! Here is the child already knocking at the door of the world . . . and we with but half a roof above our heads . . ."

"And if you go on shouting," Mary told her calmly, "you'll fetch down the remnant. Can't you understand the simple truth – Matt does not believe in a divinity?"

"Belief is it! And what about certificates of birth with *illegitimate* written all over them in red ink – does he believe in them, eh? What about common-law widows left without their inheritance for lack of paper? Does he suppose he is still nothing but a plain labouring man to whom such trifles are of no account?"

Mary bit her lip in vexation. Her mother was right, of course. To those who possessed nothing, such considerations meant nothing. The bastard child would never aspire to professional rank; the mud hovel and its chattels would be of no interest to even the most grasping Commissioners of Revenue. Conversely, if Matt were a duke, his mistress would be pensionable and his bastards accepted everywhere. Thus the two extremes of society were united by their indifference to these certified annoyances; only the "fortunate" inbetweens, suspended, as it were, between the scum and the dregs, needed be careful.

But Matt dug in his heels. No phantom Engineer-Above-the-Clouds was going to bless their union. A master of one of the most ancient human mysteries – the Just Working of Metal – had already done that. Iron from the Earth, instilled with Fire and quenched by Water, over solemn vows borne upon the Air – these had sealed their elemental marriage. Flowery speech from a cleric who couldn't tell a hod from a hammer would demean it, not dignify.

"But our children," Mary argued. "The inheritance . . ."

"Fathers disinherit sons all the time," he pointed out. "There's no iron in legitimacy."

He too, was right, of course; both her mother and husband were right – and she was pinioned in confusion between them.

The family were by then established – if only just – in the dry wing of the old mansion. The deed of conveyance had gone swiftly enough once his lordship's agent had seen they were in earnest. Mary, knowing how vastly she could improve the quality of the land, considered they had outsmarted the estate in the bargain. Matt, graduate of a school of harder knocks, was less certain. He thought it might suit the estate very well if one small farm (small, that is, in terms of the marquis's vast holding) improved its yield many-fold. They could then come down like a wolf on all their tenants around, pointing to the Flinders farm as an example, and raising the rent in anticipation of the achievement. He did not think the name of Flinders would be toasted at too many tables around the district in years to come. He always took care to call it the Flinders farm, though it had a Sullivan for its mainspring.

Be that as it may, the two welded letter Ms were nailed above the door.

Their occupation was complete by the end of March, some six to eight weeks before the baby was due. It left little time to hire the servants, scrub out the habitable rooms, refurbish the chimneys, fix new casements in the windows, ferret out the rats, fumigate with sulphur candles, equip the kitchen, and a myriad other household preparations. And with spring drawing on there could be no lull out-of-doors, either. There were farm hands to hire, horses to buy – along with their implements – fields to plough, night soil and lime to draw and spread, seed to purchase . . . there was no end to it. The hours passed like minutes; it seemed to Mary that no sooner had she seen Matt off on his Monday run northward to Manchester than it was Tuesday and she was listening out for his passing posthorn on his way south, then Thursday, for a brief exchange of windblown kisses as he went north once more, then Friday and he was home again – and Punch with him.

The Flinders of the Barony of Inchiquin in County Clare was happy, too. He passed his time in surveying the ruined portion of the house and finally announced that it would take six months to complete the survey, a year to draw up plans for the rebuilding (upon the finest modern principles of the art, to be sure) and perhaps ten to complete the task.

"Ten years without the distraction of the Grand Cork-to-Bristol Chain Ferry or the Great Aerial Balloon Train to Cathay!" Mrs. Flinders chirped joyfully to her daughter. "You are indeed our angel, my child."

In May, with the baby due at any minute, there came a fretful and querulous letter from Old Q. His agents had apparently timed the *Silent Sullivan* over a couple of recent runs. "Her velocity upon the level Pounds between Locks is no more than 8 miles to the Hour," he declared. "It requires ninety minutes to traverse the 12 furlongs of Harecastle Tunnel. And tho' the Locks are all to his Favor, each wastes eight minutes. If the Terms of the bet stipulate no Steam Engine and the Vessel not to quitt the Water, there exists no conceivable Means whereby you may fulfill the Wager. 'Tis said here on all hands that you take

Example of the recent Imposture of Mr. Hooke for no other Purpose than to bring your Service to the Publick's attention – and hang those who lose the Wager by consequence of it!"

This Mr. Hooke, a theatrical person, had advertised that he would, on stage and in full view of the spectators, shrink a female of voluptuous charms (the evidence of which would be but scantily concealed) to such a size that she would climb into a common quart wine bottle through its neck, wherein she would dance, sing, and whistle to the edification of all, who could freely pass the bottle from hand to hand the while. It had, of course, been a hoax but Mr. Hooke, to say nothing of some hundred-aught pounds in entrance fees from "a lascivious and gullible publick," was safely in France by the time of its exposure.

"How say you to this charge?" the duke concluded.

She answered him by return: "We answer Your Grace: with such cunning Ingenuity it will greatly credit you and dumbfound all who *dis*credit the Possibility."

Four days later she bore a son. Her travail upon the birthing stool was greater than she had expected but less than she had feared, which, as her mother said, put her on all fours with most other women who had gone this road before her. At the height of Mary's roaring, Matt had been seen on his knees, and his lips in silent motion, though he later denied the impeachment. Nevertheless, he raised no further objection to the name of her choice, Mark, despite its biblical linkage to his own. Mark Declan Sullivan the boy was called, his middle name being for Punch, his honorary uncle.

Matt could have stayed all month and dandled the child and marvelled at the azure of his eyes, the power of his lungs, the tiny perfection of his hands and the impossibility that they should ever grow into such great paws as his own . . . but the day of the wager – the *Impossibility Stakes*, as they were now universally called – was drawing on apace and there were the final arrangements to be made. The immediate joys of parenthood, together with its chores and impositions, were perforce left to Mary, her mother, and the entire distaff household.

Throughout that spring there had been the most extraordinary labour beside the flights of locks at Sandbach, Kidsgrove, Stone, and Curdworth. The towpath had been widened to twelve feet or more, and made to one even rake, and bedded deep in hardcore, and rolled smooth with an infill of quarry dust that set hard as stone in the sun and rain. With two weeks to go, the *Silent Sullivan* was withdrawn from service – in order, it was said, to make experiments at the passage of sundry locks. Curiously enough, those locks were the ones where the towpath had been altered.

Thereafter she was to be seen daily, fouling cables, breaking pulleys, and in general making dangerous work of locking manoeuvres she had safely mastered these months past. Gamblers and their spies looked on in glee, while the odds grew evermore desperate.

While Matt was making such a public parade of his incompetence, the *Silent Sullivan II* was secretly launched in far-off Birmingham. And the following day a strange, hollow vessel, built all of rivetted iron plate, was launched in Coalbrookdale. It was rumoured to be a giant boiler for the largest steam engine in the world. The owners of this mighty machine must be in desperate need, too, for the vessel was towed by six fleet-footed carriage horses who got her speed up beyond twelve knots on the level pounds between locks.

By night, while the spies were safely abed, a quite different series of experiments proceeded upon the slopes between the Brindley and Smeaton cuts of the Birmingham Canal. They involved that giant steam boiler and the *Silent Sullivan II*, weighted down with stones to represent her cargo of gentlemen. These secret trials were as successful as the public ones were a disaster.

Two days before the race a barge went north from Birmingham carrying four ingeniously furnished carriages of iron; their tyres were the broadest ever seen. She unshipped one at each of the widened towpaths. The gambling fraternity laughed with incredulity. Now at last the purpose behind all those manoeuvres through the locks with pulleys and tackle was clear. Matt Sullivan had decided that by opening all the locks in a staircase to create a sort of artificial rapids, he could, by means of these iron carriages and the so-called "greatest steam engine in the world" (which no one had even seen), haul the *Silent Sullivan* up in one swift operation! The vessel would not "quit the water" and nor would she sport an on-board steam engine.

But what a fool the man had turned out to be! The best Boulton & Watt engine could not manage above six strokes a minute, at twelve feet per stroke. Even with a certain amount of gearing, that wasn't going to haul the *Silent Sullivan* up her man-made rapids at any very alarming pace. The upper pounds would empty before she had been hauled halfway. It was a shame to accept the man's money. No one would now take any bets, not even at the thousand-to-one-on that was widely touted.

"Well?" Mary asked as a happily exhausted Matt slipped into bed beside her that night.

"We can't lose, love. Barring accidents."

"Or malice. Let us not forget the coaching faction."

The following night they were in Birmingham, ready against the dawn of the Impossible Day.

# PART FIVE

## IMPOSSIBLE TIMES

# CHAPTER FORTY-FOUR

EN SECONDS TO GO!" called out Lord Savory, the official timekeeper for the race. Then, "One, two, three, four . . ." A loud pistol shot marked the hour. It was eight of the clock on a fine Thursday morning in June and the greatest boat race in living memory had begun.

The first of what would ultimately be ninety relay teams of horses was whipped by Steam Punch to a gallop. It jerked the deck from beneath the feet of every gentleman aboard. A great cheer from both banks of the canal followed in their wake; everybody knew the race was hopeless, of course, yet some little devil of human contrariness wished Matt the chance to win, even among those who had wagered against him.

Matt himself was at the helm and Mary at his side – not so much to give him moral support, for he was utterly confident of winning, as to distract Old Q when his querulous fidgeting became unbearable.

"This is nowhere near thirty miles an hour," he complained almost at once. "We have no hope of winning at this snail's pace."

"Fine day though, Duke," Matt laughed.

His grace turned near-purple at the familiarity.

There were whistles of surprise and raised eyebrows when, less than four minutes later they reached the first milepost at Tyburn Road. At Tyburn itself, three good miles from the start, there was open astonishment to find the clock not yet at 8.13. As the Newtons among them were quick to point out, their average velocity was more than fifteen miles an hour. Never before had a vessel of such size achieved such speed.

At Tyburn, too, came the second relay of horses. Thanks to his hours of practice with a special hitch of Matt's devising, Punch had the changeover completed before the *Silent Sullivan II* had even caught up the slack. Old Q's stopwatch clicked yet again; he had hardly ceased pressing the button since the off. "Valiant, valiant," he said grudgingly, "but nowhere near enough. We're still going to lose by hours."

The air was thick with calculation: one hundred and fourteen miles . . . fifteen to the hour . . . seven and a half hours . . .

"Possible, possible," said the pessimists.

"But the locks, you see," countered their more sanguine friends, "the locks will defeat the man. And the tunnels. Set your fears at rest – the race is already lost. Our wager's safe as all Lombardy to a china orange."

Mary glanced at Matt to see how he was taking it; he winked back. She looked at his hand upon the tiller. The knuckles no longer showed white.

There was great excitement just beyond where there were three locks within half a mile. Again the stopwatches clicked like open day in a knitting academy. With all the locks set in their favour, and with a certain devil-take-tomorrow attitude as to their filling, they averaged just over four minutes a lock.

"Is that good?" Mary asked Matt.

"Better than in practice."

"But still not *enough*," Old Q insisted. "Egad – I might as well have my breakfast. If I can face all those good-natured friends commiserating over my losses."

He went below, though "below" on the *Silent Sullivan II* was no more than the shadow of a piece of taut canvas stretched over the well of the ship and supported on delicate iron rods; those rods stretched from gunwale to gunwale and served all the structural functions of a true deck. A single plank ran the length of her midline. In the open space all down each side, between gunwale and that one plank, there were seats where the passengers might sit, looking for all the world like respectable galley slaves who had lost their oars.

The *Silent Sullivan II* had created a great stir before the off. There had even been arguments as to her eligibility, for never had a vessel been so stripped down for her maiden voyage. The ideal racing vessel, Matt maintained, would fall apart the moment it crossed the finishing line; if any two elements held together longer than that, she had been too strongly built – which is another way of saying too heavy. In constructing the *SS II* he had come as close to that ideal as he dared; and the alarmed faces of the passengers as they had been invited to step aboard showed how well he had succeeded. But the continuing revelations of those endlessly clicking stopwatches were all the justification his policy required.

The general surprise at the sight of the vessel was as nothing to the astonishments awaiting them five miles farther on, where eleven locks mark the descent from Curdworth to Bodymoor Heath.

"Oh no!" Mary cried out in dismay as they approached the first of them. Though opened in their favour it was already occupied by another vessel. She glanced at Matt and, to her surprise, found him smiling.

Then she smiled, too. "Is that *it?*" she asked quietly.

He nodded.

"You said a giant boiler. It looks more like a sunken ship."

"It is."

"We're lost! Lost!" Old Q came wavering aft, wringing his hands and biting the remnants of fried egg and ham from his lips.

Matt paid him no heed.

The duke brightened suddenly. "It's been sunk in there deliberately. Look, you can see the spars they rolled her down – and the trolley on which they brought her. By Hades – they took no care to cover their tracks!"

They were now close to the lock and Punch stopped his team, which was already the fifth relay of the day. Young Jacko, the lad deputed to look after the lines, unhitched up forrard and came racing aft along the one-plank deck like a barefoot saltimbanco. There, using Matt's ingenious quick hitch, he had the towline fixed in a trice. Punch turned the horses about and held them ready to brace the vessel to a halt at precisely the right moment.

Old Q was happier now. "The bets will have to be called off," he said several times. "This is deliberate malice. Tottenham's behind it, I'll be bound."

Mary pricked up her ears at that.

"Hello . . . I say . . . what's here?" The party aboard had just noticed the great trolley at the lockside. Their speculation had little scope, however, for it now became clear that not only was the sunken vessel so badly damaged that both her bow and stern were split wide open but that Matt was steering straight for the gap.

"Stop, you madman!" they cried.

Old Q even tried to wrest the tiller from him.

Then it was cries of "Ho!" and "What's here?" and "For pity's sake!" as the *SS II* literally drifted into the open, waterlogged maw of the sunken boat. Punch's team braced them to an exact halt. The fit was as a hand to a glove. When the dark engulfed them, one wag had the presence of mind to cry out "Down, down – hats off!" – just as if they were in the theatre and the curtain about to rise.

But it wasn't the curtain that rose, it was the hull of the sunken ship. Hauled by some outside agency, she rose from the canal bed; and as she did so, her two halves came together, trapping the water within her. By the darkness at the bow, Mary saw that the same instantaneous "repair" had been effected there, too. The *SS II* was now afloat *within* the iron vessel. There was no more than three inches of freedom all around, but she was afloat.

In the pitch dark Matt cried out, "Gentlemen, soon you will see the light!"

They began to rise, not vertically but steeply sideways, toward the towpath. Mary, holding tight to Matt's arm, felt a tension there. "This is the part we were unable to test," he murmured. "The hydraulic cylinders didn't arrive until yesterday."

She closed her eyes and held her breath.

Then came the most extraordinary sensation. Later people described it, according to their several temperaments, as being like flying, like hanging out over nothing, like being drunk, like falling through treacle, like dying. Mary could not say what it was like but it was certainly like nothing she had ever experienced before; "falling through treacle" came nearest. The sensation ended with a great clang of iron on iron, though the shock of it was cushioned by the water in which the *SS II* was still floating.

Moments later there was sunlight, hurtful after the dark. Hatches along the scuppers of the iron vessel were being opened

328

from the outside. Like black howitzers the gentlemen's hats popped up into the light and they peered about them with dazed eyes.

"It's an iron maiden!" cried the wag, and from that moment the nameless vessel lost her anonymity, the *Iron Maiden* she was.

Old Q stood pensively staring, first at Matt then at the vessel-within-a-vessel. At last he gave out a laugh that raised the skies. "You dog!" he cried happily. "You utter rogue!"

"Time this now," Matt told him.

The *Iron Maiden* sat atop the great trolley. Ahead of them Punch had hitched in his team.

"Do we have brakes?" Mary asked anxiously.

Matt nodded. "The most ingenious on earth." He touched a great lever that came up from the trolley. With his other hand he took up a bright yellow flag and waved it vigorously.

"Giddyap!" Punch touched his leader. The lightest pull started the trolley in motion. Soon they were rattling down the slope at a rare old pace – rare enough to whiten the gills of several passengers. Most of them were too busy holding onto their hats and making their peace with their Creator to notice that, whatever the slope beneath their wheels, the *Iron Maiden* always maintained an even keel. And of those few who did notice, none connected it with young Jacko, up at the bows, moving a second lever back and forth, with one eye on the terrain ahead and another on a spirit level built into the gunwale.

Once her speed was established, Punch's team galloped before them on a slack line that needed no more than the occasional tweak where the slope eased toward the level.

Old Q took his courage from Matt, put both hands to his hat, giggled, and looked about him like a little boy.

Like all boyish treats, this mile-long descent was over all too soon. Nine locks they passed in . . .

"Time?" Matt asked as he braked her to a halt.

The duke snapped the button and stared at the watch with a keenness that turned to open disbelief. He shook it, held it to his ear, stared at it again. "It must have stuck," he said crossly.

"Two minutes fifty-one," came a cry from down the boat.

Old Q looked again at his watch. "I have two forty-three."

"Two forty-seven," cried a third.

Mary's calculating fingers raced and her eyeballs turned white before she announced, equally incredulous, "Twenty-five miles an hour!"

"Faster than I expected," Matt said modestly. He forbore to add that there were moments during the descent when he had been quite certain of the death of all on board.

The return to the water was even swifter than the exit from it had been. And now the party aboard could see how it was done. The diagonal rails, which were carried on hinges on the trolley, were folded outward again, their ends being furnished with flat pads that rested on the bed of the canal. Then, by an arrangement of pulleys, the *Iron Maiden* was lowered into the water until she floated. Jacko and Punch turned a crank at her stern, whose two halves soon parted wide enough to let the *SS II* float out into the canal.

"Twelve minutes and twenty seconds for the entire operation!" Old Q said triumphantly. "By heavens, you've saved us three-quarters of an hour!"

"Closer to fifty-five minutes," Mary corrected him.

He clapped his hands and danced a little jig. "Are there many more such places as this?" he asked.

Matt held up four fingers.

"And how many locks do they represent?"

"All told?" Matt lingered tantalizingly before he said, "Thirty-four."

"Huzza!" The duke almost threw his quaint old three-corner hat into the air. "Thirty-four . . . thirty-four. Let me see now. I reckoned eight minutes a lock. Thirty-four by eight . . ."

"Four and a half hours," Mary said. That's off *your* calculation."

"Are all downhill?"

"Two up, two down," Matt said.

Old Q's face fell. "We shan't be so fast uphill."

Matt chuckled. "Will you accept fifteen miles an hour, Duke?"

His grace found it so acceptable he did not even notice the familiarity this time.

Others had made similar calculations for now the cry was,

"Three to one on a win!" as the heaviest gamblers among them sought to hedge their no-longer-so-certain wagers.

Old Q chortled in delight; but his pleasure was short lived for now he looked about them and cried out in dismay, "Egad, but we're imprisoned here!"

And indeed it was so. The *Iron Maiden*, waterlogged again, now blocked their way to Manchester. But the reason soon became apparent for the moment the *SS II* was free of her, Punch and his team hauled her partly out of the water to let her drain. Then it was a matter of moments to seal off her bows and stern. As soon as she was watertight again they practically let her fall back into the canal, throwing a great launching wave over a number of spectators on the farther bank. Then, hitching in a fresh team, the best of the drivers from Summerley Farm hauled her light and empty shell forward at a pace that would easily outrun the *SS II* and have her in position at the foot of the next staircase of locks.

Old Q frowned unhappily. "Now we have *two* vessels to get to Manchester."

Matt corrected him "Sandbach."

Only partly to divert him, Mary said, "You mentioned Tottenham, Duke? Is he back in England?"

Matt gave her a grateful smile. Jacko hitched Steam Punch's new team up forr'ard and a cheer went up as they set off at canter in the wake of the *Iron Maiden*.

"Not alone back," Old Q grunted. "He has somehow acquired influence with Lord Thurlow."

Matt raised an inquiring eyebrow.

"The Lord Chancellor," Mary told him. "So he's untouchable?"

"While his credit there lasts – whatever it may be. At all events, Tottenham's going about openly at his old haunts."

"The young fellow, Pitman – he recovered, I hear."

The duke nodded. "That would help, to be sure."

"Is that prizefighter, Con Murphy, still with him?"

He scowled. "Aye, and Jack Horley also."

Mary almost asked if that meant Crystal, too, but the duke's anger had already answered her. He saw the sadness in her eyes and said, "Flotsam and scum, me dear – it don't float all over the harbour, you know, but blows with the wind and gathers all of a hotchpot in some foul corner."

There were times when she had cursed his intuition for the great power it gave him over the women he had used in his long, selfish life; but this was not one of them.

## CHAPTER FORTY-FIVE

Dux was waiting for them at the foot of the upward flight in Stone, a few miles south of Summerley Farm. Naturally he would not have ventured farther, into the territory of the Birmingham & Fazeley and the Coventry canals. These latterday robber barons, who controlled the passage of goods and exacted their tolls with an efficacy more sure and deadly than their medieval counterparts, were no less jealous of their fiefdoms. Besides, with the astounding growth of canal fever over these last few months, the poor man could barely stick his nose out of doors without instantly acquiring a Gadarene claque of would-be investors, gentlemen with but one thought in their minds – that Dux was off to a shareholders' meeting – and one fear in their livers – that they would miss it if they did not cling to his very coat-tails. They stood there now, all about him, a sticky thicket of blue and buff serge, of silver and scarlet brocade.

Mary hardly had time to wave before the *Silent Sullivan II* vanished inside the *Iron Maiden*. His grace's eyes were almost popping out in astonishment, for, like the rest of the crowd, he had failed to grasp the purpose of this strange, half-submerged tube of iron.

When the vessel-within-a-vessel had been hauled upon the second of the four special trolleys and the hatches were opened, Matt cried out, "Come aboard, your grace!"

Dux almost refused, but the thrill of a ride in this iron

juggernaut proved too tempting and he bade farewell to his companion, an upright man, military by his bearing though he was dressed in civilian clothes. A hundred eager hands helped the duke aboard. The church clock struck noon as he clambered down beside the Matt at the helm. "By thunder, Sullivan, you're an hour ahead of our most sanguine expectations. You'll do it with time to spare."

He and Old Q exchanged cheerful, if slightly wary greetings. "For once we're betting on the same side," Old Q said. He did his polite best to conceal his disgust at the dirty, dishevelled state of his peer; he himself had always been a fastidious man, as the legends about his bathing in milk confirmed.

Dux, as careless in observation as in dress, nodded affably. "And since we've each been right about half the time, let us hope our two half-rights will now make one downright whole."

There was no time to chop more logic for the ascent was about to begin. Until now, not even Mary had quite believed Matt's promise of fifteen miles an hour uphill, but when she saw a team of sixty great carthorses, already spanned to the haulage cable and waiting with that nervous impatience which always besets horses in the company of gambling men, she knew it was true.

The flight of locks was, in fact divided into two sets – four at Stone and the remaining three at Meaford on the northern edge of the village. The total rise was just over seventy feet in slightly less than a mile. Because the canal had an awkward dog leg between the two sets, and the trolley was not readily steerable, Matt (to the delight of the populace and the amazement of the highway commissioner) had made up the carriageway along a straightish line from below the town to Siddall's Bridge, near the top of the hill. There the trolley could be eased once again onto the towpath.

Just as they set off, Matt noticed a man pushing his way through the crowd until he was almost under the wheels of the trolley. He was shouting a warning when he realized it was Croxley. He invited him aboard, too, but the engineer waved a dismissive hand and kept his eyes firmly fixed upon the arrangement of the hydraulic pipework beneath the trolley.

He was joined by the gentleman who had been Dux's companion – who seemed no less interested in the engineering detail. They almost jostled each other for vantage; but whereas Croxley merely peered and marvelled, the other took out a small black-bound notebook, embellished with the government cypher, and began scribbling away like any old penny-a-liner.

The horse drover was a Romany master – no whip, no reins, nothing but whistles and cries. He gave a single, piercing blast from his lips and those sixty magnificent animals moved as one to take up the strain. The ropes complained, the rivets of the *Iron Maiden* gave out frightening cracks, the axles groaned . . . and the whole assembly swiftly gathered pace. They were, however, tilted forward rather noticeably; water was spilling out at the bows.

"Trim her, Jacko!" Matt called.

"I've no power till she gets her speed, sir!" the lad shouted back.

Everyone looked at Matt to see how he took this mysterious but worrying news. "Is it bad?" Mary asked quietly.

He was holding his breath, too tense to answer.

Then, as they gained speed and the crank from the bogie began to power the pump, Jacko's pull upon the lever took effect and the vessel trimmed to the horizontal. Matt gave out a vast sigh of relief. "Thank heavens we were canted forward!" he told her.

"Why, what was the danger?"

He tilted his hand downward and explained "Pressure. All at one end."

Croxley had been so fascinated by this brush with disaster that he almost precipitated one of his own. Had it not been for the prompt action of the older man beside him, he would have been swept under the trolley wheels and spread all over the highway. But he did not even notice the rescue. "Sheer genius!" he marvelled, still oblivious to his own peril. He caught Matt's eye and shouted, "Amazing!"

But no words could carry above the cheers of the crowd; Matt pointed to the hilltop, implying they could talk when the ascent was complete.

The highway formed a lazy *S* but the drover knew exactly how to offset his horses so that, although there was no steerage in the trolley, its wheels were dragged just far enough sideways to face it into the next straight. After they had negotiated the first slight bend, Matt relaxed completely. Only Mary, holding his arm and feeling the tension in his muscles, realized how under-rehearsed were so many of this day's wonders.

"Are you pulling on the brake?" she asked, having noticed that he kept his hand to the lever.

He shook his head. "Only if the rope parts."

Faster than a man could easily run, especially uphill, they soon reached the summit.

"Twelve minutes!" Old Q said, moving upwind of Dux as the *SS II* slipped backward into the canal out of the *Iron Maiden*. He kept his tone deliberately nonchalant to show that he was by now a veteran of such amazements.

It was Dux's turn to enthuse, which he did with a gaiety and exuberance rare in him these many years. He patted Matt on the back and repeatedly asked those gentlemen who had stopwatches to confirm the miracle. "And how did that young lad keep us level through all the changes in slope?" he asked at length.

The *Iron Maiden*, drained and closed down, was already back in the water and setting off for Stoke.

"No time for explanations! We must be off," Old Q said peremptorily.

But Matt shook his head. "We have four minutes."

"But why? I . . ."

"Trentham lock." Matt nodded toward the dwindling outline of the other vessel. "Only two miles."

"It's either wait here or there," Mary interpreted.

Old Q shrugged with ill grace.

Matt began to explain the mechanism to Dux but at that moment Croxley arrived, out of breath and flushed with happiness. The other gentleman was hard on his heels. As he drew near he gave Dux a nod. The duke immediately turned to Matt and said, "I'll accompany you the rest of the way, Sullivan – and, by the by, I have one further passenger for us."

"Impossible!" Old Q exploded. " 'Twill slow us down too much."

But Dux was already running his eye over the rest of the company, seeking two he might prevail upon to yield their places.

A bank proprietor and the owner of a large manufactory did not wait to be "asked" but gave up their coveted places with every outward appearance of enthusiasm – having first made quite sure that Dux knew their names and businesses.

Dux's friend thanked them most courteously, too, as he clambered aboard.

Bridgewater was a stickler for the correct form. No matter that Matt was a labouring man, he was now captain of the vessel; and so Colonel-Commandant Carmody of the Royal Engineers was presented to him rather than the other way about.

"The name is well known," Matt told the colonel, glancing at the duke.

"He's a distant kinsman of mine." Dux turned to Carmody. "Sullivan has met your niece Rowena."

"Poor fellow!" The colonel gave an ambiguous smile.

Dux then introduced him to Mary. Matt turned to Croxley. "What were you trying to say down below?"

"Marvellous – marvellous! How did you think of it?"

Matt shrugged. "I was just about to explain to his grace here."

"I don't follow it," Dux said.

"Ah!" Croxley drew breath and took over, enthusing at Matt's ingenuity with hydraulic valves and . . .

"Surely that's been four minutes?" Old Q interrupted.

. . . and cocks and cylinders and . . .

"We're wasting time," Old Q insisted.

. . . and pistons and thrusts. And, above all, Matt's genius. "How did you even think of it?" he asked.

Matt shrugged. "I couldn't see any other way."

"Any *other* way!" Croxley laughed at the very idea.

Now that the *Iron Maiden* no longer obscured the view of the trolley, Carmody's pencil was flying like a bobbin over the pages of the little black book.

"Why is it so remarkable, Mr. Croxley?" Mary asked – not that she doubted it but she wanted the world, and especially Dux, to know.

"We're losing the race!" Old Q was growing angry.

"Oh, it opens up so many possibilities for action at a distance, you see," Croxley explained. "If power can be formed at one central pump and conducted by means of water pipes to any number of remote points . . . why, the possibilities beggar the imagination!"

Carmody nodded in fervent agreement.

336

Matt, seeing Old Q about to explode, gave Punch a nod and the *SS II* set off with her usual all-fall-down jolt. Croxley, now trotting beside them, was already falling behind. "Wish I could go with you," he called out. He halted, holding his side against a stitch and breathing as if air were about to be taxed. "See you at Manchester!" he gasped.

Matt gave him a cheery wave.

"So!" Old Q stared sourly at the colonel. "Whether we beat the clock or no, Sullivan, 'tis plain *you* won't lose by it!"

"That's unworthy, Duke," Mary told him crossly. She almost added that Matt would force him to eat those words – when it occurred to her that such was precisely the old man's purpose. She smiled at his cunning.

Old Q tried not to smile back.

Matt, unconscious of these cross-currents, kept his eye on Punch and the next bend.

Beyond Trentham lock they began to look out for the wharf at Summerley Farm, where everyone would be turned out to watch them go by. And sure enough they were. The little family party of masters and servants began to cheer as soon as the boat hove into view.

"Is this your place?" Dux asked, looking keenly at the fields and the old mansion.

"We dispute the ownership with the rats and the rooks, Duke," Mary replied.

"A pretty enough *situation*," he answered, after a fruitless search for something more complimentary to say about it.

The party on the wharf were now jumping up and down in their excitement, greatly to the peril of the structure. With alarm, Mary saw that her mother was holding up baby Mark so that he could see over the heads of the little crowd; the fact that he could, as yet, discern very little beyond the reach of his ten-dozen fingers (as they sometimes seemed to number) troubled his grannie not a jot.

"Back," Mary yelled at her mother. "Not safe! Back on the field!"

But there was not the remotest chance she might hear the warning above all the excitement. Only when the gentlemen aboard took up the cry and repeated the gesture, did Mrs. Flinders grasp their meaning and comply.

Had it not been for this distraction, Mary would have noticed much sooner than she did that the man beside her father was none other than Aaron M'Grotty.

## CHAPTER FORTY-SIX

SHE NUDGED MATT. "That's a man who says he knows you. I forgot to tell you we met."

Matt followed her gaze and froze. M'Grotty grinned, put a finger to the brim of his hat, and gave it a small, ironic flick.

"Hey!"

"Where away!"

The cries of his passengers brought Matt back to the here and now, to the danger of colliding with the farther bank; he straightened course just in time to avoid an oncoming boat. The owner shook a fist at him and then, recognizing Dux, turned pale and snatched off his hat. Moments later, *he* fouled the bank, to the amusement of everyone.

Except Mary. "Who is this M'Grotty?" she asked.

Matt seemed about to reply to her question, then he pursed his lips and answered her with one of his own. "Where have you met him?"

She told him. She also mentioned that the man had befriended her parents on their way to Birmingham last autumn. "I must say he spoke of you quite warmly," she added.

Matt grunted.

"Well, who is he?" she pressed.

"The devil in moleskins."

"No friend to us, you mean."

"You may say so."

"But why? Matt – I must know. He's standing there with Mark . . ."

"We worked on a tunnel together. Croxley was the engineer. He got French wages."

"Because of you? Or something you did?"

He nodded. "Did you remark his missing teeth?"

Mary came to a decision. "Put me off," she said. "I'm going back."

Matt laughed, not altogether convincingly. "Oh, he can't hurt us."

"If you don't slow down, I shall jump off anyway."

Old Q, who had caught the tail end of their conversation, was furious. "What fancy is this, young madam?" he cried. "Are you aware how much money is afloat here?"

To shame the pair of them, she turned about and jumped off the stern, knowing that the canal was less than five feet deep at this point and that she was only a mile or so from home.

Again Matt almost crashed the boat, this time into the abutments of Sideway Bridge. The last he saw of her, as the stonework of its arch cut off his view, she was clambering upon the bank. "Find Croxley!" he shouted – and hoped that her answering wave was one of comprehension.

"Creatures of impulse," Dux said scornfully.

"Oh, bless 'em for that!" Old Q told him. "At least she had the kindness not to delay us." He consulted his watch for the thousandth time, scratched his brow and, finding no specific cause for complaint, concluded darkly, "It is all going *too* well."

Matt, remembering that scornful tip of the hat from M'Grotty, could not disagree. While he told the two dukes of his fight with the fellow, he cudgelled his brains to imagine where he himself would strike if he were bent on wrecking this race.

At Stoke the original plan had been to use the *Iron Maiden* on the third trolley to bypass the five locks in the usual way – and then to remain inside the iron vessel until they had passed through the Harecastle Tunnel. Ideally he would have built two *Iron Maidens* and had the second one waiting at the far end of the tunnel, where it was needed for bypassing a couple of dozen locks in two downhill flights near Sandbach. But, since that had not been possible, this compromise – hauling the two vessels as one through Harecastle – would be a lot faster than hauling them independently.

Now Matt looked at the trolley, ready for them on the bank at the foot of the Stoke flight; he looked at the festive crowd, at the second great team of horses, at the especially widened towpath . . . and he felt in his bones that somewhere here, in this combination, M'Grotty had contrived to lose him this race – else why give himself a public alibi so close to the scene?

At once he came to a decision. They were by now inside the *Iron Maiden*, ready to be hauled onto the trolley. "Stow that!" he shouted to Punch. "We'll ascend the flight in regular order."

The crowd was furious; he had cheated them of the year's grandest diversion.

Old Q was furious, too, though he saw the point of Matt's caution. He was slightly mollified when Matt reminded him how swiftly they could, in fact, negotiate a lock if they broke all the rules – which, to boos and catcalls from the bank, they now proceeded to do.

"In any case," Matt explained to Dux, "we must traverse Harecastle Tunnel inside the *Iron Maiden*."

Dux cocked an ear at that. "With leggers?" he asked.

"No." Matt shook his head. "That's why we must go as one combined vessel. I'm using the dodge we tried for a while at Cannock. Ropes and horses. Your grace didn't travel down by canal then?"

"No. I rode." Solemnly he added, "Canals are devilish slow things, don't you know."

Matt grinned. "You'd have seen it else."

Half an hour later, they arrived at the Chatterley end of the tunnel, where a stout manilla rope lay coiled on the towpath immediately before the entrance. One end of it vanished into the waters of the tunnel; cork torpedoes had been lashed to it, to float it clear of the bed.

"Won't they slow us down?" Dux asked.

"The drag of the clay bottom is worse."

Old Q noticed that Dux accepted Matt's word on almost everything – quite contrary to his reputation for having a mind all his own where canal matters were concerned. Was that reputation undeserved, he wondered, or was it a measure of his grace's respect for this Sullivan fellow?

Punch had the hitch half formed as the *SS II* nosed in toward the bank. He threw it over the bow timber, completed it, and, with a quick wave, set off on a single horse to go over the hilltop.

Matt drew a pistol from a cabinet at his side and fired it at the canal. It was loaded blank, shards of singed wadding danced in the ripples of the blast.

"Will some obliging gentleman recharge that for me?" he asked.

Dux took the pistol from him and unscrewed the cap of the powder horn. He said, "You have a second one ready, I see."

"One to go, two to stop."

"You've thought of every contingency."

"I hope so."

From the hilltop came the winding of a posthorn, relaying the signal to the team at the farther end of the tunnel. Matt stared expectantly at the rope around the bow; so did everyone else, taking their cue from him.

"Come on, come on!" he said impatiently.

"That devil back there has cut the tow," Old Q exploded.

But at that moment the rope came taut and the *Iron Maiden* and her cargo lurched forward into the black of the tunnel. It was a very relieved cheer that echoed off the weeping brickwork.

But the fretful duke was only partly reassured. "What if the tow does part?" he asked.

Matt shook his head.

"How d'you *know* it won't?"

"Checked every inch myself, sir."

But a short while later they all lurched forward as the boat settled back in the water and lost headway. Old Q rounded on him. "Checked every inch, sir!"

Ignoring him, Matt drew out both pistols and fired them, one after the other.

"Recharge," he said, dropping them on his seat. He had already kicked off his shoes and was stripping his shirt and breeches.

"Are you going in?" Old Q asked, somewhat superfluously, as Matt, doubled up because of the low ceiling, raced ape-fashion, the full length of the boat. A splash told them he had gone in. More splashing revealed that he was swimming away, deeper into the tunnel, as fast as ever he could.

The lapping, gurgling silence he left behind became oppressive. The tunnel was a mere nine feet wide at the waterline, leaving less than a foot of freeboard on either side of the boat. The few lamps had been lighted before they entered the tunnel; they cast a sombre illumination on the seeping bricks that arched overhead – uncomfortably close to those who now had time to look about them.

"Is there *nothing* we can do?" Old Q asked crossly.

An amused smile twisted Dux's worried features. "There is," he said as he clambered up into the narrow space between the one-plank deck and the vault above. "This is something I've always wanted to try for myself."

To the amazement of all he lay upon his back, head toward the bows, and began legging the vessel forward. "Come on, Duke!" he laughed. "Show us those fine calves of yours can move more than ladies' passions."

Everyone laughed – even, to give him his due, Old Q himself. "What do I do?" he asked, accepting help from numerous hands.

"Lie on the plank and simply walk," Dux said.

On most barges the cabin roof is the only flat area close enough to the tunnel wall to be useful to a legger – or two leggers; but here, thanks to the extra height provided by the *Iron Maiden*, that one-plank deck, running the full length of her, gave scope for up to a dozen.

Soon there was not an inch of lying space unoccupied along the entire spine of the boat. A marquis, two earls, a viscount, three baronets, a lord lieutenant, a colonel, two canal-company chairmen, three masters of foxhounds . . . and sundry other personages, each awesome in his way – all lay like schoolboys on an outing, giggling and chaffing one another, and legging for all they were worth. Or, not to exaggerate, legging for some part of what they were worth, since, excepting the two dukes, every man of them had wagered against a win. However, being gentlemen, not one of them would claim the wager if it should turn out that the tow had been deliberately fouled. Those who could not find a place on the deck pushed from the sides with their hands.

Some nautical man among them began on *Farewell and adieu to ye fair Spanish ladies*. They all took it up, roaring out the tune even when the words escaped them, and soon every leg was thrusting in unison. The effect was astonishing. They could feel the boat leap forward at every push.

"By Harry!" Dux cried out in excitement, "we'll beat the horses yet!"

Matt heard the singing begin just moments before his thrashing arms came down on one of the cork torpedoes; gratefully his fingers closed about the rope. He gave out a roar of triumph. Obviously his double shot had been heard at one or other end of the tunnel – or both – and had been passed on to the driver of the horses, who must then have stopped.

Hours later, or so it seemed, though calculation showed it could not have been above five minutes, he and the hearty leggers had closed the gap between them. Eager hands raised him in one lift from the water. He did not realize how cold he must have become until he tried to throw a knot around the towing post. In the end one of the nautical gentlemen did it for him.

"Fire once!" he called aft as he ducked beneath the decking and scuttled back the length of the vessel. The explosion seemed enormous in those confines – but would it carry? They must now be about three-quarters of a mile in, near the halfway point.

The leggers were still hard at it. One or two of them had suggested giving up once the tow was secured, but the rest had hooted with derision and kept going. Matt could hardly believe his ears when, as he struggled back into his shirt and breeches, he heard one highly respectable company chairman say to an equally worthy magistrate, "Come down, you beastly hog, it's my turn now!" – sentiments that cannot have passed those august lips, at least not in such puerile form, for thirty years gone.

Despite the valiant efforts of so many noble and gentle legs, they were making much less headway than the horses would have managed. Even without the delay, the tunnel would take more than forty minutes at this pace instead of the thirteen he had planned. Anxiously he watched the rope, which now curled back behind the *Iron Maiden* in a great, slack loop.

After an agony of moments it twitched; the torpedoes, dimly visible in the light of the lanterns, dipped beneath the surface and then rose again in sequence as the strain reached them. Soon the difference in speed became apparent as the rope flew past them, churning white water.

"I hope he's not galloping out there," Old Q said nervously.

"I hope he is," Matt contradicted.

"Would there be enough stretch to absorb the shock?"

Matt nodded confidently. "Two miles of rope!"

Even as he spoke, his assertion was put to the test. It was a close-run thing but the rope held and the dual vessel almost leaped forward, sending a great surging ripple ahead of it – which it then raced toward that still-infinitesimal pinpoint of light in the distance.

The gentlemen leggers cheered and began to run, upside down, something faster than a trot though still short of a sprint. They were sweating and laughing and gasping for breath by the time they emerged at the Church end of the tunnel. While Punch, ready and waiting with his new team, threw young Jacko the hitch, the gentlemen clambered down, guffawing, clapping one another on the back, dabbing away the sweat, calling for ale, and – above all – discussing the formation of a new club, to be known as The Gentlemen Leggers of the Grand Trunk.

While Matt was shouting his thanks – and his congratulations on their presence of mind – to the owners of the other horse team, who were already hauling in the two-mile rope, one of the company was sketching the design for the club coat of arms: a triad of legs azure courant upon a field sable pale embattled with bricks or.

The *Iron Maiden*, with the *SS II* still floating inside her, was being hauled out of the water at Hollin's Wood before the Gentlemen Leggers reached their consensus on a motto: *Manibus pedibusque* – with hands and feet (though there were more ribald translations).

The timekeeper, Lord Savory, now formed an *ad hoc* handicapping committee to determine how much to allow for the skulduggery with the rope. The clean knife-cut, three quarters through the rope at the breaking point, was all the evidence they needed.

The tunnel had taken forty-seven minutes to traverse, compared with Matt's estimate of thirteen. After much gentlemanly argument, in which everyone took any side but his own, his lordship turned to Matt and said, "We seem agreed upon an allowance of forty-five minutes, Mr. Sullivan. Does that seem fair to you."

No gentleman had ever called him mister before. He filled with pride – a pride which made him reply, "I think we may yet manage without allowance of any kind, sir."

Dux looked angry enough at this but Old Q was beside himself with rage. He stood before Matt and harangued him like a fishwife until the air between them turned purple.

When he paused for breath, Matt looked him in the eye and said calmly, "Make your peace with the world, Duke. These next four miles, you shall find eternity knocking at our wicket gate."

The duke gulped and fell silent.

The *Iron Maiden* was now on the fourth and last of her trolleys; Punch kept his eye on Matt, waiting for the signal to be off. Colonel Carmody, who had been sketching the trolley, leaped aboard and said to Matt, "Even more interesting, sir."

Soon everyone was looking at Matt, wondering why he made no move. But he strode forward and had a quiet word with Jacko. The lad's eyes went wide with shock. Then Matt jumped down and spoke to Punch; he, too, grew alarmed and seemed to argue against whatever plan Matt was unfolding.

But Matt insisted.

Punch shrugged his shoulders and threw up his hands.

With a confident grin Matt returned to the vessel. As soon as he had his hand to the brake lever he gave the signal and they were off.

"What was the debate?" Dux asked with more calm in his voice than there was in his breast.

Matt pointed ahead. "Four miles. Twenty-four locks downhill."

Dux nodded. "Two hundred feet or more. I know."

"Two hundred and fifteen. My original intention was to ride from here to Lawton salt works, then back afloat to Hassall Moss – bringing the trolley on by road – then out of the water again to ride again past Sandbach. Ninety minutes."

"But now?" Dux asked in mounting alarm, for he already had an inkling of the answer.

Matt wafted a hand at the steeply falling landscape before them. "Ride past all twenty-four locks. Fifty minutes."

"But have you made up the roads all the way?"

The only reply was a laugh.

Word of this harebrained plan spread down the ship; her gunwale was suddenly ringed with white knuckles. The boyish good humour of the Gentlemen Leggers had quite evaporated.

"All because your damned pride won't take an allowance of forty-five minutes!" Old Q said fiercely.

The atmosphere became somewhat easier when the colonel, who had spent a while inspecting this trolley, revealed that it sported one or two extra features. In the first place its front axle was on a central pivot, making it steerable. Secondly, there was a hand-cranked pump to power the hydraulic system that kept the vessel level.

"Why these elaborations?" he asked Matt.

"It seemed clever at the time," was the reply.

He had intended the steerable wheels for taking the sharp corner after Lawton Gate, to get back to the canal at the salt works. Now he went straight on at that particular intersection, but the steering was used at Thurlwood, half a mile farther on. There they also had to negotiate a steep downhill bank, leading to a short, more level stretch, followed by another steep bank, again downward, at Chels Hill.

At the top of the hill, where even the most valiant among them took one look at the slope and hid their eyes with a groan, Jacko jumped down and began to turn the handwheel like a demented gatekeeper. Matt meanwhile let the brake on and off, inching her forward to conform to the tilt. To every man aboard the effect was a marvel: The road now fell away before them but the vessel remained on her old and even keel. The weak laughter of amazed disbelief rose on every hand.

Carmody scribbled busily away.

As soon as they were trimmed to the slope Jacko leaped aboard again and, with Punch's team hauling ahead and Matt braking her astern, they were off down the hill at a good brisk trot; the small changes of slope they encountered upon the way were easily within the normal pumping action provided by the road wheels, but at the foot of the hill, before a brief level stretch, they had to repeat the process in reverse . . . and then go through the whole performance once more at Chels Hill.

It all took slightly longer than Matt had expected, but they were still going to gain plenty of time.

At the foot of the second hill was the long straight of Capper's Lane, all on a more-or-less even downhill slope. Here they were able to trot out in grand style, along a road whose surface was every bit as good as those Matt had especially improved.

"I see why you smiled when I asked if you had made up the road all the way," Dux said.

"Why?" Old Q cut in.

"'Twas done for him sixteen-odd centuries ago." Dux pointed to the highway. "We're on a Roman road."

At Dean Hill they had to stop and trim her by hand again for a brief, sharp descent to the ford of Betchton Brook. Jacko cranked the handle with the same demonic energy – but then, quite suddenly, he stopped.

Matt leaned over the side and shouted at him to go on.

The lad looked up, white at the gills, and said, "You'd best see for yourself, sir. 'Tis plain we've sprung a leak."

# CHAPTER FORTY-SEVEN

EVEN AS HE JUMPED down Matt was cursing himself for not having noticed how alarmingly the *SS II* had settled within the *Iron Maiden*. By now there could be no more than an inch of flotation left.

"'We'll manage well enough without any allowance!'" Old Q mocked in fury from the deck above.

"Give the man a chance," Dux remonstrated.

"To do what? Hang himself and us!"

Jacko inclined his head toward the stern, where the leak was plain enough. Two riveted plates had parted. The gap was no wider than would accommodate a gentleman's card but even that was wide enough to permit a frightening gush of water.

"Get the oakum and tar," Matt told the lad.

He glanced inquiringly at Colonel Carmody, who had jumped down beside him. The only response was a sympathetic smile – sympathetic . . . and watchful.

A temporary repair was soon carried out, but how long it

would last was anybody's guess. As he rammed in the caulking with his steel knife, Matt was thinking furiously.

If they were going on another couple of miles, then the lost water ought to be replaced. The thinned down shell of the *SS II* needed that cushioning between her and the iron hull of the *Maiden*. It was infuriating to see so many thousands of gallons of water gushing underfoot, just a few yards ahead at the ford, when a few hundred of them would be enough to restore the margin of safety. But how to raise even so small a quantity by those few feet – and get it from outside the iron shell to inside it?

Punch came up. "We could get her afloat again at Hassall Green," he said, nodding toward the left-hand turn just beyond the ford. "That's not too far."

"And lose all we've gained."

"Or not lose more."

Matt sighed. It was the sensible course – get back on the water as quickly as possible. There were no more flights of locks where the *Iron Maiden* would be needed. Once they were through the short tunnel at Preston Brook there were twenty-three miles of the Bridgewater Canal between there and Manchester, and not a lock in all that way; if they flogged the horses to death over that stretch, they might still make it.

The miller and his men came out to see what all the commotion was about. When they had overcome their surprise the miller asked Matt if he could be of any assistance.

But for that question, as Matt later admitted to Mary, he would have done the sensible thing. Instead he asked, "Have you any pails?"

"Half a dozen, I daresay," was the reply.

While the millhands went off to assemble every container they could lay hands on, Matt got Punch to pull the trolley forward into the middle of the ford, where they would have the least distance to raise the water.

But the moment the vessel straddled the stream he saw the real answer to his problem and laughed for joy. Why were all life's great moments sheer accidents?

The drain tube of the hand-pump now lay beneath the surface of the water. All he needed do was open the drain cock, crank the handle in reverse, and the pump would lift the water directly from the stream into the *Iron Maiden!*

The workers returned to a forest of dismissive hands and cries of "Easy off, lads!" and "Not needed!" Matt, Punch, and Jacko spelled one another at cranking the handle as fast and as hard as they could. In five minutes the water was overflowing the gunwales and spilling down about them.

Dux gave Old Q a silent smile of triumph, as if Matt were his star pupil. The only response was a malign grunt and a lift of the eyebrows that said, "We shall see!"

Scribble-scribble went the pencil in the little black notebook with the government cypher.

With a wave and a cheer they were off again, praying that the temporary caulking would hold and that no more rivets would yield. They galloped through Sandbach, floshing water in great sheets over the highway; with less than two miles to go, smoothly downhill over the old Roman road to Dragon's Lake Bridge, Matt felt they could afford to be a little reckless. The truth was, they couldn't afford *not* to be.

The gamble paid off, for, although they arrived at the bridge, where the fresh team was waiting, with more than half the refill water spilled again, they were still afloat inside the *Iron Maiden*. Soon they were afloat again outside her. And now, for the first time, the *SS II* took precedence. The old iron vessel had a somewhat forlorn air, derelict and abandoned, half in the canal and half out, as they raced away from her. Dux raised a wineglass in salute. "She served us well," he said. Then, more practically, "But you won't just leave her there?"

Matt nodded toward the farmer who had supplied this particular relay of horses. "He'll see to it."

The hour wanted ten minutes to four. They were well behind the schedule but not hopelessly so.

The lad Matt had sent ahead to warn the teams to inspect the tunnel ropes now returned. His mare was lathered to exhaustion but he brought the good news that the ropes had not been interfered with.

M'Grotty must have gambled his all on spoiling the race at Harecastle. To have done more would have doubled his risk of being caught and would, in any case, have been so extensive an interference that all bets would be called off and Matt would have been left as the moral winner.

Matt fired his starting shot and the unseen team at the far end took up the strain. The *SS II* came through the 572-yard Barnton Tunnel almost before Punch could get over the hill; a furlong or so farther on, they actually beat him through the 424 yards of the Saltersford tunnel. He came thundering down the final stretch of the towpath to ironic cheers from the ship's company.

After that it was no surprise to anyone aboard that they surged through the 1,240 yards of the Preston Brook Tunnel in under five minutes. It was by then just gone a quarter past six. They had little over ninety minutes in which to complete the remaining twenty-three miles – an average of fifteen miles to the hour.

It was not utterly impossible, especially as there were no further locks to impede them. Nonetheless, Matt began to wish he had been less cavalier about spurning the forty-five minutes allowance Lord Savory had proposed. They reached the halfway mark, at Warrington Lands, just after eleven minutes past seven. It took Old Q's racing mathematics just a few seconds to compute that, if they could manage the remainder of the course at fifteen miles to the hour, they would win by a margin of less than three minutes. But, as the next stage in that same calculation revealed, they had so far failed to maintain a pace of fifteen miles to the hour.

"It's the bridges," Matt explained. "Twenty-three bridges since Preston Brook. The towpath beneath them narrows to single file."

"And how many bridges ahead?"

"Not so many."

"But exactly?"

"Twenty," Dux told him.

More calculation ended in a dour shake of the head. "We shall fail," Old Q said.

Curiously enough, now that the real crisis was upon them, his testy, querulous spirit deserted him. He stared keenly about them, as if he thought the landscape might suggest some expedient – which, in a sense, it did.

The country to the south rose moderately steeply through well-tended parkland to a stately pile at the crest, less than half a mile ahead.

"What place is that?" Old Q asked.

"Grappen Hall," Dux replied.

"Yours?"

He shook his head. "Lord Pembridge's."

Old Q gave a little laugh. "Not Duffer Pembridge? With the quaint teeth?"

Dux chuckled. "The same."

"Oh, I helped him once, when he looked like to sleep out the night in the watch at St. James's."

"I don't see what good that is to us. There he comes now, by the way."

"Lord – *he's* changed!"

Like every landowner along their way, Lord Pembridge had ridden out to watch the canal race of the century. His tenantry, who also lined the bank, parted respectfully around him.

"Splendid place, Pembridge," Old Q called across to him.

His lordship frowned, searched for the speaker, located him, and burst into a smile – a somewhat guarded smile, Matt thought.

"Kind of you to say so, Duke," he called back as he trotted beside them. Then, noticing Dux there, too, gave a respectful nod and bade him good evening.

"Lend us that nag of yours," Old Q persisted. "I want to ride him to Manchester." Under his breath he added, "Egad, but she'll do. She's as fine a piece of horseflesh as I've seen in years."

Lord Pembridge looked down at his mount; the watchers could almost hear his mind at work, searching for the least offensive form of refusal.

"By Jupiter, but it's good to clap eyes on you again," Old Q went on. "Haven't seen you since . . . oh, when was it?" He fixed him with a beady eye and vowed, "It'll come to me in a minute, I daresay." He drew out his watch and actually began to time that minute.

Lord Pembridge was furious. He could not possibly suffer his tenants to know that he had almost been forced to spend the night in a watch-house, however long ago that might have been; but nor did he want to lend out so fine and promising a filly as this – not even to an experienced rider like the duke.

"St. James's!" Old Q said, as if it were all beginning to come back to him.

Lord Pembridge bared his teeth. If he had had pistols he would have drawn them and put a ball through the duke's tongue.

Old Q flashed another moment of recall. "Yes! That was it – by the watch in St. James's!"

"I'll meet ye at the next bridge," Pembridge snarled. "But if you break her wind on me . . ."

"Hah" the duke replied scornfully. " 'Twas a different tune in 'forty-six, when I rode Roderick Random for you at Newmarket. Won twice the price of that thing you're on now."

But when they met at the bridge below Agden Brow his tone was more conciliatory. "I merely wish to ride a short way ahead of the boat," he explained. "Make sure there's no nonsense to delay her. 'Twill be a swift trot or a slow canter most of the way. You'll get her back with this summer belly sweated off her – and all the better for it."

Pembridge chuckled. "You'd never have called it out, would you, Duke? The watch in St. James's? Not really?"

Old Q shook his head. "No more than you'd have refused me your mount, old friend – not really!"

The *Silent Sullivan II* was by now well off down the canal and the duke had to gallop directly over Woolstone Croft, cutting off the corner and rejoining the canal where it crosses the River Ribble. The filly was intelligent and willing. She seemed to sense the urgency in her new master's manner and responded to it with a will.

They were now just a hundred yards ahead of Punch and his present team of horses, whose canter, restrained by the drag of the boat, was matched by the filly's brisk trot. Over his shoulder, the duke explained to Punch how he would help at the overbridges.

The next such bridge was at Dunham Massey, little less than a mile ahead. When Punch arrived he found the duke waiting in the rushes beside the towpath. He pulled his team to a halt, undoing the hitch as soon as there was an inch of slack in the line. In the same unbroken movement he threw the shackle to Old Q, who caught it like a juggler, effortlessly. There was now enough slack for the whole line to drop to the ground and for Punch's team to trot smartly over it and up the embankment to the roadway above. The entire way was broad enough for the team to remain spanned in pairs. Meanwhile Old Q was carrying the line beneath the bridge on the brief, narrow section of the towpath. He ducked low – indeed, he almost vanished into the filly's back as they passed beneath the arch. By then they were ahead of the boat once more. Just beyond the bridge Punch was slipping off the lead horse's back, ready to catch the shackle as it was thrown to him by Old Q, who was already starting out on an easy canter toward the next bridge.

Dux watched in amazement. "The secret of eternal youth?" he mused aloud. "That man will never die while he fears he may lose a wager."

"Or a woman," Lord Savory added.

Punch caught the shackle, snapped it back in place, leaped again onto the lead mare's back and spurred them forward to resume the tow. The *SS II* had barely lost way at all.

Everyone aboard cheered – even those who stood to lose most heavily by a win against the clock.

"I wish I'd thought of that," Matt said to Dux.

Bridgewater merely laughed. "I don't think you'll face too many complaints about the things you failed to think of, Mr. Sullivan. That would be the shortest list in Lancashire."

These foreseeable – yet unforeseen – setbacks gave Matt no ease. Dux looked at his timepiece and chuckled with confidence; Old Q, delighted to be doing something at last, was grinning as if the triumph were already secure. Matt alone, knowing better than any of them how many things could still go awry, stood at the helm with his guts churning and his lip bitten cherry red.

Seeking some distraction – for steering was now his only occupation – he nodded in the direction of the colonel and asked Dux if the army had taken up wagers on the race, too.

His grace simply laughed. "Have you no imagination?"

Matt frowned quizzically.

"Can't you see that moving people swiftly from place to place is very much a military preoccupation? When today's tumult and rejoicing's over, you'd best prepare yourself for some interesting talks with Colonel Carmody."

There was scant time left for Matt to absorb this news; the race was almost over. Thanks to Old Q's stratagem, the bridges had ceased to pose any obstacle; the *SS II* reached Waters Meeting, a mile or so from their goal, with more than five minutes in hand. But he had not reckoned with the crowds who now lined the canal along both banks. All eighty thousand souls in the city seemed to have turned out to welcome them. Old Q, useful as he had been in negotiating the overbridges, proved a hundred times more useful now as a one-man cavalry charge, clearing the towpath of people who would otherwise have been taken completely unawares by the sheer speed of the boat.

But one man, even a duke, against a city proved losing odds. Old Q fought valiantly but by the time they hove in sight of Castle Field all their margin had gone. A mere ninety seconds – an impossible ninety seconds – was left.

The first thing Matt noticed – and only because he was straining so anxiously to see it – was the party of waiters, each holding his tray at the ready. The precise condition was that at least one gentleman aboard, having partaken of breakfast at their departure from Birmingham that morning, and not having left the boat all day, should swallow one mouthful of his dinner before the twelve hours were up.

Matt tried to lick his lips but his tongue was dry. They might just make it to the wharfside in time – indeed, they probably would. But in whatever few seconds might remain, could a waiter leap aboard and serve one morsel and could the gentleman thus served both chew and swallow it?

The blood deserted his hand upon the tiller; it drained from his face; it fled from his boots, quit his guts, shunned all his skin. He shivered with more than cold. His vision narrowed to that one dot, the leading waiter on the canal bank. All else ceased to exist – the wide summer skies, the city outline pierced with the spires of a dozen churches, the cheering mob, frantic in their enthusiasm to see him win.

In that tunnel-view their goal seemed impossible miles away when Lord Savory began to count out the final sixty seconds: "One, two, three . . ."

*Too fast surely?* Matt thought. The canal water seemed to have turned to treacle.

"Thirteen, fourteen, fifteen . . ."

*Too slow!* Now he meant Punch and the horses; they'd never be able to cover that distance.

"Twenty-four, twenty-five, twenty-six . . ."

The bow wave lapped over the canal banks, washing up to the ankles of the onlookers as they crowded back in the wake of Old Q's valiant trail.

"Thirty-five, thirty-six, thirty-seven . . ."

If the horses had been cut free suddenly, they would have bounded clear over the spire of the Collegiate Church, a mile distant.

"Forty-six, forty-seven, forty-eight . . ."

Miraculously they were at the wharf. The leading waiter made a spectacular leap over the blackwater gap, landed on the gunwale, almost lost his balance, but, even in the act of regaining it, spoonfed a warm potato into the nearest of a dozen open mouths in that human pack of nestlings, all clamoured about him for the honour.

"Fifty-seven, fifty-eight . . ."

The eyes of the chosen diner bulged as he attempted to swallow. None dared touch him, though all wanted to help, for fear of claims of hindrance.

"Fifty-nine . . ."

He managed it at last. His eyes went wide with the pain as that enormous wad of half-masticated potato went down his rebellious gorge.

"Sixty!"

A monstrous belch was Triumph's clarion. It's tail end was drowned in a roar of huzzas and a thunder of applause, which then continued for several minutes. Men who had just lost thousands of pounds stamped and shouted their delight, outdoing even those – and few they were – who now had winnings to count.

Indeed, it seemed as if everyone had won. Certainly everyone wanted to shake Matt by the hand, clap him on the shoulders, hoist him overhead, carry him through the streets. His feet quite literally did not touch the ground between Castle Field and the Assembly Rooms in Levers Row, where he was seated at the chairman's right, taking precedence over even the two noble dukes. Not only was he treated to a right royal feast, he was also elected President of the Gentlemen Leggers of the Grand Trunk.

It was several hours later, at a time when very little of the world any longer made sense, that Colonel Carmody found the moment to murmur in his ear, "Hark'ee, Mr. President, don't quit Manchester before we've had occasion to speak at our leisure, eh?"

# CHAPTER FORTY-EIGHT

THE FOLLOWING DAY, when the euphoria had all died down, the worrying business of Aaron M'Grotty reclaimed Matt's attention. Usually his return home was marked by a ritual how-fare-ye catechism that began with Mary, the baby, her parents and so on, widening out until even the health of the ploughboys and their teams was assured.

That evening, when she met him at the landing stage and they went a-strolling about the fields, there was but one question: "M'Grotty?" he asked.

Mary shook her head. "Young Ben Tiddy, the stockman's brother, led a valiant chase but your man lepped the canal above the bridge and slipped them." She pointed vaguely toward the Potteries, black and almost beautiful in the slanting sunlight.

"Leaped the canal?"

"Well, three-fourths of it. Can he harm us, Matt?"

Her husband shifted his gaze uncomfortably. "He'll emigrate if he values his neck. But I fear he'll go on trying. We'll just have to make it plain to him that . . ."

"It's little Mark I'd fret about the most."

"I'll set two men to guard the place and two more to hunt him down – there'll be no scarcity of volunteers for *that* office! And" – he brightened – "happen we may afford it easily enough now."

With this partial reassurance she allowed herself to be diverted. His tone suggested he was referring to something above and beyond their considerable winnings. "Oh?" she asked. "What's afoot?"

He told her what Colonel Carmody had proposed.

It was all this talk of riot and insurrection, he explained. Revolution preached at every street corner. And now these disturbances in France. "We've not paid it much attention, love. But . . . well, I never saw men more worried."

"I still don't see why they want you," she objected. "A less likely taker for the king's shilling . . ."

He smiled. "It's the movement of men, see? The rapid movement of men. How to get a crack company of Grenadiers from London to Liverpool in sixty hours . . . that sort of thing. And how to follow with the rest of the regiment inside another twenty-four."

She felt a sense of anticlimax. This was not the sort of exciting new challenge for which his enthusiasm had half-prepared her. "And who better to ask!" she said dutifully. The breeze played all about them, rattling the ripening oats, golden in the evening sun. She looked back across the fields, toward the house, which was far enough away for the dilapidations not to show. Could they not be content with this small empire? Was it not ten thousand times greater than their entire wealth had amounted to this day twelvemonth? Why should anyone want more?

She sighed. Without being fully aware of it she was beginning to invent a peaceful past beside which the present, and still more the future, could not help but seem strident, hectic, perilous.

"How now?" Matt asked.

She faced it head on: "Why should you pull their chestnuts out of the fire?" she asked. "They deserve their uneasy sleep. Down the centuries they've done nothing but flog and hang and transport the populace – and the lucky ones, the ones who escaped such reforms, faced nothing but starvation and beggary. And now, when the worm shows signs of turning, they can think of nothing better than the militia and the Riot Acts. And to top it all they have the effrontery to ask our assistance . . . as if we are of their company!"

He cleared his throat, uneasy at the strength of her passion.

"Do *you* feel we're of their company?" she pressed.

"Well . . . I am to be elected to the Staffordshire Club. And I'm President of the Gentlemen Leggers of the Grand Trunk – by unanimous decision. And Lord Savory says once I can sit a horse . . ."

"Matt!" Mary turned and, taking him by the arms, gave a violent shake. "Are you drunk?"

"Isn't it true?"

"Of course it's not true! Can't you smell out their deception? 'Tis the same one they sought to practise on me and which I so nearly yielded to. You're the latest nine-day wonder – as I once was. I must needs have 'done a Gunning' and married a duke or else sink back into oblivion when the next wonder hove in view. And 'tis the same with you – once your novelty wanes, the moment your usefulness to them is at an end . . ."

"Ah! But when will that be?" he asked truculently.

"When you least expect it, of course. When you think you're indispensable to them. Oh Matt!" She turned and clung to him. "I don't want us to end our days in some pokey little villa with twice-too-much furniture and nothing but bickering from breakfast to supper. We have no need of these people. Let's be content with what we have, eh? Even better – let's be happy to know we could have had more and yet spurned it."

"Such wild fancies!" he laughed.

"Tell them no, Matt. We are yeomen here who may thumb our noses at the fine world of fashion. And we have an enterprise too convenient to the useful classes – the men of trade – for the useless ones, the gentry, to dare oust us there. Why must we yearn to become mere dependants of patronage – which is what will happen if . . ."

"It's not that bad," he said soothingly. "You had a bad experience."

"Ergo – I know full fine what I'm saying!"

"Shall we go home? In this field I can think only of M'Grotty."

"At least promise me you'll ponder what I've said."

"Of course." He laughed to have escaped so lightly. "Indeed yes and to be sure at all, I will."

In the end, though, her entreaties made small difference. No one could tell Matt his mountain top was a valley floor; he had to see it for himself. Even on that homeward walk he said, "Yon Colonel Carmody – I could have furnished him with his rapid-militia scheme inside ten minutes."

"Why didn't you – and be done with it?"

He gave a cunning chuckle. "Does the doctor say, 'Take this salve, a penny if you please, next customer!'? Not him! He plucks his lip and knots his brow and turns up his eyes and wheezes . . . until you're that sure that, but for him, you'd be stiff and cold come the dawn. *Then* he draws forth his herbs and simples – and asks the full shilling for his skill!"

His confident humour justified her forebodings. "You're going to assist them, no matter what I say. I can tell."

He cleared his throat, scratched his ear. "I will take care, though, love. You're right in what you say, but happen we may extract the best of both."

There was another pantomime of indifference before he added, "And you'll help us, eh? With the pen and ink side of it?"

She gave a shrug of resignation. "I've no better way to keep an eye on you, I suppose."

He strolled beside her, contented and silent. It hurt that her opinions counted for so little with him. At length he spoke again: "You're right when you say they're not like us, love. Carmody now – he's a trained engineer. Good as Croxley. He took down all my plan of the two vessels and the trolleys in his little book. I thought that's what he wanted us to do for the military."

"And isn't it?"

Matt shook his head. "He said that now 'twas shown to the world, there were ten dozen engineers could repeat it. But what they couldn't do was . . . can you guess?"

"What?"

He chuckled. "This shows you how they're not like us. He said the real genius of our Impossibility Race wasn't the *Iron Maiden*, nor wasn't the *Silent Sullivan*, nor wasn't the trolleys and the hydraulics and all that. It was how we'd arranged all them teams of horses and drivers – how they were all there when wanted – and keen as volunteers to see us win, all pulling their bowels out. He said that's what made us win. The engineering was small beer beside it."

"Well . . . he has the right of it, has he not?"

Matt gave a dismissive laugh. "If there's some great art in saying, 'See here, Farmer Brown, if I pay you a fiver, and double if we win, will you have a drover and four shire horses at such-and-such a place on the towpath at such-and-such a time?' . . . why, where's the art in that!"

Mary laughed at his simplicity. "Oh, Matt, me darlin' boy!"

"What's that supposed to mean?"

"You can't see it? You say, 'Where's the art in it?' To Carmody and the likes of them 'tis a lost art. They'd *command* your Farmer Brown under pain of a flogging – and then wonder why the trace parted or one of the horses was a touch lame, and why your man had that little smirk on his face when he paraded his ten thousand difficulties."

The following day the pair of them sat down with pen and paper, a map of England, and a list of the country's canals and navigations.

Notwithstanding Matt's confidence, the task took more than a ream of paper, more than a dozen pen nibs, and more than one well of ink. It also took more than a week – for, naturally, the question he had been asked to solve was not how to move men swiftly from London to Liverpool but from anywhere to anywhere. And, being thorough government men – who know that every stone must contain at least *one* drop of blood to squeeze – they wanted what they called "contingency" plans, using canals that as yet were but a gleam in their speculators' eyes.

As Matt saw it, the military had no need of a dozen *Iron Maidens*, all rusting away in some warehouse against this or that "contingency." There were enough flyboats plying a daily trade upon the canals for the government to be able to commandeer half a dozen within twenty miles of any given barracks. And the average flyboat, though not even halfway to being a *Silent Sullivan*, would suit the army well enough. And in any event, if his *other* plans now bore fruit, there would soon be *Silent Sullivans* on every trunk waterway in the kingdom, ripe for commandeering and at a profit to them all.

He concentrated instead upon the logistics of the plan.

As it moved from outline to fine detail, Mary's misgivings strengthened rather than faded. She had a picture of some poor family in a wretched hovel on the outskirts of, say, Manchester – living copies of the creatures whose misery had so shocked her at the approaches to Dublin. There would be a rise in the price of bread. Jolly Farmer Browns, out hunting in the shires, would clap one another on the back and drink down their stirrup cups in justified glee. And mothers and children already at the gates of death would pass through. The survivors would riot . . . and what then? Why, within hours that tide of misery incarnate would lap at an iron line of riflemen. But how so swift, they'd ask? And why not worn and footsore? Thank you, Matt and Mary Sullivan!

"But what if there's war with France?" he asked. "When the Frenchie militia lands on one of our backdoor coastlines and finds itself staring at that same iron line? That's when those same folk'll say thank you, Matt and Mary Sullivan!"

She stared at him, furious that he had found this argument.

He grinned and yielded a small concession then. "Nay, love. Thou art right. That's not my reason – neither to quell the mob nor frustrate the Frenchie. It's the challenge of it. You know me. I can never resist a challenge."

# CHAPTER FORTY-NINE

DESPITE THE CUNNING of Matt's plan, the generals decided they did, after all, want a couple of *Iron Maidens* of their own, at least to take advantage of that section of the Grand Trunk where Matt had so obligingly improved the canalside path to allow the passage of the heavy trolley. Carmody commissioned him to design them. The actual building went to ironmaster-friends of the government, of course – though Matt had to supervise the work.

Carmody also insisted that Matt should ride every main canal bank in the country, partly to look for obstructions or other features that might frustrate the plan, and also to enlist the aid of those farmers, farriers, liverymen and copers who would play a part in its working. "Riots following an increase in the price of bread" was a powerful argument. As each newly completed canal was opened, Matt had to inspect its towpath and architecture with the army's needs in mind.

And as if that were not enough, he was also appointed to a War

Office committee to deal with the military implications of every new canal proposal submitted to parliament. Since ten times as many proposals were submitted as there were canals built, the job was no sinecure.

These divers employments lasted into the spring of the following year.

By then Mary was well advanced in the carrying of their second child. The threat of M'Grotty had receded once again. The men pursuing him lost the trail within days. They learned that in Chester he had assumed the name of Amos McGill. A publican down by the Liverpool dock remembered a man of that same name and M'Grotty's description staying with him on the night before an emigrant ship had sailed for New Orleans; he was sure "Amos McGill" had boarded that vessel. All in all, it seemed a fair conclusion that M'Grotty had fled the country; but, though Matt paid off the two bulldogs, he knew M'Grotty's malevolence well enough not to relax the day-and-night watch upon the farm.

The fame of the regular *Silent Sullivan* service had spread throughout the land as news of the Impossibility Race and its outcome reached every distant alehouse, assembly room, hunt meeting, and tea party. Steam Punch took over the management of the "Sullivan Line." His shrewd grasp of men – and his easy way with them, too – had, as Matt readily allowed, contributed vastly to the arrangements that had so impressed the colonel. New vessels appeared on fresh stretches of the canal almost monthly; and soon there were *Silent Sullivans* skimming the waters between London and the Midlands, Birmingham and Bristol, Gloucester and Oxford, Liverpool and Manchester . . .

Old Q had made such a fortune on the Impossibility Stakes that he now complained of being unable to get decent odds against him in any likely wager; nor was his complaint entirely jocular, for past success was never balm against present failure. He did, however, pay two visits to Summerley Manor in the months following the race. Dux called by, too, always a day or so after Old Q had left. He had also made a killing in wagers, which had rekindled the gambling spirit of his youth; and, though now it was checked by crabbèd age and the dour misogyny of a lifetime, he was not above the gentlemanly flutter against fools upon a copper-bottom certainty – which commodity seemed to stick to His Grace of Queensberry like leeches to a wealthy invalid.

The Duke of Bedford, too, paid them one brief call when he visited the Marquis of Stafford. Anybody's Mrs. Nancy Parsons was not of the party. His grace strolled jovially over the rejuvenated acres of Summerley Farm, listened to Mary's tale of the improvements she had made, advised on those that were still in the air, and jokingly consoled the marquis, who hovered at her other elbow, on the loss of such good land so cheap.

Stafford turned purple.

"Dear God," Mary scolded nervously. "Your grace would ruin a body's life for a quip. Indeed, the truth kicks toward the other goal, for didn't my Lord Stafford know exactly what game he was at when he sold these few acres to us?"

Stafford himself was surprised to hear it but he calmed down and began to nod sagely.

"Ah?" Bedford smiled encouragingly at his fellow peer. "Tell away, my lord."

The marquis turned to her, passing on the encouragement.

Mary smiled at the duke. "Now isn't it plain?" she asked. "His agent may cajole the tenants hereabouts with, 'Go to, thou sluggard, and do likewise – else you'll not afford the rise in rents that's coming next year.'" She smiled admiringly at Stafford. "Have I not found you out, sir?"

"Hang me if you haven't, ma'am," he agreed, giving the duke a triumphal grin.

Now it was Bedford's turn to be displeased.

"And yet," Mary interjected hastily, turning back to the marquis, "his grace is the real architect of your design, Lord Stafford. For nothing that has been achieved here at Summerley could even have been ventured had I not first enjoyed the run of the Woburn library. Not to mention" – she risked giving the duke's arm a friendly squeeze – "enough candles to put the sun itself to shame."

An image of Mr. Page danced before her mind's eye. What would he make of her – racked between these two ridiculously proud and dignified noblemen, fawning with the worst! How would she explain it?

She would tell him that, stripped of their pretensions and mirrored in the cast of a cool eye, they were as vulnerable as any man and as interesting as most . . . that pride dealt them the greater wound in that they must live with it every day . . . that

363

needless wealth was more curse than blessing. But would it answer him?

Indeed, was it really Mr. Page she needed answer? Had the memory of him not become some convenient post on which to hang ideas she could not bring herself to own. All her life she had followed her parents' habit and dreamed of wealth and property. Landless, she had nonetheless been reared in the landed tradition; its duties were in her very bones. Yet that same rearing had skirted as close to poverty as makes no odds; those bones knew the pauper grind, as well.

Thus she was and always would be two people, villein and freeman, royalist and republican. Worse than that – she was both those factions *and* their referee. She – if she was anyone – was at heart more interested in seeing which of them would win the battle for her heart than in forging alliances with either.

Why had this twinning of her soul only recently become apparent? Because of the property, of course – the property, the money, the need to stop thinking from day-to-day, hand-to-mouth, and develop instead that instinctive, rich man's sweep of Time's horizons.

Still, the poverty of her youth might yet be the saving of her. The new art of inoculation was then all the go; and the idea that a small, mild infusion of an otherwise virulent sickness could protect a body from the main attack came to her as a great comfort. The sterile pretensions of her childhood were proof against all present temptations to *folie de grandeur*. It did not then strike her that Matt's very different upbringing had endowed him with no such immunity.

Be that as it may, the effect of these several ducal visits was to throw the locality in a whirl. No hostess knew what to *do* about Matt and Mary Sullivan. Matt was so often away, leaving Mary to state that the pair of them were bent upon their trade (a word spoken with a certain apologetic shiver) and had no intention of "going about" in society. For its part, society, long-skilled at slamming the door in the faces of ten thousand hopefuls, had no training at all in the subtler art of throwing wide that same door and inviting the indifferent to approach, or at least to cast a glance in its direction.

Lady This and the Hon. Mrs. That would set out to catch these confidants of dukes and end up having trawled – yet again –

nothing larger than those two minnows: The Flinderses of the Barony of Inchiquin in County Clare. *She* had enough airs for a cathedral choir, and *he'd* plague the world, early and late, with grandiose plans for growing cork in Connemara – or was it for rearing connemaras in Cork?

The man best placed to penetrate the Sullivans' indifference to society's mixem-gatherums was, of course, Colonel Carmody, for his acquaintance with them was ambiguously poised betwixt and between – neither trade nor friendship but a curious amalgam of both. When Matt's latest report was ready, including his long, carefully compiled lists of canalside horse suppliers and drivers, all in Mary's slightly wayward but quite legible hand, he invited the pair of them to a longish stay at his country seat, Hawkshead Hall, forty miles away in the ancient Forest of Arden. They deserved this time of relaxation, he said, and while his hospitality was not exactly sybaritic, they would enjoy good plain food, noble vistas, fresh air, tame walking, and above all – the best of company.

A sardonic glint in his eye told them he did not refer to himself and Mrs. Carmody in this final item of enticement.

"Pray, who else will be of the party, Colonel?" Mary felt prompted to ask.

But he would not be drawn beyond saying that it was certain ladies and gentlemen who had long wished to meet them.

Of course, they had little choice but to accept this amiable invitation. The baby was not supposed to be due for a couple of months yet. The weather was improving, the spring sowing done, and the farm and business were in competent hands; what cause, then, to turn the colonel down? Once they had reached their decision, they began looking forward to the break, telling each other it was something they should think of doing more often.

Then, just two days before they were to set out, a violent storm passed over the Midlands, leaving in its wake a great pall of raincloud, which just sat overhead in the breezeless air and discharged itself in a fine, unremitting downpour. Rivers overflowed and roads became impassable, at least to carriages. But there were still the canals, if they did not burst their banks.

The Coventry Canal passed within a few miles of Hawkshead. In other circumstances they could have ridden so short a distance – indeed, Mary was all for it now; but Matt would not hear of such a thing. They stood at their bedroom window on what should have been the morning of their departure and watched the rain as it continued to fall. Great sheets of water stood upon the fields; some were united with the swollen Trent in the west, others to the canal in the east.

"A few more inches and the waters will conjoin," she commented.

"That would be one of your Remarkable Occurrences," he said. "You could add it in your own autograph hand to your book."

But she shook her head. "Too dull, I fear. Now at Highbickington, in Devonshire, five years ago, thirteen large elms were moved by floods a furlong from their native spot, whereupon they continued to flourish as formerly." She sighed. "We'll never see such marvels here."

He squared his shoulders and came to a decision: "We'll just cry off," he said. "Best anyway. Tea parties, tame walks! Who'd want to start *that* caper?"

Despite his brave words she could sense the disappointment in him. "Listen," she said. "This rain can't last for ever. If it stops tomorrow, the floods will be down in a couple of days and the roads would open again by the end of the week. So why wouldn't you go ahead, and I'd follow you in a day or so . . ."

It took many more pleas and cajolings than that for her to persuade him to this plan, but she knew how well he rubbed along with the colonel and how keenly he had anticipated this visit. She played on that until, at last, and still against his best judgment, he let himself be persuaded to go alone.

In fact, the rain did not stop on the morrow – nor the next morrow, nor the next. It persisted for a further week, at first continuously, then with breaks, which, like the lakes upon the fields, grew longer and wider and eventually coalesced into one great continuum. At last the world dared raise its eyes skyward and say, "I think it's over." But it was a further week before the waters subsided and the roads became anything like passable again.

The first visitor to Summerley, when the manor reverted from island to peninsula, was Punch. Mary saw him leap off the original *Silent Sullivan I* as it passed by on its regular run to Manchester.

Her heart danced. She knew he had been about Sullivan business on the Coventry Canal, not far from Hawkshead; naturally he would have called at the colonel's to confer with Matt. So now he was here with messages for her.

As fast as her condition allowed, she hastened below to greet him.

But as he walked toward her up the last furlong of the drive, she remarked a nervous, hasty solemnity in his gait. Something was amiss. When he drew closer and she saw his face, her misgivings were confirmed.

"What was it?" she asked before he was even indoors. "Something to do with Matt? Is he all right? Are you after coming from Hawkshead?"

"Hawkshead!" he said darkly. "Mixem-gatherum you called it – aye, and so it is."

"Tell me plainly, Punch. A gatherum of whom? Is Dux there? Is it some cabal of navigation people?"

He shook his head, reluctant to go on. At last, with further prompting from her, he forced himself to say, "Tottenham."

She gasped. "Is *he* there?"

"Didn't I see the man himself, at his ease on the lawn, bold as a whippet!"

Her heart fell. Yet why, she asked herself, should this news seem so worrying? In what way could Tottenham threaten Matt, even if he wanted to – especially under the colonel's roof? But against that, if his presence were innocent, why had Carmody said nothing about it?

"There's more," Punch warned.

"Well, I suppose Saint Ignatius Murphy is with him?"

He nodded.

But that was hardly surprising. "Sure where the master goes wouldn't the cur follow?"

Punch sighed. "He's not the only Tottenham cur."

"Jesus!" Mary exploded. "Must I bate every word outa you, man?'"

"At first I thought 'twas good news, but now I can't tell. Jack Horley is there. Whether cur to Tottenham or crony . . ."

"And Crystal?" she interrupted, heart in mouth.

"To be sure. She's his bitch. There's no doubting that! I didn't see Jack and Crystal, mind, but I was told of it. I was told a Lord Dent is there but the name means nothing to me."

She sucked her lip between her teeth and began to pace about the room. "This makes me so uneasy, Punch. But why? What did Matt make of it all? Did he say aught to you?"

"Sure he looks at me with that aisy grin of his. 'Haven't I the measure of these fine folk?' says he."

"That's a quare thing to be saying. What may he mean by it?"

Punch shrugged. "They were wild altogether. I doubt there's been much sleep beneath that roof. Hadn't he great dark half-moons on him here beneath his eyes?"

"But why would he come out with a thought like that? Doesn't it show he feels – or felt – himself under some sort of a threat?"

"Why, indeed, ma'am."

She resumed her pacing. "What I still don't see is why didn't the colonel mention this when he invited us? Did he think it would be a *pleasant* surprise? Surely not."

"Aye, surely not ma'am," Punch affirmed.

Something in his tone alerted her. "Is there more?" She looked at him and held her breath.

His eyes said it.

Her arm shot out and clasped his, involuntarily. "Rowena Carmody! Oh God, why did I not think of her? She's the colonel's niece, isn't she? Well . . . she has good reason to be there, I suppose."

"She has doubled it, then, for isn't she Lady Tottenham now."

Mary's jaw dropped. "She *married* him?"

He nodded. "And they're as well matched as any brace of cat and dog, or so I hear."

Clutching at a straw Mary said, "But come, that explains it, so – why Tottenham's there at all. Else were this coincidence too much. And Jack and Crystal got in very thick with him that year that went past now – so we can account for them. Sinister's not in it, after all. And yet – why did the colonel say nothing of it? We keep foundering on that rock."

"That's what I was pondering meself, ma'am, all the road here. And God forgive me, I couldn't hinder the reflection that Matt Sullivan's usefulness to the colonel is now gone by."

"True enough," Mary was reluctant to concede. "But even so, the man has no cause to fall out with . . ."

"You and I know that, mistress. And so does Matt. But does the colonel? That's the question, now. We all saw what happened at Worsley Old Hall that night when Matt went a-window-cleaning, ladder in hand. And whether or not Dux had the right or the wrong of it, he'll surely have told the colonel. And the colonel will just as surely have asked young madam to explain herself. And couldn't the clever serpent's tongue of that little colleen burn a hole in the page of truth itself?"

Mary put her hands to her swollen belly and cried the two words she never thought to hear her tongue utter at any flesh of hers: "Damn you!"

Punch put a reassuring hand to her arm. "I was thinking now, ma'am. Colonel Carmody may not be the only player in this game to bend Madam Coincidence to his will. That gun has *two* barrels."

"Meaning?"

"Wait while I tell you now. There's a new branch of the Coventry Canal, a private one. The Forest Branch, they call it, for it goes up to a great forest and lumberyard not a mile from Hawkshead. Indeed, the colonel's gardens are that grand, they run all the way to the canal itself, where the water is made ornamental. And though 'tis not yet opened to traffic, 'tis puddled and ready for inundation. Indeed, it's half-inundated already with the rains. They're just higgling over the price of the water. 'Twould only take some blackguard to open the feed from the summit reservoir and a pair of lock gates and you could float as sweet as a custard to the colonel's very door."

She laughed for delight. "In what? Have we . . ."

"We've a new *Silent Sullivan* to launch next week, but she's navigable now. She could be got here to Summerley and taken on to Hawkshead by this time tomorrow. The way of it would be smooth as any midwife could wish."

Mary threw her arms about him in an awkward, angular hug. "Are you still here, man?" She kissed his ear. "What in God's name is holding you?"

# CHAPTER FIFTY

Matt THREW ANOTHER LOG on the large withdrawing-room fire. Despite the warm spring days, the evenings were chill – and Rowena, baring so much skin to the darkening air, must surely feel it worse than he.

"You should get a footman to do that," she told him.

"Life's too short," he answered with a smile, trying to make her smile, too. For the past two weeks he had done his best to avoid being alone with her, but the situation between himself and Lord Tottenham had now reached such a pitch that he had to risk her solo company in the hope of worming some information out of her.

"Lost your nerve, then?" he asked suddenly.

"I beg your pardon?" Her heart leaped almost into her mouth.

"'Better Good Company than Bad Society,' you said once. Yet now you're Lady Tottenham?"

"You are impertinent, sir."

He shrugged. "I could have told you he's a bad 'un."

"Matt!" Her eyes raked the ceiling. Then she made a conciliatory gesture, inviting him to sit beside her. "One just does not talk to people in this fashion."

He accepted the invitation, saying, "But isn't it true?"

"I give up." She stared at the log, which was now beginning to burn brightly.

He ran his eyes down her fire-gilt skin.

"Even if it is true," she told him quietly, "there's no helping matters now. So there's an end to it."

"*Marriage à la Mode*," he commented. "Mary brought back a

set of those prints from London. You'll know them, of course?"

She tossed her head impatiently.

"The husband ends up murdered and the wife swallows poison. You want to be careful."

"On the contrary," she said quickly. "You are the one who should heed such advice."

Outwardly he betrayed none of his sudden interest. "Me?"

"Yes. You should be careful of Tottenham. He'll harm you if he can. Why will you not just agree to differ with him and avoid a direct engagement? You can never leave anything just *be*, can you!"

"A challenge is a challenge."

"My husband trades on that illusion. You'll end up looking down the barrel of his pistol one of these dawn mornings. And, clever as you may be, you won't . . ."

Impatiently he interrupted: "But why go and marry him?"

She burst out: "Hey nonny no! It was that or disgrace. You can have little notion, Matt, of the combined power of a family like the Carmodys – or you wouldn't even ask. They'll reword Holy Writ when it suits them: 'If thy daughter offend thee, pluck her out.' I had no choice but Tottenham."

"And your offence?" he asked.

She could not meet his eye.

Taking a chance he said, "Hark, lass. If you've wronged me and now regret it, the offence is doubled by leaving me in ignorance."

She grew taut as a bowstring but did not – could not? – speak.

He pressed on. "Did Dux ever learn the truth touching thee and me, that night at . . ."

"No!" Her vehemence was genuine, he felt sure.

His gaze returned to the window. "Did . . . anyone else?"

She was silent again.

"Your uncle?" he suggested.

"No," she sighed. "I told Tottenham. God forgive me – I made it seem you were the seducer and I the mere victim. Oh, Matt, I'm so sorry."

"Spilt milk, lass. You thought our paths would never cross again – so where was the harm? Like as not I'd have done the same myself. More to the point now – might Tottenham have told your uncle?"

"Of course not!" She laughed as if the very idea were impossible. "Why d'you seem to think my uncle knows?"

"I detect a coolness in him that was not there before."

She chuckled. "And you cannot fathom it, yourself?"

He shook his head.

"Why, man, he is vexed at your most pointed neglect of Crystal Horley and me!"

"Ah, is that all?" Matt was vastly relieved.

She laughed again. "You're a law unto yourself, right enough, Matt Sullivan."

"Aye. And the first Act in my personal Book of Statutes provides for the Safety of Navigation among Pretty and High-Spirited Females – of which you and Mrs. Horley are two prime examples. Are you sure the colonel doesn't know?"

"If he did, then, believe me, you'd not pass one further minute beneath his roof. There's no guile in him. He could never play the Judas goat, leading you to Lord Tottenham's poleaxe – if that's your fear."

He accepted her assurance at that. "And what does your husband say of me?"

"That you are a cypher that he cannot read. He would dearly wish to see you ruined, yet cannot envisage how to encompass it, though he has ruined so many before."

"Aye, I feel it. And yet he is so careful."

"Because you respond like no other man he's ever met. His favourite ruse is to get his victim drunk and then either cheat him out of a fortune or provoke him to a duel. Or both. But he calls you the Glass Mountain. He can't seem to get a-hold of anything."

Matt kept his peace, hoping for more.

"He thinks of little else but you," Rowena went on. "He maintains that your indifference to society puts you among the revolutionaries. Is that true? Do you want to hang the entire peerage?"

His laughter implied the question was not worth an answer. Then he added: "I'd settle for one or two."

"But seriously?"

"Your kinsman Dux is the true revolutionary. What he's not done for the mobility of mankind, eh! And Bedford, too – farming and that. But then look at Old Q. What's he ever done for the populace at large – except assist its increase? If the peerage was all like him, they could hang the lot tomorrow and who'd grieve?"

Tiring of the subject, she stretched her arms languorously and murmured, "Tell me more about your Navigations among Pretty and High-Spirited Females."

He smiled briefly into her eyes. "What were those rocks in olden times – used to lure poor mariners to founder upon them? And the only salvation was blindfolds and beeswax?"

Her tongue lingered on her lip. She wished he would look at her for she knew how enticing the gesture was to men. "And what of the shoals that lie in wait, concealed beneath the foam in some channel where the vessel cannot help but founder?"

"That is what prayers are for," he said, giving the conventional answer quite mechanically – and not realizing it could bear two quite opposite interpretations.

Lord Dent joined them at that moment. From the composure of his smile Matt wondered whether the man had been listening at the door for some time. Probably not. He always moved silently – and was hardly ever to be seen without that shrewd little smile on his lips, which suggested not only that he saw right into you, but also that you weren't to let it worry you – for he wouldn't breathe a word about it.

He nodded to each in turn as he crossed the room to join them. "Lady Tottenham . . . Sullivan." He made their two names sound like an interesting list, worthy of some delving.

Rowena felt discomfited enough by it to blurt out, "We're talking about the nobility of the utility, Lord Dent – I mean the other way about." And she went on to summarize what Matt had said.

Dent was amused. "Dear me, Sullivan – is it all so utilitarian, then? You don't think the nobility was ordained by God, as some say?"

Matt smiled. "Where might we look for a Plantaganet *these* days?"

"Egad, you make me question my own purchase on life."

"The country survives your lordship's long absence from London."

Dent seemed to lose interest in the subject for he turned to Rowena and asked, "And how does your ladyship?"

"She thrives, too." It was Tottenham himself who spoke, standing just inside the door. "I feel lucky tonight," he added, apropos nothing, as he advanced toward them. He and Dent exchanged a meaningful glance.

Matt watched them. He'd never met such a crowd; half their communication took the form of raised eyebrows, pursed lips, significant shrugs, and other devices of silence. Even silence itself could shriek a sentence or two among them, when properly shaped.

"Are none of you dying of thirst?" Tottenham asked, directing the question particularly at the two men. Only then, as a studied afterthought, did he include his wife.

"I'll keep you company, my dear," she replied, in tones so warm that his expression turned to surprise.

He had a most self-satisfied way of pulling the bell sash and rubbing his hands as he waited. Yet again Matt wondered what his darling Mary had ever seen in the fellow, apart from his undoubted good looks. Still less could he understand why, despite all he had done to harm her, she still had a certain soft spot for him. She herself would deny it hotly, of course.

"I suppose you'll follow your usual abstemious path, Sullivan?" Tottenham asked as the footman filled the glasses.

Matt raised a finger, a gesture that might have had half a dozen meanings, or none. Then he stood and left the room. A few minutes later he returned and, taking up a glass of wine, held it toward Tottenham in half-ironic tribute before he took a sip.

Crystal and Jack were of the company by now. She and Rowena were smiling at each other like the dearest of sisters.

"German habit this," Tottenham was saying. "They don't drink wine with the meal. The French do, of course. We've borrowed the best of the two customs."

"Us borrow from them?" Jack said truculently. "From the crouts and mossoos? It's plain to me, sir, that they're the ones who did all the borrowing – *and* got it wrong."

"What d'you say, Sullivan?" Tottenham asked, turning to him in the most companionable way.

Matt relished a gulp and patted his belly. "Like Parson Jones's barn – always room for more."

The laughter was condescending – all except Dent's. He smiled at Matt and then stared at the others as if they had missed the real joke. "You take to it like a cat to cream," he told Matt.

Matt's response was strange: He took out his kerchief and, almost guiltily, wiped his lips.

The colonel and his wife joined them at that moment, swelling the numbers beyond the point where one single conversation was easily sustained. As the men reseated themselves, Dent made some remark to Tottenham, the colonel and his wife engaged Rowena, leaving Crystal and Matt alone in a whirl of bright inanities – to which he now added his own. "A long way from Sapperton," he said.

"Sapperton?" she echoed. "Longer for you than for me."

"Is it?" He inclined his head gently toward Tottenham and let his eyebrows reinforce the question.

She followed his gesture but said nothing; her face was immobile.

"Is Jack and him falling out?" he asked.

She stared at him open-jawed. "You go at it like a bull at a gate, fellow. There's ways and ways, you know."

"Ah well, 'tis no business of mine."

"I'll toast that sentiment." But her glass did not stir. "If you're seeking an ally," she went on, almost in a whisper, "I wouldn't look toward my dear husband. Just a friendly word, now." Then, catching Jack's eye upon her, she added in a louder, more casual tone, "I wish your Mary were here."

"To be honest, so do I."

Crystal's laughter brought several other conversations to a momentary halt but Matt persisted. "When she first persuaded me to come on my own, I'll be candid, there was much in me as welcomed it. D'you understand? I wanted to touch into this sort of caper" – he nodded vaguely at the company, who were now busy once more at their own conversations – "without her interpretation at my elbow."

"And now?"

"I'd be glad of any explanation."

"Of what in particular? Perhaps I can help?"

"I've known labouring men who dream of lives in idleness. But give them two days of this and you'd be killed in the rush to get back to their shovels."

"You can't wait to be gone, eh?"

He nodded. "It's like a life spent in waiting."

"And does Mary agree with you? Oh, I do wish we lived closer, Matt. I would so love to know you both better." There was a tenderness in her eye, hinting at degrees of loss that could not be broached in any other way.

As they went into dinner, Crystal on his arm, she gave a nod toward Tottenham, safely beyond earshot, and murmured, "Do be careful at cards tonight."

He grinned.

She had expected a different response – surprise, alarm, curiosity . . . but there was only his confident grin. What could one make of him? He was like someone from a far country, she thought, a country where they happened to talk English (of a kind) but shared no other recognizable ideas or customs.

Tottenham was liberal with his host's wine during the meal. Jovially he challenged Matt to pace him glass for glass. At first the offer was refused. Then Lord Dent warned Tottenham that a frame accustomed to hard labour could, by its very nature, withstand the assault of spirituous liquors more stoutly than one reared in idleness. Jack countered this with the learned opinion that "Wine is different." Tottenham agreed. "'Tis breeding tells," he said, with as much of a sneer as the occasion allowed. "And all the animal brawn in the kingdom will not avail against it."

"There's a challenge if ever I heard one," Matt said, toasting the man with an ironic lift of his wineglass.

By the end of the meal, Tottenham was two glasses down – or rather *not* down; they stood, ready filled, beside his place, while Matt, by now truculently tipsy, having drunk the bottle down to its island, invited him to concede.

Mrs. Carmody was at first alarmed by their childish and unbecoming behaviour, but a nod and a wink from her husband quelled the rebuke on her lips. Sullivan had proved a curmudgeonly guest with the ladies; he hoped to see the man lowered a peg or two.

"I don't want their puke all over my new carpet," she told her husband in a deafening whisper.

He gave her a comforting nod that was no comfort at all.

Rowena tried to prod Matt with her foot, under the table. Everyone now realized that the situation between Matt and

Tottenham was at last coming to a head. Rowena believed she knew why and feared that her words had been the cause of it. She didn't want Matt drunk but . . . well, *navigable*.

They played solo whist that evening, Tottenham, Matt, Crystal, and Jack at one table, the rest at another. Tottenham let Crystal win some twenty-five guineas; he did it so blatantly that Matt marvelled Jack did not leap to his feet in protest a dozen times or more. At length Crystal yawned and complained of having breathed too much fresh air that day. With no attempt at sincerity she asked Tottenham if he minded her withdrawing while she was ahead of him.

He half-rose, toasted her with his glass, and wished *she* might always be ahead of *his* withdrawal. Jack laughed as loud as he. Matt turned toward Rowena, to see how she took it, and found her staring directly at him in what she trusted was an appealing gaze. But he saw only what he expected to see, a miserable, waiflike young woman.

Mrs. Carmody chose that moment to retire as well. The colonel and Rowena started at a two-handed game they called "German" whist while Lord Dent took Crystal's place at the now all-male table.

"What say we try this new 'Boston' whist?" he suggested, adding that it made the stakes more lively. "A penny a counter?" he went on.

They all turned to Matt, who said, "Indeed, why not? In for a penny in for a pound, as they say."

"Gentlemen say guineas," Tottenham told him jovially.

"Guineas." Matt accepted the correction.

The "Boston" rules certainly did make the game more lively, as Matt soon discovered. It was nothing for a thousand of the white counters to change hands on a single deal.

*Four pounds odd on one hand!* he thought. Or four guineas, almost! Mary would kill him if she knew – pounds or guineas.

"It concentrates the mind wonderfully," Dent said.

Matt tried to look as if he were concentrating the mind wonderfully.

They played the American system, which accelerates the game still further; in this, the successful bidder (who plays single-handed against the other three) is not paid for any tricks he may take beyond his bid. Thus if he bids seven and achieves them, the rest of the hand need not be played out to the end. Instead, a new round of wagers could begin at once. The system thus encourages all the players to bid to the limit of their hands, there being no reward for timidity.

For four solid hours they played. The conversation, aggressively jocular to begin with, slowly petered out until at last an electric silence gripped them. Rowena had long gone to her bed. The colonel – and the three-fourths of a bottle of port that now swilled through his veins – snoozed before the dying fire.

Matt was fuddled, too, for he had kept up Tottenham's challenge and was now a whole bottle ahead. His hands dithered when he sorted his cards; he swayed as he searched his opponents' faces for signs of their true intentions. He dropped cards, he revoked, he played out of turn – all of which cost him forfeits. When they called it a night – though it was by then early morning – he discovered to his horror that he owed sixteen thousand counters, mostly to Lord Tottenham.

"Impossible!" he said, more incredulous than angry.

Tottenham passed him the reckoning, which Matt studied upside down until the other righted it for him; even then it made no more sense. Never had he felt at such acute disadvantage.

"Sixteen thousand!" He gave a disbelieving laugh. "Thank heaven Mary's not here. She'd eat me a mile off! Though I'll say one thing for her – she'd work it out quick enough. What's it come to – sixty-aught pound?"

"What are you talking about?" Tottenham asked coldly.

"Sixteen thousand counters at a penny a counter – that must be sixty-seventy pound near enough. God, I'll not dare go home! You'll not deny me a chance to win it back tomorrow, I trust?"

His eyes begged them in turn.

"Pence? *Pence?*" Tottenham's voice grew even more icy. "*Guineas*, I think you agreed?"

# CHAPTER FIFTY-ONE

MATT LAUGHED AND clapped Lord Tottenham hard on the shoulder as he made his uncertain way toward the door. "Good try!" he said, wiping amusement and fatigue from his eyes. "A guinea a counter!"

"Sullivan!" Tottenham's voice cut like a rapier.

Matt turned.

"You're not going to rat, are you? It is sixteen thousand *guineas* you owe us."

Matt managed a tipsy grin.

"Ask either of these gentlemen," Tottenham invited.

Matt looked at Jack, who gave a sympathetic shrug and lowered his eyes . . . then at Lord Dent, who seemed far more interested in Matt's response than in confirming the worst – though he did that in passing.

Matt turned pale. "But, lookey-here now." The speech was blurred and halting. "I haven't *got* guineas – not sixteen thousand."

"I dare swear we'll accept mortgages."

Matt stumbled toward the mantelpiece and leaned upon it, staring into the dying embers. "Utter misunderstanding," he murmured.

The colonel awoke and looked sharply about him, dabbing the slumber from his lips and eyes. "What's here? What's here, eh?"

"A man who'll not honour his pledge, it seems," Tottenham replied scornfully.

"I gave no such pledge," Matt said.

"These other gentlemen heard him," Tottenham countered.

"Gentlemen, indeed!" Matt sneered. It was a mistake. Hostility froze the very air.

Tottenham told the colonel his version. When it was done, Carmody turned to Matt.

"I just said, 'In for a penny, in for a pound,'" Matt objected. "A common enough saying."

"Well, we all took it you were proposing to play for pounds. I even asked you if you didn't mean guineas, and you said it yourself: guineas! We all heard you." He looked around.

The other two nodded.

Matt turned to the colonel, who gave him the same Judas smile as Jack, sympathetic but stern. "The count is against you, Sullivan. I'm afraid it's pay up or . . ."

Matt stared at the fire. "And no chance to win it back, I'll be bound." He spoke more to himself than to the company at large.

Tottenham was quick to get in his sneer: "You said yourself – you haven't even the sixteen thousand you already owe."

But Lord Dent chipped in, surprisingly, with: "Of course you'll have your chance, Sullivan. Think what ill you please of us, there's one denial you'll not make. We *are* gentlemen."

Tottenham looked daggers at him for this intervention but he had to mumble his grudging agreement.

And on that unhappy note they departed for their beds; Matt stumbled twice upon the stair and had to be helped by two footmen.

Thirty minutes later, though, it was an entirely different man, in full control of every muscle and sinew, who crept stealthily back downstairs. He went directly to the withdrawing room, where, after fanning the cinders enough to light a single candle, he expertly picked the lock of the bureau where the playing cards were kept.

He took the pack and spread them face down upon the green baize table, the battlefield of his ruin. These, he felt sure, were the secret army that had procured his defeat.

But try as he might, he could see no mark to distinguish one card from another. The black outline of the design was printed from a block; but the colour infill was done by hand. To engrave fifty-two different blocks for a single pack would, he reasoned, be an expensive way of doing cheap business. Any cheating variation was far more likely to be found in the hand-colouring.

He made piles of each suit but saw no common variation – at least none that could be reliably detected by the dim light of a candle, the light in which many a game must be played.

The design was mostly given over to rich swirls of acanthus leaves and roses. Could it be that a darkening of this leaf betokened an ace . . . of that flower a king . . . and so on?

He was so absorbed in his scrutiny that he did not hear a second pair of feet come tippytoe downstairs and across the hall; nor did he hear the door open, nor the footfall on the carpet behind him.

A voice whispered, "Gather them together and riffle the pack, my friend."

In a mixture of guilt and surprise he dropped the few cards he held as he spun round to face his advisor.

Then, with redoubled astonishment, he cried out, "Crystal!"

She giggled. "And who did you expect?"

He turned again to the cards. "A whisper may be man or woman. It crossed my mind you were Lord Dent."

Her eyebrows shot up. "Why him?" she asked.

He shrugged. "Something about that man gives me the shivers."

From beyond the windows came the shriek of some night creature. They both stiffened – and then relaxed. She barred her smile with a warning finger and nodded toward the cards, meaning he was to do as she had bid.

"So they *are* marked?" he said.

"If they weren't, we'd starve."

"The way Tottenham was playing into your hand this evening, I didn't think either of you needed a marked deck as well!"

"That's his humour at work – rubbing poor Jack's nose in it. But never mind that. The reckoning's at hand." She pulled up a chair opposite him and, gathering most of the cards, began sorting them into sequence and suit. "I knew you were at some devious game, this evening," she said. "I couldn't bear to stay and watch. You must have a head of granite." She pointed at the empty bottles on the sideboard. "How did you down so much and yet stay sober – as I see you are?"

"Oh . . . there's a way."

She raised her hands. "No, don't tell me. I'm sure it's nothing pleasant. Did you manage it – whatever you had purposed?"

He scratched his chin. "I knew the deck was marked. I thought I might spot it, but I couldn't. I got in very deep." He told her of the confusion between pennies and guineas, which in his part at least had been genuine.

"Well, never fear," she said. "It's your lucky night after all." Her smile invested the words with a meaning that was more than immediate.

While she worked at sorting the deck, her nightgown parted slightly, serving a feast for his eyes. She, either oblivious or simply careless of the exposure, began a tutorial on "fly" cards: "The thing to remember about a physicked deck is that the marking must all be in the top inch, and preferably towards the right-hand edge." Briefly she held the pack as if it were a dealt hand. "D'you see why?"

"Mmm?"

"Do. You. See. Why?"

With guilty intensity he refocussed on her hand of cards, then nodded. So simple and obvious – why had he not worked it out for himself?

With a laugh, she handed him the now-sorted deck. "When you cog it, Matt, you're going to marvel it didn't blind you the moment you sat down to play."

He touched his stomach. "I was too queasy. That trick to stay sober – 'tis nothing vile. Drink a half-pint of thick cream first. A pint if you can stomach it."

"And you . . . stomached it?"

"Just!"

A memory struck her. "*That's* why Lord Dent made a remark about the cream – the cat that got the cream, or something."

"That man unnerves me," he confessed. "His eye misses naught."

"He unnerves everyone." Crystal gave a vague smile. "But come, this is nothing to our purpose. Riffle the pack."

At last she clutched her nightgown to her – but held it so tight that the revelation continued, different in mode but identical in form. He compelled himself to consider the cards.

Now they were in sequence he saw it at once – and, as she had predicted, it seemed extraordinary he had not noticed it before. Each corner was bordered by a design of thirteen leaves. The number thirteen alone should have been clue enough.

To a casual glance, the leaves at the top-right (and, of course, bottom-left) corners seemed identical to those on the two remaining ones; but the moment he riffled the pack it became clear that on each card the outline of one of those thirteen leaves had been artfully thickened. As if by magic his riffling seemed to move on a minutely broader, darker-edged leaf along the top, around the corner, and down the side.

More detailed inspection revealed that with the twos, the black line around the first leaf was slightly thickened; with the threes, it was the outline of the second leaf – and so on, the ace being marked in the final, thirteenth leaf.

"But it still doesn't tell the suits apart," Matt said, selecting the four kings and spreading them face down.

She leaned forward and pinned the cards with one firm finger. Air warm from her body assailed him with all the spices of the Orient. "You are looking directly at it," she told him. "You must be going blind."

Hastily he transferred his attention to the four kings – and, as before, immediately saw the trick: Though all of them had a thickened twelfth leaf, the precise location of the thickening varied. An excited scrutiny of other cards confirmed it: The black suits were thickened on the left-hand edge of the appropriate leaf, the red ones on the right, clubs and diamonds toward the leaf stem, hearts and spades near its tip.

He chuckled with delight at the forger's cunning and began performing pseudo-conjuring tricks, naming the cards before he faced them. She brought him back to earth. "Have you any idea how to use this knowledge against Tottenham?" She laid a hand on his arm, ostensibly to halt his clowning; but the caress lingered.

Reluctantly he broke the contact. "Play his game, I suppose. You're the card player. You tell me."

Between them they devised a scheme whereby he would alter the coding only on the five cards from seven to knave in each suit. Tottenham would require just that much longer to discover that his tampering had itself been tampered with. By then Matt would have had the advantage of every close-called game.

"What code will you use on the ones we change?" Crystal asked.

He winked. When he had sorted out his target cards he used

spittle and a leftover napkin to restore each enlarged leaf outline to its original, printed form. Then he took up the pen and gave it the code that belonged to the card that was next in line. Since the cards had been shuffled again, they now bore a quite random marking.

She giggled to think how it would puzzle and vex Lord Tottenham. "But what code will you use?" she repeated. "To mark them the way you'll know them again?"

He tapped the deck and said, "As is."

"But they're all at haphazard," she objected. "Twenty cards. You'll never remember that many."

He smiled. This dependence upon order and system among those who were literate always amused him.

As he worked they talked, in low voices, often descending to a whisper. He asked her first why she was helping him. Was she not merely biting the hand that fed her?

She gave out a bitter sigh. "God, Matt, I could have killed you before dinner tonight, when you were prying about me and Tottenham. Don't you realize that from the day Lord Ferrers stole Jack's inheritance, my life has been consumed with but one single purpose?"

"You disguise it well." He meant it as a compliment, not hearing the overtones of possible sarcasm until the words were out.

She took it the wrong way and had to count down her anger; the sparkle in her eyes was magnificent. When she trusted herself to answer, it was in a vehement whisper: "Oh, you'd have done it so easily, to be sure! Like Jack – a sword through the belly or some such martial nonsense, eh? Lord, but you men are simpletons."

Then, warming to the admiration – and desire – in his gaze, she continued more gently, "From the first, I realized we had no hope of a direct assault on Ferrers. His legal position and his standing in the country at large are both inviolate. We had to choose someone – a good friend to him, a good, corrupt friend, as dastardly as himself – who would turn the screw for us. That's why my heart leaped up at Mary's mention of Tottenham. An omen from on high, I thought – and think it still, in truth."

"Tottenham?" Matt was incredulous. "Turn the screw on Ferrers?"

She nodded. "Tottenham is our faithful Trojan horse."

"Sired by Dolt out of Kindness-of-Heart, I suppose?"

She stared at him askance. "Sometimes, Mr. Sullivan, your simplicity is frightening. Tottenham will turn the screw on his crony Ferrers when the constriction upon himself becomes intolerable."

"Oh! Easy!"

She smiled and looked down at the cards. "Yes – it will be now!"

As he replaced the deck in the bureau he noticed a second pack, half-hidden among some loose scoresheets. Their backs were a uniform jet black. "Could they be marked in the glaze?" he suggested.

She grew thoughtful. "You know more about this game than you pretend, Matt."

He drew four cards at random and pocketed them, saying, "Better safe than sorry."

Then he held the telltale napkin, besmirched with indian ink, above the candleflame until it was well ablaze. Before it could burn his fingers he tossed it into the dead ashes of the fire. When it was completely consumed, he raked its darker fibres in among the grey of the cinders.

"I do so admire a man who is *thorough*," she told him.

"I hide this as thoroughly as you hide your dislike of Tottenham."

Coolly she countered, "Did you drink the cream tonight for pleasure or for purpose?"

"For purpose."

"And did that take away its pleasure?" She laughed. "Can I help the way I'm made?" She let fall the hand that clutched the seams of her nightdress together. "D'you dislike the way I'm made, Matt?"

He smiled at her and blew out the candle. Her bright eyes danced before him in the dark. As he made for the door, she crossed swiftly to join him, clutched at his arm, and complained: "These eyes of mine were not made for the dark." Her unseen grin was as loud as cannonfire.

"Dark?" he echoed with jocular sarcasm. "This is morning to a working man."

"Oh, for a working man!" she sighed. "One not limp with the drink." She squeezed his arm. "Still, if you really do feel 'tis morning, Matt, my dear . . . well . . . hardly worth sleeping, is it.

Shall we rack our brains for some other occupation?" She clung tighter yet. Her body brushed against his so firmly that, even had he been the world's most natural monk, he could not have failed to count how few were the threads of warp and woof that separated her supple, tender flesh from his.

At the stairhead she did not turn toward her own chamber, but to his. She discovered that his nightshirt was borne before him like a proud spinnaker.

Her delicate fingers investigated.

He melted in an ague of longing.

In a trembling dream they glided through the doorway. Their clothing fell from them. Her naked body was like a furnace, his like a burning torch.

Gossamerlike they floated the last few paces to the bed. Into its soft embrace they sank, limbs already clasped, opening, closing, squirming, prepared for giving, ready to receive.

A short, sweet eternity later, in goosedown sheets that still held the lingering traces of Crystal's warmth, Matt composed himself to sleep out the dawn alone. He had barely nodded off when he was awakened by her return.

"What's here?" he asked with brittle tenderness, still half-drowned in slumber.

"What's here, my sweet, is *what prayers are for!*"

The laughter was not Crystal's but Rowena's.

## CHAPTER FIFTY-TWO

THIS UNEXPECTED WARMTH in his young wife bewildered Lord Tottenham. Crystal, too – who had grown mighty cool of late – was suddenly showing him a quite unwonted tenderness. To complete the puzzle, wife and mistress were each clearly taken aback by the other's startling good humour.

Delicately the two women began to probe the mystery that had seemingly engulfed them overnight. Crystal omitted to call Rowena "dear treasure"; Rowena no longer addressed Crystal as "sweetest heart." Their mutual bafflement only deepened.

Until now not a meal, not an outing, had gone by without one or other of them officiously commanding her "dearest friend's" comfort against every imagined assault – which might range from a stray draught of wind to some "unintended" barb of wit whose plotting had cost many a sleepless hour. But today their breakfast chatter would not have yielded the smallest crumb to the most malicious scribe upon the most scurrilous journal in the whole of England, not even in the dullest week of the year.

Such mutual complaisance marred for Lord Tottenham what should have been the most triumphant day of his life – a life already rich in such pretty triumphs.

Another puzzle was Sullivan. "Normal" was not the first word one would *ever* use to describe his behaviour, even in "normal" circumstances – but today he was more erratic than ever. For one thing, he kept nodding off. Five hours of drunken slumber should leave a man heavy and too sore-headed for sleep. Impending bankruptcy should make him dour and solemn – and too *worried* to sleep. And, as if that were not enough, the prospects of a second night's trouncing at the gaming table should reduce what was left of his nerve to one vast, insomniac twitch.

Yet here was Matt Sullivan, nodding off all over the place like a hibernating bear.

By the time luncheon had come and gone, and no sign of unease in the fellow, his lordship was so thoroughly disturbed that, for his own peace of mind, he simply had to creep into the withdrawing room and inspect the cards. Damn the risk!

Ever since he heard Crystal direct a calmly offhand, mildly pleasant "good morning, my dear" across the breakfast table at his wife, and receive a mildly pleasant, calmly offhand "I trust you slept soundly?" in return, it had crossed his mind from time to time that one or other of his *dear* ladies had tipped Sullivan the wink and that the fellow had then tampered with the cards. How else explain his odd calm?

With both ears strained keenly toward the door, Tottenham took the pack from the bureau and began to examine it, card by card: king of spades . . . marked on the twelfth leaf, left-hand side, top. Good. Two of diamonds . . . first leaf, right-hand side, bottom. Perfect. Queen of clubs . . . eleventh leaf . . . no tampering there, either. His fears were beginning to seem groundless.

He riffled the pack and saw the doctored leaf jumping about its corner at random, exactly as it should. He picked one final card, the ten of clubs, and began to inspect it, too.

There was a sudden footfall at the door. Guiltily he replaced the card, squared up the pack, and settled as if about to lay out a hand of patience.

It was Lord Dent.

Tottenham relaxed. "You!" He gathered up the three cards he had managed to lay.

"What folly's this?" the other asked angrily.

"Sullivan's behaving so dashed odd, I felt compelled to inspect the deck."

Dent, too, relaxed somewhat and smiled. "I feared – when I heard you riffle the pack – I feared it was Sullivan himself, making the discovery. I could understand it if *his* suspicons were by now aroused. But what has provoked your lordship's mistrust of him, eh?"

"Surely you've noticed this alarming and quite unjustifiable warmth between my wife and Mrs. Horley?"

The smile turned to laughter. "Ah! Well, you'd be more attuned to that than I, my friend. What, Totters – have they ganged agin' ye at last, eh? Tweet-tweet in the Sullivan's ear?"

The other nodded unhappily. "Such at least is my fear."

"So you supposed he must have swived the deck? And has he, indeed?"

Tottenham shrugged. "Not that I can see."

"Best put them away at once, then. You were a fool to risk it."

With some reluctance Tottenham complied. "But why," he asked as they left the room together, "is the man behaving so oddly? He's no actor. He couldn't . . ."

"You think not?"

"Allow me the occasion, my lord – for I haven't told you yet."

"I mean, you think he's no actor? I disagree."

Tottenham frowned. "How so?"

"I believe he has not blinked an eye, snored a snore, picked a tooth, nor drawn a passing breath this day – but for one constant purpose."

"And that?"

"Why to unnerve *you*, my lord! And has he not succeeded? He'll have you beat to a frazzle before you've even dined."

A new fear struck Tottenham, his eyes narrowed as he turned to Dent. "Now, see here, my lord – he's mine to pluck. I hope you have no scheme afoot to lift him from me. Find your own gull, sir!"

Dent's smile, which did not waver, grew icily fond. "I think," he said calmly, "that the plucking of this gull will be more amusing to observe than to assist. For who *is* the gull, my lord?"

Tottenham was too furious to answer.

His humour grew no better when, twenty minutes later – and beneath his very nose – Crystal buttonholed Matt and suggested a stroll to the farthest end of the garden. "We may inspect the new canal from that pretty little marble summerhouse," she said.

"Oh yes!" Rowena enthused, as if the suggestion automatically included her. Then, turning to her husband, she added, "How says my lord?"

Tottenham, not daring to ask whether this were invitation or mere canvassing of opinion, snarled that Crystal might do as she or the Devil pleased (implying there was little choice in it) but that she, Lady Tottenham, was to go to her room.

Crystal was at first put out by Rowena's importunity, but Matt – with a tiny wink, a hint of a smile, a minor inclination of his head toward Rowena – reconciled her to it pretty smartly.

This did not escape Lord Tottenham's eye, though such had plainly been the intention. He turned on his heel and strode from the room – never for one moment believing his wife would disobey him. But ten minutes later, having delayed to make her sweat, he entered their chamber, only to find it empty of her ladyship. A hint of distant laughter called him to the window, where he was just in time to see, far off down the garden, Matt Sullivan, strolling among the shrubbery toward the new canal – and flanked by silk and satin.

Tottenham's first, infuriated instinct was to rush madly after them; but then, remembering his conversation with Dent, he decided that was just what Sullivan wished – to stir him into a passion and then double it with a fine display of heart-on-sleeve. The jealous husband would rush upon them with a dozen witnesses – and find them taking turns to read to one another from *The Faith and Practice of a Christian!*

"Ha! Not me!" he said aloud. "You don't catch me!"

Anyway, what cuckoldry might his lady practise with Crystal there? And what infidelities could Crystal invoke with Rowena standing by?

"So there's naught to fear," he told the furniture. And himself.

He was still reassuring himself that all was well as they settled to cards again after supper. Crystal sat with Matt and the two lords; Jack, Rowena, and the other two Carmodys settled to watch. The air was charged with a subdued excitement. Fortunes, positions, even lives, were at stake tonight, and they all could sense it.

"Boston whist?" Tottenham suggested. "Solo again?"

"The hair of the dog," Matt agreed. This evening he had touched neither cream nor wine – nothing but Leamington water.

"And guineas?"

"In writing if you will."

Such ostentatious confidence went some way to calm Lord Tottenham's fears. He had sat opposite, and fleeced, so many in that mood.

But not, it seemed, this evening. Overnight, Matt had discovered the art of bidding, and to a fine hair. When Tottenham's hand was strong, Matt collapsed and mere pin money changed hands. When Matt was strong, Tottenham could see it, of course, and took care to play slow and tight; again, little was won or lost. But somehow, on the middling hands, when little seemed at hazard either way, the man would step in and make a killing; not on every hand, just some of them – and always the right ones from his point of view.

Within an hour he was able to announce jovially that he had reduced his debt to something he might almost contemplate paying. He gave Dent a peculiar grin as he spoke. But Dent, as Tottenham was quick to notice, seemed discomfited by it.

They were plainly up to something, that pair. Tottenham determined to watch them closely.

"You have revoked, my lord."

"Unh? What? What?" He surfaced from his angry preoccupation and stared for one uncomprehending moment at Crystal's smiling face. "Revoked, you say?"

"Indeed, sir. Last trick you had no diamonds. Now we see you had the four all along."

"The last trick was in spades." He remembered it clearly. His mind's eye could still see Dent's fingers pulling the seven of spades.

In fact, looking down now at the trick in question, he could see the marking still.

"Look!" he pounced on it and turned it over. "The seven of spades!"

But it was the knave of diamonds.

Bewildered, he faced it down again. And there was the undoubted mark: the seven of spades!

But . . . but . . . but this was impossible. He rubbed his forehead. Was he beginning to forget the code?

Concentrate! Concentrate! He broke out in a sweat.

The revocation cost him heavily. He began at last to pay attention to those middling cards, which Sullivan seemed to be managing so well. This scrutiny was quite alien to his lordship's usual style, which was to study the strong cards (whose doctored leaves were all to the lower end of the array) and the weak ones (where the leaves were at the very beginning), and to ignore those of middling worth (which were confusingly scattered either side of the corner). The full horror of his situation struck him when Dent pulled out what ought to have been the eight of clubs yet played the nine of diamonds. Matt, by a revealing coincidence pulled out the nine of diamonds (by its marking) yet played the ten of spades. Later in the hand, when Tottenham played the eight of diamonds and Crystal scooped up the trick with a trump, he saw that the back of his card proclaimed it as the ten of spades – the very card Matt had played a few tricks earlier.

Tottenham felt the blood pause on its round as he realized the full enormity of what had happened. Someone, a man of almost infinite cunning, a man who not only knew of the physicked cards but who had studied Tottenham closely enough to perceive his indifference to those of middle rank – a man of phenomenal memory, too – had altered only those cards, thus leaving

Tottenham in ignorant bliss to play his usual game with the court and the riffraff.

Sullivan? It had to be Sullivan for he alone was making any profit by it. And yet the man was an illiterate bumpkin; by no stretch of the imagination had he the skill or memory to carry off so bold a masquerade.

Lord Dent? Now that was more likely. He played many a game for unseen ends; he'd cheerfully kiss farewell to thousands if some deeper purpose demanded it. But what could that purpose be here?

All at once Tottenham saw it: Of course – Dent wanted Matt Sullivan back in full rhino so that he could fleece the man for himself! All this pretence at salvaging the Tottenham honour from the Sullivan's insult upon Rowena – that was so much froth! The sacrificial lamb in this affair was to be Tottenham – that was Dent's game. Tottenham would bring Sullivan to the door of debtor's gaol – where, magically, Dent would appear and rescue him: *See – the cards are bent! But make no fuss, my friend, no public accusations. Tottenham's too good with sword and shot for that! Just – allow me? – change the markings on the middle cards. See? Thus . . . and thus! I've observed his game, watched it grow careless. By the time he's noticed these unremarkable changes, your debt will have halved. By the time he's worked out the new code – without anyone noticing him as he does so – it will have vanished entirely!*

The viper! No wonder he was so watchful of the locked bureau all day, so furious to find Tottenham there, with the pack in his hand – close to the discovery that would have ruined all!

Tottenham came to a sudden decision. The twice-doctored cards gave the other two men an impossible advantage. Better to do the *almost*-unthinkable – play with a straight deck – than with one that left him so weak. "These cards feel sticky," he said. "Shall we take a new deck?"

Dent turned to Sullivan – which confirmed Tottenham's darkest misgivings, for why else would so exalted a nobleman turn to such a very common commoner, unless there were some game afoot?

"It can do no harm," Matt said mildly.

They fetched the all-black deck from the bureau. Tottenham was bank. When he had finished dealing, Crystal said, "Twelve. I have only twelve cards."

They all counted their hands.

"Twelve."

"Me too."

Matt gathered up the defective deck and fastidiously tidied it as he watched Tottenham flounder.

With a laugh Crystal took up the marked deck again. "Sweaty or no, my lord, the acanthus leaves are your only hope."

Tottenham froze. That laugh gave it away. What a blind fool he had been! Of course! Crystal lay behind it all. She knew the marking on the cards better than any other; why, she could read them at a dozen paces by the light of one taper. What her purpose might be, God alone knew; only fools dignified the whims of women with reason. But that it was Crystal who lay behind his present trouble he had not the slightest doubt; her eyes confessed it. Her laughter was all the confirmation he required.

"We'll play no more tonight," he said quietly. "These cards are marked."

There was a stunned silence. Half the company knew the truth about the deck, yet none had the means to cope with its public announcement.

Except Matt. Though Tottenham stared directly at him while making his shocking accusation, Matt seemed not to notice. He brushed the tainted deck aside and gathered up the all-blacks. "You must have your chance, my lord," he said, giving them a good shuffle. "Double or quits?"

"But the pack's incomplete," Tottenham replied, angry that his announcement had produced so feeble a response.

"Five cards. You draw first. I'll try to match or top you. Aces high. First with five tricks wins. Draws don't count. We don't need no full pack for that. Double or quits." With a fastidious finger he nudged the pack out into the middle of the table and invited Lord Dent to cut.

"No!" Tottenham burst out.

"Mrs. Horley, then?"

Tottenham's fist came crashing down on the pack. "No one touches them!" he hissed. "We'll play with them as they are. Double or quits, eh?"

Matt nodded and made a gesture inviting Tottenham to draw.

You could have heard a pin falling, never mind drop.

Tottenham licked his lips and drew . . . the ace of spades. He gave a sigh of relief.

Calmly Matt drew: the knave of hearts.

The next pair was a draw – two threes. They were discarded.

Tottenham drew the ten of clubs. Matt the two of diamonds.

Now his lordship had a brace of tricks to gloat over. But Matt, with only green baize to look at, was still calm.

Tottenham drew a four. A sigh went around the table.

Matt, not taking his eye off Tottenham, drew . . .

"Another three!" Crystal cried out in vexation.

"Yes, three!" Tottenham echoed with a laugh as he placed the trick beside the other two.

The next was a pair of queens, discarded.

Tottenham drew the eight of spades.

Matt – as if it had not the slightest significance – turned up the five of hearts.

He looked around at their faces. Pity and terror vied for expression – mingled with admiration at his calm.

Tottenham drew another ace, this time of hearts. "It's all over, Sullivan," he crowed. He even had the temerity to turn up Matt's card for him.

A great cackle of triumph went up from all except Matt, for the card he had turned up was the ace of diamonds. Matt simply went on staring at Tottenham.

The man's hand shivered slightly as he turned up his next: the four of clubs.

Amid the bustle of renewed excitement, Matt pulled out a clasp knife and used the tip of its blade to flip over his card: the six of hearts. There was a communal sigh of relief but Matt behaved no differently at his first win than he had at his four earlier losses. He continued to stare deep into Tottenham's eyes, making him more nervous with every second that passed. The others looked on in fascination, none more so than Dent.

Tottenham drew a seven; Matt flipped over an eight – again without registering the slightest emotion. Now it was two to four.

The next was another draw: two fives. "That's them gone," Crystal whispered.

Rowena gave a quiet scream of frustration, which caused Tottenham to round on her in fury.

394

"Does your lordship feel fit to continue?" Matt asked solicitously.

Tottenham took a grip on himself and, with fingers he could barely master, turned over his next card, a knave.

With maddening slowness Matt eased the tip of his knife under his card.

"Oh, for Christ's sake!" Tottenham roared. "No one's going to accuse you of . . ." His voice tailed off as he saw the queen that fell to Matt.

So now it was four to three.

Furiously Tottenham turned over a nine.

So did Matt. He was even calmer now, if that were possible. He moved as if there were some divine penalty for any superfluous action. That incredible stillness of his held the entire company in a spell, all except Tottenham, who, in an even greater fury, turned over a four.

Matt's card, when he at last managed to turn it over was . . . also a four.

A roar of disbelieving frustration enveloped them. In a flash Tottenham turned over his next card: the ten of hearts.

Matt flipped over the knave of clubs.

"No!" Crystal shrieked in disbelief. "Each time you've beaten him by one!"

Matt gave no sign of hearing her. Even now he kept his eyes fixed on Tottenham. "Four all," he said mildly.

The man reached forward. The blood had left his face. His mouth twitched in manic grimaces. The hand that fingered the depleted deck shook uncontrollably. Hardly daring to look, he turned over his card.

There was a gasp, for he had drawn the king of clubs. All turned again to Matt, their pity rekindled.

Matt pretended to count the cards they had already drawn – though he knew that thirty-one had gone, including the other three aces. Add in the four missing cards and the deck was now reduced to . . . "One chance in seventeen," he said calmly to Tottenham. "Sixteen to one you'll beat me, my lord."

"Draw, for God's sake!" Tottenham cried.

"How stands the debt betwixt us?" Matt continued evenly.

"Two thousand," Dent told him.

"Four thousand to nothing," Matt mused, almost as if they

were discussing some famous wager made several generations ago. "What if we put another ten thou' each side of it, eh?" He smiled at Tottenham, whose mouth was now working so fast he had small nipples of foam at the corners, like a well-schooled horse champing at a bit. "Fourteen from me if I lose, ten from you if I win? Fair enough?"

"Fair?" Dent cried. "At sixteen to one! Come on Totters, you can't refuse."

Tottenham licked his lips, discovered the foam, and wiped it off into the crannies of his fingers. "Very well," he scowled.

Matt smiled and then – to the astonishment of all – sat back in his chair and waved a hand toward the pile, inviting his opponent to turn the top card over for him. His manner suggested that, almost from the day of his birth, he had known precisely what that card would be.

Tottenham seemed paralyzed. Dent laughed. "Aye! Remembers what happened last time he turned one up, what, eh!"

Tottenham could bear it no longer. His hand was almost locked in rigor but he managed to grip the card and turn it over.

Crystal and Rowena hugged each other and wept for joy. Jack and the colonel stared at the card with incredulity. Dent alone, after that first cursory glance, turned his gaze full upon Matt . . . Who was still staring at Tottenham in that same calm way.

It drove Tottenham over the brink. "You knew it!" he screamed. "I don't know how, but you could read every card in that deck. You knew it was the ace of clubs!"

## CHAPTER FIFTY-THREE

TOTTENHAM HURLED THE card table furiously aside but Matt, anticipating the action, caught it by the corner and prevented any great damage. Cards and wine spilled across the carpet.

The softened fall of the table redoubled his lordship's rage.

"Can't stomach your own medicine, eh?" Matt scoffed, watching him keenly.

Tottenham was already looking for something else to attack. His eyes darted wildly about the room. Then Matt's words seemed at last to penetrate the red mists of his fury and he turned to his opponent. "What did you say?"

He ground his teeth as he awaited the reply.

"You're a swindler, Tottenham," Matt said calmly. "The very worst kind – which bleats and whines when it suspects . . ."

"Ah! So you admit you swindled me!"

Slowly Matt shook his head. "The fox smells his own hole first."

"Sullivan!" the colonel barked. "For you to accuse a guest under my roof of cheating is serious enough. But do I understand you to admit that you, convinced of his deceit, have yourself been cheating him?"

"I give you my word, Colonel . . ." Matt began.

But Tottenham interrupted. "Beware of this man's word, sir. I have this day learned that he is the seducer – the would-be seducer – of your niece at Wortley Old Hall."

"No!" Rowena cried, moving toward her uncle.

But Matt stepped between them. "It's the truth," he said. To Rowena he added, "Let me spare you the lie, my lady."

Their eyes locked in silent contest. "If you confess to this, Mr. Sullivan, then" – she inclined her head meaningfully toward her husband – "God help you."

"That's what prayers are for," he told her.

"See – the dog has the temerity to smile!" Tottenham raged.

Again the colonel's voice commanded their silence. "If this be true, Sullivan, then you must quit my house this very hour. Now tell me, as you hope to stand before your Maker, did . . ."

"It is true," Matt said. "The lass was in no way to blame. I'm sorry to lose your company, sir, for I've grown to esteem you highly. But there it is . . ."

"Not so hasty!" Tottenham said. "I suppose you believe, you ignorant peasant, that your lowly birth and mean rank put you beyond the gentleman's code of honour. But you are wrong, sir! You are, indeed, so wrong. You have traduced my name and I demand the opportunity to restore it."

Matt stared around at the company. "Have I a second?" His eye fell on Jack but it was Lord Dent who stepped forward. "You have, sir," he said.

"Aye, I thought as much!" Tottenham sneered. " 'Twas you or La Horley! What is your choice of weapons?"

"Hey!" Jack's ears picked up at Tottenham's jibe. "What's this?"

"Surely you pretend your ignorance," Tottenham turned on him with icy pleasantness.

"Eh?"

"She's his whore, man. The whole world is party to it. The Glass Mountain and the Cave of Crystal!"

"Liar!" Crystal shouted. "Why the man's demented. Colonel— you cannot allow this scandal to continue. *There's* the creature you should drive from this house." Her finger stabbed toward her accuser.

Jack stared around at that ring of faces, pitying, bewildered, stony, contemptuous; for the first time since he had fled his home, the world was expecting an honourable decision out of him.

"You dare!" Crystal warned him.

That was all it needed. The years of blind-eyed complaisance rose like a hornet swarm, priming him with a venom he would otherwise never have found. "Yes, whore!" he said. "Well, madam, you shall learn fidelity hereafter. As for now . . ." He turned to Tottenham, clearly intending to second him.

"Horley!" Matt cried out. "For God's sake, man, how can you lay such an accusation? If you'd had the conviction of that fine, flowery oath you swore that night beneath the moon — if you'd had the stomach to enlist in some foreign army, then . . ."

"No, Matt!" Crystal almost screamed. "Say nothing as to that." She rounded on her husband in fury. "You dare call me whore—and then second the man whose name is on the bill. Well, *second* you are and *second* you always were!"

Everyone began shouting at once.

"Cease your brawling this instant!" Carmody roared. "Lord, what's here! We squeeze the pimple of a few marked cards and it turns into a festering boil with as many heads as those here present — and all running foul matter and blood!"

At last his wife awoke. "What? What?" she asked anxiously.

"Where?" She began a close inspection of the carpet, saw the spilled wine, and rang furiously for the servants.

Dent took advantage of the interruption to say, "Carmody, you'd not wish it put abroad that you allowed one of your guests unfair advantage over the other in an encounter of honour? If Sullivan is to sleep in the stables, so must Tottenham also. Or they both sleep in their beds tonight."

The colonel gave a brusque shrug. "Sleep in them, you say? If these vile revelations be true, it'll amaze me if they can even *find* 'em."

The servants arrived and Mrs. Carmody set them to picking up the cards and dealing with the spilled wine.

"We return to the choice of weapons," Tottenham reminded them.

Dent looked at Matt, who gave a noncommittal shrug. "Bring both swords and pistols," Dent told Jack. "We'll make our choice upon the field. You can furnish all we require, I trust, Colonel?"

"Oh dear," Mrs Carmody complained. "Is there to be a duel?" She looked vaguely about her for things to protect.

"I'm afraid so, my dear. Yes, I can furnish swords and pistols for an entire platoon, if you will."

"I shall retire for the night," his wife said. "If you must engage in these stupidities, please be sure to move well out of sight from the house before you commence. And let me tell you now – I shall tolerate no corpses indoors."

When she had gone everybody turned to Carmody, almost as if they expected from him a prayer or a small homily to round off the day. "At dawn, then," was all he said.

It was a chill note on which to suspend so hot a quarrel.

The dawn itself was even chillier. Matt had spent much of the night wrestling with the undoubted fact that, swords or pistols, Tottenham already had him as good as nailed in his box. But what other weapon could he choose that would remove his lordship's advantage? This sacrifice of precious sleep had produced an idea or two, but whether they were the work of an overheated mind or not, only the gentlemen here gathered could decide.

They were standing in the stable yard; footmen were carrying out boxes of pistols and cases of duelling swords for their inspection and choice. It was all very calm and businesslike, though a fevered turmoil lay just beneath the surface.

Into this calm Matt tossed his first salvo. "Er, this is a matter of . . . honour?" he asked.

They all turned to him in surprise.

"Of mine, at least," Tottenham said. Then, remembering his host, he added, ". . . with which that of my wife is inseparable, to be sure."

"And of mine," Jack added, testing the balance of a brace of pistols.

"Then here's a thing I often meant to ask." Matt turned to Carmody. "If the finest swordsman in the kingdom ran his blade through the least-tutored novice, how great is the honour he would thereby gain?"

"Hah!" Tottenham crowed. "The question asked by cowards down the ages."

"Not at all," Matt answered him jovially. "Indeed, if such affairs of honour are intended to weed out the cowards, then I have in mind the grandest test of honour ever devised by man. But I just wanted to be sure I'd caught the notion aright."

Dent chimed in; his soft voice and all-knowing smile added a menace that the plain words did not bear: "If a novice faced a master, fair and square – whatever the weapons they chose – the novice would show the heart of courage. As to what the master would show, that is for the world to judge, but you, my lord" – he smiled coldly at Tottenham – "mentioned . . . cowardice?"

Tottenham made several vicious slashes at the air, pretending to test his rapier. "Sophistry," he cried. "These are topics for a ladies' debating academy. We have manly affairs to settle, and all the world knows how."

But the others had not forgotten Matt's promise: "the grandest test of honour ever devised." The colonel prompted him to explain. He seemed eager for some way out of the whole affair, either to please his wife or because this cold dawn had brought with it the realization that Matt Sullivan, the certain loser, was worth ten thousand times more to his country than his opponent.

"Oh . . ." Matt was diffident. "Perhaps I exaggerate. I just thought that if the two contenders were placed in circumstances that put their courage to its ultimate test . . . see who withstands it the longer . . . that sort of thing."

400

Tottenham's response was the last thing Matt expected. He had felt sure the man would angrily reject any suggestion that did not confer a grossly uneven advantage. Instead, his lordship said, "What precisely had you in mind?"

Matt was so taken aback that he continued for a moment or two along his original line. "It seemed wrong, you see, for me to choose a weapon that would leave your courage snug in bed, my lord . . ."

"Yes, yes!" Tottenham grew impatient. "I grant all that. Say what you had in mind – or is it *your* courage that falters, after all?"

"I had this picture of us, sat back-to-back on a barrel of blasting powder, with a fuze steadily burning toward it. Who leaps down and takes to his heels first – he's the loser."

"And the winner dies!" the colonel protested.

But Tottenham cut this objection short with a simple, "I accept!"

Carmody repeated his protest: "The winner may die."

"And is such a death unknown," Tottenham asked, "even in the most conventional of duels? Colonel, I'm sure you and your Engineers can furnish the necessary means to conduct this novel trial of honour?"

## CHAPTER FIFTY-FOUR

LONG BEFORE DAWN the following day large crowds began to assemble; their little fires dotted the hillside, and the colonel's groundsmen were on constant patrol, driving the bolder intruders from the actual gardens. It looked for all the world as though some famous divine were to preach there that day.

Word of the great Gunpowder Duel had spread for miles. It

would have taken an army to keep people entirely away – and a second army to quell the resulting riot. So, bowing to the inevitable, and to his wife, the colonel had set the stage as far as possible from his home – in that "pretty little summerhouse," normally so secluded from the public gaze, where Matt had exhausted the afternoon with Crystal and Rowena.

The description hardly did it justice, for it was a pavilion rather than a summerhouse, arcadian rather than pretty, and quite large enough to shelter an elephant. Nor would such a creature have found difficulty getting in, for, apart from the six slim columns that rose to support the gleaming, marble-domed roof, it was open to the elements on all sides. Though it stood on a small knoll, there was higher ground all about, both in the garden itself and beyond the "ornamental waterway" that was, in fact, the Forest Branch canal. To those pastures and hayfields the mob had been driven and, more or less, confined; persons of quality, on the other hand, were conducted to privileged sites within the grounds. Yet all, whatever their vantage, agreed that the colonel had chosen well; no other site could have afforded half so much of a view to one tenth as many viewers.

Talking of halves, the waterway was, as yet, only half ornamental, being only half filled – and that by heavenly, rather than human, arrangement. The quarrel as to which of the two canal companies was to purchase water from the other, and at what rates, was still in progress. But today that deficiency was all to the good, for it left more room to the spectators; the front row of "the gods," as it were – the vulgar crowds who had to stand beyond the canal – could sit on the bank and let their feet dangle over dry clay that was intended soon to hold back water.

An hour after dawn, when the more fickle elements in the crowd began to grow restive, the local rifle corps band appeared and started to play stirring music that, paradoxically, settled the mob again. At nine, with the sun climbing well up the sky, they gave way, amid cheers, to a heavy cart manned by the colonel's own regiment, the Royal Engineers, all resplendent in their red tunics and pipeclay belts. Marooned in the centre of its flat deck, roped and spiked like some ferocious beast, stood a large keg. The crowds groaned at the size of it, and those who stood half a mile off began to look somewhat less enviously at those with the ringside vantage.

Ten minutes after the Engineers had withdrawn, and there was still no sign of the party from the house, the crowds again grew restless. The band put on a smart display of marching but the time for such distractions had passed; the music was drowned in that bloodcurdling chant of the mob when the gallows cart is tardy to appear: "We w a a a n t you! We n e e e d you!"

At the height of it the shrubbery parted at the hillcrest, directly between house and pavilion, and the two contenders appeared. The chant turned into a roar of greeting.

The colonel looked magnificent in full dress, gold helmet, plumes, and all.

Matt halted a moment and stood there, taking in the scene.

Behind him Mrs. Carmody pictured the litter so vast a crowd would surely leave behind but for once held her peace.

The whole party came to a pause.

"Is all well?" Jack asked.

Matt merely smiled at him . . . at Crystal, at Rowena, at all the world; he was wondering how so magnificent a breakfast could leave a stomach so void.

"Well, Murphy – what's the betting?" Jack asked Con, who came up to join them at that moment.

"Evens, master," was the reluctant answer.

Tottenham's lips curled in disgust. "What an age is this we live in, eh, Dent! When the courage of a labouring bumpkin is wagered even with that of a sixteen-quartered nobleman! Ye gods – perhaps it *is* time to be quit of it."

Matt's smile faded at these words and he turned to stare at his adversary.

Tottenham met his gaze. "Well, Sullivan?" he asked, patting himself where rib and belly meet, "is this ephemeral rubbish worth ten pence, eh? Never mind your ten thousand!"

"Guineas?" Matt asked lightly.

Everyone laughed, even – to give him his due – Tottenham. Matt's smile, however, soon faded; this fatalistic mood that seemed to have settled upon his opponent did not augur well. Fatalists and gunpowder make poor playfellows.

The cheers of the crowd redoubled as the champion party resumed its gentle descent to the pavilion. The roar rose through a crescendo until the moment the contestants arrived; then, as they mounted the steps, a great silence fell – a silence that could have blunted a knife.

The colonel stepped forward. "You both know the rules" – he gave a forced laugh – "damme, you invented 'em!"

But the others were now too tense even to smile. The silence seemed to hem them in.

Hastily, he went on "You are to sit back to back upon the barrel, which contains enough powder to put you and this pavilion up among the stars. During the contest neither is to make such movements as the other might construe as yielding the contest – unless, to be sure, you *are* truly yielding it. The fuze will be laid the moment you're seated. It will be lighted at once and the contest goes to him who braves it out the longest. Leave it too late . . . and . . ."

Whatever fine flower of speech he had prepared for ending this sentence, one look into the eyes of the two men was enough to silence him. Neither needed nor wanted any reminder of what might happen if he did not run in time.

They doffed their cloaks and let themselves be guided backward by their seconds until each felt the rim of the barrel pressed against the backs of his thighs.

"Take your positions," the colonel said.

As they sat down a strange sort of sigh, almost a groan, went up from the crowd. It was accompanied by a general inward movement that almost squeezed the front rows of the gods into the half-filled canal.

The rest of the party began to withdraw from the pavilion.

Prompted by them, everyone for several hundred yards around withdrew a little as well. Fear was on the very air; it welded that vast throng into a single *animus*, which breathed as one, moved as one, and whose heart beat to the rhythm of that one great dread.

Crystal glanced back over her shoulder at Matt, her eyes brimming with tears. He looked down, saw her, and gave a knowing wink – not realizing that this exchange of secret glances was followed in every detail by Jack.

The engineers spilled a trail of powder across the marble floor to the very edge of the pavilion; the bombardier came forward with a smouldering touchrope. He looked toward the colonel.

"Are you ready?" Carmody called out.

Both men raised a hand and lowered it.

The colonel's sword rose through its ceremonial arc.

A trumpet flourished over a rolling of drums. The crowd, which all this while had slowly revived the murmuring, the shouts, the laughter, fell again to that thrilling silence, so absolute, so eery.

When the fanfare ended the drummers went on beating out the seconds – *durrum . . . durrum . . . durrum!*

"Gentlemen, I salute you!" The colonel placed the hilt of his sword to his lips; the blade, vertical and rock-steady, flashed above the plume on his helmet, silver by bright gold. In one swift cut he lowered it diagonally until it pointed at the ground a yard from his boots.

The bombardier applied the touchrope and at once the trail of black powder burst into sparkling life.

The two men watched in silent fascination.

Beyond the plinth, the greensward fell gently to the ornamental lagoons – or what would become lagoons when the canal was filled. The crowds of people ranged about them melted into a single blur of colour and shade. The silence was total except for the *durrum . . . durrum . . . durrum* of the kettledrums.

Matt tried to pick out individual faces; it was useless. Young or old, man or woman, rich or poor, they shared but a single expression – a rapt fascination compounded of horror and pity. Its strength cancelled out all differences among them, reduced them to a common, human observer – waiting for one or both to die.

Never before had Matt been so aware of his own transience. Within the minute – how slow that fuze was burning! – he would probably cease to exist. Tomorrow, his memory would already be fading. This crowd would remember this day's events as long as they lived, but they'd have to jog each other's memories for the names. If the *Silent Sullivans* lived on, passengers would one day be surprised to hear there was once an actual living man behind the name – like phætons and hackneys. Was there ever a Mr. Phæton or a Mr. Hackney, he wondered?

"The damned thing's gone out," Tottenham said.

The trail of powder certainly seemed as dead as when it was laid. The bombardier began a cautious and reluctant retracing of his steps toward the pavilion, but before he had covered half a

405

dozen yards the trail sputtered back to life and the man took to his heels in terror.

*Durrum . . . durrum . . . durrum!*

"Is this not absurd?" Matt asked. "What do we prove by it? If I cut and run, does that prove you never marked the cards?"

*Durrum . . . durrum . . . durrum!*

Tottenham was silent.

"We're a pair of lunatics," Matt concluded.

*Durrum . . . durrum . . . durrum!*

# CHAPTER FIFTY-FIVE

THE LATEST *SILENT SULLIVAN* was surely composed of lead. The water of the Coventry Canal had beyond doubt turned to treacle. "Were those horses fostered by snails or what?" Mary called out to Steam Punch.

The thunder of the galloping hooves and the bright gurgle of rushing water beneath the bows drowned her words; the few that Punch heard he took for encouragement and waved cheerfully back at her.

At the Glascote locks in Tamworth she had a chance to vent her frustration. She looked at the fresh team of horses and declared scornfully that they were reared for the bog. "Sure, look at them! They'll test each pace before they'd trust it."

Punch gave her arm an encouraging squeeze. "Speed's not all that's in it, colleen," he said. "Begod, they're not going to *invite* us into that lock, you know."

"How shall we shift, then?"

He winked. "The way I have it conspired, now, they'll have to open those gates as they only way to keep the main canal in service."

"You'd better tell me," she said, checking her impatience.

To save time, she had come down the canal from Summerley on the regular boat from Stoke and had met Punch at Fazeley, which they had now left a mile or so behind them. From here they were to race hell-for-leather – and certainly hell for horseshoes – on toward the junction with the new Forest Branch. The enforced pause at these locks was her only chance to hear the latest, and necessarily final, version of the plan.

"The main thing," he said, "is they have all the water we'll need. Without that new rezavoy, the Anker would have bursted its banks weeks ago. So when we get to Grendon . . ."

"How far's that?" she interrupted.

"Ah, but five or six miles. As the fella said – speed's not the thing at all. But cunning is. The junction to the Forest Branch begins with a lock, a single-step lock of nine-foot-four . . ."

"How close to the main line?"

"Sure, if 'twas any closer, we'd go through the side of it."

"And how many more locks between there and the Hall?"

He grinned. "Divil a one! Nor one betwixt here and Grendon, neither."

She clapped her hands for delight. "So all we need do is get into that one lock, open the lower gate, and go!"

"*And* open the sluices to the rezavoy. *And* make sure no one shuts them after we've gone. Indeed, that's *all!*"

Her face fell as she began to grasp the complexity of the operation. "But how . . . I mean – have you arranged . . ."

"Isn't that what I was after telling you? Craft is more friend to us than speed. I have a little ridgement of men hidden at Bradley Green. They'll do what's needful once we're away. But there's only one fella can get us through."

"You," she said.

He shook his head. "Have you ears of oak? 'Tis our old friend, Mr. Charles James Foxy Cunning."

There was no time to tell her more; the lock was full, the gates were opening, the summit level stretched southward before them, inviting a gallop. Only when they were off once more on their helter-skelter journey did she realize he had not told her precisely how he intended to trick the canal keepers into opening the as-yet-unused lock.

The next five miles seemed like fifty. Between Tamworth and

Amington some lunatic builder, lost in love with bridges, had been given free rein – which now prevented Punch from doing the same with his horses. And from there to Polesworth the line of the canal was a serious of lazy zigzags. Each bend seemed to promise a good run beyond, only to deny it as they negotiated the end of the curve. Then at last, half a mile or so past Polesworth, one final bend brought the line back to its true, southerly course and a more-or-less straight run of water beckoned.

They made good speed over that next mile but as they drew close to Grendon her heart fell. It became clear that the way ahead was blocked. Two boats had collided and their crews were involved in a heated exchange. At the moment it was only of words but, as the *Silent Sullivan* drew closer, it was plain to Mary that they were squaring up for a fine old ding-dong.

Her frustration boiled over. "As if we hadn't enough to contend with already!" she shouted to Punch. "Can you unhitch one horse and run ahead to stop them?"

He threw up a hand in disgust but evidently decided to press ahead as fast as he could – which was certainly much too fast for the situation that would soon be upon them.

"Slow down!" she yelled at him.

He raised a hand, as if to signal his obedience; yet still he forged ahead.

Mary looked at the fast-approaching impasse, speechless in her disbelief. At this rate, if she swung the tiller hard, they'd almost leap out of the water and up over the grass. Indeed, for one wild moment, she found herself wondering if that were not perhaps his plan for getting them off the main line and into the lock!

Two men – canal servants by the cut of them – came racing up the towpath toward them. Punch seemed at last to awaken to the danger they were now in, for he reined back and prepared for a stand. Mary threw him the stern line as she whizzed on by but – most unusually for him – he missed it.

She yelled out in frustration. To have come so far, to be so near to their goal, and be cheated of its achievement by that one moment of carelessness! If only she weren't so heavy with child, she could have thrown the line a little bit farther – and then perhaps he would not have missed it.

The thought of the baby made her fearful of the crash that was now quite unavoidable. The impact would certainly throw her forward. Above all, she had to avoid that. And yet she did not dare leave the tiller. In the few moments that were left she drew in some of the slack stern line and wound two or three wet coils about her body, just beneath her arms. Then she braced herself for the smash.

The fighting crews were at last alerted to her danger – and, indeed, to their own. They raced forward to man the gunwale of the boat nearest her and held out planks, gaffs, boathooks, oars, hands . . . anything that might be used to fend her off or break her impact.

She became aware that several of them were pointing toward the east, emphasizing the gesture with repeated, vigorous stabs, and yelling unintelligibly at the tops of their voices. She followed their direction and saw that the oak piles which formed the canal bank at that point were of a different size.

Then she saw it was not their size that changed, it was their direction.

A fraction of a second later she saw why: They formed the inlet – concealed from her until now – to a side branch.

The Forest Branch! It suddenly dawned on her. This was the opening – the way she had to go.

The point where the branch entered the main line had been enlarged into a winding hole. In a flash she realized that if she could use that space to bring the stern round smartly enough . . .

But no. The bows would still go crunching headlong into the piling on the opposite bank.

Perhaps . . . an idea began to take hold. She glanced at the near corner of the inlet. Could she clip it without stoving in her sides? That might just slew her round enough to avoid that headlong smash.

She had possibly three seconds left in which to make up her mind. In fact, the certainty of crashing into the farther bank made it up for her. She swung the tiller hard round and braced herself for what she hoped would be a mere grazing impact.

It never came.

She had forgotten Punch and his two-ton team of steaming muscle. A pair of the great shire horses were jerked forward into the water, but their massive inertia had done the trick by then. The bow was held at the very entrance to the branch while the stern, gathering all the momentum to itself, swung broadside round and, with a little help from her at the tiller, headed the craft for the first of the lock gates.

As Punch had warned, those gates were just a few yards into the cut, not even half a boat's length. By slewing sideways she had dissipated a great deal of her forward momentum; enough was left to bring her to a nudging halt against the very timbers of the lock.

In the confusion the two barges in dispute of the main line somehow drifted forward (against the wind, which was odd) and wedged the *Silent Sullivan* fast where she was.

All hell broke loose. The two company men swore and foamed at the lips. Punch lost his head and shouted a dozen contradictions without drawing breath. Mary loosened the coils about her and gave the tiller one or two ineffective waggles. The crews of the two barges piled incompetence upon misfortune and made it finally impossible for men, horses, poles, or wind to shift what were now three fast-wedged and welded vessels.

They all fell to silence, somewhat in awe of the magnificent confusion they had created, a confusion that had now set like concrete.

"Jesus flaming Christ!" said one of the canal men, tipping back his cap and scratching his head as he stared at the scene in utter disbelief.

"How in the name of all that's holy . . ." The other began before he, too, sank into awestruck silence. All the words in Oxford were no match for this debacle.

"Is them gates rusted or what?" Punch asked.

"Can't touch *them*," the taller of the canal men said quickly. "Proprietors' orders."

Boats were drawing near from both north and south. Their masters whistled and tooted their posthorns in impatience at what they could see from far off. But what they saw from much closer-to brought a dying fall of incredulity to their noise. Within minutes there were a dozen generals upon the bank, all handing out commands at the tops of their voices – and not a soldier left to obey them.

The consensus, however, was that the lock gates would simply have to be opened. Mary, who had twigged the whole plan by now, fought hard not to smile. The canal men were adamant, though – the proprietors had forbidden them to open the new lock gates, practically on pain of death.

"We're scuppered!" a lad shouted from the deck of one of the locked barges.

Everyone turned to see and, sure enough, she was going down by the bows.

That settled it. Brushing the two canal men aside, and their protestations with them, the assembled crews opened the lock gates and let the *Silent Sullivan* inaugurate the facility.

"False alarm!" shouted the lad on the sinking boat. "The bung in her drain got kicked out in the fight." He gave a sheepish laugh but by then Punch was already closing the gate behind them.

"Here, there's no need for that!" shouted one of the keepers.

But a new amazement caused his voice to tail off yet again. From all about him, from hedges and ditches, from fields and lanes, came a small army of navigationers, farmhands, city labourers, vagabonds, pedlars . . . everywhere he looked he saw them coming.

"Nay!" cried his fellow but it was too late. Half a dozen burly blackguards stood between them and the lower gate, which another two-dozen men were trying to force open.

They made little progress until, in response to some unseen skulduggery at the summit reservoir beyond, water filled the sluice and backed up the half-filled canal to equalize the pressure. Then the gate swung open in a rush and the *Silent Sullivan* leaped forward upon the last few miles of her journey.

A great cheer sped them on their way.

And a great wave of water did the rest. That part of it, at least, Punch had not planned. He knew the impulse of water from the reservoir would carry them some way along the canal – which was why the fresh horses were waiting out of sight around the first bend. But he would never have imagined that the huge inrush of water would surge forward in one endlessly curling wave, upon whose forward slope they now chanced to find themselves balanced.

It seemed a miracle the water did not, as it were, slide forward beneath them and level off into one smooth, though ever-rising surface; it was almost as if some unseen impediment on the clay bed of the canal actually plucked at the water and held it back – so that the liquid higher up, impatient to press on, almost stumbled over its own feet. Indeed, at times it did, for the wave would break and hasten them even faster toward their goal.

They raced past the waiting farmhand, his team of horses all at the ready.

"Can't stop!" They waved. "Can't stop!" And they left him staring after them, his gawping flycatcher of a mouth making a gash of black in the white oval of his face.

Scenes of rural charm flashed past. Astonished cattle stood on their own short shadows in the knee-high grass of spring. Coppices of ash, lone and ancient oaks, new barns and dilapidated dovecotes, hedgerows, cottages, farms, and lanes . . . all sped by as they rode that wave through the fields of Leicestershire.

Mary laughed for joy. All the frustrations of these past days were surely behind them now. Punch stood at the bows, fending off one bank or the other whenever they loomed close enough to threaten an upset. Having nothing better to do, she went forward and joined him.

"There's a wave like this runs for miles up the River Severn," she said. "Twelve foot high at times."

"Praise God we're spared that." He was not as delighted as she had expected to find him.

"Is aught amiss?" she added.

He turned a worried face toward her. "Only this," he said. "How in the name of God are we going to stop when we want?"

## CHAPTER FIFTY-SIX

A MILE SHORT of the Hall the canal was spanned by a new stone bridge. And upon the bridge stood a man, a young fellow with a daredevil way about him. As the *Silent Sullivan* drew near, it became obvious he was preparing to leap down upon her deck.

Instinctively Mary hefted her boathook, ready to prevent him; but Punch shook a finger at it. "An extra pair of hands could be useful," he said and, turning to the young fellow, cried, "Jump *with* us!" He pointed urgently forward. "*With* the boat."

The fellow was quick on the uptake. He abandoned his preparations to leap down on the approach side of the bridge and, taking a short run and a flying leap as they passed beneath its arch, landed between them, as lithe as any fairground tumbler.

"Well, shipmates, this is the way to travel!" he said as he rose to his feet again. "The name is Weston. Charley Weston." He laughed. "My, but shan't we arrive in style!"

Mary introduced herself and Punch. "Arrive where?" she asked.

"At the field of battle – isn't that where you're going? The Carmody place. The whole world's gone there today"

The other two exchanged glances of foreboding. "Battle?" Mary echoed. "Is the colonel staging some battle?"

"Indeed, you may say so, Mrs. Sullivan." His voice tailed off as he spoke her name; the smile faded. "Sullivan," he repeated. "Oh Lord, but this is awkward."

*Durrum-durrum-durrum* . . .

Matt watched the flame sputter its malevolent way toward them. Everything had come to seem unreal.

"I've lost my fear," he said to Tottenham.

It was not a boast but an announcement of genuine loss, touched with sadness.

"I give not a damn for what *you've* lost!" the other replied quietly. "D'you realize what you've done?"

Matt said nothing.

"This is no duel between you and me, Sullivan. As far as I'm concerned, you might as well go now. Each of us is fighting his own self. The winner cannot spare the loser. The loser takes all! Do you love your Mary?" he went on, in quite a different tone.

Matt remained silent.

"I do," his lordship said. Then, looking at the advancing fire, he added, "Bright serpents of death!"

Charley Weston waved a hand toward the multitude and said, "Didn't I tell you?"

But no words could have prepared Mary and Punch for the sight that now greeted their eyes. It looked as if the entire population of a fair-sized town had been transported *en masse* into the countryside. As the boat drew nearer and more of the grounds came into view, the numbers increased apace.

The most uncanny thing about them was their silence. Just before the boat had rounded the final bend there had been a flourish of trumpets; now, in the spinechilling hush that followed, the steady *durrum-durrum-durrum* of the drums was almost deafening.

Often in dreams – and more especially in nightmares – we have a sense that we know what is about to happen; not *everything*, just the immediate events that lie ahead. Indeed, this tantalizing half-gift of prophecy explains the peculiar terror of nightmares, for it makes each event seem inevitable; it forestalls our intervention.

Such a terror now held Mary as the eternal wave of water carried them at last into full view of the pavilion. There was the landscape – exactly as young Weston had foretold. Between his description and her imagination, nothing was left to surprise her: the marble building, gleaming in the sun; the grassy slopes, packed with fine ladies and gentlemen; the hillside *hoi polloi*; the drummers and the band; the military in their sprightly uniforms . . . and there at the heart of it all, perched upon a common powder barrel, a couple of idiot baboons, daring each other not to die.

Tottenham, she now saw, was the nearer of the two; Matt was three-quarters turned from the river.

A dark dread overcame her that whatever was about to happen, it was ordained so from the very beginning. Nothing she might do or say would change it by a jot – indeed, quite the reverse: Whatever she did or said, it was already part of that inevitable unfolding.

Feeling more hopeless than at any time in her life, she drew breath, opened her lips, and cried out: "Matt!"

*Durrum-durrum-durrum* . . .

The grounds were briefly suffused with darts of pink as faces turned toward the source of this interruption, but only those in the immediate path of the water paid any greater heed. Even then, as they scrambled for land they hoped would remain dry, they returned their eyes to the pavilion and kept them glued there.

"Matt!"

Obsessed though he was with the approaching flame, the cry penetrated his absorption. It was not real, of course, but some trick of memory, conjured into play by Tottenham's words.

"Matt!"

There it was again.

But this time it seemed too real, too far outside his own head, to be mere imagination. Some ruse of Tottenham's?

It was, of course, by far the likeliest explanation.

"Well, I'm damned!" Tottenham murmured at his back.

Unable to help himself – and, indeed, no longer caring whether he broke the rules or not – Matt turned toward the source of that cry.

Punch's worries about not being able to stop proved groundless in the event. When the wave reached the gardens, it found half a dozen invitations scattered about its path – little canals and blind lagoons, the ornamental works that had induced the colonel to part with any land at all. Not knowing which route to choose, the water chose each indifferently and dissipated its energies among all. The *Silent Sullivan*, carried broadside-on into one of the blind inlets, nudged to its final rest against some scaffolding prepared for the reception of a marble water-god, who presently lay in numbered segments on the grass.

Without even testing its firmness, Mary leaped upon the structure and thence, by means of a stout plank, which gave a gentle incline to the lawn, she began to run uphill toward the pavilion.

The moment Matt saw her he lost all heart for this contest in absurdity. He leaped from the barrel, crying, "You have the contest, my lord!"

A groan went up from the crowd. He ignored it, even when it turned to jeering and taunts of cowardice.

"I win, therefore I lose." Tottenham's reply was in tones so strange that Matt, though now desperate to be with Mary once more, was compelled to halt and turn.

The nobleman was staring at the flame, which he was now at perfect liberty to kick to the four winds. The catcalls petered out, drowned in a new and rising note of panic among those nearest.

All around the pavilion there began a terrified movement outward – uphill, down toward the water, outward into the shrubbery . . . anywhere away from the coming explosion.

"Didn't you hear?" Matt asked. "Can't you see? You've won!"

"Didn't *you* hear?" Tottenham mocked. "There's but one way to win: The loser takes all."

The sputtering fire had only inches left to burn. Matt, seeing that flight was now useless for himself, ran toward the fuze and began to scuff at it furiously.

But it was too late. His vigour left whirls of powder in its wake, enough to bridge the gap. Every kick moved some of the powder, but it rearranged the rest and scattered the sparks among it. At last he dropped on all fours and used the flats of his hands. "Fool!" he screamed at Tottenham. "Idiotic bloody fool!"

He almost won. In fact, he believed he had won. With the sweat gushing from every pore, he breathed a great sigh of relief and sat back on his haunches. And only then did he notice a tiny spark at the very rim of the barrel. Less than a second now separated him from certain death.

"No!" he yelled in anguish as he hurled himself at it.

"No!" Mary screamed as she laboured up the hill, fighting her way through the panic-stricken mob of former gentlefolk.

The last image in Matt's mind, before the world turned white-hot about him, was of his hand, frozen, like his entire body, in mid-air, poised useless inches from its goal. The last feeling in his heart was for Mary.

The delighted crowd upon the hillside saw ladies and gentlemen trampling one another in a frenzy, saw a gallant officer standing his ground, saw a noble lord justifying nobility's pride over common clay, saw the great Matt Sullivan grovelling in terror . . . saw all this vanish in a sheet of flame, saw black smoke engulf the entire pavilion in its pall of death.

# CHAPTER FIFTY-SEVEN

THE INTERPLAY OF FORCES between the chief reagents in my powder is stoichiometric in all save its exothermic relations," the young chemist had promised.

"Quite, quite," the colonel had said, nodding sagely. He knew the Greek and Latin roots of the words, of course, which gave him the illusion of almost understanding the actual sentence.

His bombardier had put it better, though, after the first secret trials of what was later officially known as powder, blasting, manoeuvres, for use upon. "It's louder than gunpowder," he said. "Makes more smoke. And a brighter flash, too. But that saps all its strength, seemingly. What's left couldn't pull the skin off of cream."

"Quite, quite," Colonel Carmody had said to that, too – and with more conviction.

Of this pair of descriptions of the new powder, it was the latter that came into his mind as he strode toward the pavilion, eased the wadding from his ears, and waited for the smoke to thin.

Even before it was half cleared he saw the idiot Sullivan staggering about, trying to get to his feet; the idiot Tottenham was stretched out on the floor, a few yards away. "For God's sake lie down, man!" he called out. "If they see you've survived that, we'll have a riot on our hands."

"Can't hear you, sir," said the bombardier. "I'll attend to it."

He ran into the smoke and flattened Matt with a tackle.

"Stretchers!" the colonel shouted. "Brace up, you bearers – at the double now!"

"Such a dreadful *mess!*" cried an anguished Mrs. Carmody.

When the smoke finally drifted away it revealed a sorrowful party making its way back to the Hall, taking with it two burned and mutilated corpses. Bringing up the rear was a big, powerful man carrying in his arms a dead or dying woman, heavy with child.

"Matt?" Mary murmured, blinking her eyes open again.

"Hush, woman," Punch clasped her tighter yet. "Your man's well enough. We're withdrawing from sight while they still think we've our dead to mourn."

Mary groaned. "I believe the baby's on its way."

Martha Sullivan was born some eight hours later, a small, thin, hairy child, not quite as premature as their calculations would have predicted, and thus in no immediate danger of expiring.

Mrs. Carmody had no birthing stool; such things were for the ignorant peasantry. In the days of her fecundity she had lain upon her own linen until there was risk of soiling it, whereupon she had transferred to a pile of sacking and straw at the bedside.

Mary refused to do that.

Crystal tied together a pair of chairs by their front legs and then pushed the backs apart to make a V-shaped void between them.

Ingenious but uncomfortable, Mary said.

Mrs. Carmody supervised the rolling-up of the carpet and the laying-down of a year's back numbers of the *Leicestershire Mercury*.

In the end Matt, having recovered somewhat from his stunning, perched himself over the open V and she sat on his lap, the way he could put his arms around her from behind and bear down on the baby when she told him. "You were there at the sowing," she said, "so you might as well be in at the harvest, too."

Every female in the house was present, it seemed. A pair of old kitchen maids tried to comfort Mary with tales of monstrous and painful births they had witnessed – and, indeed, experienced – over the years. Once Matt had banished them from the room, the affair went smoothly.

Baby Martha did not even cry. The woman wiped her down and handed her to Mary, who gazed into those calm eyes and grinned. "God love us, Matt, but we're one of a kind now – all four of us."

He gave her a fond hug. "All one of you," he murmured.

418

The doctor arrived when it was all over; the weatherbeaten roads were only half to blame. "The world's full of fools," he complained as he downed a compensatory rum toddy. "Lady Venton, out for a drive by the canal, on her way to this morning's Theatre of Dolts, takes a whim into her head (for I'll not call it a *mind*, hark'ee) to have her coach washed. Drives it half into the canal, says she'll sit within until the job is done. Five minutes later another pack of fools decide it's time to inundate the works. How she 'scaped drowning we'll never know."

He investigated Matt's partial loss of hearing (which indeed was highly partial, being capable of listening out for his new daughter's whimpers but quite unequal to picking up his wife's opinion of his recent behaviour) and declared it to be temporary.

"We mend swiftly, we Flinderses," she assured him. "My mother was up and about two days after she bore me."

"Then you don't need me at all," he answered gruffly.

He investigated Tottenham's somewhat more serious wounds and said he *hoped* his lordship might still be capable of siring an heir. "A beefsteak poultice and a diet of oysters," was his receipt as he pocketed his fee and left.

His lordship's only comforter was Jack, who came to sit at his bedside.

"I said beastly things about you, Horley," Tottenham mumbled after the doctor had withdrawn. "Beastly unforgivable."

Jack smiled. "Then I brand you liar, Totters. My forgiveness you have already earned."

Tottenham lay back on his pillows and gazed at his visitor through half-closed eyes. "Indeed, sir? May I ask how?"

"Your courage this morning!" Jack said, as if that were all the explanation the Recording Angel himself might require.

"You call that courage?"

"Well – you were not to know the powder was all sound and no fury."

"The truth, man," Tottenham urged. "What is it you really want of me?"

Jack lowered his eyes; his voice fell to a whisper. "I wish to know what has passed between that villain and my wife."

"'Passed between them'? I imagine it was the usual squirt of human yeast – though of somewhat commoner manufacture than she's accustomed to. Why d'you need to ask?"

Jack's eyes flashed with rage at these taunts but he said nothing.

"Ah!" Tottenham simulated discovery. "I begin to read you now. No usual little dusting of gold was there to mask the transaction! This time 'twas for pleasure's sake alone. Is that it? Your honour's been taken cheap, eh?"

Jack spun on his heel and made for the door.

"Stay!" Tottenham cried. "I'm sorry. It must be the pain. Put it down to the pain."

Jack paused unwillingly. The apology was too pat to be credible, yet long habit held him now at Tottenham's whim.

"You must have wanted something more than that small nugget of intelligence? Surely you knew it already?"

"I swear to you I did not."

Tottenham gave a weary laugh and closed his eyes. "God's wounds – how am I to unravel you, Jack Horley? You make no bones of it when she beds with me, yet . . ." He let the rest of it hang.

At length, Jack's silence forced him to open his eyes again. He expected to find the man speechless with rage; but no rage was there, nor sorrow, nor bewilderment either – only an odd kind of baffled hesitation.

Suddenly it dawned on him. "Ah, at last I begin to comprehend. You raised no objection in my case because you knew she can't stand hide nor hair of me; she'd as soon see me stretched as well fetched! But Sullivan is different, eh? Isn't that the way of it?"

"From the moment they met!" Jack said vehemently. "The very morning of our bridal night, she could not take her eyes off him." He was lost in memory awhile; then he added, in a more everyday tone, "I should never have left home. London was the ruin of me."

"What will you do about Sullivan?"

Jack looked at him in surprise. "He can't still be of interest to you, surely? He yielded the honours, and thousands saw him do it – what more could you want?"

"Is that what you think?"

"Think? I know it. I saw it. And so did . . ."

"Oh, be quiet! If you saw that, then you saw nothing. Let me tell you what I saw – which is what you should have seen: I saw a man of infinite cunning there today. He planned it all – except perhaps the colonel's deception with the powder – he plotted every move: from the first turn of the cards, that night he pretended to be so drunk, from then until my death."

"But you survived."

Tottenham gave a bitter laugh. "Yes, I 'survived.' And that merely adds to his victory."

"Victory! Oh, Tottenham, have you gone . . ."

"Hold your tongue!" Tottenham thundered. "You're a good soul, Jack. A stout, simple, honest fellow. But you must understand – I *want* you to understand – Sullivan has walked circles round us all, even Dent, who (or so I suspect) wished to pluck the gull for himself. When Sullivan 'yielded the honours' to me this morning – as you so innocently put it – he yielded trash. That most convenient arrival of his wife, in the very nick of time – and in so dramatic a fashion, too! – why that was all his plot. See how he faced me outward, that I might see her first! Then how he ran to her, leaving me to die, the victor. Victor? Hah!" He laid a finger on each cheek, pointing to his eyes. "My last vision, the picture I was to carry, printed here, into eternity, into the purgatory Matt Sullivan had prepared for me, plotted with such cunning care, was of her running to him, him running to her, the pair of them in love's embrace." He turned his mild, mad eyes upon his cuckold-friend and smiled, as if to say, "Now do you see?"

A man less stout, simple, and honest than Jack Horley would have pointed out at once that Matt had not, in fact, raced down the lawn. Indeed, he had chosen to die (not knowing the colonel's trick with the powder) in trying to save his opponent. It took Jack the best part of a minute to bring himself to raise the objection.

Tottenham dismissed it with contempt. "'Tis plain I foiled him," he answered simply. "I told him – the winner tastes no victory. The loser takes all. At first he did not see I had tumbled to his plan. But when he did (though 'twas by then too late), he saw he had to save me. He had to keep me alive for another day. The duel between us still rages."

Jack, though unconvinced, saw no point in opposing further. "What mean you to do next?" he asked.

"Can you not see? Is it not obvious?"

"Not to me."

"That image he intended for my eyes . . . to burn in here" – he

made a mock spit of his two fingers and on them impaled his skull
– "through all eternity . . . that fair, that beauteous *brand! . . . I
must pluck . . .*" He paused, lost in private reverie.

"Yes?" Jack urged, on tenterhooks to hear the obvious.

Tottenham gave him the oddest look, as if he thought Jack
might have left the room hours ago.

"Mary Flinders?" Jack prompted. "You said you must . . .
what?"

"Ah – yes! I must pluck her from him."

## CHAPTER FIFTY-EIGHT

BABY MARTHA FELL ASLEEP at Mary's breast, her milkwet lips
parted in the rictus of satisfaction. "Venus and Bacchus," she
mused as she lifted the drops on her finger. "Sure, 'tis two-in-one
to them."

It prompted Crystal to recall the numerous fine gentlemen she
had observed in a similar condition – that fleeting rigor mortis of
the soul. Though she smiled at the scene, she could not help a
twinge of envy. "Did you hear that Colonel Carmody has
ordered Tottenham from this house," she asked. "The moment
he's fit to stand, never mind travel."

"But why?"

"I believe that Rowena confessed that Tottenham had, in fact,
doctored the cards and that Matt pleaded guilty to her seduction
only to shield her honour."

"Oh, I've no patience with any of it," Mary said. "I think I
shall leave tomorrow myself. And the babe shall start with her
wet nurse."

"D'you feel able? Will you not wait here for Matt's return?"

"God, I was never better. I could have up and left the day after this one came. As for Matt, he can return as easily to Summerley – and more safely, too, for *our* neighbours will not grudge his survival as they do hereabouts. Lord, what is it in the mob that craves the deaths of others?"

"Aren't you pleased, at least, that he's back in cahoots with the colonel?"

"Indeed and I am not," Mary said vehemently. "His work for the military is done. This present visit to the War Office rings down the curtain, and I wish he may never do more for them. What's left now but that they will seek to translate my Matt into a smart gentleman?"

The scorn in her voice left Crystal scandalized. "Where would be the harm in that?"

"Where's the *harm* in a dog on its hinder legs? Matt has a fine, great enterprise to build. Let our children be gentry, if they've no more sense, we . . ."

"Such bitterness, Mary. You were never so before."

Mary rearranged her bodice and laid the baby over her shoulder to ungripe her. "Crystal, dear," she said casually. "I wish you'd tell me what was happening here in this house before I arrived."

"I wish I knew myself," Crystal answered, somewhat too eagerly. "I was no party to it."

"There was some plot to discredit Matt – or ruin us?"

"As I said, I was not privy to any of it. Dear God, they'd have schooled the Borgias." She frowned. "Though, to be fair, 'tis my belief that in the action against Matt, Tottenham alone was to blame."

And she went on to outline the events (or some of them) that led up to the Gunpowder Duel. "I showed him how the cards were marked," she confessed proudly. "He used the knowledge to regain all he was cheated of the night before. But – and here's the oddest thing, Mary – the game by which he won that bet for ten thou' was played with the *other* deck. It belonged to the colonel and the backs were of jet-black, So I'm sure they weren't marked. Even so, Matt seemed to know every card that was coming." She smiled. "But there again – he's as secretive as any of them. He hasn't their duplicity, to be sure, but you'd never know what the Silent Sullivan was thinking, would you. I wonder . . . *did* he know those cards?"

"He assisted a conjuror for a time once, when he was in France. But whether cards were in it, I couldn't say. I thought their marvels were chiefly with the illuminating gas – the thing I told you about that morning we first met. Aiee – doesn't that seem like another lifetime now!"

"I didn't know he'd been to France. Can he speak French?"

"Worse than a Normandy peasant."

By way of chance comment, baby Martha vented a rasher of wind. Mary called in the nurse to take the little mite off to her crib.

When they were alone Mary said, "It's such a lovely day, shall we send for our shoes and shawls and go out?"

As they strolled down the lawn, aiming for no particular destination, she returned to their earlier theme, saying, "I wonder if Miss Rowena had a hand in any of this?"

Crystal cleared her throat and glanced briefly toward the house. "Lady Tottenham seems, if anything, most favourably disposed towards Matt."

"You mean she would certainly dispose her favours toward him!"

"Mary!"

"Come out of your cupboard now, Crystal. Doesn't the whole world know what happened between that one and Matt up at Dux's place."

"Happened? Or *almost* happened?"

"In the heel of the hunt, what's the difference?" Mary smiled and tapped her temple. "If it happens here, it happens."

Crystal arched her eyebrows. "You're mighty complaisant about it, I must say."

"I wasn't married to him then."

"Ah – would that make a difference? You'd condemn it now?"

"Ach – where's the point!" Mary shrugged. "All the world and his wife dance that same blanket hornpipe, wherever they can, whenever they may. If chance came my way, who's to say what side I'd fall? I'd as soon condemn snuff at a wake, so I would."

Crystal digested this opinion in silence. They reached the path that led toward the temple. She raised her eyebrows and looked toward Mary, who shrugged and chose it. "What way will you shift now?" she went on. "If Tottenham . . . God, isn't it the quarest thing to be talking about the man and him lying so near!" She turned back for a final glance toward the house.

"If he what?" Crystal prompted.

"Well, if he doesn't pay his debt to Matt, he can hardly return to fine society, so called."

Crystal stared intently into a clump of Solomon's seal – a search that yielded nothing. "'Twas done with anyway," she said at length.

Mary gave her an accusing nudge. "Is that regret I hear?"

The other sighed as they resumed their stroll. "I don't understand it. I love my Jack. For all his faults . . . I know he's the weakest . . . I mean, he has the noblest ideals, and yet at the merest puff of wind . . ." Her voice broke but she quickly regained control. "We should never have gone to London. At home his ideals would never have been challenged."

Mary tried to think of some neat way to change the subject. But Crystal went on, with sudden sharpness, "Anyway, I'm not the only one."

The accusation in her tone made Mary say, "The only one who what?"

"You're as bad! I see how you flutter when Tottenham's near. And how you *must* talk of him, even though . . ."

"But, Crystal – I can't bear the man!"

"And you think I can? There's the torment of it – that I can know him for the devil he is, and yet . . . when he's near . . . just the touch of his hand, the caress of his eyes . . ." She shivered. "How can such things be?"

Mary felt the sudden pace of her own heartbeat.

"Be honest now," Crystal said, smiling, trying to make light of it.

Mary felt it safe to join the game if humour were its terms. She grinned and asked, "Is it so obvious?"

"Only to a fellow sufferer."

"I thought 'twas done with. The farm, the children – and my darling Matt, whom I adore as you do your Jack – I thought all business with Tottenham was a folly long past, buried with so much else beside. Yet I only need one sight of him – not even that – and . . . I agree – 'tis past all explanation."

"Some are formed for celibate lives," Crystal said. "Some for monogamy. Some men should have a dozen wives. And I, of husbands, twenty-three.''

Mary laughed. "That's a good one. I didn't see it was a pome until . . .''

"Tottenham devised it. He put it all about town. Everyone knew it was a lampoon upon me, of course.''

"Oh no!" Mary's smile vanished. "Him of all people! The man's a . . . a gobshite! I'm sorry, but there's no other word.''

Crystal sighed. "Twenty-three's a cruel slander, but the cruelty feeds most on the truth within it. From the moment I was blooded in the world's oldest hunt, I knew no one man would ever suit me. Well, well. There it is, so. I seem to have acquired two short heels and must live with myself as I am.'' She looked up and said sharply, "And what of you, my dear? Has your own table been so indifferently garnished you have acquired no appetite to dine abroad?''

"To the contrary!" Mary flared up. "Why, it has been such a banqueting and carousing . . . night upon night . . .''

Agreement burned hot in Crystal's eyes. Mary saw it and paused, too astonished to complete her protest. Crystal, supposing that passionate memories had robbed her tongue, nodded with something more than mere understanding.

Mary, who had begun this conversation to quieten her mildest and most natural suspicions, who had hoped – at best – for some stumbling confession of infidelity with Matt, followed by tearful prayers for mercy and forgiveness, and who, moreover, had not the slightest idea how she would respond to them when they came, was astounded at this bold confession-in-passing, so gleeful, so wanton, so lacking in pleas for mitigation.

She was even more astonished to find herself filled not with anger but rather with a kind of grim satisfaction. That moment of revelation in Crystal's eyes – proof enough to her of Matt's infidelity – had released her from . . . from what? From some constraint of which she had not even been aware, and which even now she could not name.

She was free, a voice said within.

But free from what?

Free *for* what?

They walked on toward the temple. Neither saw the figure that stepped out from among the shrubbery and watched them pass beyond sight. Once there had been a time when Aaron M'Grotty would have taken a chance such as this to make off with Mary – to spite his old arch-enemy. Now nothing would do but the man himself.

Mary was nothing more to him than bait.

## CHAPTER FIFTY-NINE

A SUMMER STORM WAS threatening to break. Fitful lightning flashed over the Peak District, away to the northeast. The preparations for Tottenham's departure went on regardless.

"But he's still a sick man," Mary said to Rowena. "Surely to God the colonel wouldn't expect him to leave in *these* conditions?"

"For my part I wish he'd left last week. I wish he'd never come at all. I wish he was smothered at birth. I wish I'd never met him."

Crystal fanned her face in pantomime. "Well, that answers *my* question! I was about to ask if you were still intent upon remaining here – not going with him, I mean?"

"Would *you*? The colonel has offered me the protection of his roof for as long as I wish, which, in practical terms, means for as long as I can bear my aunt's obsession with fluff and filth – but certainly long enough to be rid of my lord. I'm sure neither of you would do otherwise, if you were in my shoes." She tossed her head. "I shan't even bid him farewell."

"Well, someone must," Mary said.

"Must!" Rowena echoed angrily.

"Else it will seem so unfeeling." Mary looked at Crystal, who shook her head, vigorously.

"Sure, it can hardly be me," Mary said.

"Jack'll see him into his coach," Crystal promised. "And if he gets no female farewell here, you may be certain of one thing: He'll find a female to welcome him somewhere. He's never short of the 'commodity,' as he calls it."

Rowena giggled. "Aye – say one thing for him – in that exchange he's bullish enough!"

And thus it was that, an hour later, Tottenham began the descent of the stairs, supported only by the faithful Jack.

Mary, who by chance was, at that same moment, going from the morning room to the library, where she hoped to find a better light – a path that would take her to the foot of that same staircase – turned back and waited in the shadows for the man to be gone.

But he must have seen her, for, as he reached the foot of the stair, he called out, "Mrs. Sullivan?"

She stopped breathing.

"We'll go that way," Tottenham told Jack. "She was there a moment ago, I'll smack calfskin on it."

Mary realized she had no choice but to step forth into the light and brave it out.

"There!" Tottenham grinned hugely. "She couldn't bear to see me depart alone!"

"Didn't I think you'd gone these two hours," Mary countered. "With the Earl of Hell playing your welcome there, over the Peaks beyond."

His lordship laughed. "Ah – that fire i' the eyes! D'ye mark it, Jack?"

His companion laughed too, immoderately.

"This is the jade we should have fought over, you and I," Tottenham continued. "Not that brace of milk-veined trollops we call wives."

Coldly Mary walked toward him, reviving her original intention to go into the library; but as she swept past he shot out a hand and seized her by the wrist. Instantly she was transported back to the morning of their first meeting, when he was carried indoors; then as now he had been enfeebled by a duel; now as then she was bound to him by ties she could not understand. His coal-black eyes, burning deep in his pale, drawn face, held her prisoner.

"You'll at least bid me farewell," he told her harshly.

It was not the grip of a sick man. "You're hurting," she said.

He relaxed his hand at once, gave her a dazzling smile, and said, "Please?"

She had forgotten his mercurial shifts of mood – or, rather, had forgotten their effect on her. She was as putty in his hands – only for a moment, but it was long enough to start her feet on the short journey to the stable yard.

Like a man who has tamed a fractious filly, he paid her no further heed, but walked ahead, much more briskly than he had seemed able to descend the stairs, and out into the stable yard.

It had been the colonel's express command that he was not to depart from the front door to the Hall.

"No wives to sweeten our departure, I see," Tottenham said the moment they were outside. "As I foretold." He turned around and said – with no trace of sarcasm, "You're worth any number of them, Mary."

She knew precisely how little such an opinion was to be valued and yet she felt absurdly pleased at it. A wild thought crossed her mind – that this was, in some obscure way, one of the truly important moments of her life. There was something she might say – if she could just pin it down – that would shatter Tottenham's composure and completely reform his character, as he pondered her words in the weeks and months of exile that lay ahead. It would be a Remarkable Occurrence, a shift in the spiritual landscape of England even more marvellous than the migrations of trees and hills that so fascinated her.

Desperately she sought those words within her. Nothing was there. Only the idea – smooth, perfect . . . and formless. Nothing to grip it by.

Then she was distracted by the sight of Con, wearing a coachman's coat and sitting in the driving seat. He gave her an ambiguous smile that left her uneasy.

Tottenham almost leaped aboard the coach. His agility was returning swiftly in the electric evening air, as though the house and its people had pressed down his spirit. The exit from the yard faced east, where the heavens were black as ink. Against that backdrop the evening sun upon his face gave him the look of a warrior-hero, a fine painting come to life, adding to the vitality of his living flesh all the classical grandeur of art.

He turned in the open carriage doorway. Con put all four reins in his left hand and raised the whip. The horses trembled to be off; one of them cantered on the spot.

"Don't go!" she said, still searching for those words.

"On the contrary . . ." Tottenham smiled and gave a brisk nod over her shoulder.

At this signal, Jack seized her roughly from behind and bundled her in. He made no sound and Mary herself, thinking it no more than foolish horseplay, denied them the reward of a scream – until she was secured. Then her shout was of anger; but too late. The door was shut, the window up, and Con's cry, "Gitaaaap!" and the thunder of the hooves drowned every syllable.

Her fury swiftly turned into weary annoyance. It really was too absurd! Where could the fool take her that would be safe from discovery? How could he travel without leaving a trail as broad as the Shannon? Besides, he was too close a . . . well, 'friend' was hardly the word! – too close for theatricals of this sort to seem anything other than comic.

To prove it she laughed; but he joined in, so she stopped. "Well and good," she told him. "Vastly amusing, my lord. Now will you turn about and set me down?"

There was a hammering at the window. Mary was surprised to see Jack hanging there, upside down, and grinning like a schoolboy. Tottenham made a gesture of annoyance and, reaching forward, drew across the blind. In the last moment, before it cut him off, she saw Jack's expression turn from bewilderment to pain.

"Damn the fellow!" Tottenham said. "I hoped we'd left him behind."

"I thought he was to travel with you . . . to, well, wherever you intended going?" Mary said.

The other laughed. "Aye – and so did he! But that office is now yours, my lamb." The coach began to slow down. "Oh double-damn the fool," he added.

He drew breath to shout to Con that he was to drive on, but then had a better idea. With a smile he eased his stick behind the door handle and then let back the blind again. Jack was not in sight, but as the coach pulled to a halt he leaped down from the roof and turned to face them.

He was grinning again. "Ha ha!" he shouted. "The jest's over, man. It's cold as wet toads out here. Open up, there's a sport?" He clutched his arms and gave a theatrical shiver, just in case Tottenham doubted him.

But Tottenham did not even glance his way; he stared ahead with a look of weary resignation. "You're turning into a bore, Horley," he shouted. "Go back and embrace that Scotch bedpan you married. She'll be desolate by now for the loss of me." He winked at Mary and added under his breath, "That'll heat him ten degrees!"

She felt the most terrible Judas, fighting back a smile, and watching Jack turn purple outside.

The moment the poor man had caught his breath he hurled himself at the door, only to find it stoutly barred. He leaped up, peeped within, and, seeing that the other door was not secured, made a dash around the back.

It was all Tottenham had been waiting for – and (thanks to long association) so had Con – for the machine lurched forward even as his lordship uttered the first syllable of, "Drive on!"

The violence of its motion hurled Mary across the carriage and into his arms.

"Two birds with the one stone!" he said delightedly. "But I vastly prefer my little Irish linnet to the squawking Gloucester turkeycock."

She struggled, but he was too strong for her. Indeed, it was a contest of will more than of muscle, and his will at that moment was far more powerful than hers. A terrible fatalism came over her, bringing a lassitude that robbed her limbs of any mere physical strength they might have used.

Later she had a thousand reasons. At the time, though, reason wasn't in it.

Lightly his lips caressed her downy cheek. "I love you," he whispered. "You are the only woman in all the world I have ever been capable of loving like this."

She closed her eyes and tried to will herself to resist; the best she could manage was to suppress the shiver he aroused within.

"You are the most wonderful woman who ever lived," he went on. His lips sought her ear; his soft, warm tongue found it.

His quiet voice, so close, the warmth of his breath . . . this time she could not even suppress the shiver. *Matt!* She made a silent prayer. *Oh, darling Matt, forgive me this one trespass . . .*

431

She was still in disarray from that tumble across the carriage. "Such sweet disorder of your dress!" he said, taking gentle advantage of it with fingers that no longer held her prisoner.

*. . . as I forgive yours.*

"You know I hate you," she told Tottenham. "You are the vilest, most odious . . ."

But he only laughed at her – while the coach raced on into the teeth of the storm.

## CHAPTER SIXTY

BEHIND THE SHUTTERS on the servants' top stair Rowena and Crystal waited, half-hidden, to watch Tottenham's ignominious departure.

"It's plain to see Mrs. Carmody never comes here," Crystal said, trying to wipe the grimy windowpane with the moistened corner of her kerchief.

"You're only making it worse," Rowena complained. "Oh, I say – it's the Murphy creature who's driving." She shivered theatrically. "I cannot abide him."

Fortunately a serving maid came by and they were able to send her for a large kitchen clout, liberally soaked in water.

And thus they saw the entire episode – or almost.

"The minx!" Crystal said the moment Mary appeared in the yard with their two husbands.

"She's welcome!" Rowena commented.

"Not to my Jack."

"Look at her – gossiping away like a mop fair. I know Tottenham's besotted with her."

"And she's more than slightly nuts about him," Crystal said. "She was speaking of it only the other week."

"Here! You don't think they're eloping together?" Rowena asked, biting her lip like a naughty schoolgirl.

Crystal shook her head. "She has more sense than that."

"Still – poor Matt! He'd be in dire need of consolation."

Their eyes dwelled cheerily in each other's for a moment, though they knew it was mere daydream. And during that moment Jack bundled Mary inside the coach. All the two women heard was the rumble of wheels as it fled; all they saw was Jack, leaping up behind and hanging on for dear life.

And all they *didn't* see was Mary, turning from the coach and coming back indoors.

"Where is she?" Crystal asked, pressing her eyes to the pane and squinting toward every angle of the yard.

"She must have come in while we weren't looking."

"She was quick about it, then. Let's go and ask what his famous last words might have been."

With that intention in mind, they set their steps toward the withdrawing room. But even before they had quit the servants' quarters, second thoughts prevailed.

"If we come so swift upon their departure, she'll guess we were watching," Rowena said.

"We could have heard the carriage wheels."

"It would show we were straining our ears to listen."

"You're right, as ever, my dear. We shall say nothing."

"Indeed, we shan't even go seek her out."

Less than two hours later, when dinner was about to be served, there was a commotion at the front door. Dogs barked, servants came running, and then the word spread through the house: "The master's back. The master's home."

Matt, of course, was with him.

"My dear!" Mrs Carmody called out happily – though she wrung her hands at the mud and gravel the two men had trailed indoors. "We did not expect you until this day week."

The colonel waved an expansive hand toward Matt. "You must blame this man, my dear. He never uses two words where one will do – nor any at all where none will serve better. Before the withering fire of his silence, committees of generals have turned and fled in disarray. Has Lord Dent been here?"

The three women exchanged bewildered glances. "Was he expected?" Mrs. Carmody asked.

"Half and half," her husband replied. "I thought he might have called by. Toby Wharton told me he'd left on a mission to the North Country – and then later denied it. Said it was all a mistake. Something's afoot. Nothing about that man is ever straightforward."

Matt raised his eyebrows at Crystal.

"What?" she asked. "I'm no reader of minds."

"Mary?"

The women exchanged bewildered glances. It was, indeed, slightly odd that the commotion which had brought everyone else running to the entrance hall had failed to stir Mary to join them.

"She's been so tired lately," Rowena said. "We'll go and find her."

But Matt would not hear of it. If she were asleep, she could wake in her own good time. He'd finished his wanderings and his War Office committees at last. There was no urgency.

He went upstairs and tiptoed into their bedroom; but she was not there. He came out and found Crystal and Rowena waiting.

"How is she?" Rowena asked.

He shook his head. "Not there." Catching the smile that passed between the two women, he said, "You *know* something?"

Rowena shook her head. "Our knowledge, dear Matt, is all pluperfect."

"Oh yes!" Crystal giggled. "Plu-, plu-perfect!"

They collapsed on each other in laughter.

"Devil take this!" He stalked off.

Crystal was the first to pull herself together. "Perhaps Mary has nodded off in the library?" she suggested in a tone of soothing apology.

But Mary was not in the library. Nor was she with the baby in the nursery, which was Crystal's next suggestion.

Still no one was worried – not really worried. A slight twinge of puzzled anxiety, perhaps, but nothing you might call worry. But when she proved not to be in the morning room either, they looked at each other and realized that comforting explanations were growing alarmingly scarce.

They split up then and, taking a candelabra apiece, searched all the rooms on the ground floor. When they met again in the main hall and saw the hope in each other's eyes fade, they knew the hunt was now in earnest.

"Colonel!" Matt's shout echoed among the old beams.

The butler came running, muttering excuses for the meal being delayed.

"Never mind that," Rowena said. "Have you or any of the servants seen Mrs. Sullivan?"

"I've not seen her since luncheon, madam. I'll inquire among the others."

"Send first to your master," Crystal told him. "Say we believe she's missing and . . ."

"Missing? Who's missing?" It was the colonel, up on the landing. Clad only in a dressing gown, he was pink from the bath in which he had been removing the grime of his journey.

While Crystal explained matters to the colonel, Rowena told the butler to go and inquire among the others. "Any who saw her, bring them here, be they scarecrow or village idiot."

"I'll get dressed again," Carmody said and vanished from sight.

While they waited for the inquiry among the servants they made a second search of the ground floor. This time they found a handkerchief of Mary's. The circumstances were so absurdly like a Discovery Scene in a melodrama that they went out of their way to treat the find as trivial.

"My maid will see it's laundered," Rowena said, tucking it casually into her sleeve.

Moments later the butler returned with a stable lad who said he'd seen Mrs. Sullivan bidding farewell to Lord Tottenham and Mr. Horley.

"When would that be?" the colonel asked, taking charge now that he was dressed once more.

But the time of day was a mystery to the lad.

Crystal looked at Rowena. "It must have been around six," she said. "A little before, perhaps."

"Yes," Rowena confirmed. "I think I heard carriage wheels at around that hour."

Matt consulted his watch. "Just about two hours," he noted. "You said no farewells."

Rowena gave him a withering look – then softened it by saying, "Perhaps she went for a stroll down to the summerhouse. She might have twisted her ankle."

When Aaron M'Grotty saw a great party of masters and servants, all furnished with lanterns and sticks, coming his way, he thought his game was up. But when he heard them all shouting, "Mrs. Sullivan!" and "Mary!" he did no more than withdraw to a safer distance and keep them under scrutiny.

He'd almost had that bastard Sullivan, not half an hour ago – had him in his sights and could have despatched him to hell in a trice. But the colonel had been too near.

He toyed with the idea of stalking his quarry in silence now and finishing him with a knife; but the place was alive with lanterns and muscle. Best to bide his time a little more. He felt in his bones it would not be too long now; some kind of crisis was plainly upon the household.

After twenty minutes of fruitless searching the butler came to the front door, stood upon the steps, and blew a whistle with his fingers. They all came running.

"Tom Sowerbutts, sir, who lays the hedges on the Hinckley road, says he saw them."

"Them?"

"It seems Mrs. Sullivan may . . . well, you'd best hear it from his own lips, sir."

Tom Sowerbutts had never been in so grand a room. He stood there, marooned in the middle of Mrs. Carmody's new carpet, tucking in his elbows, pressing his knees together, trying to fold himself into as small a space as possible.

"Now what's all this?" the colonel asked as he came in.

His wife, who was immediately behind him, shrieked, "Oh, the carpet!" She dispatched a maid to fetch a newspaper.

"An it please you, sir, Colonel Carmody, I was laying the hedge out at Vose's Farm on the Hinckley road, when . . ."

"What time?" the colonel asked.

"Was there a lady?" asked Matt.

The man screwed up his face. "The vespers was rung, but not long – so 'twas gone six." He brightened. "Yes, sir. The *exact* time was between six and seven, near enough!"

"Go on."

"The lady . . ."

"Let him tell it his way, Sullivan, or we'll be here all night." The colonel turned to the man with a smile of encouragement.

The newspaper arrived. Mrs. Carmody snatched it and went to kneel behind old Tom.

"Well, this coach-and-four come by, see."

Mrs. Carmody raised his right leg and placed it on the spread-out sheets. He looked down in alarm.

"Go on, go on!" the colonel thundered, meaning the anger for his wife.

Poor Sowerbutts, taking it to be aimed at himself, grew even more frightened. "There's not too many o' them on that road, not coaches and four."

Mrs. Carmody stood and pushed at him, like a stubborn beast in the market ring, until he stood four-square upon the paper. "Don't stir," she hissed.

The old fellow fixed the colonel with a petrified eye and continued, "The last one I remember was four year ago, when . . ."

"Never mind that," the colonel told him. "Tell us who was in this coach?"

"It was Michaelmas quarter-day – that's how I remember it, see?"

"Was it drawn by four greys?"

The man screwed up his face. " 'Tis a long time to remember a thing like that, sir. But . . ."

"No! *Today's* coach, man! Was today's coach drawn by four greys?"

Sowerbutts gave a dignified sniff. "As I was *about* to tell you, sir . . . yes. Magnificent horses they was . . ."

"We know the creatures," Matt put in, fighting back his impatience. "Just tell us about the coach – and who was in it."

"Just the two, sir – the gentleman and the lady."

"Not two men? You're quite sure?"

"No doubting it was a lady, sir," he said with slightly lickerish emphasis. Then, seeing what a chill response this drew, he wet his lips and stared around uncertainly. "There was two men," he added. "One inside and one on top."

"That was Jack," Rowena said impulsively.

Crystal looked daggers at her.

Matt caught the exchange and frowned inquiringly at Rowena.

"Oh, very well," she said crossly. "I watched them go. I was at a window upstairs."

"What window?" Mrs. Carmody asked.

"No matter," Matt said sharply. "Was Mary in the coach?"

Rowena gave an awkward shrug. "I don't know. The Murphy creature was driving. I saw that much."

"Hell and damnation, woman!" Matt cried.

"I don't know!" she shouted back. "I don't know! I don't know! She walked across the yard with them. I didn't see everything. They talked for a short while, then I was distracted by something, then I heard the carriagewheels and I looked back and they were going out the gate as if the Angel of Judgment were after them. Jack was clinging onto the roof for dear life. And Mary . . . well – she wasn't there." She turned directly toward Matt and added, "I swear by all that's holy, it never crossed my mind until now that Mary might have been in the coach. We both – I mean I – thought she'd come back indoors."

"We both thought it," Crystal said quietly. "We were both watching him leave and we both believed Mary came back into the house." She turned to Sowerbutts. "Can you say what this lady looked like?"

He relaxed and took an aimless step – which brought a peremptory shriek from Mrs. Carmody. He shrivelled back into the centre of his paper island and gave a description that left no doubt: The woman in the coach was Mary Sullivan.

It took Matt a second or two to absorb the news. When he looked around at the others he was astonished at what he saw. There is a subtle difference between the pity shown to a man whose wife has been abducted and that shown to one whose wife has simply chosen to run away. The pity in their eyes, every man and woman among them, was of the second kind.

He stared back at each, briefly, in turn, shaking his head ever more violently against their unanimous assumption. "No!" he roared at last.

The colonel, staring awkwardly somewhere beyond Matt's left shoulder, said, "You'll go after 'em, nonetheless?"

Matt ignored the question. "You're wrong!" he shouted, raking them with his eyes. "She would never have gone of her own free choice."

Crystal made a gesture of hopelessness and looked at Rowena, who pointed out, "None of us has said it, Matt. What voice are you seeking to drown?"

Matt's look of reproach cut her to the very core.

The colonel, trying to distract the company rather than unravel the knot further, asked Sowerbutts, "The fellow on the roof — would you know him again?"

"I *did* know him again, Colonel, sir — when he passed me on foot about ten minutes after."

"On foot?" A buzz of amazement went among them.

"You mean he came back?"

Sowerbutts saw Crystal turning toward the door. "Not back here, ma'am," he said. "He's down the Lord o' Warwick now, drowning his sorrows."

"Sorrows?" Crystal echoed angrily. "By Christ but I'll give him sorrows he couldn't drown in seven oceans of gin!"

At that moment there was a great roaring and crashing from the hall beyond; it sounded as though a whole suit of armour had been brought down — which, indeed, they discovered to be the case as soon as they reached the scene. Sitting dazed in the middle, drunk as a pig, was Jack, tears streaming down his face.

"Sullivan!" he cried as soon as he focussed on Matt. "My pal!" He raised both his arms in a kind of symbolic hug; his body, deprived of their support, wavered and fell back among the shards of aegis, cuirass, heaume, and visor, making more racket than a shall-I band.

Matt bent to assist him. "Where's Tottenham?" he asked. "Is Mary with him?"

Jack shook his head violently, as if seeking to dislodge something from his ear. "Plucked her," he muttered.

"What!"

"Did he say plucked?" Mrs. Carmody whispered to her husband.

"So I hope," he murmured in reply.

"What?" Matt roared even louder.

Jack blinked at him. "Plucked her," he repeated, as if he thought Matt were the simpleton. "Pluck! Pluck! . . ." His repetition of the word degenerated into an imitation of a hen.

"Useless!" Matt shouted at him in disgust.

He let go and rose to his feet. Jack fell back again. "Plucked the brand!" he said, delighted at the brilliance of his memory.

Matt spun around. "Tottenham's words?" he asked.

Jack grinned and gave a huge, careful nod. "Very words. She is the brand . . . the brand . . . something-something-something . . . before mine eyes. He has set to burn before mine eyes. I must pluck it from him. Very words. Oh, Sullivan, my old pal, I am so bloody sorry."

Matt bent down at his side again and once more helped him to a sitting position. "Sorry for what, Horley? Did you play a part in it?"

Jack gathered his few remaining wits and, lifting a ponderous, wavering finger, said, "Because of you, you see."

"Yes – me. All right. But tell me what you did?"

Jack shook his head impatiently. "Not me. You did it! Human yeast. You . . . and . . ." He began a minute search of each face in the rough circle about him. He passed Crystal's and had to come back. "Her!" he cried triumphantly. "You and her!"

Crystal turned scarlet. "He's in his altitudes," she explained to Mrs. Carmody. "His mind's wandering."

"Just tell us what *you* did, Horley," Matt continued patiently. "Mary's been abducted. That's a hanging offence. Did you have any part in it?"

Jack nodded – and went on nodding long after he had forgotten what he might be assenting to.

"What did you do, Jack?" Rowena asked sharply.

"Pushed her in. Shut the door. Only just managed . . ." Tears welled in his eyes.

"Where is the man taking her?" Matt cut in.

Jack blinked at him. "Who?"

All eight of Matt's knuckles turned white. Crystal hastily knelt at her husband's other side. "*Think*, darling! And tell us, do. We have to know. Where is Tottenham taking her?"

"To Hull." He gave a cunning grin and tugged at his lower lip – a canting gesture to show that the truth has not yet left the mouth.

"But?" Crystal prompted.

"His *coach* will go to Liverpool, but *he* . . . to Hull." He nodded with huge satisfaction, as if revealing some plot of his own.

"And Mary with him? To America, I suppose?"

Jack frowned. "Brazil," he said at last.

"Liverpool or Hull, we'll receive him at the dock," Matt said, rising. "If you can sober up as fast as you got in that state, Horley, you may join us."

He helped Crystal to rise. In the middle of stretching her limbs, which were on the verge of pins-and-needles, she stopped and looked all about her, peering into the shadows. "Where's Rowena?" she asked.

Everyone stared at everyone else; no one had seen her go.

In fact, at that moment she was leaping into the saddle of the first horse she had found in the stables – just as she had flung herself into the first warm overcoat and booted spurs that came to hand. That all these items happened to belong to Matt was sheer coincidence.

"Gitaan!" she yelled at the horse, who emerged from the stable at full gallop.

She did not take the back gate – the way she had seen her husband leave. She knew his mind well enough to be sure that if he started east he would soon turn west. And west, for any outlaw – as Tottenham now surely was – could only mean Liverpool. She'd shoot him there.

Matt's horse was so large and powerful she had to duck her head as she went out by the other gate, the one that led to the front, otherwise she would have dashed out her brains on the lantern that swung there in the gathering storm.

By the light of that same lantern Aaron M'Grotty saw that his chance had come at last. All he had to do was sit and wait and it would come directly to him.

He pulled back the hammers on both pistols and cuddled the flints beneath his arms, lest one stray drop of rain should ruin so many years of waiting.

PART SIX

REMARKABLE OCCURRENCES

# CHAPTER SIXTY-ONE

HE FIRST BALL grazed Rowena's neck at its junction with her shoulder. The horse, frightened at M'Grotty's sudden emergence from the bushes, gave one mighty bound, like a lamb in spring, and came back to earth in a jolting, four-prong halt that flung the unprepared Rowena forward onto its neck. The movement undoubtedly saved her life, for M'Grotty, who had expected the creature to shy to one side, was caught off guard and prevented from aiming his second shot.

"Stand, you devil!" he cursed.

The horse reared wildly on its hind quarters. Moments later its flailing hooves bore the assassin to the ground. As he dropped he fired in panic into the creature's belly, but either his powder was poor or it had been affected by the damp, for the pistol produced the merest pop. The iron buckle of the girth deflected the feeble shot into Rowena's left calf, with just sufficient impulse to break the skin. She fell stunned into the shrubbery where, moments earlier, M'Grotty had lain concealed.

The riderless horse ran in terror about the lawns for a circuit or two and then bolted for the stable yard. The rain had now turned into a downpour.

M'Grotty lay, fully conscious, in the middle of the drive wondering why his body felt as if had been neatly sliced in half. With his hands he could feel his hips and thighs, but those parts of him – indeed, everything below the midriff – yielded no sensation whatever. Nor, as he now discovered to his alarm, would any of those muscles obey him.

445

Back indoors there was consternation and uproar. Moments after they discovered Rowena's absence they heard the clatter of hooves in the stable yard. They all ran in that direction but before they reached the yard door they were halted by the sound of the first pistol shot from the direction of the drive, not too far from the house. Then came the shriek of the horse, coupled with a brief, piercing female scream, which, in turn, was drowned by a male bellow of pain and rage. Finally came a second shot, much feebler than the first. Then a silence marked only by the steady drumming of the rain. Weaving in and out of it they could just discern the thunder of hooves on the turf.

Despite the rain they all crowded out into the yard, where, moments later, they saw Matt's horse come galloping in, saddled but riderless. A stableboy caught up its dangling rein and began trying to soothe its fear; the light of the single lamp over the gate made it glisten like a new-varnished carving.

Matt himself had disappeared. In fact, he was already racing off down the drive in the direction from which the shots appeared to have come. The head lad, bearing a storm lantern, was close behind. Crystal was all for going, too, but the colonel asked her to go indoors with his wife and help Jack sober up; then he sent for more lanterns and set off into the dark.

And Tom Sowerbutts, marooned in the withdrawing room, a rustic Crusoe on his island of paper, listened to the distant commotion and wondered how long it would be before rescue came.

Panic seized Aaron M'Grotty. Like a drowning rat he lay in the middle of the drive, knowing in his bones that the footsteps now approaching were those of the man he thought he had killed, and knowing, too, that he was a helpless cripple from the waist down.

In the dark Matt actually tripped over him and fell at full length into the bushes, not two feet from Rowena, who was just coming to. In getting to his feet he overbalanced and half-fell against her. She gave a little cry in which drowsiness, fear, and bewilderment were equally mingled.

"Rowena!" he said, feeling for her head.

"Matt?" She tried to sit up. "My leg's gone to sleep."

By now the head lad had arrived with the lantern. "There's a man stretched cold here in the drive, Mr. Sullivan," he called.

"Never mind him. Bring light here."

He gave Rowena a quick but careful inspection, enough to find both her wounds and make sure she was not bleeding heavily from either. He winced to see how close the ball had gone to the great vessels of her neck but said nothing to her of it.

"You'll do fine," he said. "Just be brave while I carry you within." And, soaked as she was, and weighted down in his great coat, he hefted her in his arms and bore her back toward the house.

"What of this blackguard, sir?" the lad asked as they passed M'Grotty in the drive.

Matt, not wishing to delay getting indoors, turned him over, none too gently, with the toe of his boot. "Aaron M'Grotty!" he gasped, but his surprise died as quickly as it had risen. "Of course! I might have guessed." Anger now seized him. "All for what, man? For *what?*" He gave him a vicious kick in the thigh. "On your feet!"

"The devil take you, Sullivan," the other snarled. There was no bellow of pain, as there ought to have been from such an assault.

"Satan's hands are full enough this night. Come on – gittup!"

He kicked harder still, so that even Rowena cried stop. But again there was no sign of pain.

The colonel joined them at that moment. "The man's paralyzed," he said. "Seen it often."

Rowena winced at the hurtful tingle from her reviving leg. Matt wasted no more time with M'Grotty but set off directly for the house. "Leave the bastard!" he shouted back over his shoulder. "Some carriage will finish him off."

The colonel and the lad dragged the helpless villain by the legs across the lawn and into one of the stables. He screamed from the pain in his back and the bumping of his skull until he fell unconscious. They left him, a misshapen bundle of wet rags, on a pile of dirty straw. The head lad was sent to fetch the constable.

Arrived indoors, the colonel found his wife and Matt inspecting the flesh wound in Rowena's calf. Crystal and Mrs. Carmody had removed her wet clothing and replaced it with dry; they had also covered both her limbs with a sheet, leaving only the wound in the calf exposed. The two younger women found these precautions amusing, which caused Mrs. Carmody to raise an eyebrow or two.

"She seems to have lost a little blood," Matt told the colonel. "But it looks clean enough."

The wound in her neck was even lighter – though, from the way she had fallen, not so clean. "Nothing to fuss about here," the colonel said. "The bullet's saved the expense of leeches. You'll heal in a week on your own, dear niece – or, if you'd prefer a month, we'll send for the surgeon."

"Who was it?" Rowena asked. "Did Tottenham leave a man there to . . ."

"His name's Aaron M'Grotty." Matt told them briefly of the circumstances. "He tried to kill you because you were in my coat and on my horse."

But Rowena would not believe Tottenham wasn't in it somewhere. "You must leave me at once and go after him," she insisted. There was a cold, hard light in her eye that none had seen there before.

The colonel laid a gentle finger on her neck, near the wound. "You can see to that, Mrs. Carmody," he told his wife. "There's something to be said for all this cleanliness, I daresay. Personally I think a handful of maggots does wonders for any wound."

She made no response, being long used to such provocation, but Matt grinned to see the distaste on Rowena's face. "Seems you'll live," he told her.

"I'll live to see him hanged. Listen – if Jack says Tottenham headed for Hull, he'll really be making for Liverpool."

"Why did you run out like that? Were you going after Tottenham?"

She nodded. "To shoot him." She grew impatient. "For God's sake, Matt – just go, or I'll rise and do it for you!"

By now Jack was sober enough to stand, though he could add little in the way of rational debate. There was no hope that a party on horseback, making its way through unfamiliar lanes, in pitch dark and pouring rain, could gain on a coach and four that had the advantage of several hours' start by daylight. In any case, there was by now no certainty that it any longer contained their quarry. The balance of probability, though, was that Tottenham would do the opposite of what he had planned with Jack – go to Liverpool while the coach went on to Hull.

It was decided among them that the colonel and the still-dazed Jack should follow the generally northeastward trail of the original coach, asking at every inn and livery along the way where Tottenham might have switched to a new conveyance, leaving the original to lay its false scent to Hull. Matt, meanwhile, would head directly for Liverpool, a route that would take him past Summerley, where he could recruit Punch and all the manpower he needed. "I'll follow the canal towpaths," he said. "Thanks to you, Colonel, no man in England knows them better."

The constable and his deputy came for M'Grotty just as the two parties were checking their mounts. When they heard the particulars of the outrage, they decided to bring him directly to the gaol at Leicester, where, at the next assize, he would be sent to the gallows. "If he survives this journey," the constable said.

"Oh, be sure he does not die before his time," the colonel ordered, and he made them shake out a good thick layer of straw beneath the man and cover him with an oilcloth. They put him in leg-irons, despite his paralysis, and fettered him to fixed gyves in the side rails of the open cart.

The constable's decision to go to Leicester suited Jack and the colonel very well, for the cart would give them guidance during the first couple of hours. By then the storm might have passed. If the clouds thinned, there would be a good moon to light them until dawn.

The prospects were fair. The wind had greatly moderated and the steady downpour of rain had turned much gentler – more like a summer shower with occasional squalls. They all set off simultaneously, the cart and its followers along the Hinckley road, Matt down a lane that led to a bridge over the Forest Branch canal. They parted in great cheer, being certain that despite his lead of several hours, Tottenham had no hope of escape by any port in the land. By tomorrow's daylight the military semaphores would get messages not merely to Hull and Liverpool but to Dover, Plymouth, Glasgow, and every other likely point of embarkation – long before Tottenham could possibly arrive at even the nearest of them.

Within a quarter of a mile the towpath led Matt to the ornamental water that marked the canal's passage through the grounds of the Hall. There, standing on the Chinese bridge, barely discernible against a thinning of the cloud on the northwestern horizon, stood what he at first took to be a highwayman.

449

Matt reined in and drew his pistol, keeping it dry beneath his cloak. "Who's there?" he challenged.

The laugh gave her away – it was Crystal. She wore a pair of Jack's britches and sat astride a mettlesome little arab mare, a gift from Old Q.

"Don't be a fool," he told her as he spurred his own mount onward.

"How can you stop me?" she called as she settled to follow.

"I'll tell the first canal servant we meet that you're not of my party."

All the way to the main canal she begged him to change his mind. Anything might happen before he reached Summerley. He could be thrown. His horse might go lame. He might be glad of someone to send off with a message. And anyway, when they found Mary, she ought to have the support of someone of her own sex.

"Please, Matt?" she begged. "Say I may follow?"

He would not give her that assurance. When they passed the lock keeper at the junction, he hesitated. Crystal gathered her little steed, ready for a dash along the bank. Then he said, "The lad and I are bound off to Liverpool on military business." The man waved them on without demur.

"There's a tormenting streak in you," she called to him when they were alone again.

"That smile," he said, "between you and Rowena . . . the way you laughed . . ." He could not voice the rest of his accusation.

But Crystal divined it. "As I stand before Judgment, Matt, my dear, neither Rowena nor I knew one whisper of this."

"You saw them leave together."

"Without knowing it – aye. I swear to you, we told the truth . . . Oh, Matt! There is guilt enough here in what *did* happen, without adding to the scales what did *not*."

When he remained silent she prompted, "Say you believe me?"

All he answered was, "Guilt!" And his tone accused himself more than her.

The rain eased off completely between there and Nuneaton. When they drew near the town, they were challenged again, but the moment the watchmen heard Matt's voice they stood aside and waved the pair of travellers through. Just before they reached Fazeley, the clouds thinned and a full moon began to show its brilliance; after the almost total darkness of the storm it was painful to the eyes.

Before the clearance they had not risked anything faster than a trot; in the seeming daylight that now bathed them they stretched it to a slow canter, a loping sort of pace that both horses could maintain for hours. Midnight chimed from Meaford clock as they drew within sight of Summerley.

They rode straight round to Punch's cottage, the former bailiff's lodgings in the days when Summerley had been the manor house. The moment the fellow heard what had happened to Mary he flew into a rage and was all for leaping on Matt's horse and galloping to Liverpool.

"And you so calm!" he shouted at them. "How can you?"

"You weren't there two hours ago!" Matt replied. "We've had time to think, time to make plans." And he went on to outline them.

As Punch listened his immediate anger was channelled into an eagerness to join the chase and be in at the kill. "I'll get fresh horses," he interrupted, already walking toward the stables. "You may tell me the rest as we go."

Matt turned to Crystal. "We've no time to rouse a maid. If I bring you to the pantries, can you put together a bag of vittles – enough for six – while I prepare pistols and powder?"

He soon had their armoury together and went out to help Punch with the horses, telling him what little remained to be told as they worked. Punch had roused the three youngest, fittest, strongest hands, who joined the party as soon as they had struggled into their clothes.

And so, a mere ten minutes after Matt and Crystal had arrived, they and the four new riders set out on the most deadly pursuit of their lives.

# CHAPTER SIXTY-TWO

BY THE TIME their coach was approaching Derby, Mary had managed to convince Lord Tottenham that nothing could please her more than to be running off with him. She hoped that the first change of horses might offer the chance for her to escape – especially if his guard were well and truly down by then.

It *was* all bluff on her part. Looking into his eyes, so dark and troubled, so powerful, even in the dim light of the carriage lamp, she had to remind herself of that.

"Derby!" she said when he told her that was their immediate destination. "D'you recall the last time we were in that town? On the great Pic-to-Pic race? We had no time to rest then, either. I wonder will our lives ever be anything but helter-skelter?"

His agreement was morose; his eyes remained downcast.

"Oh, so sombre!" she protested and threw herself onto his lap again.

He tried to respond but there was no more arousal left in him. "You'll kill me," he protested.

"Too many past debauches to your discredit. Isn't that the truth of it?"

With an oddly shy note of apology in his voice, he asked, "Do I greatly disappoint you?"

"In *that* way?" She kissed his forehead. "What d'you think now?"

"In that way – in any way?"

"Sure your character could do with some of that holy soap."

He buried his face in her neck, as if even the dim light from the carriage lamp were too harsh. "What a fool I have been, Mary," he murmured. "And what would I not give to be able to go back now to that morning on which we met."

"You never told me the truth of that. There was some compact between you and Con Murphy, wasn't there."

"The man's a . . . I don't know. There's no word for him."

"Useful creature?" Mary suggested.

"Lower than the beasts of the fields."

"But useful!"

"When he described you to me . . . he had no idea. He put before me the picture of a wild young Irish rose with her head full of dreams. A rose in bud, ripe for picking . . ."

Mary gave an ironic laugh. "Was he so wide of the mark?"

"A bloom to wear at one's collar for her brief season, and then discard. That's all he saw in you. He said for ten guineas he could bring you to London and lay you before me. I beat him down to seven, when I should have rewarded him with all I had. Oh, Mary – with you I could have been such a different . . ." The words dried within him.

She rubbed her cheek against his ear. "And when he delivered me . . . why did you not yield?"

"Yield?" He looked at her in bewilderment.

"You know what I mean," she insisted.

"On my honour I do not."

"Those first days in London, and during our journey to Manchester – anytime up to when you let out the bull – you know full well . . ."

"What bull? I let out no bull."

"Please, Tottenham, don't take me for a child still. 'Tis all past now, anyway. I bore no real rancour then and I bear none now. You opened the gate that . . ."

"But I swear to you, I know nothing of any bull. The moment you crossed that finishing line, just within the appointed hour, I had to vanish. I heard nothing of this."

She believed by now that she could tell when he was lying; these protestations were oddly convincing. Slightly less sure of herself she said, "Your last words to me during the race, on that hill near Buxton, when Old Q passed us out in his carriage and was his usual kindly and considerate self, you said something about my having cause now to frustrate him."

"Indeed, I remember that," he said hotly. "And you looked daggers at me and replied you had cause to frustrate me!"

"I did not!" she protested.

"Not in so many words, perhaps, but such was your meaning."

"Indeed and it was not. You took me entirely wrong, so. But, whatever and all about that, you surely rode on and opened the gate to let that bull go straying . . ."

"I rode straight to Manchester and . . . well, what I did there is naught to my credit. But I saw no gate, no field, no bull. That much I'd call on God himself to witness."

She caressed his cheek. "Then I have blackguarded you. I'm sorry."

His lips pressed against hers. She began to melt again. "Did you truly think I had unleashed . . . oh, Mary! The reason I left so hastily was that I could not hurt you further. I tried – and could not bring myself to it. And so I had to look to the saving of my own miserable skin."

He pulled his head away to see into her eyes, but she clung tighter to prevent it. Visions of all that might have been began to assail her.

"That night of the thunderstorm," he went on. "You spoke then of yielding, too. And I said you would yield everything but your heart. So, too, I say it now."

"My heart?" she echoed. "But you are no babe in such matters, my dear. You can read a woman's heart and mind when Venus first puts that cup to her lips. You knew you had only to snap a finger and I was yours – yet all you did was play with . . ."

"Play!" he roared. "Play? But I have been in torment over you. Listen!" He lifted her bodily off his lap and sat her beside him. "You rob me of reason when you sit so close." He shut his eyes and gathered himself. When he was quite calm again he continued, "You say snap my fingers and you'd be mine. But what would have been mine? Certainly not your heart – though you protest it a thousand times. Your charms? Not even them. Oh, you would seem to grant me that favour – as, indeed, you have seemed to do these past hours – but it is a very *seeming* gift. You give me your body as a man might 'give' a brace of pheasant to his cook."

"It is a strange cook, my lord, who is known to be at the broth

454

early and late, and who pays, more often than not, for the privilege of dipping his ladle in the stews!''

He laughed at her wit but was not provoked by it. "True or not, my lass – and, of course, it is true – it is nothing to my argument. You have used me this day for your own wanton pleasure, as I have used countless of your sex before. I confess it. You do not. That is all.''

"You speak as a man,'' she told him crossly. "For a woman it is never so simple. Tell me – why did you carry me off today? What hopes had you?''

"I took you'' – he grinned as the idea struck him – "yes: in order to yield to you at last!'' But the smile faded and he became serious again. "The reason I did not 'snap my fingers,' was that I knew what would happen once you came to me. You are no common jade, Mary; your star rules once a century. Old Q saw it the instant he met you. He could no more have touched you then than I. You transform those whose lives you enter. And the last thing Old Q wanted, at his age, was to have his life entered and transformed; and such was the case with me, too. Then.''

"And now?''

"Now I can no more escape it than . . .''

At that moment they thundered beneath an archway and emerged into the yard of the Derby Ram. He flung open the door and leaped down without waiting for the steps to be unfolded. "Quick as you can, now,'' he said to Con. "We shall change horses here and press onward at once.''

Then he held out his arms to lift her down. When her feet were on the ground he continued to hold her by the waist, staring into her eyes, throwing her into a fresh confusion. Finally, as if the gesture were part of some ritual, he snatched his hands away and held them high and open.

"You are free,'' he said simply.

She frowned.

"Yes, free. We shall be here about five minutes. I'll go within and procure some brandy and madeira. No one will watch over you. Slip away if you will – I shan't pursue you.''

Ten minutes later, as the fresh team cantered out of Derby on the road to Mansfield, she watched the smile on his face and knew she had been wrong not to take him at his word. She could have walked away from the inn and he would not have stopped her.

At the time she had told herself he wasn't to be trusted. He was merely testing her. The first move she made toward freedom, he'd have pounced and she'd have continued the journey bound hand and foot with no chance whatever to escape. Now his guard really would relax.

Also, at some less rational level, she did not want to "escape" by his leave. She wanted to thwart him, to make him hurt.

And at an even deeper level, where her mind resisted its own invitation to explore, she wanted to make Matt hurt, too. She felt herself to be in no real danger from Tottenham. There would come a thousand chances for her to escape between here and whatever dockside he had chosen for their embarkation. In the meanwhile Matt would be going out of his mind with anxiety. And the next time Crystal or some other low-heeled wench offered to spread the gentleman's relish for him, perhaps he'd remember this present dread of losing her and tie a knot in it instead.

Her feeling for Tottenham played some small . . . very minor . . . part in the decision, of course. He was right. She had just used him for her pleasure – no question of anything deeper than that – which was why it was so completely safe to go on, just a little farther, with him . . .

When they had left the last outlying hovels of the town behind, Tottenham, still wearing that vastly satisfied smile, pulled her upon his lap and slipped his tender, skilful hands into the folds of her dress . . . and her reasons for staying with him grew confused and oddly unimportant.

About a dozen miles out of Derby, just beyond the village of Alfreton, they turned off into a little byway that led a bumpy mile or so to a farm, where they were obviously expected. The farmer was out in his yard, waiting to greet them, lantern in hand. His wife stood at the kitchen doorway, nervously wiping her hands upon her pinafore, again and again.

"Welcome, master," the man said. "And you, too, young mistress. Welcome. Come away within, and you'll find we have all prepared as your man desired it."

Con leaped down from the driver's seat – but not to unhitch the horses and lead them to shelter. Instead his place was taken at once by another, who turned them about and set off down the lane, back toward the highway.

"What now?" Mary asked.

Tottenham smiled at her. "I'm buying us time. I told Jack that I'd send my coach empty to Liverpool, to draw off the hounds, while I – that is, we – went on to Hull."

"But he'll tell them now."

"Exactly. But d'you suppose they'll believe it!"

She laughed. "You mean thing! So we really are going to Hull?"

"To Hull and beyond! Oh yes – far, far beyond!"

## CHAPTER SIXTY-THREE

DAWN WAS BREAKING when Mary and Tottenham set out the following morning. After a few miles they came to Mansfield, where they took the Sheffield road – a long way round if they truly were making for Hull. Two hours later a tired Colonel Carmody and an exhausted Jack drew near to that same junction.

They, too, had changed mounts at the Ram in Derby, where they learned that Tottenham had gone before them last night, and by this same road.

"Rum thing," the colonel said unhappily. "D'ye think she's bolted with him?"

"Never!" Jack replied, with a guilty inclination of his head. "You'd never say so if you'd seen what force it required to bundle her into the carriage."

"Hate speaking ill of a lady, Horley, but it's a damned rum thing. The genial Boniface of the Ram told me Mrs. Sullivan was at liberty there for five minutes, yet she made no attempt to run, what? With the constabulary three doors away, the vicarage in the next street, and a watch house on the corner, eh? Yet she walks into the premises, uses the privy, and walks out again – with neither Tottenham nor his man in sight – and slips back into the coach as calm as a kyloe cow. Rum's the word for it. She looks like a bolter to me."

Jack cleared his throat uncomfortably. "Wouldn't like to think that of her, colonel. I'd prefer to believe she felt herself too closely watched, if not by Tottenham, then by someone in his pay. Any among that rabble of ostlers, curates, and serving maids could have been his lordship's agent. How was she to know? Nay, I prefer to think she was deliberately putting Tottenham at his ease, the more surely to give him the slip later."

Reluctantly, the colonel assented, mainly out of kindness to Jack. "It would explain why Sowerbutts saw her laughing," he conceded.

"Indeed, colonel. And if they have gone to Hull – of which I grow hourly more convinced – then . . ."

"But surely there's no question of that, man? We're going to Hull merely for completeness' sake – no stone unturned – that sort of caper. But, penny on the drum, the blackguard's gone to Liverpool, eh?"

Jack pursed his lips, tilted his head, shrugged unwillingly.

The colonel's eyes narrowed. "Have you been holding something back from the rest of us?"

The accusation alarmed Jack. "Only a feeling I have here." He tapped his chest. "I know Tottenham well enough by now. I know the way his brain cogs turn. He had that smile on his face. I believe he was not so much bluffing me as *double*-bluffing."

"And you thought so from the start, eh? But why let Sullivan go off to Liverpool?"

"Well . . . I have no proof, you see . . ." Jack could not meet his inquisitor's eye.

The colonel smiled grimly. "Wanted to make it up to him – isn't that the way of it? Bring the girl back and cover your shame in glory." He reached across and patted Jack on the arm. "Can't say I blame you, Horley. I'd have done the same if I'd stood in your boots. Not that you *could* stand at the time. But this does put a different complexion on things, what, eh, eh?" He pursed his lips and plucked at them before he continued. "If they really are bound for Hull, what's the gel going to do? You know her, man. What's she going to do? Is she bolting with him?"

Jack, glad at last of a direct question that was *not* aimed at him, said, "I believe she might even stay with him all the way to Hull – but by strategy rather than free choice. Where else would suit her better? Every port in the land, great or small, is alive with soldiers and marines, all on watch for the French. Knowing that, why would she risk some village constabulary or country parsonage as her only hope of sanctuary from so ruthless a man? Not to mention the Murphy creature."

The colonel screwed up his eyes, filled with doubt. "Then why risk going to the east coast at all? The west coast will hardly be guarded by more than the ordinary excise patrols. There's little fear of a French attack upon Lancashire."

"Agreed. But consider this: Tottenham's only possible port on the Lancashire coast would be Liverpool. His only safe destination's America, north or south. And within the next few hours – as Tottenham must realize – Sullivan will have the whole of the Mersey docks stitched up tighter than a refashioned virgin." He laughed. "No, colonel – the rat's in the bottle. Liverpool's the bung and Hull is the dimple where he hopes to hide – and where we shall catch him. You may stake your life on't. And I'll stake mine that she's no bolter."

They came to the junction. The colonel, not trusting the fingerboards, consulted his vade mecum. "Left to Sheffield," he announced. "Right to the Sherwood Forest."

"*And* to Hull," Jack said, turning right and setting off without further ado. The colonel, less certain of the choice, followed him uneasily.

It surprised them slightly to arrive at Retford, on the far side of the forest, and discover that no one at the coaching inns had seen a handsome young nobleman, a swaggering bull of a pugilist, and a pretty woman – a threesome it would surely be hard to disguise.

"You don't suppose they took the Sheffield road after all?" the colonel asked Jack. "Intending to double back to Liverpool?"

Jack's boundless assurance was undented. "They took some road around this place, to throw us off the scent – also to make us think his talk of going to Hull was all bluff."

But the colonel remained dubious. "He must change horses somewhere – and carriages, too – if he is truly bent on thwarting us."

To Jack this was no objection at all. "He will have arranged it all at farmhouses and inns on the byroads. His man Murphy was

absent all last week and most of the week before that, remember –
well, you were away yourself, so you'd hardly know. But he
was. And now we see why. He was arranging this elaborate trail,
this seemingly empty trail, for us *not* to follow.'' He laughed.
''And so we shall follow it – and we shall surprise him at Hull.''

''To *Hull?*'' Matt halted his latest mount and stared at Crystal in
disbelief. ''But that's where Tottenham said he was going.''
Suspicion darkened his eyes. ''Did you speak with Jack before
you waylaid me? Is this some plot between you?''

''No!'' she protested vehemently. ''Good heavens, Matt, how
could you even . . .''

''You're holding something back. That's plain.''

Her eyes fell. ''Only a suspicion. Nothing I could prove.''

''A suspicion of what?''

''I know Jack well enough by now. He had that certain light in
his eye. He'' – she fought for the exact words – ''well . . . he didn't
look to me like a man setting out on a wild-goose chase. Did he
to you? The colonel – yes. He had the air of a man bent on mere
duty – a conscientious huntsman determined to leave no covert
undrawn, but with no real hope of finding quarry. Jack, on the
other hand – well, you saw him.''

Matt bit his lip. ''Hull, eh?'' he murmured and gauged the
height of the morning sun. ''I still don't understand you, lass –
why you said nothing of this while now.''

She closed her eyes with a weary sigh and turned her face away
from him, toward the sun, luxuriating briefly in its warmth. Her
reins hung slack, as if she were already abdicating control over
her immediate destiny.

He watched these signs with sinking heart. ''Is there more?'' he
asked.

She nodded reluctantly, and then said, like a child offering an
excuse: ''It has just occurred to me, this last half-hour or so.''

''For the pity of Christ!'' he begged.

She drew a deep breath, squaring herself to the decision. ''You
remember when we first met, by the canal at Sapperton?''

He nodded tensely, hardly breathing.

''And we told you how Lord Ferrers had cheated the Horleys –
you remember the tale?''

''Indeed.''

460

"Well, Sapperton Hall is not the ancestral home of the Ferrers. In fact, this present lord treats it as little more than his southern hunting lodge. His real home is at Molescroft Grange near Beverley, which is not a dozen miles beyond" – she paused and then uttered the name that seemed to be on everybody's lips that day – "Hull!"

She waited to see its effect on Matt.

"Go on," he told her.

"Well, Jack can hardly ever bring himself to mention that man's name, but I'm sure, at the back of his mind, he believes that Tottenham is indeed making for Hull – not in order to embark for the Continent and Brazil but merely to *seem* to have done so."

"While in reality he goes to earth with Ferrers at Molescroft Grange! Oh yes – this has a dreadful likeness to truth! But, for heaven's sake, why did Jack say naught of this?"

"Oh, Matt!" Crystal gave him a pitying smile. "Do you really not know?"

"Not for the life of me."

"Because he is in such awe of you, man."

Matt gave a mirthless laugh at the absurdity of this statement.

"But it's true," she insisted. "You are everything he wishes he could be. He talks lion and acts lamb. Night after night he dreams he's of Sir Galahad's company – and then he awakens to find the same old court shoes upon his feet, ready as ever to dance to another's tune. Have you ever imagined what it must be like to *be* such a creature? I love the man, so I know it in the very pit of my heart."

Matt was too moved to mock the thought again.

"And then consider," Crystal went on: "Fate suddenly deals him this wonderful hand. He and he alone will outwit the cunning Lord Tottenham and restore Mary Sullivan to her one true love and master."

"Such a fool!" Matt exclaimed. "Yet such a noble friend! Such a noble, foolish friend!"

But then the tears that had started in his eye were swiftly halted. "Yet *I* am now the one upon the wild-goose chase!"

Crystal's next remark dried his eyes still further. "And if, in the course of the affair, he just happens to see his sword on both sides of Lord Ferrers a couple of dozen times . . . well, well. Regrettable, but such things happen."

Matt came to a swift decision. "When we reach Preston Bank, we'll send word to Liverpool to watch the port and every road, lane, and ginnel leading to it, but we ourselves shall turn inland — for Manchester and Hull."

"*Not* to Hull?" Mary asked in bewilderment. They had paused for some early-evening refreshment at a farmhouse and were now standing in its parlour. "But I thought you told me . . ."

"This *coach* is going to Hull," Tottenham said, pleased as a dog with seven tails. "And good old Murphy is going with it. And so are two obliging servants of Ferrers . . ."

"Ferrers?" Mary interrupted. She suddenly remembered that Crystal had mentioned Tottenham's connection with him the first time they met.

"Who else?" Tottenham was annoyed at her interruption.

"But then . . ." she continued, risking his further displeasure. Deep foreboding now gripped her as it finally dawned that this abduction was no spur-of-the-moment prank.

"What now?" he snapped.

"Well . . . why did we change coaches last night?"

"Lord!" he answered sarcastically. "It would be a fine thing to go all the way in the same coach! Even the three blockheads we now dangle in our wake might not swallow that."

*Blockheads!* Mary thought. There lay Tottenham's weakness. "You've gone to mighty pains, my lord, to throw these 'blockheads' off our scent."

"Ah, let me tell you!" His humour returned. "You haven't heard the half of it. These two servants of Ferrers are also going by this coach to Hull. They will bear a most astonishing resemblance to you and me — especially as they will be wearing the clothes that presently adorn us — and in which, as half the constabulary in England may know by now, we set out from the Hall yesterday afternoon."

"But I don't wish to exchange apparel with some woman I've never even . . ."

Tottenham silenced her with a kiss. "D'you think for a moment that I would inflict such indignity upon you? Fie! Even as we speak, my pet, your new costume awaits you above."

"Above?" She was bewildered again.

He nodded. "They await us in the room this good farmwife

has so obligingly put at our disposal. Ferrers won't be here for an hour or so yet." He held her tight, shivering with rekindled longing – which swiftly recruited her senses to the same purpose – and murmured, "Please to tell me – what further inducement d'you require before you'll climb the stair with me and disrobe?"

In fact, it was nearer two hours before Ferrers arrived – to find them both exhausted and asleep. "I'm sorry to be so late," he told them archly when they were dressed in their new clothes and fit for company once more. "The byways in some of the parishes between here and Beverley are in a shocking state. There seems to be a rule – the finer the commissioner's house, the worse the metal of his roads. But" – he laughed – "being a highway commissioner myself, I do not inquire too closely into the matter."

"At least you were not seen?" Tottenham asked anxiously. "You're sure of it?"

"Not by any who know me – that I'll smack calfskin to."

Mary was fascinated to meet Lord Ferrers at last. From Crystal's descriptions, coloured by her own moral imagination in the days of her innocence, she had pictured an ogre – something like Hogarth's portrait of the gross and warty Simon, Lord Lovat, the infamous traitor, in his death cell. But now her later experience of life prevented her from being altogether surprised to find him both young and fairly good-looking.

"Where are the two who are to impersonate us?" Mary asked him, thinking it might be amusing to see a living representation of herself and Tottenham.

Ferrers lifted an inquiring eyebrow toward his noble friend.

"Fear not," Tottenham laughed. "She's here of her own free will. She's had a dozen chances to escape and has taken none of 'em."

Ferrers was not entirely reassured.

"Cheer up!" Tottenham redoubled his effort to persuade. "You should be even more glad of it than I. Abduction's a hanging matter; all you're doing now is abetting the criminal conversion of a wife's affections – something you probably do every week anyway."

Ferrers laughed.

"I suppose they've gone already?" Tottenham asked.

"Aye." Ferrers rose and began to struggle into a heavy

coachman's overcoat. "A good half-hour since. And we'd best make a start also."

When she and Tottenham were in the coach and on their way once more, Mary asked, "If not to Hull, then where are we going?"

"To Liverpool, of course. If our pursuers gave it even a moment's serious thought – which, of course, they won't – they'd realize it's our only possible port of escape."

"Is it?"

"Of course. France is too perilous for Englishmen now. The Americas are our only goal."

"But every road will be watched and guarded."

He nodded. "So no one will even notice the two cockle-pickers walking wearily homeward along the strand, carrying between them the creels they've filled in a day of backbreaking toil." He laughed at the cleverness of it.

"But what when we draw near to the port?" she asked.

Still smiling, he shook his head. "We never shall. Those same two cocklepickers, when they reach somewhere not a million miles from Bootle, will take to the water in their little rowing boat, presumably bound for their humble little cottage on the farther bank of the estuary. And if, by the remotest chance, some local quidnunc with spyglasses happens to be watching them – why, all he will see is a ship, outward bound, whose captain has obviously taken some whim to buy a pailful or two of cockles. Through his glasses our spy will observe the two go aboard to show their wares. And a moment later he will see them – or some couple indistinguishable from them at that distance – returning to their boat, where they will resume their journey to the farther bank. Our enemies will be watching the port and we'll board a boat that has already left it." His voice fell to an ecstatic murmur. "Just think, Mary, my dove – by this time tomorrow we shall be on the high seas and bound away for Brazil!"

# CHAPTER SIXTY-FOUR

JACK AND THE COLONEL drew blank at Newark, too.

"But it's impossible," Jack said, looking at the roads that fanned out in all directions from the market place. "No matter what roundabout way they took, all roads lead to Newark. They'd have to come through here."

The colonel restrained himself from voicing the obvious conclusion. They returned to the smithy, where the master was reshoeing one of their horses. Jack sniffed deeply at the fumes of scorched hoof, which had a reviving effect on his tired brain. "You're absolutely sure that no Lord Tottenham – or no Lord *Anyone* not native to these parts – has passed through here of late?" he pressed the blacksmith.

"Well, now, I never went so far as to say that," the man replied guardedly.

Jack clutched at the straw. "You mean some unknown nobleman has passed this way? And was there with him a . . ."

"I 'udn't say unknown," the smith interrupted.

"Well, what would you say?" Jack asked. " 'Strange to these parts'?"

"That all depends on what you'd call 'these parts', sir."

Jack clenched his fists and counted down his anger. The colonel intervened. "Has any nobleman passed this way, whether known to you of old or not?" he asked.

There was something in his military briskness that commanded a reply, and no nonsense. The smith straightened and said, "Yes, sir. A nobleman known to me when I was 'prenticed at Kingston-upon-Hull passed this way not two hours since and I remember remarking . . ."

"His name?" the colonel barked.

But it was Jack who answered, and in a voice hushed by foreboding: "Ferrers?"

The blacksmith looked at him shrewdly and nodded. "The same, sir. And I remember remarking that the turnpike between here and Lincoln must be in sore want of tolls, for he was mired to the axles."

"What has Lord Ferrers to do with it?" the colonel asked Jack.

"I'll explain as we go, colonel." Jack struck his own forehead with his fist. "I was right – and yet so wrong." He turned to the smith. "Describe his coach to us. And tell us which road he took from here."

Matt and his party left Manchester by the Oldham road, making for Littleborough and the old pass through the Pennines to Todmorden.

"I've been trying to picture these events from Mary's point of view," Crystal said.

"And?" Matt prompted when no further thoughts seemed forthcoming.

"And why she was laughing and seemed at her ease when Sowerbutts saw her in Tottenham's . . ."

"Oh, Lord!" Matt said wearily. "I know you all believe she went of her own choice, but if only you . . ."

"I think no such thing," Crystal protested. "Yet can you be sure, my dear, that Mary, though taken by force, would wish to escape *at the very first opportunity?*" She watched the anger darken Matt's face before she spoke further: "We must change horses again soon, my dear, if we're to make good progress through those hills."

They stared for a while in silence at the turbulent upland before them, a rolling, heaving skyline, dark and forbidding – a land to get lost in, where outlaws might hide for ever.

Then Crystal, after glancing all about her to be sure the others were beyond earshot, added, "And we should rest ourselves, too, Matt. Shall we choose an inn where you may lie with me?"

He turned and stared at her, aghast. "How can you even suggest such a thing!"

She raised her eyebrows. "Do you mean that we shall never taste those joys together again?"

He said nothing.

"Perhaps I am suddenly distasteful to you?"

Silence.

"You have found another?"

"Crystal!" he begged. "Cease this provocation."

"Then tell me why you will never bed with me again?"

"You know why."

"Tell me nevertheless."

He scratched his head awkwardly and, like her, checked that the others were far enough away before he answered. "We amused ourselves. I shan't say I didn't enjoy it, but . . ."

"I should hope not!"

"But love was not in it. To call it love is . . . Well, no matter. 'Tis all past now. I'd sooner forswear all such moments than risk losing the wife I love so dearly."

"Ah!" She pounced. "We have it at last. You do, perhaps, see some connection between your own behaviour and the sight of Mary, happy and at ease in . . ."

"Of course," he snapped angrily. "My new resolve has everything in the world to do with Mary – for she is everything in the world to me."

"And she knows it?"

"Indeed she does."

"Because you tell her so? And often?"

"She knows it without needing to be told."

"Lord, such a paragon! And yet to look at her you'd say she was a woman much like any other."

He shook his head. "I no longer follow you."

"Can you follow this, then: Any woman whose husband takes her love and understanding so much for granted might not grieve too sorely at his sufferings – his *temporary* sufferings, two or three days' worth, let us say – especially if they led him to declare that he'd sooner forswear all future peccadilloes than risk losing her."

"But Mary knew nothing of all that."

Crystal gave out a silvery peal of laughter. "And are you ready for more, asks Mother Goose!"

"You mean she did?" He was shocked. "You spoke of it?"

"Not I, but she – in general terms. Or seemingly general terms."

He closed his eyes and shook his head. "Oh, I cannot follow all this female . . . devious . . ."

"But you are, Matt. You are! This is a female, devious scent across half England." She laughed, not unkindly, but not forgivingly, either. "And you *are* following it. Mary is speaking to you, every step of the way. But are you listening?"

He slumped. Indeed, he seemed to shrivel inward from contact with his own clothing. "But why? Why did she go with" – his lips curled in distaste as he uttered the name – "Tottenham?"

Crystal pretended the question was genuine. "May it have something to do with his sublimely good looks?" She almost purred the words in his ear. "Or with his beautifully turned calves? His compelling voice?"

"Stop!" he cried.

"Or those enticing fingers – so gentle yet so skilled?"

"Enough!"

"And, to be sure, the one thing he has in common with *you*, dear Matt."

There was a long pause, during which he did an imitation of a steam boiler rising to its working pressure. At last he could contain himself no longer. "What has . . . what could we possibly . . . that creature and I – in what fashion . . ."

"The fact that sooner or later you both make a conquest of every pretty woman whose path crosses yours. That's something a woman can feel the moment she draws near to man. We need no advertisement of it. And you have no idea what an enticement it is to our poor, frail, susceptible hearts, my love."

He looked her straight in the eye and asked, "Why are you telling me these things now?"

She smiled. "In order that you may vent your spite on me, my dear – for, like you, I have done much to deserve it. Then, when we have our Mary safe again – as surely we will – you need show her nothing but your better side."

While Matt's party began the long, gentle eastward climb through the hills, Tottenham's coach was leaving Harrogate, making for the byroad that twists and turns westward, ever rising, up the valley of the Nidd, over the Yorkshire Dales, and down again into Lancashire. Both roads lead through the uplands, the central spine of northern England, but even at their nearest approach they are still a dozen miles apart – a dozen miles of treeless moorland barred by potholes, mires, and limestone crags, not to mention dashing mountain torrents and rock-embosomed tarns. For all their chance of meeting, the two parties might as well have been in separate hemispheres.

Night and the weather defeated them both. Long before sunset the skies to the west began to thicken. The dying day filled the clouds with a ghastly pallor, sulphurous and streaky. Before the last of it had fled, the heavens opened and the rain simply poured down in bellropes. Every half mile the roads were crossed with white water, spilling over the choked drains and culverts. There was no hope of progress until the rain eased off. Matt's party was granted shelter for the night in a barn above Sowerby Bridge. Tottenham, Ferrers, and Mary were only slightly more comfortable in a big truckle bed in a water bailiff's lodge at Lower Birstwith.

The bailiff, one William Bell, said he'd be out after poachers until dawn; his wife said it would suit her as well not to use the bed as she was all behind with her baking.

Ferrers gave a great groan and declared he never believed any coachman earned his keep before this day. Then he flung himself beneath the blankets and began almost at once to snore.

Mary and Tottenham soon joined him on the mattress; she gave her lover a suggestive caress and was pleased to be answered by a disbelieving groan. He settled himself toward sleep with a gratifying display of purpose. Within ten minutes his breathing, too, was deep and regular. She allowed him a further ten and then slipped from the bed.

From the kitchen came the most gorgeous smell of baking. Mrs. Bell was standing at the open oven door, turning the first batch of rolls, as Mary entered; she smiled. "What – hungry again?"

Mary gratefully accepted a hot roll, though it wanted another minute or so for perfection.

"Our two best appetites," the woman said ruefully. "And both will swell our bellies!"

Mary wasted no time in telling her story – or a version of it that begged the fewest questions and recruited the greatest sympathy. By the time she had finished, the bailiff's wife was all for fetching the chopper from the woodshed and hacking the two lords to tatters as they slept. But Mary managed to channel this indignation into the more practical business of aiding her escape under cover of this dreadful night. If she could only reach Harrogate, she would find both freedom and security there.

"I should have leaped from the coach as we passed through that town," she admitted. "But these men will stop at nothing – especially Lord Tottenham. I have convinced him I am coming of my own free will, so I daren't disillusion him until my escape is entirely assured."

Mrs. Bell tied her a small bundle of cheese and fresh rolls and then dashed through the rain to an outhouse to fetch one of her husband's hooded capes made of oilcloth. The outhouse door made an alarming racket, which perhaps woke Tottenham. At all events, Mary heard him dragging his slippered feet wearily down the passage at the same time as the woman came running back, slop-slopping through the puddles in the yard.

Both arrived simultaneously and stood, framed in their respective doorways, an open-mouthed *tableau vivant* of suprise.

"See what a fine bundle of fresh bread and cheese Mrs. Bell has made for us to take tomorrow," Mary said to Tottenham. "And she says we may borrow her husband's oilcloths while we hitch the horses and load up." She turned to encourage Mrs. Bell into collusion with the lie.

For a moment the woman looked as if she'd prefer to give Tottenham the top of her mind but she caught sight of Mary's imploring eyes and accepted the imposture. "Would your lordship care for a roll?" she asked as she raised her pinafore to dab the rain from her face. Unfortunately a pin or some snag caused her skirts and petticoats to be uplifted as well – exposing her plump thighs and giving the invitation to "a roll" a somewhat different gloss.

When they had finished laughing, the ice was well and truly broken. He said, "I shall accept your *bread* roll gladly, Mrs. Bell." Then, biting into one, he pronounced it the most scrumptious he had ever tasted.

The woman's eyes shone at the compliment; Mary saw that his old familiar spell was working on her, too.

"Oh, but your lordship is quite the wag . . ." Mrs. Bell's remark ended in a little scream of laughter as Tottenham rose and caught her by the wrist.

"Come with us!" he pleaded. "Be our cook! Or must I abduct you, too?"

She stopped laughing; her eyes went wide in shock.

"Oh – didn't Mrs. Sullivan tell you? I'm abducting her. Actually, we're running off to Brazil together. In common parlance we are 'bolting.' But to give it spice we pretend I am abducting her and that her husband is after us, brrrristling with pistols, swords, and potions." He laughed.

Mrs. Bell gazed from one to the other in bewilderment.

Tottenham looked to see Mary's response; she put her head on one side and stared back with pitying acidity.

"I thought you might have told her," he said with a shrug. Then, turning back to the other, he added, "In point of fact, Mrs. Bell, the lady's husband, Matt Sullivan, the *great* Matt Sullivan, the king of silence, is safely abed and tucked up with his whore."

Tottenham's only mistake was not to have his eyes on Mary as he spoke these words, for he would have seen her face turn livid white, her eyes flash, her nostrils flare. Instead, all he saw was the smile as it fled from Mrs. Bell's lips; all he heard was Mrs. Bell saying, "Well, sir, a joke may reach only so far."

Tottenham turned to Mary then, but she, realizing he was out to entrap her by just such a provocation, fought back her anger and, with a gentle tolerance far from her true feeling at that moment, said, "Eat your bread and cheese, my dear – and keep your wit for those who love you and forgive."

As far as he was concerned she had passed the test. He relaxed and broached a fresh barrel of charm. "I jest," he confessed. "And in poor taste, too. But when we reach Mersey's banks tomorrow night, I promise you . . ."

"Reach where?" Mrs. Bell interrupted.

"Liverpool," he said.

"You'll need a good set of wings, then," she told him. "Tomorrow night, did you say?"

"Is it not possible?" The blood drained from his face as he asked.

"Well . . ." She spoke as people speak of impossibilities. "If you left this minute, on a bright, clear moonlight night, and had four or five changes of horses . . ." The recitation ended with a dubious cast of her lips.

He rose abruptly, overturning his chair. "Then we shall leave at once, moonlight or no, fresh horses or no. We have to catch that ship and no other or we are damned. Mary – come pack your belongings. I'll wake Ferrers and we'll start on the horses."

He ran back up the passageway to the bedroom; before he was half way he repeated his call to her.

She stayed only long enough to right his chair. As she turned to go, her eyes met Mrs. Bell's and she begged her: "Misdirect us, I implore you, Mrs. Bell. As you wish to see your place in Heaven, send us into some blind mountain fastness where we may be traced and trapped? Please?"

There was pity in the other's eyes – but bewilderment also. "I can't make head nor tail of either o'ye," she said. "But especially him." She nodded toward the passage.

"D'you suppose it's any easier for me?" Mary answered. "He has me killed with a confusion."

## CHAPTER SIXTY-FIVE

JACK AND THE COLONEL faced a second long night without rest. From Newark they had returned the way they came, as far as Mansfield, where they took the Sheffield road. Heroically the colonel withheld the comment that *he* would have gone that way in the first place. On the other hand, Jack could have pointed out that, but for their mistaken meander to Newark, they might never have learned of Lord Ferrers's active engagement in this affair.

From Sheffield, which is on the eastern edge of the Pennines, about forty miles south of Harrogate, they held to the low road north, encouraged by a dubious report that Lord Ferrers's coach had gone that way not two hours before them.

"Must have cut through Sherwood Forest, or we'd have met them on our way to Newark," Jack said. "But," he asked for the hundredth time, "why is Ferrers coming this way at all? If Tottenham's seeking sanctuary with him . . . it makes no sense."

"It makes even less sense," the colonel pointed out, "that they sometimes use the turnpikes and sometimes take to the byroads, which any man in a hurry would never do. No, my friend" – he shook his head dolefully – "there's some new wild card in this hand, and we've not spotted it yet."

In Barnsley, a dozen miles or so north of Sheffield, they had the good fortune to hear of two positive sightings of Lord Ferrers, whose mudstained coach was something of a moving landmark. There was also a less firm sighting of Tottenham – or at least of his man Murphy, who was well known in pugilist circles and had a following far outside London. One amateur of the art was almost ready to swear he had noticed the great man driving a coach out along the Wakefield road. "And I were fair capp'd to see it," he added – to the bewilderment of both gentlemen, who gave him fourpence and hoped he might soon recover from the condition.

They took fresh mounts in the village and pressed on toward Wakefield. There, to their dismay – and further bewilderment – they found no one who had seen either lord or his coach.

Trusting to luck they continued their northward progress, making now for Leeds. They had gone barely a mile when a lad came running after them, crying, "Sirs! Sirs!" at the top of his voice. They turned and galloped back.

He was so winded that his tale was hard to follow, but the gist of it was that the pugilist Murphy had just been sighted driving a coach and four along the Pontefract road, eastward from Wakefield. The lad himself knew no further particulars, but the man who had sent him would furnish them with more if they cared to return to the village.

They gave the youth sixpence for his pains and galloped back to Wakefield for dear life. Their informant was standing in a small crowd outside the Jolly Rig tavern with an empty, or, more precisely, a newly emptied, tankard in his hand.

"Was Murphy driving fast?" they immediately asked the fellow.

He waved the tankard suggestively. "George Pennefather, maisters," he said jovially. "At your service."

Jack took out a golden half-guinea, which caused even the colonel's eyes to widen. After that there was no more prevarication. Con Murphy, the noted pugilist, was seen not ten minutes ago, driving Lord Tottenham's coach and four along the Pontefract road.

"You know the fellow by sight?" Jack asked.

"Didn't need to, sir. He introduced hissen to us wi'out a by-your-leave. 'How far may it be to Selby, good fellow?' he says to us. 'Permit me to introduce missen: Ignatius Murphy, Lord Tottenham's man.' So I asked him straight out, I said, 'Art tha yon bareknuckle prizefighter, Lump Hammer Murphy?' 'T'very same,' says he."

"And was Lord Tottenham with him?" Jack asked impatiently.

Penefather gave him a withering look, much as to say that he was about to get to that part of his story. A serving wench brought out some pies, which they paid for and ate greedily, with much drawing-in and blowing-out of breath to cool the meat.

"There were two gentry within the coach," the man went on, anxiously eyeing the pocket where Jack had parked the coin while he dealt with his handful of food. "A lady and a gentleman."

"Describe them," the colonel asked. "How were they dressed?"

Of course, the description matched exactly those clothes that Tottenham and Mary had been wearing when they left the Hall. The two men exchanged glances that dared at last to hope against hope.

But a skeptical bystander chimed in: "And how came *you* to observe their dress with such scrupulous attention?"

"Nay, there were little art to that," the man replied mildly, "for they both descended to stretch their bones."

"And when they resumed the journey," Jack returned to the original question, "was he driving fast?"

Pennefather shook his head. "More of a walk nor a trot, maister. And a fair jovial man he is, and all. He'll give the time of day to any as care to stop."

He got his half-guinea at that.

"He'd have told you all for half a crown," the colonel commented drily when they were safely on the Pontefract road.

"Hark'ee, colonel, if this costs me twenty guineas before we're done, I'll not grudge a farthing of it to Matt Sullivan. This entire business is all my fault."

The colonel rode on in uncomfortable silence before he said, "Now see here, Horley. You're not the only one with a peck of remorse in his knapsack. I abetted Lord Tottenham, too, you know, when I thought him an honourable man."

Jack agreed hurriedly, eager to talk of other things. But then the colonel, wishing no doubt to change the focus of their conversation, said, "What were your reasons, eh? Ah . . . something similar?"

"Quite," Jack said. "Yes. Indeed. Nothing to it, either. You know how one can misread a glance? Misconstrue a sigh. That's all it was, you know – a glance and a sigh." He looked at Carmody, anxious to see whether this somewhat lame gloss on his behaviour were taken seriously or not.

"To be sure, to be sure," the colonel replied awkwardly, and spurred his horse to a brisker trot.

Jack added, "Poor Mrs. Horley, you know. Such a weak, tender vessel. So susceptible to glances and sighs. Yet I love her to distraction and would forgive her anything – though, you understand, 'tis never more than glances and sighs with her."

"By God, there's our man now!" the colonel said with vast relief. He did not, however, put spur to flank at once, but reached out a hand to restrain his companion. "Let us watch him," he said, "before we plan our approach."

Their trot had brought them through the hilly country to the west of Pontefract. At the moment, it so happened, they were at the crest of a small rise and able to look down on a good half-mile stretch of the road ahead. The coach was undoubtedly Tottenham's and the man driving it, even though they could see only his back, was equally certainly Con Murphy.

"Why are they merely sauntering along?" Jack asked.

"And see!" The colonel pointed at the coach, which had come to a halt. "Why stop and talk to all the world?"

Con had, indeed, raised his hat and was now in earnest conversation with a passer-by.

"By harry, they *wish* to be seen!" the colonel said.

"To risk being taken up by some patrol?" Jack put in dubiously.

The colonel shook his head. "What's the wild card?"

"Here's Tottenham and his man, Murphy . . ." Jack's tone was speculative. "Sought by every thieftaker in the North – and for a hanging matter, too – strolling along the king's highway, in broadest daylight, almost handing out their cards to the populace. Mad as it may sound, colonel, I'll swear you're right. They *wish* to be taken up!"

His friend gave one curt nod. "It's a feint, man. No other cause will fit. They wish to be taken up because the two souls within that coach are *not* Lord Tottenham and Mary Sullivan – they merely wear their apparel."

Jack nodded, yet he was not completely happy with the explanation. "But, upon their being taken up, we would spot the imposture at once," he pointed out.

"Oh, *we* would spot it. That I grant. 'Twas the risk they took. Yet, as they planned it, how small that risk must have seemed! What possible chain of circumstances would put you and me – or Matt Sullivan – or any other pursuer known to them – upon a cross-road from the village of Wakefield along the north bank of the Humber! No, my friend, they wish to be taken up by those who do not know them – who will, of course, send word to us that the birds are netted . . ."

". . . neatly drawing us off the true scent! There we have it!" Jack rubbed his hands in delight. "Well now – what is our riposte? We must surprise them."

"I think I have that, too," the colonel said grimly. "A fine little surprise."

Con Murphy was beginning to sweat, and not merely from the heat of the afternoon sun. For more than twenty miles he had driven a coach, containing a man who was supposedly the most sought after person in the land, at a full leisurely pace and in broad daylight, stopping to pass the time of day with all and sundry, giving out his name as if he were in trade – and he could not have been less troubled by the law had he spent the day in the innermost court of St. Giles's rookery. What was wrong with the world?

"Sure isn't it the truth?" he called down to Lord Ferrers's footman, who sat within, wearing Lord Tottenham's clothes. "They're never there when you need them!"

As he drew into Pontefract and caught sight of the constabulary at the crest of the rise, he decided to take the bull by the horns. As they drew level with the house, he reined in his horses and sprang down. "I'll ask the way direct," he explained to the two servants inside the coach.

He went over to the window and tapped upon it. A burly constable raised the sash a few inches and snapped, "Your business?"

"Begging your honour's pardon, your honour," Con said.

"The name's Ignatius Murphy, by the way. Lord Tottenham's man. I'm after bringing his lordship to the port of Hull." He nodded backward toward the coach. "And we desire to be put on the right road."

The constable's eyes narrowed as he gazed over Con's shoulder. "And who's the lady?" he asked.

Con made an excellent fist of turning pale. "There's no lady, your honour," he said uneasily.

"Damn you, man, but there is. I can see her now."

Con looked at the coach, gave out a feeble laugh, and said, "Oh, *that* lady. Ah . . . that's . . . she's . . ." Inspiration came: "A female servant!" He laughed more robustly. "No lady at all, your honour. Just a female servant."

Someone behind the constable, invisible to Con, spoke a few words. Con heard the voice but not the actual command.

The constable turned back to Con. "Come in here," he snapped.

The last person Con expected to see as he entered the constabulary was Lord Dent – or anyone who would know his lordship and Mary by sight.

"Well now, Lump Hammer, here's a fine howdedoo!" he said by way of welcome.

Truth to tell, the sudden appearance of Lord Dent had also surprised the colonel and Jack when, not ten minutes earlier, they had ridden cross-country to get ahead of the coach and had entered the Pontefract constabulary with a plan of their own to deploy.

"So it was true!" Carmody said. "Toby Wharton told me you'd been dispatched up here."

"Dispatched?" His lordship bridled at the word.

"Later denied it, too. What's the mystery, eh?"

Dent smiled thinly. "No secret now, I suppose. I'm inspecting the northeastern coastal fortifications."

"Oh? And pray, when is the next high tide in Pontefract?" the colonel asked drily.

Dent laughed. "It could be a high tide of frenchies – and it could be sooner than we all suppose. There's a difference of opinion as to where the main rear garrison for the Humber should be. In this town? Or more forward in Selby? But say, what brings you both here?"

When Dent heard their game he cut himself into the hand – which was why he now faced the wretched Murphy and reduced him to a trembling aspen.

Clutching at any straw, Con blurted out the tale he was supposed to have kept to last: "An it please you, my lord, all I'm at is a-bringing of two o' Lord Ferrers's servants back home to Beverley." Now that his eyes grew accustomed to the gloom he began to discern other figures in the background.

Dent ignored the explanation. "Your master is abducting Mrs. Sullivan, man. And you are aiding and abetting. 'Tis a hanging matter." He spoke in tones of friendly regret. "And there's but one way you may save your neck. Tell us what road they took and where they are destined."

"Sure, they'd never tell me such things," Con protested.

One of the background figures came forward. "Do as he advises, my old friend," he said. With sinking heart Con saw that it was Jack.

The other spoke, too, and his spirit hit bedrock, for it was the colonel. "The longer you delay, the more certain your hanging," he said.

For a moment Con teetered on the brink of betrayal; then the old, simple loyalties reasserted their grip. "Hanging for what, sir – if I may make so bold? What crime is here? You may speak of abduction . . ."

"Stop wasting our time," Jack shouted angrily. "Or it will go worse . . ."

"Aye abduction!" Dent interrupted. "And well you know it."

Con was regaining his composure by the second. "Abduction is it! Who abducts her onto his lap! Who abducts her arms around his neck! Who abducts her lips to his! Who abducts the laugh that's never quiet between them!"

The colonel stepped past Lord Dent and struck Con upon the cheek. But he might as well have slapped a forest oak. Con merely smiled as he said, "*Ab*duction? You may spell it with an S and an E!"

"There's Tottenham's wit," Jack commented. "Spoken by his parrot."

"Now it's we who're wasting time," Dent said briskly. "It's plain our man won't talk. Bring in the other two."

Murphy made a half-hearted gesture of barring the door

behind him. "Sure, they know nothing," he said. "Even less than me."

Dent smiled grimly and gave a nod to the constable.

The poor footman and the ladies' maid, demoralized at so swift an unmasking of their imposture, terrified at the prospect of the gallows (when their master had promised them he was doing no more than play a jape upon a friend), capitulated before the first question was even put to them.

Five minutes later Dent, Jack, and the colonel set off up the Great North Road toward Harrogate, armed (thanks to Dent's position in the government) with full powers to recruit whatever size of military detachment they might later require.

At the same time, riders were despatched to patrol every trans-pennine road Matt and his party might conceivably take – if he took any at all. If they failed to meet him, they were to converge on Liverpool and put men on the strand north of Bootle. From Bradwell Peaks in the south to Langstrothdale in the north, no pass was left uncovered.

## CHAPTER SIXTY-SIX

Mr. ƧULIVAN TURN RITE, read the sign that was tacked to the stunted, blasted oak – the only tree in sight in this fierce, Godforsaken upland. The whole party came to a halt.

"I never knew *turn* was spelt like that," Matt said, quietly proud of being able to read the message at all.

Crystal, thinking he was jesting, gave him an exhausted smile. "If this be not the end of our journey, my dear, then it's certainly the end of me."

Their party had not even settled to sleep last night when there came a great hammering at the barn door from a deputized constable with a message from Pontefract.

Since then they had ridden along bridleways and packhorse trails, over Oxenhope Moor to Haworth, then Ilkley Moor to Skipton, and so into even wilder fell country, to Malham Tarn and beyond. Now, just after dawn, they and their horses were ready to drop.

"I'd sooner walk to Galway Bay and back," Punch said, "than go through such a night again."

"And me," Matt muttered to himself.

Crystal pricked up her ears. "How's this?"

He looked at her balefully. "And you're to blame for it as much as anyone."

A narrowing of the path enabled them to spur ahead, a little out of earshot of the others. "What you said yesterday," he explained, "about not talking to Mary, not telling her things – taking her for granted – I vow to you, I got that low about three o'clock last night, I couldn't think of one good reason for her to stay with me while Lord Tottenham was on offer, too."

"Oh, Matt!" Crystal was horrified that her modest, though serious, rebuke had bitten so deep. "It was nothing as severe as that . . ."

But, like many a new convert before him, he was now determined on a public wallow in his own past sins: He had treated Mary as less than half a person . . . had never taken her seriously . . . had hardly ever consulted her on important matters, nor held her opinion precious even when he had . . . and so on. He had stared into Hell last night and life could never be the same again.

As the confession unwound, Crystal relaxed. In her tiredness she was filled with a warm half-love for this strange, untutored man of quiet extremes. What would life be like, she wondered, if no one ever went to extremes? What a frightening, unpassionate thing it would be if everyone who saw the error of his ways was able to apply exactly the right and modest correction, with never an ounce of excess.

Her words of protest – that he was now going too far the other way – died unuttered; his remorse should have its scope. He could shy a ton of mud at his own reputation; when it was over, enough would stick to make him a better husband than before.

And what else mattered?

When the breast-beating became just a trifle wearisome, she found the trick to silence him: She began heartily to agree with each stricture as it fell from his lips. The strictures dwindled; the lips finally closed.

The "turn rite" led along a barely distinguishable track at the foot of a limestone scar. As the brim of that great inland bluff rose, marking an abrupt edge to the fell at its crown, so the path by its foot began to dip downward. Within a mile they were traversing the base of what could only be called a mountain. The wall of rock to their left was plainly the site of a long-vanished waterfall, half as wide as mighty Niagara and almost as high.

Where its tumbling curtains of water had once smashed themselves to a boiling fury, there now lay nothing more dramatic than a waste of giant boulders, half-entombed in grass. And among those boulders stood . . .

"Jack!" Crystal shouted in delight.

The whole party turned and waved urgently at her to keep her voice down.

"Lord Dent's there, too," Matt said.

"We must hope he's not hand-in-glove with Tottenham," Crystal commented. "You never know with him."

Punch added his pennyworth: "Sure, even if that man drew a pistol and shot Tottenham dead, you still couldn't say. He has the eye of a travelling rat. I'd not work for him if I was paid."

The mutual greetings of the two parties were effusive but subdued.

"Did I give the game away?" Crystal asked anxiously. "Calling out like that?"

Jack shook his head. "Most probably not. But we must be careful. Here's how the land lies. Tottenham, Ferrers, and Mary rested this night at the house of a water bailiff. About eight miles yonder." He pointed away to the east. "They had intended to wait out the storm there but the housewife told them they had little enough chance of reaching the Mersey as it was." He broke off to ask, "The messenger told you what their plans were for getting aboard ship there?"

Matt answered with a shiver. "'Twould have succeeded, too."

"Howsomever – when Tottenham hears how fine he's cut the journey, he wakes up Ferrers and says they must be off. But

Mary, God bless her – no doubt at risk of her life – finds occasion to beg the woman to misdirect them up here upon the fells. Which, not to make a Canterbury Tale of it, is what she has done."

"So they're trapped!" Matt said delightedly.

Jack confirmed it with a huge grin.

"How?"

"D'you see this ancient waterfall behind us?"

They nodded as they stared at the vast, eroded rockface, still unable to equate its serenity and calm with the turmoil it must once have displayed.

"Now follow the ancient watercourse down into the valley. Past that ruined abbey . . . beyond the wood . . . those two great fields of sheep . . . and then a farmhouse – d'ye see? And beside it what looks like a line of white sheets flapping in the wind?"

"I see it," Matt confirmed.

"If you had arrived here by our path from the east you would have passed those 'sheets' and seen them to be a mighty cauldron of upwelling water. It is . . . majestic." He trembled for lack of the proper words. "Greatly swollen by the recent rains, to be sure. And the source of all that water is" – he turned again to the cliff – "up there." He made a hooking gesture with his finger to indicate the fell beyond its rim. "The great river that once poured over this bed has more lately found an underground passage through the limestone beneath our feet. Put your ear to the ground and you may hear it rushing through its measureless caverns here below. And the point where it enters the ground, up there on the fell, is a vast pit, enclosing a tarn in which they say you could hide the whole of York Minster, spire and all – the Great Gawpen Ghyll, folk call it hereabouts. And the tarn is filled by a mountain stream that runs north-south, the length of the valley. Today it is a mighty torrent that completely bars the ancient trail which traverses the valley from east to west."

Matt smiled. "And Tottenham is up there now? On that very trail? Does he know his way is blocked?"

Jack consulted his fob watch. "He has probably just arrived at that conclusion. I think we should start to spring our trap."

# CHAPTER SIXTY-SEVEN

HELL'S TEETH!" Tottenham roared as he turned the head of the lead horse about for the fourth time. "What was that old hag prating on about? There's no way through this valley at all – much less her wonderful short cut."

When they had found the way barred at the ford, they had gone northward up the valley, seeking either the source of the stream and a way around the head of it, or some place where it might broaden out and become shallow enough to ford. They had discovered the source easily enough; and the moor beyond was as smooth as you'd like it. Unfortunately, a great fault ran across the land at that point – which was why the source bubbled up there and nowhere else – so the smooth moorland was the upper surface of a big shelf, raised between four and ten feet above the rocky valley wherein they were still trapped.

Ferrers, who had the point of vantage up there in the driver's seat, ran his eye east and west along the line of the shelf. "No way up," he reported glumly. "We'd need block and tackle and an army of hauliers."

Tottenham's anger subsided as quickly as it had flared. He faced the team down the slope, back the way they had come, and said, quite calmly, "We shall just have to go back and wait for the torrent to abate. Surely it must soon expend itself? These upland streams are mighty floods one minute and purling brooks the next."

"I can cope, going back," Ferrers said. "No need to hold their heads." And he made room for the other to jump up beside him.

Tottenham grinned. "I'll travel within."

He opened the door and swung himself easily inside as the coach gathered pace. "Well, my dove?" he said with a smile that was almost tender, even shy. He was exhausted, too. "It has been amusing to try it this way, but I think we must now steel ourselves to failure. What say we go home and take the dull road to South America? Have you the stomach enough for that?"

She frowned. "The dull road?"

"Aye." He waved at the carriage and more vaguely at the landscape. "There is no need of all this. To be candid, I'm ashamed of it now." He reached across and pulled her easily into his lap. "I love you so much, my darling, I'll face any humiliation, crawl through any amount of public mire, if only you are there at the end of it all. You have transformed my life. What an idiot, wastrel fool I've been all these years!"

Tears came into her eyes. She buried her face in his neck. "Please, my dear?" she whispered. "No more."

"What is it you wish?" he murmured. "You have but to name it."

"I no longer know. To sleep – that's all I can think of."

"Now that you admit you love me, what can Sullivan do about it? Imprison you? You can swear your affidavit and then we may walk without let or hindrance onto any ship we choose. What d'you say, eh?"

She hugged him tighter still in her misery. "Oh my dear, why were you not like this three years ago?"

His lips sought her wet cheek and tried to kiss away her tears. "What matters it now? You know the reasons."

She burst into a new spate of tears, even more bitter than before.

"Tottenham!" Ferrers's urgent cry broke in upon them. "Come out here and look at this."

With that catlike agility of his, Tottenham lowered the window, swung himself out backwards and up onto the roof. Even before he had joined his companion she heard him give out a foul oath.

Heart in mouth she sprang to the opened window and poked out her head – only to draw it in again almost at once.

She sat there, white to the gills and hardly daring to breathe. Matt had come at last – and Punch, and Jack and Crystal, and the colonel, and others she could not identify in so brief a glance.

"Mary!" She heard Matt's voice above the roaring of the waters, for they were approaching the impassable ford once more.

Why did she not respond? Why did she sit there, paralyzed with fear and guilt? Because she knew she did not deserve one tenth – not one hundredth – part of the efforts they had made to rescue her. She had meant only to teach Matt a gentle lesson and had ended up learning a far more bitter truth about herself: She was not worthy of him. Tottenham was, indeed, just about her mark. If now, by way of punishment, she was to spend the rest of her life with him . . . well, the Angel of Vengeance himself could hardly devise a penance more fitting.

Yet that was not the only voice to clamour at her inner ear. There were others, telling her she was in no fit state to judge her soul – which, in any case, was the prerogative of Another. Her duty was to do what was right and leave judgment to the Mercy Seat.

Tottenham lowered himself onto the bench beside Ferrers. When he had left Mary in response to his friend's cry, he fully intended to give himself up. After all – what could he suffer? Damages for the criminal conversion of a wife's affections were more of a commercial transaction than a legal penalty – a way for men to buy and sell their wives. Then, with that behind him, he could take the sensible path toward the life of an oversea planter, with Mary at his side. But the sight of his pursuers, ranged against him and closing in, proved too much. It roused the old risk-all urges within him.

"No need for you to hazard your life, old sport," he said. "When I give the word, jump for it."

"What on earth are you planning?"

Tottenham was about to say that he would ride harum-scarum at the little knot of his tormentors, scattering those with wit to run, trampling those who lacked it, and make for the highway once more. But just at that moment the colonel put a whistle to his lips and the resulting blast brought a whole army out of hiding. Soldiers, mounted gamekeepers, constables, and every Tom, Dick, and Harry they'd been able to recruit for the day came out from their lairs behind rock or tussock and began a steady march toward the ford. They seemed to be walking down the spokes of a vast, invisible wheel.

485

"I shall try to break through the ford!" Tottenham gave a wild laugh.

"You're mad!"

That laugh again. "I'd be even more mad to yield to that rabble. You jump off – you're in no danger." He seized the whip and reins from his friend and lashed the team to a gallop.

"Stop!" Matt Sullivan began to sprint toward him. "Mary! Mary!"

It only made him more determined to go on. "Jump, you fool!" he shouted at Ferrers.

But Ferrers, who had known Tottenham too long to have any very high opinion of his altruism, grew suspicious of these constant urgings to go. "Why me?" he shouted, holding tight the rail with all his strength. "Throw the jade to the wolves. She's what they're after."

They reached the bend where the track down the valley intersected with the one that, on normal days, crossed the ford. Matt and Punch were in the forefront of the rescuers, racing as fast as muscle could carry them toward that same intersection.

Tottenham hauled hard on the rein and, by the skin of his teeth, not to mention a little accidental help from the terrain, made the bend without overturning. For a moment or two, the horses had to slow to a trot. With Tottenham's frenzied use of the whip they soon returned to full gallop, but in that moment of hesitation Punch, with an effort that ought to have torn his muscles from their ligaments and burst every vessel in his frame, made it to the side of the coach and leaped for the handle of the door.

Matt, meanwhile, by an effort no less superb, had gained the luggage boot, where he clung to Tottenham's trunk for dear life.

If the window had not been down, Punch would have fallen, almost certainly beneath the huge rear wheel. But then the door fell open and he just managed to grasp the window sill.

His danger brought Mary out of her paralysis. She sidled toward him and saw at once that he was trying to swing himself inside. Heedless of her own danger she knelt and, bracing herself against the seat, stretched down to grab anything in reach.

First it was his ankle, which she held until his boot was within a whisker of its goal – only to have it slip from her grasp. Fortunately he felt it coming, or he would have lost his hold on the sill. The wild swinging of the door was no help at all.

They were now almost upon that leaping, tumbling torrent of white water. "By God, you might do it!" Ferrers said incredulously. "Keep up this speed and you'll get us over."

Tottenham gave an ancient war whoop. "I have to make these creatures more frightened of me than of that flood." He bared his teeth in a snarl and, yelling like a demon, lashed the surging flanks of the two leaders without mercy.

By now Matt was on top of the trunk, grimly clutching its securing straps. But as to his making any further headway, the chances were slim. There was no back luggage rail to leap up and grasp. And upon each side of him those huge, murderous wheels were spinning like dervishes. His only hope was to hang on and wait for the pace to slacken; his most powerful weapon was surprise, for he was sure that neither Tottenham nor Ferrers had seen him leap aboard.

On the second attempt Mary got Punch's' foot upon the threshold, moments later the rest of him fell over her, safely inside the carriage body. At the very next instant the leading pair of horses gave a scream of fright and hurled themselves across that impossible fury of water.

They actually made it to the farther bank, but their momentum by then was halved. The second pair, lacking that forward impetus, were less fortunate; like a mighty fist the rushing stream battered them sideways, off the road and toward the rocky bed. There it knocked the feet out from under them.

The piteous struggles of those leviathans of muscle left at least two onlookers, the two lords in the driving seat, in no doubt as to the outcome of any contest between their own puny frames and that massive torrent of death.

The body of the carriage was even more easily brushed aside. Its treatment by the water was almost contemptuous. The swivel beneath the coach struck a rock, shattering the joint whereby the shaft was attached. The team, being now free of their burden, leaped forward into the slightly less boisterous water on the farther side.

Ferrers, seeing his only chance to leave a sinking ship, made one flying leap for the shaft and harness they still trailed behind them.

And missed.

He vanished beneath the foam and never rose again. No one

saw him go over the rim of Great Gawpen Ghyll – a couple of hundred yards downstream – but none could doubt that there indeed was his grave.

The appalling swiftness of his disappearance, the obvious futility of whatever struggle he might have made, and the certainty of his end brought home to Tottenham the utter folly of what he had done.

In the corner of his eye he saw the horses bolt away, still terrified but free. The coach – with Mary inside it – now teetered in this monstrous current, whose power nothing could withstand unless it were rock and rooted deep in the earth.

For the present the bodywork was impaled. Some underwater spike of stone held it back from that terrible last journey to the pit of Gawpen Ghyll. But with every passing second the torrent dealt a fresh piledriver-blow that shook its tenuous grip. Any minute now it would tear or lift and float away, down that last mad furlong of boiling fury where no power on earth could save them.

Mary! She was all that mattered now.

He turned and found himself staring directly into the eyes of Matt Sullivan.

Matt, clinging one-handed to the front luggage rail, was already drawing back his fist when he heard the man say, "Mary! Mary's inside. We must save her! Form a chain and save her." He nodded toward a point somewhere over Matt's left shoulder. "Look!"

By now the entire ambushing army had arrived. Several men had ropes, which they began casting toward the stricken coach.

Crystal held her hands beside her eyes, ready to blot out the terrible sight that could surely not be long postponed. She watched the coach as it rocked about its point of impalement and did not notice that she had forgotten how to breathe.

It was her day for forgetting. She had watched Ferrers being swept to his death and in that dreadful moment not one atom of her recalled how often she had prayed for even worse fates to befall him.

One of the ropes struck Matt's foot. Swift as an acrobat he clasped his ankles together and trapped it. "Hold me!" he yelled at Tottenham.

Trusting to that grasp, Matt half twisted his body, bringing his ankles up toward him and reaching down with his hands. After a perilous moment his fingers closed about the hemp and a great cheer went up from the bank.

He immediately bent the rope around that rail at the edge of the roof. In so doing he leaned over and peered inside. Punch saw him first. "God be praised!" he shouted.

"Mary?" Matt shouted back. With leaden heart he saw her voluminous skirts floating in the water.

"Putting on my britches. Get us more rope."

Matt soon had the first line bent. He turned to the party on the bank and screamed, "More!"

They had already thrown a second line, which Tottenham had caught and was now bending to the same rail, about two feet from where Matt had worked.

Matt caught the third, and then had to waste precious seconds in persuading them that he did, indeed, wish them to let go the other end. The moment he had it all coiled in one untidy hank upon the roof he seized it and passed it below to Punch.

The coach received a mighty buffeting at that moment, which almost threw the two men off the roof. Matt just managed to hold on but Tottenham was flung into the water – temporarily behind the shelter of the coach, where he clasped the open window frame for dear life. He made a frantic lunge and got himself half inside.

Steam Punch's fist almost knocked him senseless.

"No!" Mary cried and leaped forward to stop him finishing the man off.

He turned and looked at her in surprise.

"We all need each other now," she shouted. She could not be sure he heard her above the roaring of the water but at least he made no further assault. Instead he resumed his task of tying the line around her waist.

"Where's the other end?" Tottenham asked, oblivious to his bleeding nose.

Punch pointed vaguely at the water. Tottenham fished for it, found the free end, and took it to the window, where Matt's great hand was already hanging, impatient to receive it.

Punch put his lips close to Mary's ear and, miming with the words, shouted: "This rope – other end – secure. You – safe."

Shouldering Tottenham aside he led her in a protective

bear-hug to the window and pointed out the two lines that now linked the coach to the shore. Again he mimed that the rope around her waist was now tied to one of those above.

"And you?" she asked.

"Out!" he cried, giving her a brusque push.

Matt reinforced the message by tugging urgently at the rope. She looked out at the rushing water, at the small yet impossibly furious gulf which separated them from safety. Not wishing to die in anger of any man she turned back to Lord Tottenham and kissed him on the cheek, where Punch had struck him. Then she braced herself for the ordeal of the waters.

Behind her back Lord Tottenham touched his cheek and gave Punch a smile of triumph. It was too dark in there for him to see the hardness enter the other man's eyes.

At that moment the water won its battle with the rock that, until then, had held the coach. With a crunching, splintering, grating sound – which they heard more through the soles of their feet than their ears – the frail timbers of the floor yielded to the invincible tug of the torrent and were dashed away.

Being held at the top by two stout ropes, whose other ends were now fastened securely around the living rock of the river bank, the rest of the coach began to tilt on its side. Before the doorway vanished beneath the surface, Punch pushed Mary out. He and Tottenham then made a leap for the other door, which by then, was fast rising.

Moments later the body of the carriage broke up and raced away downstream. Matt was clinging to the last remnant, the roof, which was secured by lines to the shore. Unfortunately, he had not had time to take up the slack in Mary's line; there were two or three fathoms to pay out. She made a desperate grab for his hand but the sudden tug of the water was too powerful and she was swept away.

Death was surely upon her. Now that she was travelling with the water, no longer resisting its force, the peace was beyond all description. She felt more than resigned to death, it was almost welcome – the crowning of her. Her final thought was of Matt; it filled her with a great happiness.

Then came a jolt that almost severed her in two. The slack had paid out and she was now a twitching, half-drowned marionette, to be won in a duel between Matt and the raging waters. A surge of the current thrust her to the surface, where her desperate lungs sucked greedily on the air. The blackness of oblivion, which had been closing down her vision, began to break up into blotches of translucent pink. In the middle of one of them she saw that the roof of the shattered coach, still secured to the bank by its two ropes, had swung in an arc, closer to the bank and into the lee of a great boulder. All at once her entire attitude was transformed. Their chance of survival, she now realized, lay just on the hopeful side of zero. Paradoxically she herself was now in the most dangerous position of all – dangling at the end of a line and still in mighty turbulence.

But Matt, taking advantage of his own slack water, was steadily hauling her to safety.

Now some drowned portions of the vehicle, momentarily pinned against this or that underwater obstacle, began to break up. The debris flashed past Mary at a frightening speed; one of the front wheels missed her by inches.

The light, frail structure of the roof, still secured at the end of the ropes, became a mere plaything of the raging water. Punch and Tottenham, who had escaped by the skin of their teeth, had meanwhile worked their way around the luggage rails to the point where the ropes were secured. Their combined strength made short work of hauling Mary to safety.

The suck of the torrent had tugged her many times beneath the raging surface. She was spluttering furiously when they at last got her among them, but at least she was conscious and breathing.

Now the water proved their ally. Matt lifted the ropes over a low rock that had prevented them from swinging even nearer to the bank. Moments later the four survivors were swept to the water's edge, where dozens of eager hands waited to pluck them back into their element.

The first out was Tottenham. Punch and Matt remained, arms linked in a protective cordon around Mary. Tottenham and the colonel took one of her arms each and pulled her ashore. She was still conscious and, with Crystal's help, was able to stand and walk after a fashion. They made straight for one of the coaches.

Meanwhile Tottenham had hauled out Matt, who turned to do the same for Punch.

But he would not be helped. "You go after Mary," he shouted, almost angrily, as he reached a hand up toward Tottenham.

He was halfway out of the water when, just at the most precarious point of balance for both of them, he suddenly shifted his grip to clasp Tottenham around the waist.

"What the devil!" the man cried. But his anger swiftly turned to alarm, for Punch now bent his legs at the knees, unbalancing them both completely. He then deliberately straightened his legs in a mighty, backward leap that carried the pair of them into the most turbulent stretch of water.

Mary heard Tottenham's last awful cry and spun around, just in time to see the white, churning water close about the two dark shapes of them.

They were barely ten yards from the edge of the Great Gawpen Ghyll when they surfaced again, for the first and last time; both seemed to be staring straight at her.

Tottenham's last agonized cry was still ringing out as he vanished for ever, down the precipice of water and into that vast, dark cauldron of rock. Most of those present heard only the shout of a scoundrel unprepared to meet his Maker, a formless bellow of rage and hate. But Mary knew otherwise. Tottenham had carried with him into eternity the unfinished crying of her name.

Who raised her from her collapse, who carried her to the waiting carriage, and brought her to the warm bed where she later awoke, she could not say; all she remembered were the tears she thought would never stop – tears of pity for the two drowned men.

One had poured upon her all the love that death had denied his wife and daughters – a love that had brought him to make this last, awful sacrifice that she might live free.

The other had found, too late to be of any use, the ancient, simple truths of love and the human spirit. Dishonoured by his Honour, degraded of his own Nobility, he had nonetheless loved her truly. And because of that he had taken with him to his final judgment – to balance out a life of infamy – nothing but a few hours' insight of all that might have been.

And her prayers.

God alone knew whether that was enough.

# ENVOI

STEAM PUNCH LEFT A WILL. It was not at all the sort of document
to be proved – or contested – in a court of law, yet not only did it
perfectly express his last wishes it was also, in its turn, a perfect
testament to the man. No law could have granted it more legality
than that. It read, in part:

> Item: My good Friends the Flinderses of the Barony of
> Inchiquin in the County of Clare are to receive the Fine Bed I
> bought of late and are to make grand Usage thereof.
> Item: My good Friends Matt and Mary Sullivan are to receive
> the Silver stolen of Lord Ferrers, the which I buried at . . .

. . . and there followed precise directions to the coppice above
Sapperton Tunnel where he had concealed the haul.

A week after the tragedy that brought this noble document to
light, they, the Flinderses (now of Summerley Manor in the
County of Stafford), the Sullivans (of every canal in England
worthy the name, both grand and small), and the Horleys
(anciently and soon again of Aston Hall in the County of
Gloucester), held a mass to his memory in the Roman church at
Stoke. The following day they launched the latest of the Sullivan
fleet and named her the *Steam Punch* – in which the two younger
couples immediately set off for Gloucestershire.

The vessel had been especially adapted for this voyage, with a
cabin forward and a cabin aft, and all the keel in between. Only
moments after they had retired for the first night of the journey,
Matt and Mary felt the *Steam Punch* being rocked by a familiar

and regular bobbing motion that steadily grew more vigorous and frenzied.

"I hope that's Jack," Matt whispered.

Mary chuckled and said, "I care not fig who it may be – just as long as I know who it's *not!*"

While caressing her breasts he discovered something small and metallic hanging between them. He was horrified to think it might be a cross but a closer inspection with his fingertips revealed it to be a key.

"What's it to?" he asked.

She giggled. "To my heart."

"But seriously?"

"I never was more serious, my darling husband. 'Tis the key to this cabin."

He pondered the implications of that while they took advantage of Jack and Crystal's activity to mask their own.

Later he gave out a lugubrious sigh and said, "So that's to be the way of it! How long before you'll learn to trust me?"

"Soon." She sealed the promise with a kiss. "Forty years. 'Twill pass in a twinkling. You'll see."

Three leisurely days later they arrived at the Coates end of Sapperton Tunnel where they made fast and at once set off for the grove Punch had described. The plate was all there, badly tarnished but otherwise unharmed. The sacks had long since rotted but they had prepared for that by bringing four more, fresh from the miller.

For Mary, the sight of those sacks, bulging with silver and clanking dully, brought that long-forgotten afternoon vividly back to life.

"Isn't it like as if a grand loop in all our lives was here tied back on itself?" she said to the others as, with the load shared among them, they made their way back to Aston Hall. " 'Tis a season gone."

"And what seasons are to come?" Crystal asked.

"The best!" Jack cried.

They reached the spot where Matt and Mary had parted in such anger on that night, where he had almost decided to forget Dux and come to London with them, and where she had almost given up her London ambitions and instead thrown in her lot with him.

She reminded Matt of the incident, which he pretended to have forgotten. "Suppose I had gone with you," she speculated. "I wonder would our lives today be any different? Or do they tend toward some fixed purpose no matter what path we think we choose?"

"*Your* lives would be the same, I'm sure," Crystal asserted. "Matt would have gone to Dux and all the brilliant things he's done since would have followed. But our lives, mine and Jack's, would be utterly different. I'd now be the wife (if not, indeed, the widow) of a captain in some foreign army, or a Cuban planter . . . or something awful."

Mary sighed. "And Punch and Tottenham and Ferrers would all be alive!"

"Who's to say as much?" Crystal asked angrily. "Tottenham's life and Ferrer's were neither of them worth a groat – not while Jack and a hundred other victims breathed. And but for you, my dear, what value d'you think poor old Punch would have put on his own life, eh?"

"Sure, he wasn't all that old," Mary protested feebly.

Matt smiled to himself.

They were halfway up the hill by now. She paused and looked back over the canal, winding its way down toward the Thames and London. "But, Lord-a-mercy – I was young!"

The nearer they came to the crest of the hill the more impatient did Jack become to see his old home. Crystal pretended to be winded. "You go on," she puffed, lowering her sack to the ground. "If you don't see it soon, you'll die of a plethora."

The moment he had vanished around the next twist of the broad, woodland path she turned to Matt and Mary and said, "I'll catch up with him shortly, but I'll likely get no better chance than this to thank the two of ye from the bottom of my heart."

"For what?" Mary asked.

"You know for what – for this 'loop in our lives.' It's like a new start for us, for me. Some men are parish men and some are for the nation. Jack is of that first variety. Set him in London and he'll shrivel and die; but plant him here and he's a colossus. Come back in a year and you'll see."

"I see it already," Matt told her.

"But we'll come back anyway," Mary added with swift solemnity.

Crystal laughed. "I'll not redden your necks with further thanks. It will be different for me, too, now. I shall be . . . different."

Too embarrassed to say more, she stood there, wiping her palms on her pinafore and blinking back the tears.

Matt bent down and took up her sack, adding it easily to his own. He pointed with his eyes along the path Jack had taken. Gratefully, she turned and ran.

Matt turned to Mary, who threw her arms around his neck and kissed him. "You're the most marvellous man ever," she whispered. "There! That's this year's telling of it done!"

He rubbed his nose on her cheek and murmured, "Sure, haven't I the perfect pattern to guide me?"

Arm in arm, they set off at their most leisurely pace. "And what of those two?" Matt asked, pointing toward a break in the trees ahead, through which, silhouetted against the hilltop skyline, they could see Crystal as she caught up with Jack and threw her arms about him.

"There it is at last," Mary replied. "Our very own *Remarkable Occurrence!*"